PENGUIN BOOKS

CRIME CLASSICS

Rex Burns is the Edgar Award–winning author of eleven mystery novels. Mary Rose Sullivan is the author of three books on Victorian literature. Both of these authors have written on the subject of mystery fiction, and they together teach a course on the development of mystery fiction at the University of Colorado at Denver.

EDITED BY

REX BURNS AND MARY ROSE SULLIVAN

CRIME CLASSICS

THE MYSTERY STORY FROM POE TO THE PRESENT

PENGUIN BOOKS

PENGUIN BOOKS
Published by the Penguin Group
Viking Penguin, a division of Penguin Books USA Inc.,
375 Hudson Street, New York, New York 10014, U.S.A.
Penguin Books Ltd, 27 Wrights Lane, London W8 5TZ, England
Penguin Books Australia Ltd, Ringwood, Victoria, Australia
Penguin Books Canada Ltd, 10 Alcorn Avenue, Suite 300,
Toronto, Ontario, Canada M4V 3B2
Penguin Books (N.Z.) Ltd, 182–190 Wairau Road, Auckland 10, New Zealand

Penguin Books Ltd, Registered Offices:
Harmondsworth, Middlesex, England

First published in the United States of America by
Viking Penguin, a division of Penguin Books USA Inc., 1990
Published in Penguin Books 1991

1 3 5 7 9 10 8 6 4 2

PUBLISHER'S NOTE

These stories are works of fiction. Names, characters, places, and incidents either are the product of the authors' imagination or are used fictitiously, and any resemblance to actual persons, living or dead, events, or locales is entirely coincidental.

THE LIBRARY OF CONGRESS HAS CATALOGUED THE HARDCOVER AS FOLLOWS:
Crime classics: the mystery story from Poe to the present/edited by
Rex Burns and Mary Rose Sullivan.
p. cm.
ISBN 0–670–83207-3 (hc.)
ISBN 0 14 01.3128 0 (pbk.)
1. Detective and mystery stories, American. 2. Detective and
mystery stories, English. I. Burns, Rex. II. Sullivan, Mary Rose.
PS648.D4C75 1990
813′.087208—dc20 90–50122

Printed in the United States of America
Set in Goudy Old Style
Designed by Steven N. Stathakis

Grateful acknowledgment is made for permission to reprint the following copyrighted works:
"A Jury of Her Peers" by Susan Glaspell. Copyright 1946 by Susan Glaspell. Reprinted by permission of Curtis Brown Ltd.
"The House in Turk Street" from *The Continental Op* by Dashiell Hammett. Copyright © 1974 by Lillian Hellman, Executrix of the Estate of Dashiell Hammett. Reprinted by permission of Random House, Inc.
"The Adventurous Exploit of the Cave of Ali Baba" by Dorothy L. Sayers. Copyright 1933 by Dorothy Leigh Sayers. Reprinted by permission of Harper Collins Publishers.
"The Blue Geranium" from *The Tuesday Club Murders* by Agatha Christie. Reprinted by permission of Harold Ober Associates Incorporated. Copyright 1930 by Agatha Christie.
"Murder at the Automat" by Cornell Woolrich. Reprinted by permission of the author's estate and the agents for the estate, Scott Meredith Literary Agency, Inc.
"Death and the Compass" from *Ficciones* by Jorge Luis Borges. Reprinted by permission of Grove Press, a division of Wheatland Corporation. Copyright © 1962 by Grove Press, Inc. Translated from the Spanish © 1956 by Emecé Editores, S.A., Buenos Aires.
"Hand Upon the Waters" reprinted from *The Knight's Gambit* by William Faulkner by permission of Random House, Inc. Copyright 1939 by The Curtis Publishing Company.
"The Adventure of Abraham Lincoln's Clue" by Ellery Queen. Reprinted by permission of the author's estate and the agents for the estate, Scott Meredith Literary Agency, Inc.
"The Comforts of Home" from *Everything That Rises Must Converge* by Flannery O'Connor. Copyright © 1960, 1965 by the Estate of Mary Flannery O'Connor. Reprinted by permission of Farrar, Straus and Giroux, Inc.
"The Sleeping Dog" by Ross MacDonald. Reprinted by permission of Harold Ober Associates Incorporated. Copyright © 1965 by Ross MacDonald.
"Sadie When She Died" by Ed McBain. Copyright ©1972 by Evan Hunter. Used by permission of John Farquharson Ltd.

ACKNOWLEDGMENTS

Our thanks go to all those who helped in the production of this anthology, particularly to Lori Lipsky for her skillful editing; to Shirley Beaird and Chris Benight, proprietors of Murder by the Book in Denver, for their expert advice about texts for our course in detective fiction; and to Jeanne Lavelle and Sharon McGee, for their knowledgeable suggestions about contemporary mystery writing trends. Finally, we would like to thank our students for sharing our interest in detective fiction; to them this volume is dedicated.

CONTENTS

INTRODUCTION

THE CASE FOR DETECTIVE FICTION

The immense popularity of mystery fiction, today the single largest-selling genre in the United States and Western Europe, is not hard to fathom. Everyone likes a good story, especially one with high stakes and an uncertain outcome, and detective fiction by its nature fills the bill. Its subject matter—the solving of some puzzling aspect of a crime—is intrinsically interesting and its format engages us directly by offering an opportunity to match wits with the detective and so participate, in a sense, in solving the crime. But even an avid reader of mysteries might wonder whether a genre so rigidly formulaic—and so unapologetically entertaining—as detective fiction constitutes an appropriate subject for formal study.

The stories in this volume were selected to support the proposition that detective fiction makes a worthwhile topic of study. A comparatively recent phenomenon (originating in the mid-nineteenth century), it has flourished long enough and in such a variety of styles that it can be studied from a historical and comparative perspective. It serves as a mirror of social values, reflecting in its changing emphases shifting public attitudes towards crime and criminals. And, just as it can tell us much about other times and cultures, it can also tell us much about ourselves—including those things that do *not* change, such as our need to separate good from evil and truth from falsehood. Finally, because of its formal structure, detective fiction demands craftsmanship of the writer and thus assures, at its best, a challenging experience for the reader. Many of the stories in this present collection can be read on more than one level and all stand up well to the test of re-reading.

The tacit understanding between writer and reader of traditional detective fiction, that all the significant evidence needed to solve the case will be provided before the end of the story, imposes stringent requirements on the writer: of clarity, economy, and attention to detail. As Raymond Chandler noted, "the detective story, even in its most conventional form, is difficult to write well." Christianna Brand, in the preface to her *Fog of Doubt,* explained why: "An enormous amount of sleight-of-hand is required to produce each necessary fact, disguising its importance, its real meaning—and *not* by mixing it up with a lot of facts not otherwise necessary to the story: I like to say that no two lines could be removed from any work of mine, whose removal would not leave somewhere else in the book, a gap, which those lines referred to." Ingenuity counts but so does plausibility; the premises may be farfetched but the story's internal logic has to be airtight.

Writers have to consider not only their readers but also other writers—their rivals and predecessors. As Chandler noted, the good detective-story writer "competes not only with all the unburied dead but with all the hosts of the living as well." He or she has to create a detective figure different enough to stand out in a crowded field but one that still fits into the literary-detective tradition. (A minor convention of the genre calls, in fact, for some acknowledgment that the writer is working in a time-honored tradition, either directly, as in Arthur Conan Doyle's slyly having Sherlock Holmes call Gaboriau's Lecoq "a miserable bungler" and Poe's Dupin "a very inferior fellow," or indirectly, as in Ross Macdonald's naming his detective Archer after Sam Spade's murdered partner.) Writers have responded to the competition by working to put an individual stamp on their style, by such means as the telling or colorful metaphor—a mark of Hammett and Chandler—or the witty literary allusion—favored by Christie and Sayers. But more important to the detective writer's success than either characterization or style is a sense of structure: to paraphrase Coleridge on poetry, the right words and in the right order.

Even readers who use detective fiction for "escape" will concede that their half of the writer-reader covenant demands engagement with the details of the narrative design. We overlook at our peril anything that is said or done, we must keep track of chronology and locality and even of what does *not* happen (as in Conan Doyle's clue of "the curious incident of the dog in the nighttime" who failed to bark), and remember details for comparison with alternative versions of an incident. In an article defending the study of the mystery genre, the historian Robin Winks makes the case that reading detective fiction takes some of the same skills as reading history, in that every fact must be counted equally at the outset and none taken at face value: we learn that "to decide too early which facts are the most important is to introduce bias into one's study and (usually) to deflect one from a potentially valuable line of apparently peripheral investigation." We also have to pay close attention to narrative strategies like tone and point of view, noting who is telling us which facts and why, and to the precise meaning of words in context: what, actually, does the writer mean when he says that a room is "locked," a letter "hidden," or a murderer "invisible"? Meeting the writer's challenge in traditional detective fiction—i.e., coming up with the solution before the final revelation—calls for a reader who is both skeptical and eternally vigilant.

POE AND THE PROTOTYPE

Historically, detective fiction emerged almost simultaneously with the first appearance of a professional detective force. "The Murders in the Rue Morgue," Edgar Allan Poe's earliest story featuring the private detective Dupin, appeared in 1841, a year before the fledgling London Metropolitan Police established its Detective Department. Among the intellectual currents that contributed to the creation of Chevalier C. Auguste Dupin were the eighteenth century's Enlightenment with its worship of Reason and the nineteenth century's Romanticism with its worship of Imagination. But equally influential were the same sociological changes that produced his real-life detective counterpart: a shift in public sympathy away from the outlaw—earlier often treated in song and story as a victim of injustice or as a picaresque hero—and toward the police. Readers in the 1840s had developed what Ian Ousby, in his study of early literary detectives, describes as "a mildly salacious interest in crime and a more serious interest in problems of public order"; the combination prepared them to look on professional criminal-catchers less as "bloodhounds" (as they were known when, before the establishment of the police, they were drawn mainly from the ranks of criminals turned informers) and more as useful members of the burgeoning class of civil servants.

In making his protagonist an expert investigator—albeit not a police official—Poe was ahead of his time and, although his eccentric-genius sleuth set the pattern for all fictional great detectives, it was a half-century before another writer dared portray a detective so magisterial and so nearly infallible. Throughout the rest of the century, professional detectives in fiction were somewhat ambiguous figures, portrayed as either carrying some taint of the paid informer about them or—once the police force gained a reputation for honesty and efficiency—as working at their job conscientiously but without much style. After the appearance of Sherlock Holmes, style again became as important as substance for the literary detective. But even as Holmes's descendants—the Lord Peter Wimseys, Hercule Poirots, and Ellery Queens—dominated the fiction of the early twentieth century, a very different breed of investigator was coming on the scene: hardened, unillusioned, guided by a private rather than a public sense of duty. The shifting persona of the detective thus reflects the changing emphases over the years in society's attitudes toward the detective's double role as punisher of the guilty and defender of the innocent, as well as the detective's relationship to society.

Poe's conception of the detective recognized the psychological bonding that can take place between pursuer and pursued, a phenomenon especially noticeable in the "doubling" relationship between Dupin and his opponent, the Minister D____ in "The Purloined Letter." Poe may have been influenced in this by William Godwin's *Caleb Williams* (1794) in which the relentless pursuit of a murderer by his servant turns into an equally relentless pursuit of the servant by the master. The line between guilt and innocence finally becomes blurred as the detective and criminal each project themselves into the mind of their adversary. The idea that the detective must learn to think like the criminal—a more complex version of the old idea that "it takes a thief to catch a thief"—reappears later in many fictional detectives such as Georges Simenon's Inspector Maigret, who, like Dupin, rely more on psychology than on science to get their man.

Although the detective's persona might change—along of course with his methods, which became increasingly technological—what did not change was the format for telling his story, a format which, as Dorothy Sayers says, Poe struck off at almost a single blow in the five short stories that make up his detective fiction corpus. There is, first of all, the device of having the detective's exploits narrated by an admiring, less-acute companion who thus serves as a stand-in for the reader; there is the challenge to the reader to find the significant clue buried amid a welter of false clues ("red herrings"); and there is the detective's bag of ruses and diversions aimed at trapping the criminal—tricks that include even a rudimentary form of disguise, as in Dupin's donning spectacles to hide his gaze. There are subsidiary themes, such as the besting of the plodding policeman by the detective. Each of the stories features a particular plot twist: in "The Mystery of Marie Rogêt" it is the "armchair detective," who solves the mystery solely on the basis of newspaper reports; in "The Gold Bug" the twist is the decoding of a cipher; in "Thou Art the Man" it is the most-unlikely-suspect-as-murderer. In "The Murders in the Rue Morgue" and "The Purloined Letter," the selections included in this volume, Poe illustrates in varying ways his most crucial "principle of investigation": that successful detecting depends on learning to see not what *appears* to be there but what actually is there. The reader, like the detective, has to learn that familiarity with, or preconceptions about, an object or idea can blind one to its real significance. Just as few elements of today's detective fiction cannot be found, at least in embryo, in Poe's stories, so his key "principle of investigation" continues as a staple of the genre.

OTHER EARLY DETECTIVES

Although Poe's invention of the detective-fiction format owed much to his intellectual and social milieu, and to his own fascination with psychology, it also owed something to literary models, especially the early work of Charles Dickens. As Edmund Wilson noted, Poe was very much "akin to his European contemporaries" and he followed developments in English fiction with keen interest. His classic horror tale, "The Tell-Tale Heart," is a brilliant re-working of Dickens's short story, "A Confession Found in a Prison in the Time of Charles the Second," and his solution to Dickens's *Barnaby Rudge* (1841), published before the final chapters had appeared, was so on-target that it annoyed Dickens (and may have contributed to his obsessive secrecy about the outcome of *The Mystery of Edwin Drood* thirty years later).

While *Drood* (which has been called the "perfect murder mystery" because Dickens's death at the midpoint of composition left it forever insoluble) is the only Dickensian work that can be labeled purely detective fiction, the theme of detection surfaces repeatedly in other stories and reflects his typically Victorian ambivalence toward professional detectives. His portrait of Police Inspector Bucket in *Bleak House*

(1853) shows admiration for the efficiency and dedication of this practiced criminal-catcher but also suggests a faintly sinister element in Bucket's watchfulness and almost magical appearances (an observer becomes aware of the detective as "a third person" in the room "who was not there when he himself came in, and has not since entered by the door or by either of the windows. . . ."). Bucket's methods include bribery and intimidation as well as careful checking of facts, and his reliance on surveillance gives him overtones of the spy-informer. When the murderer he has cornered asks if he is "an angel or a devil" and taunts him with the fact that though he can run a murderer to earth he cannot restore the murder victim to life, we sense that Dickens regarded detectives as better able to punish crimes than prevent their occurrence.

Among Dickens's contemporaries, his friend Wilkie Collins made major contributions to the literature of detection in two novels. *The Woman in White* (1860) pits two amateur detectives, Marian Halcombe and Walter Hartright, against a sophisticated villain who is a professional spy. Collins's multi-perspective structure, with chapters narrated by principals and peripheral characters in turn, dramatizes the importance of detection in the struggle of good and evil; "knowledge is power," indeed, and, even if A and B both know X, A's awareness that B knows it gives A the advantage. The balance of power constantly shifts, as the two friends share the detecting task, using everything from Halcombe's feminine intuition to Hartright's dogged examination of witnesses and records to outwit a formidable opponent. In *The Moonstone* (1868) Collins introduced a professional detective, Sergeant Cuff, who is almost as efficient but more sympathetic than Dickens's Bucket. Cuff's style of well-disguised alertness became popular with later writers: his respectable appearance (he always wears "decent black") and domesticated hobby (he grows roses) are disarming ("he might have been a parson, or an undertaker—or anything else you like, except what he really was") and mask a shrewd, though not all-knowing, observer.

The American writer Anna Katherine Greene used a similarly unpretentious but proficient police investigator in *The Leavenworth Case* (1878), a novel important for introducing some variations on detection that later writers, mainly of the English country house-murder school, found extremely useful: a "closed society" (a single household in which everyone is equally suspect), the use of ballistics to establish the time of death, and reproduction of a diagram of the murder scene. Greene, the daughter of a criminal lawyer, also used realistic courtroom cross-examination to further plot revelation. She used her professional detective Ebenezer Gryce as protagonist in a series of novels, supplying him with an assistant named Amelia Butterworth who complemented his logical deductions with feminine perceptiveness (noting, for instance, that an apparently worn hat is really new because it has only one hatpin puncture). Butterworth became the prototype for sharp-eyed spinster sleuths like Agatha Christie's Miss Marple.

Surprisingly, stories featuring women as professional detectives began to emerge in England when women were still a rarity in the business and, unlike their male counterparts in Victorian fiction, they are portrayed in an entirely favorable light. In *The Experiences of a Lady Detective* (1884) W. S. Hayward introduced a genteel but briskly competent police investigator named Mrs. Pascal. Baroness Emmuska Orczy—who had used an armchair detective for *The Old Man in the Corner* (1910)—featured in *Lady Molly of Scotland Yard* (1910) an attractive aristocrat who goes into police work to clear her husband's name and who heads "the Female Department of the Yard," a position involving undercover work and a variety of risky adventures. Her exploits are narrated by her maid, who assists in solving the cases. Like their nonprofessional predecessor, Marian Halcombe in *The Woman in White,* these distaff detectives are intrepid, resourceful, and perceptive (Lady Molly, for example, deduces a disguised woman's actual appearance from the size of her hat); they rely more on logic than intuition and win the grudging respect of male colleagues and adversaries. Gender-consciousness in these stories seems to have replaced the class-consciousness evident in portrayals of male detectives, as seen in the satisfaction with which Lady Molly's maid relates Her Ladyship's shrewd deduction about the discrepant hat size: "Our fellows did not think of that," she notes, "because they are men."

One female contemporary of Dickens who was even more distrustful of professional detectives, Mary Elizabeth Braddon, nevertheless created a private investigator who proved to be immensely popular with readers and who has several characteristics in common with the greatest of detectives, Sherlock Holmes. In *Lady Audley's Secret* (1862), which mixes bigamy, imposture, and murder in the manner of many sensational novels of the period, an elegant young idler named Robert Audley, trained as a lawyer but unwilling to practice such an unsavory profession, is drawn into a mystery surrounding his uncle's new wife. Like Collins's Walter Hartright, he is motivated in his detection—

which includes exhaustive examination of records and interviewing of witnesses—only by a threat to the family honor, so that he emerges as a chivalrous hero rather than a pursuer of criminals. His style is something new: languid and slightly bohemian (he favors stray dogs and French novels), he can tell what a man is thinking by the way he combs his hair, he has a prodigious memory for details and, when the villain is finally unmasked, he has no compunction about taking the law into his own hands to decide her fate. What he will not do is lower himself to such unseemly tactics as wearing disguises or quizzing a youthful witness (tactics Inspector Bucket had adopted); "I am not a detective officer," he announces, "and I do not think the most accomplished detective would like to get his information from a child." Detecting was, it seems, an unsuitable job for a gentleman—at least until the advent of Sherlock Holmes.

THE GREAT DETECTIVES

Although Arthur Conan Doyle seems to have been unaware of Braddon's detective, he readily acknowledged a debt not only to Poe but to the Frenchman Émile Gaboriau whose detective Lecoq in *L'Affaire Lerouge* (1866) is a master of disguise, an expert reader of footprints, and given to instructing his slower-witted companion in the secrets of his art. Conan Doyle's achievement was to paint in vivid color the pen-and-ink sketch of detective-and-assistant handed on by both Gaboriau and Poe; he did it so well that he created what has been called "instant folklore." Holmes and Watson have distinct personalities, realized in an evocative setting of gaslights and hansom cabs, their adventures are told swiftly and with memorable turns of phrase ("the game's afoot"), and they involve highly inventive and even bizarre circumstances (such as a league of red-headed men). Holmesian detection relies on deduction from observation of everything from tobacco ash to ciphers and on diversions and disguises (he can even make himself shorter than his actual height), but what has captured the popular imagination in Holmes as in no other literary detective is largely his inimitable style—succinct, decisive, and unflappable.

The other "great detectives" that followed soon on Sherlock Holmes have his omniscience without his humanizing touches (brought out mainly in his relationship with Watson). Jacques Futrelle's professor known as "The Thinking Machine" caricatures the bloodless intellectual who can think himself out of a locked room, and R. Austin Freeman's Dr. Thorndyke is a forensic scientist, similarly emotionless, who relies for his detective prowess on his green box of equipment. A super-sleuth with a more human face is G. K. Chesterton's Father Brown, an unprepossessing priest—always fumbling with umbrella and brown-paper parcels—who, in the style of Sergeant Cuff and others, looks as "unlike a detective as you can imagine"; what sets him apart more significantly from other supremely successful detectives is his motivation, which is to save souls rather than to uphold the law. Chesterton is interested in the religious implications of crime, viewing it as a sickness to be cured only by confession and reparation, and the detective for him is the reader of human hearts, a spy for God. He follows Poe and Conan Doyle in giving his stories the quality of a tale—he considered that detective fiction should be a kind of fairy tale, evoking a magical world beneath the everyday reality—but for him the detective story is even more basically a morality tale. For the several writers who follow him in using a "clerical" detective, the advantages to be exploited lie mainly in the shock value—of "murder in the nunnery"—or in the opportunities afforded for access to others' innermost lives.

THE GOLDEN AGE

By the 1920s British mystery fiction had become a minor industry; women writers were particularly prominent in the form known as the "cozy," in which members of a closed group, often in a country house or village, became suspects in a generally bloodless and neat murder solved by a great-detective kind of private investigator. The "puzzle" aspect predominated and plots relied on precise chronology and setting, with the text often accompanied by railroad schedules, maps, and diagrams of the murder scene. So many writers used the format that a Detection Club was set up under the leadership of Dorothy Sayers and members swore to abide by the "Rules of Fair Play" (not to conceal a "Vital Clue" from the reader, or use "Mysterious Poisons unknown to science," or let their detective rely on "Divine Revelation, Feminine Intuition, Mumbo Jumbo" or the like). Although the "Rules" were tongue-in-cheek, writers took their obligation to play fair seriously enough that a lively controversy erupted over Agatha Christie's 1926 tour de force, *The Murder of Roger Ackroyd,* which carried the "least-likely as guilty" convention to an extreme that some claimed was unfair to the reader. (The argument continued at such length that critic Edmund Wilson wrote in exasperation an essay entitled "Who Cares Who Killed Roger Ackroyd?")

Agatha Christie went on to become the undisputed queen of Golden Age fiction in a career that spanned half a century. Two of her detectives—the little Belgian professional Hercule Poirot and the English amateur Jane Marple—remain, thanks in part to film and television adaptations of Christie stories, among the best-known of all fictional investigators. Christie is supreme as a manipulator of plots, and maintained her inventiveness through a lifetime output of more than eighty novels and scores of short stories. Less prolific was Dorothy L. Sayers, who wrote a handful of novels and several short stories featuring Lord Peter Wimsey, whose debonair style conceals a keen intelligence and much learning, allowing for dialogue full of witty literary allusions and puzzles of the crossword variety. At the height of her success with Wimsey, Sayers departed from her formula, and from the theory she had espoused that any love interest introduced into detective fiction could only dilute the proper effect, to write *Gaudy Night* (1935). Here, Lord Peter takes second place as detective to Harriet Vane, a woman he had saved from the gallows and then fallen in love with. In the course of this attempt to meld detective fiction and the "serious" novel, Sayers explores the conflicts that arise from the entrance of women into higher education as well as those germane to the genre (differences in male and female styles of detection and between real-life and fictional detecting). Harriet Vane's attempt to resolve her personal problems through the process of unraveling a mystery is a more sophisticated version of Mary Roberts Rinehart's popular detective story, *The Circular Staircase* (1908), a work in the much-derided Had-I-But-Known vein (so called because the heroine acknowledges in retrospect the risks involved in amateur detecting). Rinehart's timid spinster finds that, in venturing into forbidden places to uncover a murderer, she also opens doors to and for herself and, while Sayers's working out of a similar identity crisis is a more complex achievement by far, the similarity of theme in works so far removed from each other points to the persistence of feminist concerns in detective fiction by women. The same tendency, of female detectives to personalize the detection process, can still be seen a generation later, in such novels as P. D. James's *An Unsuitable Job for a Woman* (1972), in Amanda Cross's *Death in a Tenured Position* (1981), and in Sue

Grafton's *"D" Is for Deadbeat* (1987); in each, the woman investigator is motivated less by professionalism than by a feeling of kinship to the victim.

The term "Golden Age" is no longer used strictly to mean the years between the world wars when the British "cozy" mystery was in its heyday, but now is used to characterize a style of mystery writing. "Golden Age" crimes are ingenious and so are their solutions; the writer's tone is light and sophisticated. Writers such as the pseudonymous pair known as "Ellery Queen" successfully adapted the Golden Age format to the American scene, emphasizing the aspect of detection as puzzle-solving, or intellectual game, by interrupting the narrative in some stories to issue a formal "Challenge" to the reader to come up with a solution before reading the ending.

THE BLACK MASK SCHOOL

The Black Mask or "hard-boiled" school of writing was born in the 1920s and has been credited with changing the detective story radically from the tradition established by Edgar Allan Poe. Founded as a pulp magazine by Henry L. Mencken and George Jean Nathan, *The Black Mask* (1920–1951) initially published any kind of adventure story. But under a series of editors such as George W. Sutton and Philip C. Cody, the magazine soon focused on crime and detection as well as on series characters. The first hard-boiled private eye, Terry Mack, made his appearance in May 1923, in "Three Gun Terry," by Carroll John Daly, who would quickly become one of the period's most popular writers. The same year saw the publication of the first Continental Op story, "Arson Plus," by Dashiell Hammett, as well as early work by Erle Stanley Gardner.

But it was under the editorship of Joseph Thompson Shaw (1926–1936) that the magazine became the major proving site for hard-boiled detective fiction. Symbolically, one of "Cap" Shaw's first acts was to shorten the title to *Black Mask.* This compression reflected the stylistic aim of the new editor to achieve "simplicity for the sake of clarity, plausibility, and belief." Moreover, he saw mere action to be "meaningless unless it involves recognizable human character in three-dimensional form." In effect, Shaw was bringing to the mystery genre the literary theories of American Realism as practiced by William Dean Howells and others. He saw his magazine as providing training for

American writers as well as establishing a revolutionary direction for the detective story.

The "hard-boiled" protagonist tended to be a tough guy who nonetheless brought justice to the weak and death to those who preyed on them. As popular private eye Race Williams said, "I never bumped off a guy who didn't need it." The world of the hard-boiled hero reflected the America of the 1920s and 1930s: gangsters, political corruption, economic depression, the uneasy awareness of impending cataclysm far beyond the control of the single individual. The result was an isolated protagonist who managed to obey his own code of ethics and achieve a limited and local justice in a less than perfect world.

Dashiell Hammett's Sam Spade, for instance, remains true to his limited principle of conduct in *The Maltese Falcon* (1930): that a detective has to "do something" about the murder of his partner. Chester Himes (*A Rage in Harlem,* 1957) adapted the hard-boiled style and character to portray the kind of justice available to citizens of the black ghetto. Many writers who came after Hammett made their detectives less rough-edged and more chivalrous—Raymond Chandler's Philip Marlowe is a "man of honour" and Ross Macdonald's Lew Archer is something of a father confessor to troubled souls—but Chandler's famous statement about the modern detective's task conveys the narrowing of expectations for the hero: "Down these mean streets a man must go who is not himself mean, who is neither tarnished nor afraid." In their problematic status, the modern hard-boiled private investigators are closer to the morally ambiguous detectives of Victorian literature than to the Great Detectives of the Golden Age.

Stylistically, the emphasis in hard-boiled fiction was on compression and rapidity, achieved by the use of active verbs and concrete nouns and a diction drawn from the everyday, slangy language of alleyway and pool room. One of the finest stylists of the school was Raymond Chandler who made use of compressed, evocative description and pithy, sardonic metaphor and simile (a man has "a face like a collapsed lung," death is "the big sleep"). At his best, in novels such as *The Long Goodbye* (1953), Chandler succeeded at what he conceded was a difficult task: reworking a familiar commercial formula "to make something like literature out of it." Because his work was mainly in the novel—some of his published short stories were later incorporated into novels—Chandler is not represented in the selections in this volume, but he exerted immense influence, stylistically and thematically, on later writers of detective fiction.

The work of *Black Mask* writers exhibited characteristics shared by others in the larger literary community. Their grim attitude toward life is also reflected in the work of Eugene O'Neill and Maxwell Anderson, Ernest Hemingway and William Faulkner. Like them, the *Black Mask* writers inherited the attitudes of literary naturalism as defined by Stephen Crane and Theodore Dreiser, and looked forward to the existentialism of Jean-Paul Sartre.

THE POLICE PROCEDURAL

The general requirements of a central mystery and effective storytelling are as important for the police procedural as for other forms of detective fiction. However, procedurals differ from previous forms in their heavy reliance on a realistic presentation of actual police methods. Though an author may, for narrative purposes, focus on a single protagonist, teamwork is another requirement of the form: in real life, police agents do not work alone, and the fiction reflects this. However, the distinction between the more traditional forms and the police procedural is often tested and grows increasingly blurred. A number of detective stories feature policemen solving crimes by themselves through use of close observation and intuition—techniques familiar since Inspector Dupin and Sherlock Holmes. Such stories tend to be less police procedurals than traditional detective novels using the police environment as a background. Nonetheless, that background often rivals the detective in impact on the reader.

The foremost scholar of the police procedural, George N. Dove, dates the form's beginnings with *V as in Victim* (1945), by Lawrence Treat. Other claimants are Hillary Waugh (*Last Seen Wearing,* 1952) and John Creasey (*Gideon's Day,* 1955). Reasons for the development of the form vary from the post-World War II distrust of existing formula writing to the wide popularity of television's "Dragnet," which began in 1949 and ran for seven years.

The most popular and prolific writer of procedurals is Ed McBain, whose long series of novels and short stories set in the "87th Precinct" of a big-city police force features a team of detectives working together, often on more than one case at a time. Among the featured investigators are Steve Carella, whose happy home life seems to give him empathy for all kinds of people, and Meyer Meyer, whose role as a Jew in a largely gentile environment gives him a balancing detachment. By adopting a structure that allows him to bring to the fore first one, then another, of his detective figures, McBain skillfully exploits the opportunities for human interest and variety in sleuthing styles inherent in the police-team approach. He can also thus mix dramatic and comic tones within a single plot, a device adapted by the critically acclaimed television series about an urban police force, "Hill Street Blues."

Hillary Waugh worked a variation on the detective team by setting his police force in a small town rather than a big city and, in novels such as *Pure Poison* (1966), putting it under the direction of a folksy chief, Fred C. Fellows. The trend in police procedurals, however, is to de-emphasize the team aspect—what Julian Symons calls "the vision of sectarian comradeship inside the police force"—in favor of a less-idealized view of relationships within the force. George Dove sees Rex Burns's Denver detective Gabe Wager, for instance, as representative of a "considerable number of fictional police detectives who are able to maintain their professional integrity in spite of their own internal suffering"—suffering that, in Wager's case, results from his status as a Chicano on a predominantly Anglo force. In novels such as *Strip Search* (1984), Wager doggedly does his job, unillusioned about the bureaucratic and social biases facing him, but practical-minded enough to see that the compromising and jockeying for power around him threaten his getting the job done—if only because, as George Dove puts it, "the erosion of trust in the police force will hurt relationships with informants, without whose confidence no department can function."

In important ways, then, a detective such as Wager is more akin to loners like Sam Spade and the Continental Op than to the closely knit 87th Precinct team. Many writers of procedurals give their series investigators a similar kind of semi-autonomous stature—free of the system's politics and tendency to corruption—by having them work with, but not in, the police department: as a retired sergeant now freelancing, for example, or a university forensic expert called in as consultant, or—in the case of Jonathan Kellerman's *Over the Edge* (1987)—a psychologist helping a former patient enmeshed in the drug culture. The flexibility that such an approach affords writers for working the police scene, coupled with the current popularity of "fact crime"—as reflected in television documentaries about crime and the public's interest in new developments in forensic science—suggest that the police procedural will continue to have wide appeal.

OTHER VARIATIONS

The kind of metafiction practiced by writers such as Jorge Luis Borges, challenging the conventions of realism and carrying the deconstructing of puzzles to their logical extreme, would seem to forecast the end of detective fiction as a genre; Borges' "Death and the Compass" logically ends with the death of the detective who has become obsessed with solving the puzzle. Instead, however, recent practitioners of postmodernism, such as Umberto Eco in *The Name of the Rose* (1980) and *Foucault's Pendulum* (1989), have found the detection formula particularly suitable to their ends. Eco, for example, has said that as a writer searching for ways to capture "the pattern of the Zeitgeist" and "to reveal the reader to himself," he had only to choose, out of all the model plots in existence, "the most metaphysical and philosophical: the detective novel."

Other writers of serious fiction have used detective fiction on occasion for the purpose of exploring the social or philosophical questions Eco refers to. Susan Glaspell's "A Jury of Her Peers" and William Faulkner's "Hand Upon the Waters" both show characters discovering, and then concealing, damning evidence of a murder because they grasp dimensions of the crime—motives and circumstances—beyond the comprehension of the official justice system. Flannery O'Connor's "The Comforts of Home" also suggests the limitations of the detecting process that relies too much on objective reality and misses the psychological element in the crime. For O'Connor, the human condition is not a challenging problem to be solved but an unfathomable mystery to be accepted.

Georges Simenon, one of the most prolific and influential of detective writers, holds that even as part of an official police organization a detective can transcend the limitations of the legal system and maintain his humanity. His Inspector Jules Maigret solves cases by combining modern scientific police procedures with an intuitive understanding of the criminal mind. Like Poe's Dupin, he not only analyzes what he has seen but he broods, creatively, over what he has *not* seen. In *Maigret and the Madwoman* (1970), his absent-minded doodles turn out to be a sketch of the old woman he failed to help; sitting on a park bench, imagining her there feeding the birds, he feels his way to the elusive truth about her murder. A final clue about how to dispose of the case and the criminal comes to him not from a colleague but from his wife—evidence that Simenon belongs among those writers concerned more with the psychology than with the procedures of detection.

Many of the best of contemporary detective-fiction writers bring together several different strands in their work: the inventive plot and solution, in a realistic setting, and with characters of some depth, so that their works closely resemble serious or "mainstream" fiction. P. D. James is one who uses for her "closed society" not a country house but a hospital for the terminally ill or a forensic laboratory; Ruth Rendell's subjects are middle-class, suburban, often families torn by psychological stresses. This kind of writing is in no danger of dying out, because it deals with never-ending and universal human mysteries and still presents the satisfaction of a solution, "not by supernatural means or good luck," as P. D. James says, "but by human intelligence, human courage and human perseverance." Even writers who have stayed with the more conventional formulas of the genre have found ways to keep the material fresh, by emphasizing humor rather than violence in the hard-boiled vein of detection, as does Loren Estleman, or by focusing on a particular sub-culture (as Amanda Cross has done with academe and Dick Francis with sports) or region (as James McClure has in South Africa) or ethnic group (as Tony Hillerman has with Navajo Indians).

All these signs suggest that the mine of detective fiction is far from being worked out and that writers will continue to strike gold, often artistically as well as commercially. Somerset Maugham may prove correct in his prediction that historians of twentieth-century literature "will pass somewhat lightly over the compositions of 'serious' novelists and turn their attention to the immense and varied achievement of the detective writers."

—REX BURNS
MARY ROSE SULLIVAN

CRIME

CLASSICS

EDGAR ALLAN POE
(1809–1849)

Edgar Allan Poe was born in Boston and educated in Virginia and England and, briefly, at West Point before becoming a journalist and editor. His influence on detective fiction cannot be divorced from his contribution to the development of the short story as a form. Through example and theory, he demonstrated the importance and effectiveness of economy in construction and unity of effect. Especially vital for the detective story was his emphasis on tight plotting and "ratiocination"—logical inference through careful observation—in the unravelling of the mystery. His technique offered a highly entertaining alternative to the loosely-structured tale of mystery and terror, and made use of characteristics of plotting, such as the significant clue buried amid red herrings, still expected in today's crime puzzles. Additionally, and stemming from his interest in the psychology of terror, he moved the mystery story from a focus on the superficial trappings of eerie setting and shocking event to a study of the criminal's mind, either directly or as recreated by a detective. This latter development, and details of Inspector Dupin's style and methods, owed something to Poe's reading of the *Memoirs* (1828–29) of Eugène-François Vidocq, a one-time thief and prison-informer who rose to become head of the Surêté, the French detective force.

"The Murders in the Rue Morgue" is among the earliest and by all odds the most famous of "locked-room" mysteries, a form in which a murder victim is found inside an apparently sealed enclosure and the detective's challenge is to discover the murderer's *modus operandi.* Not only does it introduce the great detective who solves cases through a combination of deduction and imagination—sometimes studying the scene of the crime and sometimes meditating on it in the darkness of his room—but it makes ingenious use of a whole series of motifs, such as "doublings" (the ape and his master, the houses of victim and detective), that would be adapted by later writers of mysteries.

"The Purloined Letter" is considered the most prototypical of all detective stories, in that it makes the most unlikely solution to the crime the correct one and then shows that the most unlikely solution is in fact the most obvious one. Dupin's solution of a mystery that baffles the police drives home Poe's point made in "The Murders in the Rue Morgue" that in detection "There is such a thing as being too profound." It also illustrates the great detective's ability to put himself imaginatively into the mind of his adversary, a form of "doubling" that is echoed throughout the story, from the two "purloinings" to the double meanings of words like "letter," "hidden," and "see."

THE MURDERS IN THE RUE MORGUE

What song the Syrens sang, or what name Achilles assumed when he hid himself among women, although puzzling questions, are not beyond all *conjecture.*

SIR THOMAS BROWNE

The mental features discoursed of as the analytical, are, in themselves, but little susceptible of analysis. We appreciate them only in their effects. We know of them, among other things, that they are always to their possessor, when inordinately possessed, a source of the liveliest enjoyment. As the strong man exults in his physical ability, delighting in such exercises as call his muscles into action, so glories the analyst in that moral activity which *disentangles.* He derives pleasure from even the most trivial occupations bringing his talent into play. He is fond of enigmas, of conundrums, hieroglyphics; exhibiting in his solutions of each a degree of *acumen* which appears to the ordinary apprehension praeternatural. His results, brought about by the very soul and essence of method, have, in truth, the whole air of intuition.

The faculty of re-solution is possibly much invigorated by mathematical study, and especially by that highest branch of it which, unjustly, and merely on account of its retrograde operations, has been called, as if *par excellence,* analysis. Yet to calculate is not in itself to analyze. A chess player, for example, does the one, without effort at the other. It follows that the game of chess, in its effects upon mental character, is greatly misunderstood. I am not now writing a treatise, but simply prefacing a somewhat peculiar narrative by observations very much at random; I will, therefore, take occasion to assert that the higher powers of the reflective intellect are more decidedly and more usefully tasked by the unostentatious game of draughts than by all the elaborate frivolity of chess. In this latter, where the pieces have different and *bizarre* motions, with various and variable values, what is only complex, is mistaken (a not unusual error) for what is profound. The *attention* is here called powerfully into play. If it flag for an instant, an oversight is committed, resulting in injury or defeat. The possible moves being not only manifold, but involute, the chances of such oversights are multiplied, and in nine cases out of ten, it is the more concentrative rather than the more acute player who conquers. In draughts, on the contrary, where the moves are *unique* and have but little variation, the probabilities of inadvertence are diminished, and the mere attention being left comparatively unemployed, what advantages are obtained by either party are obtained by superior *acumen.* To be less abstract, let us suppose a game of draughts where the pieces are reduced to four kings, and where, of course, no oversight is to be expected. It is obvious that here the victory can be decided (the players being at all equal) only by some *recherché* movement, the result of some strong exertion of the intellect. Deprived of ordinary resources, the analyst throws himself into the spirit of his opponent, identifies himself therewith and not unfrequently sees thus, at a glance, the sole methods (sometimes indeed absurdly simple ones) by which he may seduce into error or hurry into miscalculation.

Whist has long been noted for its influence upon what is termed the calculating power; and men of the highest order of intellect have been known to take an apparently unaccountable delight in it, while eschewing chess as frivolous. Beyond doubt there is nothing of a similar nature so greatly tasking the faculty of analysis. The best chess-player in Christendom *may* be little more than the best player of chess; but proficiency in whist implies capacity for success in all those more important undertakings where mind struggles with mind. When I say proficiency, I mean that perfection in the game which includes a comprehension of *all* the sources whence legitimate advantage may be derived. These are not only manifold, but multiform, and lie frequently among recesses of thought altogether inaccessible to the ordinary understanding. To observe attentively is to remember distinctly; and, so far, the concentrative chess-player will do very well at whist; while the rules of Hoyle (themselves based upon the mere mechanism of the game) are sufficiently and generally comprehensible. Thus to have a retentive memory, and proceed by "the book" are points commonly regarded as the sum total of good playing. But it is in matters beyond the limits of mere rule that the skill of the analyst is evinced. He makes, in silence, a host of observations and inferences. So, perhaps, do his companions; and the difference in the extent of the information obtained, lies not so much in the validity of the inference as in the quality of the observation. The necessary knowledge is that of *what* to observe. Our player confines himself not at all; nor, because the game is the object, does he reject deductions from things external to the game. He examines the countenance of his partner, comparing it carefully with that of each of his opponents. He considers the mode of assorting the cards in each hand; often counting trump by trump, and honor by honor, through the glances bestowed by their holders upon each. He notes every variation of face as the play progresses, gathering a fund of thought from the differences in the expression of certainty, of surprise, of triumph, or chagrin. From the manner of gathering up a trick he judges whether the person taking it, can make another in the suit. He recognizes what is played through feint, by the air with which it is thrown upon the table. A casual or inadvertent word; the accidental dropping or turning of a card, with the accompanying anxiety or carelessness in regard to its concealment; the counting of the tricks, with the order of their arrangement; embarrassment, hesitation, eagerness, or trepidation—all afford, to his apparently intuitive perception, indications of the true state of affairs. The first two or three rounds having been played, he is in full possession of the contents of each hand, and thenceforward puts down his cards with as absolute a precision of purpose as if the rest of the party had turned outward the faces of their own.

The analytical power should not be confounded with simple ingenuity; for while the analyst is necessarily ingenious, the ingenious man is often remarkably incapable of analysis. The constructive or combining power, by which ingenuity is usually manifested, and to which the phrenologists (I believe erroneously) have assigned a separate organ, supposing it a primitive faculty, has been so frequently seen in those whose intellect bordered otherwise upon idiocy, as to have attracted general observation among writers on morals. Between ingenuity and the analytic ability there exists a difference far greater, indeed, than that between the fancy and the imagination, but of a character very strictly analogous. It will be found, in fact, that the ingenious are always fanciful, and the *truly* imaginative never otherwise than analytic.

The narrative which follows will appear to the reader somewhat in the light of a commentary upon the propositions just advanced.

Residing in Paris during the spring and part of the summer of 18—, I there became acquainted with a Monsieur C. Auguste Dupin. This young gentleman was of an excellent, indeed of an illustrious family, but, by a variety of untoward events, had been reduced to such poverty that the energy of his character succumbed beneath it, and he ceased to bestir himself in the world, or to care for the retrieval of his fortunes. By courtesy of his creditors, there still remained in his possession a small remnant of his patrimony; and, upon the income arising from this, he managed, by means of a rigorous economy, to procure the necessaries of life, without troubling himself about its superfluities. Books, indeed, were his sole luxuries, and in Paris these are easily obtained.

Our first meeting was at an obscure library in the Rue Montmartre, where the accident of our both being in search of the same very rare and very remarkable volume, brought us into closer communion. We saw each other again and again. I was deeply interested in the little family history which he detailed to me with all that candor which a Frenchman indulges whenever mere self is his theme. I was astonished, too, at the vast extent of his reading; and, above all, I felt my soul enkindled within me by the wild fervor, and the vivid freshness of his imagination. Seeking in Paris the objects I then sought, I felt that the society of such a man would be to me a treasure beyond price; and this feeling I frankly confided to him. It was at length arranged that we should live together during my stay in the city; and as my worldly circumstances were somewhat less embarrassed than his own, I was permitted to be at the expense of renting, and furnishing in a style which suited the rather fantastic gloom of our common temper, a time-eaten and grotesque mansion, long deserted through superstitions into which we did not inquire, and tottering to its fall in a retired and desolate portion of the Faubourg St. Germain.

Had the routine of our life at this place been known to the world, we should have been regarded as madmen—although, perhaps, as madmen of a harmless nature. Our seclusion was perfect. We admitted no visitors. Indeed the locality of our retirement had been carefully kept a secret from my own former associates; and it had been many years since Dupin had ceased to know or be known in Paris. We existed within ourselves alone.

It was a freak of fancy in my friend (for what else shall I call it?)

to be enamored of the night for her own sake; and into this *bizarrerie*, as into all his others, I quietly fell; giving myself up to his wild whims with a perfect *abandon*. The sable divinity would not herself dwell with us always; but we could counterfeit her presence. At the first dawn of the morning we closed all the massy shutters of our old building; lighting a couple of tapers which, strongly perfumed, threw out only the ghastliest and feeblest of rays. By the aid of these we then busied our souls in dreams—reading, writing, or conversing, until warned by the clock of the advent of the true Darkness. Then we sallied forth into the streets, arm in arm, continuing the topics of the day, or roaming far and wide until a late hour, seeking, amid the wild lights and shadows of the populous city, that infinity of mental excitement which quiet observation can afford.

At such times I could not help remarking and admiring (although from his rich ideality I had been prepared to expect it) a peculiar analytic ability in Dupin. He seemed, too, to take an eager delight in its exercise—if not exactly in its display—and did not hesitate to confess the pleasure thus derived. He boasted to me, with a low chuckling laugh, that most men, in respect to himself, wore windows in their bosoms, and was wont to follow up such assertions by direct and very startling proofs of his intimate knowledge of my own. His manner at these moments was frigid and abstract; his eyes were vacant in expression; while his voice, usually a rich tenor, rose into a treble which would have sounded petulantly but for the deliberateness and entire distinctness of the enunciation. Observing him in these moods, I often dwelt meditatively upon the old philosophy of the Bi-Part Soul, and amused myself with the fancy of a double Dupin—the creative and the resolvent.

Let it not be supposed, from what I have just said, that I am detailing any mystery, or penning any romance. What I have described in the Frenchman was merely the result of an excited, or perhaps of a diseased, intelligence, but of the character of his remarks at the periods in question an example will best convey the idea.

We were strolling one night down a long dirty street, in the vicinity of the Palais Royal. Being both, apparently, occupied with thought, neither of us had spoken a syllable for fifteen minutes at least. All at once Dupin broke forth with these words:

"He is a very little fellow, that's true, and would do better for the *Théâtre des Variétés.*"

"There can be no doubt of that," I replied, unwittingly, and not at first observing (so much had I been absorbed in reflection) the extraordinary manner in which the speaker had chimed in with my meditations. In an instant afterward I recollected myself, and my astonishment was profound.

"Dupin," said I, gravely, "this is beyond my comprehension. I do not hesitate to say that I am amazed, and can scarcely credit my senses. How was it possible you should know I was thinking of—?" Here I paused, to ascertain beyond a doubt whether he really knew of whom I thought.

"—of Chantilly," said he, "why do you pause? You were remarking to yourself that his diminutive figure unfitted him for tragedy."

This was precisely what had formed the subject of my reflections. Chantilly was a *quondam* cobbler of the Rue St. Dennis, who, becoming stage-mad, had attempted the *rôle* of Xerxes, Crébillon's tragedy so called, and been notoriously Pasquinaded for his pains.

"Tell me, for Heaven's sake," I exclaimed, "the method—if method there is—by which you have been enabled to fathom my soul in this matter." In fact, I was even more startled than I would have been willing to express.

"It was the fruiterer," replied my friend, "who brought you to the conclusion that the mender of soles was not of sufficient height for Xerxes *et id genus omne.*"*

"The fruiterer—you astonish me—I know no fruiterer whomsoever."

"The man who ran up against you as we entered the street—it may have been fifteen minutes ago."

I now remembered that, in fact, a fruiterer, carrying upon his head a large basket of apples, had nearly thrown me down, by accident, as we passed from the Rue C—— into the thoroughfare where we stood; but what this had to do with Chantilly I could not possibly understand.

There was not a particle of *charlatanerie* about Dupin. "I will explain," he said, "and that you may comprehend all clearly, we will first retrace the course of your meditations, from the moment in which I spoke to you until that of the *rencontre* with the fruiterer in question. The larger links of the chain run thus—Chantilly, Orion, Dr. Nichols, Epicurus, Stereotomy, the street stones, the fruiterer."

* and all that sort.

There are few persons who have not, at some period of their lives, amused themselves in retracing their steps by which particular conclusions of their own minds have been attained. The occupation is often full of interest; and he who attempts it for the first time is astonished by the apparently illimitable distance and incoherence between the starting-point and the goal. What, then, must have been my amazement, when I heard the Frenchman speak what he had just spoken, and I could not help acknowledging that he had spoken the truth. He continued:

"We had been talking of horses, if I remember aright, just before leaving the Rue C——. This was the last subject we discussed. As we crossed into this street, a fruiterer, with a large basket upon his head, brushing quickly past us, thrust you upon a pile of paving-stones collected at a spot where the causeway is undergoing repair. You stepped upon one of the loose fragments, slipped, slightly strained your ankle, appeared vexed or sulky, muttered a few words, turned to look at the pile, and then proceeded in silence. I was not particularly attentive to what you did; but observation has become with me, of late, a species of necessity.

"You kept your eyes upon the ground—glancing, with a petulant expression, at the holes and ruts in the pavement, (so that I saw you were still thinking of the stones,) until we reached the little alley called Lamartine, which has been paved, by way of experiment, with the overlapping and riveted blocks. Here your countenance brightened up, and, perceiving your lips move, I could not doubt that you murmured the word 'stereotomy,' a term very affectedly applied to this species of pavement. I knew that you could not say to yourself 'stereotomy' without being brought to think of atomies, and thus of the theories of Epicurus; and since, when we discussed this subject not very long ago, I mentioned to you how singularly, yet with how little notice, the vague guesses of that noble Greek had met with confirmation in the late nebular cosmogony, I felt that you could not avoid casting your eyes upward to the great *nebula* in Orion, and I certainly expected that you would do so. You did look up; and I was now assured that I had correctly followed your steps. But in that bitter *tirade* upon Chantilly, which appeared in yesterday's '*Musée*,' the satirist, making some disgraceful allusions to the cobbler's change of name upon assuming the buskin, quoted a Latin line about which we have often conversed. I mean the line

Perdidit antiquum litera prima sonum.*

I had told you that this was in reference to Orion, formerly written Urion; and, from certain pungencies connected with this explanation, I was aware that you could not have forgotten it. It was clear, therefore, that you would not fail to combine the two ideas of Orion and Chantilly. That you did combine them I saw by the character of the smile which passed over your lips. You thought of the poor cobbler's immolation. So far, you had been stooping in your gait; but now I saw you draw yourself up to your full height. I was then sure that you reflected upon the diminutive figure of Chantilly. At this point I interrupted your meditations to remark that as, in fact, he *was* a very little fellow—that Chantilly—he would do better at the *Théâtre des Variétés*."

Not long after this, we were looking over an evening edition of the *Gazette des Tribunaux*, when the following paragraphs arrested our attention.

> "EXTRAORDINARY MURDERS.—This morning, about three o'clock, the inhabitants of the Quartier St. Roch were roused from sleep by a succession of terrific shrieks, issuing, apparently, from the fourth story of a house in the Rue Morgue, known to be in the sole occupancy of one Madame L'Espanaye, and her daughter, Mademoiselle Camille L'Espanaye. After some delay, occasioned by a fruitless attempt to procure admission in the usual manner, the gateway was broken in with a crowbar, and eight or ten of the neighbors entered, accompanied by two *gendarmes*. By this time the cries had ceased; but, as the party rushed up the first flight of stairs, two or more rough voices, in angry contention, were distinguished, and seemed to proceed from the upper part of the house. As the second landing was reached, these sounds, also, had ceased, and every thing remained perfectly quiet. The party spread themselves, and hurried from room to room. Upon arriving at a large back chamber in the fourth story, (the door of which, being found locked, with the key inside, was forced open,) a spectacle presented itself which

* The first letter destroys the antique sound.

struck every one present not less with horror than with astonishment.

"The apartment was in the wildest disorder—the furniture broken and thrown about in all directions. There was only one bedstead; and from this the bed had been removed, and thrown into the middle of the floor. On a chair lay a razor, besmeared with blood. On the hearth were two or three long and thick tresses of gray human hair, also dabbled with blood, and seeming to have been pulled out by the roots. On the floor were found four Napoleons, an ear-ring of topaz, three large silver spoons, three smaller of *métal d'Alger,* and two bags, containing nearly four thousand francs in gold. The drawers of a *bureau,* which stood in one corner, were open, and had been, apparently, rifled, although many articles still remained in them. A small iron safe was discovered under the *bed* (not under the bedstead). It was open, with the key still in the door. It had no contents beyond a few old letters, and other papers of little consequence.

"Of Madame L'Espanaye no traces were here seen; but an unusual quantity of soot being observed in the fireplace, a search was made in the chimney, and (horrible to relate!) the corpse of the daughter, head downward, was dragged therefrom; it having been thus forced up the narrow aperture for a considerable distance. The body was quite warm. Upon examining it, many excoriations were perceived, no doubt occasioned by the violence with which it had been thrust up and disengaged. Upon the face were many severe scratches, and, upon the throat, dark bruises, and deep indentations of finger nails, as if the deceased had been throttled to death.

"After a thorough investigation of every portion of the house without farther discovery, the party made its way into a small paved yard in the rear of the building, where lay the corpse of the old lady, with her throat so entirely cut that, upon an attempt to raise her, the head fell off. The body, as well as the head, was fearfully mutilated—the former so much so as scarcely to retain any semblance of humanity.

"To this horrible mystery there is not as yet, we believe, the slightest clew."

The next day's paper had these additional particulars:

"*The Tragedy in the Rue Morgue.*—Many individuals have been examined in relation to this most extraordinary and frightful affair," [the word '*affaire*' has not yet, in France, that levity of import which it conveys with us] "but nothing whatever has transpired to throw light upon it. We give below all the material testimony elicited.

"*Pauline Dubourg,* laundress, deposes that she has known both the deceased for three years, having washed for them during that period. The old lady and her daughter seemed on good terms—very affectionate toward each other. They were excellent pay. Could not speak in regard to their mode or means of living. Believed that Madame L. told fortunes for a living. Was reputed to have money put by. Never met any person in the house when she called for the clothes or took them home. Was sure that they had no servant in employ. There appeared to be no furniture in any part of the building except in the fourth story.

"*Pierre Moreau,* tobacconist, deposes that he has been in the habit of selling small quantities of tobacco and snuff to Madame L'Espanaye for nearly four years. Was born in the neighborhood, and has always resided there. The deceased and her daughter had occupied the house in which the corpses were found, for more than six years. It was formerly occupied by a jeweller, who under-let the upper rooms to various persons. The house was the property of Madame L. She became dissatisfied with the abuse of the premises by her tenant, and moved into them herself, refusing to let any portion. The old lady was childish. Witness had seen the daughter some five or six times during the six years. The two lived an exceedingly retired life—were reputed to have money. Had heard it said among the neighbors that Madame L. told fortunes—did not believe it. Had never seen any person enter the door except the old lady and her daughter, a porter once or twice, and a physician some eight or ten times.

"Many other persons, neighbors, gave evidence to the same effect. No one was spoken of as frequenting the house. It was not known whether there were any living connections of Madame L. and her daughter. The shutters of the front windows were seldom opened. Those in the rear were always closed, with the exception of the large back room, fourth story. The house was a good house—not very old.

"*Isidore Musèt, gendarme,* deposes that he was called to the house about three o'clock in the morning, and found some twenty or thirty persons at the gateway, endeavoring to gain admittance. Forced it open, at length, with a bayonet—not with a crowbar. Had but little difficulty in getting it open on account of its being a double or folding gate, and bolted neither at bottom nor top. The shrieks were continued until the gate was forced—and then suddenly ceased. They seemed to be screams of some person (or persons) in great agony—were loud and drawn out, not short and quick. Witness led the way up stairs. Upon reaching the first landing, heard two voices in loud and angry contention—the one a gruff voice, the other much shriller—a very strange voice. Could distinguish some words of the former, which was that of a Frenchman. Was positive that it was not a woman's voice. Could distinguish the words '*sacré*' and '*diable.*' The shrill voice was that of a foreigner. Could not be sure whether it was the voice of a man or of a woman. Could not make out what was said, but believed the language to be Spanish. The state of the room and of the bodies was described by this witness as we described them yesterday.

"*Henri Duval,* a neighbor, and by trade a silver-smith, deposes that he was one of the party who first entered the house. Corroborates the testimony of Musèt in general. As soon as they forced an entrance, they reclosed the door, to keep out the crowd, which collected very fast, notwithstanding the lateness of the hour. The shrill voice, this witness thinks, was that of an Italian. Was certain it was not French. Could not be sure that it was a man's voice. It might have been a woman's. Was not acquainted with the Italian language. Could not distinguish the words, but was convinced by the intonation that the speaker was an Italian. Knew Madame L. and her daughter. Had conversed with both frequently. Was sure that the shrill voice was not that of either of the deceased.

"——*Odenheimer, restaurateur.*—This witness volunteered his testimony. Not speaking French, was examined through an interpreter. Is a native of Amsterdam. Was passing the house at the time of the shrieks. They lasted for several minutes—probably ten. They were long and loud—very awful and distressing. Was one of those who entered the building. Corroborated the previous evidence in every respect but one. Was sure that the shrill voice was that of a man—of a Frenchman. Could not distinguish the words uttered. They were loud and quick—unequal—spoken apparently in fear as well as in anger. The voice was harsh—not so much shrill as harsh. Could not call it a shrill voice. The gruff voice said repeatedly, '*sacré,*' '*diable,*' and once '*mon Dieu.*'

"*Jules Mignaud,* banker, of the firm of Mignaud et Fils, Rue Deloraine. Is the elder Mignaud. Madame L'Espanaye had some property. Had opened an account with his banking house in the spring of the year——(eight years previously). Made frequent deposits in small sums. Had checked for nothing until the third day before her death, when she took out in person the sum of 4000 francs. This sum was paid in gold, and a clerk sent home with the money.

"*Adolphe Le Bon,* clerk to Mignaud et Fils, deposes that on the day in question, about noon, he accompanied Madame L'Espanaye to her residence with the 4000 francs, put up in two bags. Upon the door being opened, Mademoiselle L. appeared and took from his hands one of the bags, while the old lady relieved him of the other. He then bowed and departed. Did not see any person in the street at the time. It is a by-street—very lonely.

"*William Bird,* tailor, deposes that he was one of the party who entered the house. Is an Englishman. Has lived in Paris two years. Was one of the first to ascend the stairs. Heard the voices in contention. The gruff voice was that of a Frenchman. Could make out several words, but cannot now remember all. Heard distinctly '*sacré*' and '*mon Dieu.*' There was a sound at the moment as if of several persons struggling—a scraping and scuffling sound. The shrill voice was very loud—louder than the gruff one. Is sure that it was not the voice of an Englishman. Appeared to be that of a

German. Might have been a woman's voice. Does not understand German.

"Four of the above-named witnesses being recalled, deposed that the door of the chamber in which was found the body of Mademoiselle L. was locked on the inside when the party reached it. Every thing was perfectly silent—no groans or noises of any kind. Upon forcing the door no person was seen. The windows, both of the back and front room, were down and firmly fastened from within. A door between the two rooms was closed but not locked. The door leading from the front room into the passage was locked, with the key on the inside. A small room in the front of the house, on the fourth story, at the head of the passage, was open, the door being ajar. This room was crowded with old beds, boxes, and so forth. These were carefully removed and searched. There was not an inch of any portion of the house which was not carefully searched. Sweeps were sent up and down the chimneys. The house was a four-story one, with garrets (*mansardes*). A trap-door on the roof was nailed down very securely—did not appear to have been opened for years. The time elapsing between the hearing of the voices in contention and the breaking open of the room door was variously stated by the witnesses. Some made it as short as three minutes—some as long as five. The door was opened with difficulty.

"*Alfonzo Garcio,* undertaker, deposes that he resides in the Rue Morgue. Is a native of Spain. Was one of the party who entered the house. Did not proceed up stairs. Is nervous, and was apprehensive of the consequences of agitation. Heard the voices in contention. The gruff voice was that of a Frenchman. Could not distinguish what was said. The shrill voice was that of an Englishman—is sure of this. Does not understand the English language, but judges by the intonation.

"*Alberto Montani,* confectioner, deposes that he was among the first to ascend the stairs. Heard the voices in question. The gruff voice was that of a Frenchman. Distinguished several words. The speaker appeared to be expostulating. Could not make out the words of the shrill voice. Spoke quick and unevenly. Thinks it the voice of a Russian.

Corroborates the general testimony. Is an Italian. Never conversed with a native of Russia.

"Several witnesses, recalled, here testified that the chimneys of all the rooms on the fourth story were too narrow to admit the passage of a human being. By 'sweeps' were meant cylindrical sweeping-brushes, such as are employed by those who clean chimneys. These brushes were passed up and down every flue in the house. There is no back passage by which any one could have descended while the party proceeded up stairs. The body of Mademoiselle L'Espanaye was so firmly wedged in the chimney that it could not be got down until four or five of the party united their strength.

"*Paul Dumas,* physician, deposes that he was called to view the bodies about daybreak. They were both then lying on the sacking of the bedstead in the chamber where Mademoiselle L. was found. The corpse of the young lady was much bruised and excoriated. The fact that it had been thrust up the chimney would sufficiently account for these appearances. The throat was greatly chafed. There were several deep scratches just below the chin, together with a series of livid spots which were evidently the impression of fingers. The face was fearfully discolored, and the eyeballs protruded. The tongue had been partially bitten through. A large bruise was discovered upon the pit of the stomach, produced, apparently, by the pressure of a knee. In the opinion of M. Dumas, Mademoiselle L'Espanaye had been throttled to death by some person or persons unknown. The corpse of the mother was horribly mutilated. All the bones of the right leg and arm were more or less shattered. The left *tibia* much splintered, as well as all the ribs of the left side. Whole body dreadfully bruised and discolored. It was not possible to say how the injuries had been inflicted. A heavy club of wood, or a broad bar of iron—a chair—any large, heavy, and obtuse weapon would have produced such results, if wielded by the hands of a very powerful man. No woman could have inflicted the blows with any weapon. The head of the deceased, when seen by witness, was entirely separated from the body, and was also greatly shattered. The throat had evidently been cut with some very sharp instrument—probably with a razor.

"*Alexandre Etienne,* surgeon, was called with M. Dumas

to view the bodies. Corroborated the testimony and the opinions of M. Dumas.

"Nothing further of importance was elicited, although several other persons were examined. A murder so mysterious, and so perplexing in all its particulars, was never before committed in Paris—if indeed a murder has been committed at all. The police are entirely at fault—an unusual occurrence in affairs of this nature. There is not, however, the shadow of a clew apparent."

The evening edition of the paper stated that the greatest excitement still continued in the Quartier St. Roch—that the premises in question had been carefully re-searched, and fresh examinations of witnesses instituted, but all to no purpose. A postscript, however, mentioned that Adolphe Le Bon had been arrested and imprisoned—although nothing appeared to criminate him beyond the facts already detailed.

Dupin seemed singularly interested in the progress of this affair—at least so I judged from his manner, for he made no comments. It was only after the announcement that Le Bon had been imprisoned, that he asked me my opinion respecting the murders.

I could merely agree with all Paris in considering them an insoluble mystery. I saw no means by which it would be possible to trace the murderer.

"We must not judge of the means," said Dupin, "by this shell of an examination. The Parisian police, so much extolled for *acumen,* are cunning, but no more. There is no method in their proceedings, beyond the method of the moment. They make a vast parade of measures; but, not unfrequently, these are so ill-adapted to the objects proposed, as to put us in mind of Monsieur Jourdain's calling for his *robe-de-chambre—pour mieux entendre la musique.** The results attained by them are not unfrequently surprising, but, for the most part, are brought about by simple diligence and activity. When these qualities are unavailing, their schemes fail. Vidocq, for example, was a good guesser, and a persevering man. But, without educated thought, he erred continually by the very intensity of his investigations. He impaired his vision by holding the object too close. He might see, perhaps,

* Molière's character calls for his "dressing-gown—in order to hear the music better."

one or two points with unusual clearness, but in so doing he, necessarily, lost sight of the matter as a whole. Thus there is such a thing as being too profound. Truth is not always in a well. In fact, as regards the more important knowledge, I do believe that she is invariably superficial. The depth lies in the valleys where we seek her, and not upon the mountain-tops where she is found. The modes and sources of this kind of error are well typified in the contemplation of the heavenly bodies. To look at a star by glances—to view it in a sidelong way, by turning toward it the exterior portions of the *retina* (more susceptible of feeble impressions of light than the interior), is to behold the star distinctly—is to have the best appreciation of its lustre—a lustre which grows dim just in proportion as we turn our vision *fully* upon it. A greater number of rays actually fall upon the eye in the latter case, but in the former, there is the more refined capacity for comprehension. By undue profundity we perplex and enfeeble thought; and it is possible to make even Venus herself vanish from the firmament by a scrutiny too sustained, too concentrated, or too direct.

"As for these murders, let us enter into some examinations for ourselves, before we make up an opinion respecting them. An inquiry will afford us amusement," [I thought this an odd term, so applied, but said nothing] "and besides, Le Bon once rendered me a service for which I am not ungrateful. We will go and see the premises with our own eyes. I know G——, the Prefect of Police, and shall have no difficulty in obtaining the necessary permission."

The permission was obtained, and we proceeded at once to the Rue Morgue. This is one of those miserable thoroughfares which intervene between the Rue Richelieu and the Rue St. Roch. It was late in the afternoon when we reached it, as this quarter is at a great distance from that in which we resided. The house was readily found; for there were still many persons gazing up at the closed shutters, with an objectless curiosity, from the opposite side of the way. It was an ordinary Parisian house, with a gateway, on one side of which was a glazed watch-box, with a sliding panel in the window, indicating a *loge de concierge.* Before going in we walked up the street, turned down an alley, and then, again turning, passed in the rear of the building—Dupin, meanwhile, examining the whole neighborhood, as well as the house, with a minuteness of attention for which I could see no possible object.

Retracing our steps we came again to the front of the dwelling, rang, and having shown our credentials, were admitted by the agents in charge. We went up stairs—into the chamber where the body of Mademoiselle L'Espanaye had been found, and where both the deceased still lay. The disorders of the room had, as usual, been suffered to exist. I saw nothing beyond what had been stated in the *Gazette des Tribunaux*. Dupin scrutinized every thing—not excepting the bodies of the victims. We then went into the other rooms, and into the yard; a *gendarme* accompanying us throughout. The examination occupied us until dark, when we took our departure. On our way home my companion stepped in for a moment at the office of one of the daily papers.

I have said that the whims of my friend were manifold, and that *Je les ménageais:* *—for this phrase there is no English equivalent. It was his humor, now, to decline all conversation on the subject of the murder, until about noon the next day. He then asked me, suddenly, if I had observed any thing *peculiar* at the scene of the atrocity.

There was something in his manner of emphasizing the word "peculiar," which caused me to shudder, without knowing why.

"No, nothing *peculiar,*" I said; "nothing more, at least, than we both saw stated in the paper."

"The *Gazette,*" he replied, "has not entered, I fear, into the unusual horror of the thing. But dismiss the idle opinions of this print. It appears to me that this mystery is considered insoluble, for the very reason which should cause it to be regarded as easy of solution—I mean for the *outré* character of its features. The police are confounded by the seeming absence of motive—not for the murder itself—but for the atrocity of the murder. They are puzzled, too, by the seeming impossibility of reconciling the voices heard in contention, with the facts that no one was discovered upstairs but the assassinated Mademoiselle L'Espanaye, and that there were no means of egress without the notice of the party ascending. The wild disorder of the room; the corpse thrust, with the head downward, up the chimney; the frightful mutilation of the body of the old lady; these considerations, with those just mentioned, and others which I need not mention, have sufficed to paralyze the powers, by putting completely at fault the boasted *acumen*, of the government agents. They have fallen into the gross but common error of confounding the unusual with the abstruse. But it is by these deviations from the plane of the ordinary, that reason feels its way, if at all, in its search for the true. In investigations such

* I humored them.

as we are now pursuing, it should not be so much asked 'what has occurred,' as 'what has occurred that has never occurred before.' In fact, the facility with which I shall arrive, or have arrived, at the solution of this mystery, is in the direct ratio of its apparent insolubility in the eyes of the police."

I stared at the speaker in mute astonishment.

"I am now awaiting," continued he, looking toward the door of our apartment—"I am now awaiting a person who, although perhaps not the perpetrator of these butcheries, must have been in some measure implicated in their perpetration. Of the worst portion of the crimes committed, it is probable that he is innocent. I hope that I am right in this supposition; for upon it I build my expectation of reading the entire riddle. I look for the man here—in this room—every moment. It is true that he may not arrive; but the probability is that he will. Should he come, it will be necessary to detain him. Here are pistols; and we both know how to use them when occasion demands their use."

I took the pistols, scarcely knowing what I did, or believing what I heard, while Dupin went on, very much as if in a soliloquy. I have already spoken of his abstract manner at such times. His discourse was addressed to myself; but his voice, although by no means loud, had that intonation which is commonly employed in speaking to some one at a great distance. His eyes, vacant in expression, regarded only the wall.

"That the voices heard in contention," he said, "by the party upon the stairs, were not the voices of the women themselves, was fully proved by the evidence. This relieves us of all doubt upon the question whether the old lady could have first destroyed the daughter, and afterward have committed suicide. I speak of this point chiefly for the sake of method; for the strength of Madame L'Espanaye would have been utterly unequal to the task of thrusting her daughter's corpse up the chimney as it was found; and the nature of the wounds upon her own person entirely precludes the idea of self-destruction. Murder, then, has been committed by some third party; and the voices of this third party were those heard in contention. Let me now advert—not to the whole testimony respecting these voices—but to what was *peculiar* in that testimony. Did you observe any thing peculiar about it?"

I remarked that, while all the witnesses agreed in supposing the gruff voice to be that of a Frenchman, there was much disagreement in regard to the shrill, or, as one individual termed it, the harsh voice.

"That was the evidence itself," said Dupin, "but it was not the peculiarity of the evidence. You have observed nothing distinctive. Yet there *was* something to be observed. The witnesses, as you remark, agreed about the gruff voice; they were here unanimous. But in regard to the shrill voice, the peculiarity is—not that they disagreed—but that, while an Italian, an Englishman, a Spaniard, a Hollander, and a Frenchman attempted to describe it, each one spoke of it as that *of a foreigner*. Each is sure that it was not the voice of one of his own countrymen. Each likens it—not to the voice of an individual of any nation with whose language he is conversant—but the converse. The Frenchman supposes it the voice of a Spaniard, and 'might have distinguished some words *had he been acquainted with the Spanish.*' The Dutchman maintains it to have been that of a Frenchman; but we find it stated that '*not understanding French this witness was examined through an interpreter.*' The Englishman thinks it the voice of a German, and '*does not understand German.*' The Spaniard 'is sure' that it was that of an Englishman, but 'judges by the intonation' altogether, '*as he has no knowledge of the English.*' The Italian believes it the voice of a Russian, but '*has never conversed with a native of Russia.*' A second Frenchman differs, moreover, with the first, and is positive that the voice was that of an Italian; but, *not being cognizant of that tongue*, is, like the Spaniard, 'convinced by the intonation.' Now, how strangely unusual must that voice have really been, about which such testimony as this *could* have been elicited!—in whose *tones*, even, denizens of the five great divisions of Europe could recognize nothing familiar! You will say that it might have been the voice of an Asiatic—of an African. Neither Asiatics nor Africans abound in Paris; but, without denying the inference, I will now merely call your attention to three points. The voice is termed by one witness 'harsh rather than shrill.' It is represented by two others to have been 'quick and *unequal.*' No words—no sounds resembling words—were by any witness mentioned as distinguishable.

"I know not," continued Dupin, "what impression I may have made, so far, upon your own understanding; but I do not hesitate to say that legitimate deductions even from this portion of the testimony—the portion respecting the gruff and shrill voices—are in themselves sufficient to engender a suspicion which should give direction to all farther progress in the investigation of the mystery. I said 'legitimate deductions'; but my meaning is not thus fully expressed. I designed to imply that the deductions are the *sole* proper ones, and that the suspicion arises *inevitably* from them as the single result. What the suspicion is, however, I will not say just yet. I merely wish you to bear in mind that, with myself, it was sufficiently forcible to give a definite form—a certain tendency—to my inquiries in the chamber.

"Let us now transport ourselves, in fancy, to this chamber. What shall we first seek here? The means of egress employed by the murderers. It is not too much to say that neither of us believe in praeternatural events. Madame and Mademoiselle L'Espanaye were not destroyed by spirits. The doers of the deed were material and escaped materially. Then how? Fortunately there is but one mode of reasoning upon the point, and that mode *must* lead us to a definite decision. Let us examine, each by each, the possible means of egress. It is clear that the assassins were in the room where Mademoiselle L'Espanaye was found, or at least in the room adjoining, when the party ascended the stairs. It is, then, only from these two apartments that we have to seek issues. The police have laid bare the floors, the ceiling, and the masonry of the walls, in every direction. No *secret* issues could have escaped their vigilance. But, not trusting to *their* eyes, I examined with my own. There were, then, *no* secret issues. Both doors leading from the rooms into the passage were securely locked, with the keys inside. Let us turn to the chimneys. These, although of ordinary width for some eight or ten feet above the hearths, will not admit, throughout their extent, the body of a large cat. The impossibility of egress, by means already stated, being thus absolute, we are reduced to the windows. Through those of the front room no one could have escaped without notice from the crowd in the street. The murderers *must* have passed, then, through those of the back room. Now, brought to this conclusion in so unequivocal a manner as we are, it is not our part, as reasoners, to reject it on account of apparent impossibilities. It is only left for us to prove that these apparent 'impossibilities' are, in reality, not such.

"There are two windows in the chamber. One of them is unobstructed by furniture, and is wholly visible. The lower portion of the other is hidden from view by the head of the unwieldy bedstead which is thrust close up against it. The former was found securely fastened from within. It resisted the utmost force of those who endeavored to raise it. A large gimlet-hole had been pierced in its frame to the left, and a very stout nail was found fitted therein, nearly to the head. Upon examining the other window, a similar nail was seen similarly fitted in it; and a vigorous attempt to raise this sash failed also. The police were now entirely satisfied that egress had not been in these directions. And, *therefore,* it was thought a matter of supererogation to withdraw the nails and open the windows.

"My own examination was somewhat more particular, and was so for the reason I have just given—because here it was, I knew, that all apparent impossibilities *must* be proved to be not such in reality.

"I proceeded to think thus—*a posteriori.* The murderers *did* escape from one of these windows. This being so, they could not have re-fastened the sashes from the inside, as they were found fastened—the consideration which put a stop, through its obviousness, to the scrutiny of the police in this quarter. Yet the sashes *were* fastened. They *must,* then, have the power of fastening themselves. There was no escape from this conclusion. I stepped to the unobstructed casement, withdrew the nail with some difficulty, and attempted to raise the sash. It resisted all my efforts, as I had anticipated. A concealed spring must, I now knew, exist; and this corroboration of my idea convinced me that my premises, at least, were correct, however mysterious still appeared the circumstances attending the nails. A careful search soon brought to light the hidden spring. I pressed it, and, satisfied with the discovery, forbore to upraise the sash.

"I now replaced the nail and regarded it attentively. A person passing out through this window might have reclosed it, and the spring would have caught—but the nail could not have been replaced. The conclusion was plain, and again narrowed in the field of my investigations. The assassins *must* have escaped through the other window. Supposing, then, the springs upon each sash to be the same, as was probable, there *must* be found a difference between the nails, or at least between the modes of their fixture. Getting upon the sacking of the bedstead, I looked over the head-board minutely at the second casement. Passing my hand down behind the board, I readily discovered and pressed the spring, which was, as I had supposed, identical in character with its neighbor. I now looked at the nail. It was as stout as the other, and apparently fitted in the same manner—driven in nearly up to the head.

"You will say that I was puzzled; but, if you think so, you must have misunderstood the nature of the inductions. To use a sporting phrase, I had not been once 'at fault.' The scent had never for an instant been lost. There was no flaw in any link of the chain. I had traced the secret to its ultimate result,—and that result was *the nail.* It had, I say, in every respect, the appearance of its fellow in the other window; but this fact was an absolute nullity (conclusive as it might seem to be) when compared with the consideration that here, at this point, terminated the clew. 'There *must* be something wrong,' I said, 'about the nail.' I touched it; and the head, with about a quarter of an inch of the shank came off in my fingers. The rest of the shank was in the gimlet-hole, where it had been broken off. The fracture was an old one (for its edges were incrusted with rust), and had apparently been accomplished by the blow of a hammer, which had partially imbedded, in the top of the bottom sash, the head portion of the nail. I now carefully replaced this head portion in the indentation whence I had taken it, and the resemblance to a perfect nail was complete—the fissure was invisible. Pressing the spring, I gently raised the sash for a few inches; the head went up with it, remaining firm in its bed. I closed the window, and the semblance of the whole nail was again perfect.

"This riddle, so far, was now unriddled. The assassin had escaped through the window which looked upon the bed. Dropping of its own accord upon his exit (or perhaps purposely closed), it had become fastened by the spring; and it was the retention of this spring which had been mistaken by the police for that of the nail,—farther inquiry being thus considered unnecessary.

"The next question is that of the mode of descent. Upon this point I had been satisfied in my walk with you around the building. About five feet and a half from the casement in question there runs a lightning-rod. From this rod it would have been impossible for any one to reach the window itself, to say nothing of entering it. I observed, however, that the shutters of the fourth story were of the peculiar kind called by Parisian carpenters *ferrades*—a kind rarely employed at the present day, but frequently seen upon very old mansions at Lyons and Bourdeaux. They are in the form of an ordinary door (a single, not a folding door), except that the upper half is latticed or worked in open trellis—thus affording an excellent hold for the hands. In the present instance these shutters are fully three feet and a half broad. When we saw them from the rear of the house, they were both about half open—that is to say, they stood off at right angles from the wall. It is probable that the police, as well as myself, examined the back of the tenement; but, if so, in looking at these *ferrades* in the line of their breadth (as they must have done), they did not perceive this great breadth itself, or, at all events, failed to take it into due consideration. In fact, having once satisfied themselves that no egress could have been made in this quarter, they would naturally bestow here a very cursory examination. It was clear to me, however, that the shutter belonging to the window at the head of the bed, would, if swung fully back to the wall, reach to within two feet of the lightning-rod. It was also evident that, by exertion of a very unusual degree of activity and courage, an entrance into the window, from the rod, might have been thus effected. By reaching to the distance of two feet and a half (we now suppose the shutter open to its whole extent) a robber might have taken a firm grasp upon the trellis-work. Letting go, then, his hold upon the rod, placing his feet securely against the wall, and springing boldly from it, he might have swung the shutter so as to close it, and, if we imagine the window open at the time, might even have swung himself into the room.

"I wish you to bear especially in mind that I have spoken of a *very* unusual degree of activity as requisite to success in so hazardous and so difficult a feat. It is my design to show you first, that the thing might possibly have been accomplished:—but, secondly and *chiefly*, I wish to impress upon your understanding the *very extraordinary*—the almost praeternatural character of that agility which could have accomplished it.

"You will say, no doubt, using the language of the law, that 'to make out my case,' I should rather undervalue, than insist upon a full estimation of the activity required in this matter. This may be the practice in law, but it is not the usage of reason. My ultimate object is only the truth. My immediate purpose is to lead you to place in juxtaposition, that *very unusual* activity of which I have just spoken, with that *very peculiar* shrill (or harsh) and *unequal* voice, about whose nationality no two persons could be found to agree, and in whose utterance no syllabification could be detected."

At these words a vague and half-formed conception of the meaning of Dupin flitted over my mind. I seemed to be upon the verge of comprehension, without power to comprehend—as men, at times, find themselves upon the brink of remembrance, without being able, in the end, to remember. My friend went on with his discourse.

"You will see," he said, "that I have shifted the question from the mode of egress to that of ingress. It was my design to suggest the idea that both were effected in the same manner, at the same point. Let us now revert to the interior of the room. Let us survey the appearances here. The drawers of the bureau, it is said, had been rifled, although many articles of apparel still remained within them. The conclusion here is absurd. It is a mere guess—a very silly one—and no more. How are we to know that the articles found in the drawers were not all these drawers had originally contained? Madame L'Espanaye and her daughter lived an exceedingly retired life—saw no company—seldom went out—had little use for numerous changes of habiliment. Those found were at least of as good quality as any likely to be possessed by these ladies. If a thief had taken any, why did he not take the best—why did he not take all? In a word, why did he abandon four thousand francs in gold to encumber himself with a bundle of linen? The gold *was* abandoned. Nearly the whole sum mentioned by Monsieur Mignaud, the banker, was discovered, in bags, upon the floor. I wish you therefore, to discard from your thoughts the blundering idea of *motive,* engendered in the brains of the police by that portion of the evidence which speaks of money delivered at the door of the house. Coincidences ten times as remarkable as this (the delivery of the money, and murder committed within three days upon the party receiving it), happen to all of us every hour of our lives, without attracting even momentary notice. Coincidences, in general, are great stumbling-blocks in the way of that class of thinkers who have been educated to know nothing of the theory of probabilities—that theory to which the most glorious objects of human research are indebted for the most glorious of illustration. In the present instance, had the gold been gone, the fact of its delivery three days before would have formed something more than a coincidence. It would have been corroborative of this idea of motive. But, under the real circumstances of the case, if we are to suppose gold the motive of this outrage, we must also imagine the perpetrator so vacillating an idiot as to have abandoned his gold and his motive together.

"Keeping now steadily in mind the points to which I have drawn your attention—that peculiar voice, that unusual agility, and that startling absence of motive in a murder so singularly atrocious as this—let us glance at the butchery itself. Here is a woman strangled to death by manual strength, and thrust up a chimney head downward. Ordinary assassins employ no such mode of murder as this. Least of all, do they thus dispose of the murdered. In this manner of thrusting the corpse up the chimney, you will admit that there was something *excessively outré*—something altogether irreconcilable with our common notions of human action, even when we suppose the actors the most depraved of men. Think, too, how great must have been that strength which could have thrust the body *up* such an aperture so forcibly that the united vigor of several persons was found barely sufficient to drag it *down!*

"Turn, now, to other indications of the employment of a vigor most marvellous. On the hearth were thick tresses—very thick tresses—of gray human hair. These had been torn out by the roots. You are aware of the great force necessary in tearing thus from the head even twenty or thirty hairs together. You saw the locks in question as well as myself. Their roots (a hideous sight!) were clotted with fragments of the flesh of the scalp—sure token of the prodigious power which had been exerted in uprooting perhaps half a million of hairs at a time. The throat of the old lady was not merely cut, but the head absolutely severed from the body; the instrument was a mere razor. I wish you also to look at the *brutal* ferocity of these deeds. Of the bruises upon the body of Madame L'Espanaye I do not speak. Monsieur Dumas, and his worthy co-adjutor Monsieur Etienne, have pronounced that they were inflicted by some obtuse instrument; and so far these gentlemen are very correct. The obtuse instrument was clearly the stone pavement in the yard, upon which the victim had fallen from the window which looked in upon the bed. This idea, however simple it may now seem, escaped the police for the same reason that the breadth of the shutters escaped them because, by the affair of the nails, their perceptions had been hermetically sealed against the possibility of the windows having ever been opened at all.

"If now, in addition to all these things, you have properly reflected upon the odd disorder of the chamber, we have gone so far as to combine the ideas of an agility astounding, a strength superhuman, a ferocity brutal, a butchery without motive, a *grotesquerie* in horror absolutely alien from humanity, and a voice foreign in tone to the ears of men of many nations, and devoid of all distinct or intelligible syllabification. What result, then, has ensued? What impression have I made upon your fancy?"

I felt a creeping of the flesh as Dupin asked me the question. "A madman," I said, "has done this deed—some raving maniac, escaping from a neighboring *Maison de Santé.*"

"In some respects," he replied, "your idea is not irrelevant. But the voices of madmen, even in their wildest paroxysms, are never found to tally with that peculiar voice heard upon the stairs. Madmen are of some nation, and their language, however incoherent in its words, has always the coherence of syllabification. Besides, the hair of a madman is not such as I now hold in my hand. I disentangled this little tuft from the rigidly clutched fingers of Madame L'Espanaye. Tell me what you can make of it."

"Dupin!" I said, completely unnerved; "this hair is most unusual—this is no *human* hair."

"I have not asserted that it is," said he; "but, before we decide this point, I wish you to glance at the little sketch I have here traced upon this paper. It is a *fac-simile* drawing of what has been described in one portion of the testimony as 'dark bruises and deep indentations of finger nails' upon the throat of Mademoiselle L'Espanaye, and in another (by Messrs. Dumas and Etienne) as a 'series of livid spots, evidently the impressions of fingers.'

"You will perceive," continued my friend, spreading out the paper upon the table before us, "that this drawing gives the idea of a firm and fixed hold. There is no *slipping* apparent. Each finger has retained—possibly until the death of the victim—the fearful grasp by which it originally imbedded itself. Attempt, now, to place all your fingers, at the same time, in the respective impressions as you see them."

I made the attempt in vain.

"We are possibly not giving this matter a fair trial," he said. "The paper is spread out upon a plane surface; but the human throat is cylindrical. Here is a billet of wood, the circumference of which is about that of the throat. Wrap the drawing around it, and try the experiment again."

I did so; but the difficulty was even more obvious than before. "This," I said, "is the mark of no human hand."

"Read now," replied Dupin, "this passage from Cuvier."

It was a minute anatomical and generally descriptive account of the large fulvous Ourang-Outang of the East Indian islands. The gigantic stature, the prodigious strength and activity, the wild ferocity, and the imitative propensities of these mammalia are sufficiently well known to all. I understood the full horrors of the murder at once.

"The description of the digits," said I, as I made an end of reading, "is in exact accordance with this drawing. I see that no animal but an Ourang-Outang, of the species here mentioned, could have impressed the indentations as you have traced them. This tuft of tawny hair, too, is identical in character with that of the beast of Cuvier. But I cannot possibly comprehend the particulars of this frightful mystery. Besides, there were *two* voices heard in contention, and one of them was unquestionably the voice of a Frenchman."

"True; and you will remember an expression attributed almost unanimously, by the evidence, to this voice,—the expression, '*mon Dieu!*' This, under the circumstances, has been justly characterized by one of the witnesses (Montani, the confectioner) as an expression of remonstrance or expostulation. Upon these two words, therefore, I have mainly built my hopes of a full solution of the riddle. A Frenchman was cognizant of the murder. It is possible—indeed it is far more than probable—that he was innocent of all participation in the bloody transaction which took place. The Ourang-Outang may have escaped from him. He may have traced it to the chamber; but, under the agitating circumstances which ensued, he could never have recaptured it. It is still at large. I will not pursue these guesses—for I have no right to call them more—since the shades of reflection upon which they are based are scarcely of sufficient depth to be appreciable by my own intellect, and since I could not pretend to make them intelligible to the understanding of another. We will call them guesses, then, and speak of them as such. If the Frenchman in question is indeed, as I suppose, innocent of this atrocity, this advertisement, which I left last night upon our return home, at the office of *Le Monde* (a paper devoted to the shipping interest, and much sought by sailors), will bring him to our residence."

He handed me a paper, and I read thus:

> CAUGHT—*In the Bois de Boulogne, early in the morning of the* —— *inst.* (the morning of the murder), *a very large, tawny Ourang-Outang of the Bornese species. The owner (who is ascertained to be a sailor, belonging to a Maltese vessel) may have the animal again, upon identifying it satisfactorily, and paying a few charges arising from its capture and keeping. Call at No.* —— *Rue* ——, *Faubourg St. Germain—au troisième.*"

"How was it possible," I asked, "that you should know the man to be a sailor, and belonging to a Maltese vessel?"

"I do *not know* it," said Dupin. "I am not *sure* of it. Here, however, is a small piece of ribbon, which from its form, and from its greasy appearance, has evidently been used in tying the hair in one of those long *queues* of which sailors are so fond. Moreover, this knot is one which few besides sailors can tie, and it is peculiar to the Maltese. I picked the ribbon up at the foot of the lightning-rod. It could not have belonged to either of the deceased. Now if, after all, I am wrong in my induction from this ribbon, that the Frenchman was a sailor belonging to a Maltese vessel, still I can have done no harm in saying what I did in the advertisement. If I am right, a great point is gained. Cognizant although innocent of the murder, the Frenchman will naturally hesitate about replying to the advertisement—about demanding the Ourang-Outang. He will reason thus:—'I am innocent; I am poor; my Ourang-Outang is of great value—to one in my circumstances a fortune of itself—why should I lose it through idle apprehensions of danger? Here it is, within my grasp. It was found in the Bois de Boulogne—at a vast distance from the scene of that butchery. How can it ever be suspected that a brute beast should have done the deed? The police are at fault—they have failed to procure the slightest clew. Should they even trace the animal, it would be impossible to prove me cognizant of the murder, or to implicate me in guilt on account of that cognizance. Above all, *I am known.* The advertiser designates me as the possessor of the beast. I am not sure to what limit his knowledge may extend. Should I avoid claiming a property of so great value, which it is known that I possess, I will render the animal at least, liable to suspicion. It is not my policy to attract attention either to myself or to the beast. I will answer the advertisement, get the Ourang-Outang, and keep it close until this matter has blown over.' "

At this moment we heard a step upon the stairs.

"Be ready," said Dupin, "with your pistols, but neither use them nor show them until at a signal from myself."

The front door of the house had been left open, and the visitor had entered, without ringing, and advanced several steps upon the staircase. Now, however, he seemed to hesitate. Presently we heard him descending. Dupin was moving quickly to the door, when we again heard him coming up. He did not turn back a second time, but stepped up with decision, and rapped at the door of our chamber.

"Come in," said Dupin, in a cheerful and hearty tone.

A man entered. He was a sailor, evidently, a tall, stout, and muscular-looking person, with a certain daredevil expression of countenance, not altogether unprepossessing. His face, greatly sunburnt, was more than half hidden by whisker and *mustachio.* He had with him a huge oaken cudgel, but appeared to be otherwise unarmed. He bowed awkwardly, and bade us "good evening," in French accents, which, although somewhat Neufchatelish, were still sufficiently indicative of a Parisian origin.

"Sit down, my friend," said Dupin. "I suppose you have called about the Ourang-Outang. Upon my word, I almost envy you the possession of him; a remarkably fine, and no doubt a very valuable animal. How old do you suppose him to be?"

The sailor drew a long breath, with the air of a man relieved of some intolerable burden, and then replied, in an assured tone:

"I have no way of telling—but he can't be more than four or five years old. Have you got him here?"

"Oh, no; we had no conveniences for keeping him here. He is at a livery stable in the Rue Dubourg, just by. You can get him in the morning. Of course you are prepared to identify the property?"

"To be sure I am, sir."

"I shall be sorry to part with him," said Dupin.

"I don't mean that you should be at all this trouble for nothing, sir," said the man. "Couldn't expect it. Am very willing to pay a reward for the finding of the animal—that is to say, anything in reason."

"Well," replied my friend, "that is all very fair, to be sure. Let me think!—what should I have? Oh! I will tell you. My reward shall be this. You shall give me all the information in your power about these murders in the Rue Morgue."

Dupin said the last words in a very low tone, and very quietly. Just as quietly, too, he walked toward the door, locked it, and put the key in his pocket. He then drew a pistol from his bosom and placed it, without the least flurry, upon the table.

The sailor's face flushed up as if he were struggling with suffocation. He started to his feet and grasped his cudgel; but the next moment he fell back into his seat, trembling violently, and with the countenance of death itself. He spoke not a word. I pitied him from the bottom of my heart.

"My friend," said Dupin, in a kind tone, "you are alarming yourself unnecessarily—you are indeed. We mean you no harm whatever. I pledge you the honor of a gentleman, and of a Frenchman, that we intend you no injury. I perfectly well know that you are innocent of the atrocities in the Rue Morgue. It will not do, however, to deny that you are in some measure implicated in them. From what I have already said, you must know that I have had means of information about this matter—means of which you could never have dreamed. Now the thing stands thus. You have done nothing which you could have avoided—nothing, certainly, which renders you culpable. You are not even guilty of robbery, when you might have robbed with impunity. You have nothing to conceal. You have no reason for concealment. On the other hand, you are bound by every principle of honor to confess all you know. An innocent man is now imprisoned, charged with that crime of which you can point out the perpetrator."

The sailor had recovered his presence of mind, in a great measure, while Dupin uttered these words; but his original boldness of bearing was all gone.

"So help me God!" said he, after a brief pause, "I *will* tell you all I know about this affair;—but I do not expect you to believe one half I say—I would be a fool indeed if I did. Still, I *am* innocent, and I will make a clean breast if I die for it."

What he stated was, in substance, this. He had lately made a voyage to the Indian Archipelago. A party, of which he formed one, landed at Borneo, and passed into the interior on an excursion of pleasure. Himself and a companion had captured the Ourang-Outang. This companion dying, the animal fell into his own exclusive possession. After a great trouble, occasioned by the intractable ferocity of his captive during the home voyage, he at length succeeded in lodging it safely at his own residence in Paris, where, not to attract toward himself the unpleasant curiosity of his neighbors, he kept it carefully secluded, until such time as it should recover from a wound in the foot, received from a splinter on board ship. His ultimate design was to sell it.

Returning home from some sailor's frolic on the night, or rather in the morning, of the murder, he found the beast occupying his own bedroom, into which it had broken from a closet adjoining, where it had been, as was thought, securely confined. Razor in hand, and fully lathered, it was sitting before a looking-glass, attempting the operation of shaving, in which it had no doubt previously watched its master through the keyhole of the closet. Terrified at the sight of so dangerous a weapon in the possession of an animal so ferocious, and so well able to use it, the man, for some moments, was at a loss what to do. He had been accustomed, however, to quiet the creature, even in its fiercest moods, by the use of a whip, and to this he now resorted. Upon sight of it, the Ourang-Outang sprang at once through the door of the chamber, down the stairs, and thence, through a window, unfortunately open, into the street.

The Frenchman followed in despair; the ape, razor still in hand, occasionally stopping to look back and gesticulate at his pursuer, until the latter had nearly come up with it. It then again made off. In this manner the chase continued for a long time. The streets were profoundly quiet, as it was nearly three o'clock in the morning. In passing down an alley in the rear of the Rue Morgue, the fugitive's attention was arrested by a light gleaming from the open window of Madame L'Espanaye's chamber, in the fourth story of her house. Rushing to the building, it perceived the lightning-rod, clambered up with inconceivable agility, grasped the shutter, which was thrown fully back against the wall, and, by its means, swung itself directly upon the headboard of the bed. The whole feat did not occupy a minute. The shutter was kicked open again by the Ourang-Outang as it entered the room.

The sailor, in the meantime, was both rejoiced and perplexed. He had strong hopes of now recapturing the brute, as it could scarcely escape from the trap into which it had ventured, except by the rod, where it might be intercepted as it came down. On the other hand, there was much cause for anxiety as to what it might do in the house. This latter reflection urged the man still to follow the fugitive. A lightning-rod is ascended without difficulty, especially by a sailor; but, when he had arrived as high as the window, which lay far to his left, his career was stopped; the most that he could accomplish was to reach over so as to obtain a glimpse of the interior of the room. At this glimpse he nearly fell from his hold through excess of horror. Now it was that those hideous shrieks arose upon the night, which had startled from slumber the inmates of the Rue Morgue. Madame L'Espanaye and her daughter, habited in their night clothes, had apparently been occupied in arranging some papers in the iron chest already mentioned, which had been wheeled into the middle of the room. It was open, and its contents lay beside it on the floor. The victims must have been sitting with their backs toward the window; and, from the time elapsing between the ingress of the beast and the screams, it seems probable that it was not immediately perceived. The flapping to of the shutter would naturally have been attributed to the wind.

As the sailor looked in, the gigantic animal had seized Madame L'Espanaye by the hair (which was loose, as she had been combing it), and was flourishing the razor about her face, in imitation of the motions of a barber. The daughter lay prostrate and motionless; she had swooned. The screams and struggles of the old lady (during which the hair was torn from her head) had the effect of changing the probably pacific purposes of the Ourang-Outang into those of wrath. With one determined sweep of its muscular arm it nearly severed her head from her body. The sight of blood inflamed its anger into phrenzy. Gnashing its teeth, and flashing fire from its eyes, it flew upon the body of the girl and embedded its fearful talons in her throat, retaining its grasp until she expired. Its wandering and wild glances fell at this moment upon the head of the bed, over which the face of its master, rigid with horror, was just discernible. The fury of the beast, who no doubt bore still in mind the dreaded whip, was instantly converted into fear. Conscious of having deserved punishment, it seemed desirous of concealing its bloody deeds, and skipped about the chamber in an agony of nervous agitation; throwing down and breaking the furniture as it moved, and dragging the bed from the bedstead. In conclusion, it seized first the corpse of the daughter, and thrust it up the chimney, as it was found; then that of the old lady, which, it immediately hurled through the window headlong.

As the ape approached the casement with its mutilated burden, the sailor shrank aghast to the rod, and, rather gliding than clambering down it, hurried at once home—dreading the consequences of the butchery, and gladly abandoning, in his terror, all solicitude about the fate of the Ourang-Outang. The words heard by the party upon the staircase were the Frenchman's exclamations of horror and affright, commingled with the fiendish jabberings of the brute.

I have scarcely any thing to add. The Ourang-Outang must have escaped from the chamber, by the rod, just before the breaking of the door. It must have closed the window as it passed through it. It was subsequently caught by the owner himself, who obtained for it a very large sum at the *Jardin des Plantes.* Le Bon was instantly released, upon our narration of the circumstances (with some comments from Dupin) at the *bureau* of the Prefect of Police. This functionary, however, well disposed to my friend, could not altogether conceal his chagrin at the turn which affairs had taken, and was fain to indulge in a sarcasm or two about the propriety of every person minding his own business.

"Let him talk," said Dupin, who had not thought it necessary to reply. "Let him discourse; it will ease his conscience. I am satisfied with having defeated him in his own castle. Nevertheless, that he failed in the solution of this mystery, is by no means that matter for wonder which he supposes it; for, in truth, our friend the prefect is somewhat too cunning to be profound. In his wisdom is no *stamen.* It is all head and no body, like the pictures of the Goddess Laverna—or, at best, all head and shoulders, like a codfish. But he is a good creature after all. I like him especially for one master stroke of cant, by which he has attained his reputation for ingenuity, I mean the way he has '*de nier ce qui est, et d'expliquer ce qui n'est pas.*' "*

* "Of ignoring whatever is, and of explaining what does not exist"—a phrase from Rousseau's *La Nouvelle Héloise.*

THE PURLOINED LETTER

Nil sapientiae odiosius acumine nimio.

SENECA.*

At Paris, just after dark one gusty evening in the autumn of 18—, I was enjoying the twofold luxury of meditation and a meerschaum, in company with my friend C. Auguste Dupin, in his little back library, or book-closet, *au troisième, No. 33, Rue Dunôt, Faubourg St. Germain.* For one hour at least we had maintained a profound silence; while each, to any casual observer, might have seemed intently and exclusively occupied with the curling eddies of smoke that oppressed the atmosphere of the chamber. For myself, however, I was mentally discussing certain topics which had formed matter for conversation between us at an earlier period of the evening; I mean the affair of the Rue Morgue, and the mystery attending the murder of Marie Rogêt. I looked upon it, therefore, as something of a coincidence, when the door of our apartment was thrown open and admitted our old acquaintance, Monsieur G——, the Prefect of the Parisian police.

We gave him a hearty welcome; for there was nearly half as much of the entertaining as of the contemptible about the man, and we had not seen him for several years. We had been sitting in the dark, and Dupin now arose for the purpose of lighting a lamp, but sat down again, without doing so, upon G.'s saying that he had called to consult us, or rather to ask the opinion of my friend, about some official business which had occasioned a great deal of trouble.

* "Nothing is more odious to good sense than too great subtlety."

"If it is any point requiring reflection," observed Dupin, as he forbore to enkindle the wick, "we shall examine it to better purpose in the dark."

"That is another of your odd notions," said the Prefect, who had a fashion of calling every thing "odd" that was beyond his comprehension, and thus lived amid an absolute legion of "oddities."

"Very true," said Dupin, as he supplied his visitor with a pipe, and rolled towards him a comfortable chair.

"And what is the difficulty now?" I asked. "Nothing more in the assassination way, I hope?"

"Oh no; nothing of that nature. The fact is, the business is *very* simple indeed, and I make no doubt that we can manage it sufficiently well ourselves; but then I thought Dupin would like to hear the details of it, because it is so excessively *odd.*"

"Simple and odd," said Dupin.

"Why, yes; and not exactly that, either. The fact is, we have all been a good deal puzzled because the affair *is* so simple, and yet baffles us altogether."

"Perhaps it is the very simplicity of the thing which puts you at fault," said my friend.

"What nonsense you *do* talk!" replied the Prefect, laughing heartily.

"Perhaps the mystery is a little *too* plain," said Dupin.

"Oh, good heavens! who ever heard of such an idea?"

"A little *too* self-evident."

"Ha! ha! ha!—ha! ha! ha!—ho! ho! ho!"—roared our visitor, profoundly amused, "oh, Dupin, you will be the death of me yet!"

"And what, after all, *is* the matter on hand?" I asked.

"Why, I will tell you," replied the Prefect, as he gave a long, steady, and contemplative puff, and settled himself in his chair. "I will tell you in a few words; but, before I begin, let me caution you that this is an affair demanding the greatest secrecy, and that I should most probably lose the position I now hold, were it known that I confided it to any one."

"Proceed," said I.

"Or not," said Dupin.

"Well, then; I have received personal information, from a very high quarter, that a certain document of the last importance, has been purloined from the royal apartments. The individual who purloined it is known; this beyond a doubt; he was seen to take it. It is known, also, that it still remains in his possession."

"How is this known?" asked Dupin.

"It is clearly inferred," replied the Prefect, "from the nature of the document, and from the non-appearance of certain results which would at once arise from its passing *out* of the robber's possession;—that is to say, from his employing it as he must design in the end to employ it."

"Be a little more explicit," I said.

"Well, I may venture so far as to say that the paper gives its holder a certain power in a certain quarter where such power is immensely valuable." The Prefect was fond of the cant of diplomacy.

"Still I do not quite understand," said Dupin.

"No? Well; the disclosure of the document to a third person, who shall be nameless, would bring in question the honor of a personage of most exalted station; and this fact gives the holder of the document an ascendancy over the illustrious personage whose honor and peace are so jeopardized."

"But this ascendancy," I interposed, "would depend upon the robber's knowledge of the loser's knowledge of the robber. Who would dare—"

"The thief," said G., "is the Minister D——, who dares all things, those unbecoming as well as those becoming a man. The method of the theft was not less ingenious than bold. The document in question—a letter, to be frank—had been received by the personage robbed while alone in the royal *boudoir.* During its perusal she was suddenly interrupted by the entrance of the other exalted personage from whom especially it was her wish to conceal it. After a hurried and vain endeavor to thrust it in a drawer, she was forced to place it, open as it was, upon a table. The address, however, was uppermost, and, the contents thus unexposed, the letter escaped notice. At this juncture enters the Minister D——. His lynx eye immediately perceives the paper, recognizes the handwriting of the address, observes the confusion of the personage addressed, and fathoms her secret. After some business transactions, hurried through in his ordinary manner, he produces a letter somewhat similar to the one in question, opens it, pretends to read it, and then places it in close juxtaposition to the other. Again he converses, for some fifteen minutes, upon the public affairs. At length, in taking leave, he takes also from the table the letter to which he had no claim. Its rightful owner saw, but, of course, dared not call attention to the act, in the presence of the third personage who stood at her elbow. The Minister decamped; leaving his own letter—one of no importance—upon the table."

"Here, then," said Dupin to me, "you have precisely what you demand to make the ascendancy complete—the robber's knowledge of the loser's knowledge of the robber."

"Yes," replied the Prefect; "and the power thus attained has, for some months past, been wielded, for political purposes, to a very dangerous extent. The personage robbed is more thoroughly convinced, every day, of the necessity of reclaiming her letter. But this, of course, cannot be done openly. In fine, driven to despair, she has committed the matter to me."

"Than whom," said Dupin, amid a perfect whirlwind of smoke, "no more sagacious agent could, I suppose, be desired, or even imagined."

"You flatter me," replied the Prefect; "but it is possible that some such opinion may have been entertained."

"It is clear," said I, "as you observe, that the letter is still in possession of the Minister; since it is this possession, and not any employment of the letter, which bestows the power. With the employment the power departs."

"True," said G——; "and upon this conviction I proceeded. My first care was to make thorough search of the Minister's hotel; and here my chief embarrassment lay in the necessity of searching without his knowledge. Beyond all things, I have been warned of the danger which would result from giving him reason to suspect our design."

"But," said I, "you are quite *au fait*[*] in these investigations. The Parisian police have done this thing often before."

"Oh yes; and for this reason I did not despair. The habits of the minister gave me, too, a great advantage. He is frequently absent from home all night. His servants are by no means numerous. They sleep at a distance from their master's apartment, and, being chiefly Neapolitans, are readily made drunk. I have keys, as you know, with which I can open any chamber or cabinet in Paris. For three months a night has not passed, during the greater part of which I have not been engaged, personally, in ransacking the D—— Hôtel. My honor is interested, and, to mention a great secret, the reward is enormous. So

* expert

I did not abandon the search until I had become fully satisfied that the thief is a more astute man than myself. I fancy that I have investigated every nook and corner of the premises in which it is possible that the paper can be concealed."

"But is it not possible," I suggested, "that although the letter may be in the possession of the Minister, as it unquestionably is, he may have concealed it elsewhere than upon his own premises?"

"This is barely possible," said Dupin. "The present peculiar condition of affairs at court, and especially of those intrigues in which D—— is known to be involved, would render the instant availability of the document—its susceptibility of being produced at a moment's notice—a point of nearly equal importance with its possession."

"Its susceptibility of being produced?" said I.

"That is to say, of being *destroyed*," said Dupin.

"True," I observed: "the paper is clearly then upon the premises. As for its being upon the person of the minister, we may consider that as out of the question."

"Entirely," said the Prefect. "He has been twice waylaid, as if by footpads, and his person rigorously searched under my own inspection."

"You might have spared yourself this trouble," said Dupin "D——, I presume, is not altogether a fool, and, if not, must have anticipated these waylayings, as a matter of course."

"Not *altogether* a fool," said G., "but then he's a poet, which I take to be only one remove from a fool."

"True," said Dupin, after a long and thoughtful whiff from his meerschaum, "although I have been guilty of certain doggerel myself."

"Suppose you detail," said I, "the particulars of your search."

"Why the fact is, we took our time, and we searched *every where.* I have had long experience in these affairs. I took the entire building, room by room: devoting the nights of a whole week to each. We examined, first, the furniture of each apartment. We opened every possible drawer; and I presume you know that, to a properly trained police agent, such a thing as a *secret* drawer is impossible. Any man is a dolt who permits a 'secret' drawer to escape him in a search of this kind. The thing is *so* plain. There is a certain amount of bulk—of space—to be accounted for in every cabinet. Then we have accurate rules. The fiftieth part of a line could not escape us. After the cabinets we took the chairs. The cushions we probed with the fine long needles you have seen me employ. From the tables we removed the tops."

"Why so?"

"Sometimes the top of a table, or other similarly arranged piece of furniture, is removed by the person wishing to conceal an article; then the leg is excavated, the article deposited within the cavity, and the top replaced. The bottoms and tops of bed-posts are employed in the same way."

"But could not the cavity be detected by sounding?" I asked.

"By no means, if, when the article is deposited, a sufficient wadding of cotton be placed around it. Besides, in our case, we were obliged to proceed without noise."

"But you could not have removed—you could not have taken to pieces *all* articles of furniture in which it would have been possible to make a deposit in the manner you mention. A letter may be compressed into a thin spiral roll, not differing much in shape or bulk from a large knitting-needle, and in this form it might be inserted into the rung of a chair, for example. You did not take to pieces all the chairs?"

"Certainly not; but we did better—we examined the rungs of every chair in the hotel, and, indeed, the jointings of every description of furniture, by the aid of a most powerful microscope. Had there been any traces of recent disturbance we should not have failed to detect it instantly. A single grain of gimlet-dust, for example, would have been as obvious as an apple. And disorder in the glueing—any unusual gaping in the joints—would have sufficed to insure detection."

"I presume you looked to the mirrors, between the boards and the plates, and you probed the beds and the bed-clothes, as well as the curtains and carpets."

"That of course; and when we had absolutely completed every particle of the furniture in this way, then we examined the house itself. We divided its entire surface into compartments, which we numbered, so that none might be missed; then we scrutinized each individual square inch throughout the premises, including the two houses immediately adjoining, with the microscope, as before."

"The two houses adjoining!" I exclaimed; "you must have had a great deal of trouble."

"We had; but the reward offered is prodigious."

"You include the *grounds* about the houses?"

"All the grounds are paved with brick. They gave us comparatively little trouble. We examined the moss between the bricks, and found it undisturbed."

"You looked among D——'s papers, of course, and into the books of the library?"

"Certainly; we opened every package and parcel; we not only opened every book, but we turned over every leaf in each volume, not contenting ourselves with a mere shake, according to the fashion of some of our police officers. We also measured the thickness of every book-*cover*, with the most accurate admeasurement, and applied to each the most jealous scrutiny of the microscope. Had any of the bindings been recently meddled with, it would have been utterly impossible that the fact should have escaped observation. Some five or six volumes, just from the hands of the binder, we carefully probed, longitudinally, with the needles."

"You explored the floors beneath the carpets?"

"Beyond doubt. We removed every carpet, and examined the boards with the microscope."

"And the paper on the walls?"

"Yes."

"You looked into the cellars?"

"We did."

"Then," I said, "you have been making a miscalculation, and the letter is *not* upon the premises, as you suppose."

"I fear you are right there," said the Prefect. "And now, Dupin, what would you advise me to do?"

"To make a thorough re-search of the premises."

"That is absolutely needless," replied G——. "I am not more sure that I breathe than I am that the letter is not at the Hôtel."

"I have no better advice to give you," said Dupin. "You have, of course, an accurate description of the letter?"

"Oh yes!"—And here the Prefect, producing a memorandum-book, proceeded to read aloud a minute account of the internal, and especially of the external appearance of the missing document. Soon after finishing the perusal of this description, he took his departure, more entirely depressed in spirits than I had ever known the good gentleman before.

In about a month afterwards he paid us another visit, and found us occupied very nearly as before. He took a pipe and a chair and entered into some ordinary conversation. At length I said—

"Well, but G——, what of the purloined letter? I presume you have at last made up your mind that there is no such thing as over-reaching the Minister?"

"Confound him, say I—yes; I made the re-examination, however, as Dupin suggested—but it was all labor lost, as I knew it would be."

"How much was the reward offered, did you say?" asked Dupin.

"Why, a very great deal—a *very* liberal reward—I don't like to say how much, precisely; but one thing I *will* say, that I wouldn't mind giving my individual check for fifty thousand francs to any one who could obtain me that letter. The fact is, it is becoming of more and more importance every day; and the reward has been lately doubled. If it were trebled, however, I could do no more than I have done."

"Why, yes," said Dupin, drawlingly, between the whiffs of his meerschaum, "I really—think, G——, you have not exerted yourself—to the utmost in this matter. You might—do a little more, I think, eh?"

"How?—in what way?"

"Why—puff, puff—you might—puff, puff—employ counsel in the matter, eh?—puff, puff, puff. Do you remember the story they tell of Abernethy?"

"No: hang Abernethy!"

"To be sure! hang him and welcome. But, once upon a time, a certain rich miser conceived the design of spunging upon this Abernethy for a medical opinion. Getting up, for this purpose, an ordinary conversation in a private company, he insinuated his case to the physician, as that of an imaginary individual.

" 'We will suppose,' said the miser, 'that his symptoms are such and such; now, doctor, what would *you* have directed him to take?'

" 'Take!' said Abernethy, 'why take *advice,* to be sure.' "

"But," said the Prefect, a little discomposed, "I am *perfectly* willing to take advice, and to pay for it. I would *really* give fifty thousand francs to any one who would aid me in the matter."

"In that case," replied Dupin, opening a drawer, and producing a check-book, "you may as well fill me up a check for the amount mentioned. When you have signed it, I will hand you the letter."

I was astounded. The Prefect appeared absolutely thunderstricken. For some minutes he remained speechless and motionless, looking incredulously at my friend with open mouth, and eyes that seemed starting from their sockets; then, apparently recovering himself in some measure, he seized a pen, and after several pauses and vacant stares, finally filled up and signed a check for fifty thousand francs, and handed it across the table to Dupin. The latter examined it carefully and deposited it in his pocket-book; then, unlocking an *escritoire,* took thence a letter and gave it to the Prefect. This functionary grasped it in a perfect agony of joy, opened it with a trembling hand, cast a rapid glance at its contents, and then, scrambling and struggling to the door, rushed at length unceremoniously from the room and from the house, without having uttered a syllable since Dupin had requested him to fill up the check.

When he had gone, my friend entered into some explanations.

"The Parisian police," he said, "are exceedingly able in their way. They are persevering, ingenious, cunning, and thoroughly versed in the knowledge which their duties seem chiefly to demand. Thus, when G—— detailed to us his mode of searching the premises at the Hôtel D——, I felt entire confidence in his having made a satisfactory investigation—so far as his labors extended."

"So far as his labors extended?" said I.

"Yes," said Dupin. "The measures adopted were not only the best of their kind, but carried out to absolute perfection. Had the letter been deposited within the range of their search, these fellows would, beyond a question, have found it."

I merely laughed—but he seemed quite serious in all that he said.

"The measures, then," he continued, "were good in their kind, and well executed; but their defect lay in their being inapplicable to the case, and to the man. A certain set of highly ingenious resources are, with the Prefect, a sort of Procrustean bed, to which he forcibly adapts his designs. But he perpetually errs by being too deep or too shallow, for the matter in hand; and many a schoolboy is a better reasoner than he. I knew one about eight years of age, whose success at guessing in the game of 'even and odd' attracted universal admiration. This game is simple; and is played with marbles. One player holds in his hand a number of these toys, and demands of another whether that number is even or odd. If the guess is right, the guesser wins one; if wrong, he loses one. The boy to whom I allude won all the marbles of the school. Of course he had some principle of guessing; and this lay in mere observation and admeasurement of the astuteness of his opponents. For example, an arrant simpleton is his opponent, and, holding up his closed hand, asks, 'are they even or odd?' Our schoolboy replies, 'odd,' and loses; but upon the second trial he wins, for he then says to himself, 'the simpleton had them even upon the first trial, and his amount of cunning is just sufficient to make him have them odd upon the second; I will therefore guess odd;—he guesses odd, and wins. Now, with a simpleton a degree above the first, he would have reasoned thus: 'This fellow finds that in the first instance I guessed odd, and, in the second, he will propose to himself upon the first impulse, a simple variation from even to odd, as did the first simpleton; but then a second thought will suggest that this is too simple a variation, and finally he will decide upon putting it even as before. I will therefore guess even;—he guesses even, and wins. Now this mode of reasoning in the schoolboy, whom his fellows termed 'lucky,'—what, in its last analysis, is it?"

"It is merely," I said, "an identification of the reasoner's intellect with that of his opponent."

"It is," said Dupin; "and, upon inquiring of the boy by what means he effected the *thorough* identification in which his success consisted, I received answer as follows: 'When I wish to find out how wise, or how stupid, or how good, or how wicked is any one, or what are his thoughts at the moment, I fashion the expression of my face, as accurately as possible, in accordance with the expression of his, and then wait to see what thoughts or sentiments arise in my mind or heart, as if to match or correspond with the expression.' This response of the schoolboy lies at the bottom of all the spurious profundity which has been attributed to Rochefoucauld, to La Bruyère, to Machiavelli, and to Campanella."

"And the identification," I said, "of the reasoner's intellect with that of his opponent, depends, if I understand you aright, upon the accuracy with which the opponent's intellect is admeasured."

"For its practical value it depends upon this," replied Dupin; "and the Prefect and his cohort fail so frequently, first, by default of this identification, and, secondly, by ill-admeasurement, or rather through non-admeasurement, of the intellect with which they are engaged. They consider only their *own* ideas of ingenuity; and, in searching for anything hidden, advert only to the modes in which *they* would have hidden it. They are right in this much—that their own ingenuity is a faithful representative of *the mass;* but when the cunning of the individual felon is diverse in character from their own, the felon foils them, of course. This always happens when it is above their own, and very usually when it is below. They have no variation of principle in their investigations; at best, when urged by some unusual emergency—by some extraordinary reward—they extend or exaggerate their old modes of *practice,* without touching their principles. What, for example, in this case of D——, has been done to vary the principle of action? What is all this boring, and probing, and sounding, and scrutinizing with the microscope, and dividing the surface of the building into registered square inches—what is it all but an exaggeration *of the application* of the one principle or set of principles of search, which are based upon the one set of notions regarding human ingenuity, to which the Prefect, in the long routine of his duty, has been accustomed? Do you not see he has taken it for granted that *all* men proceed to conceal a letter,—not exactly in a gimlet-hole bored in a chair-leg—but, at least in *some* out-of-the-way hole or corner suggested by the same tenor of thought which would urge a man to secrete a letter in a gimlet-hole bored in a chair-leg? And do you not see also, that such *recherchés* nooks for concealment are adapted only for ordinary occasions, and would be adopted only by ordinary intellects; for, in all cases of concealment, a disposal of the article concealed—a disposal of it in this *recherché* manner,—is, in the very first instance, presumable and presumed; and thus its discovery depends, not at all upon the acumen, but altogether upon the mere care, patience, and determination of the seekers; and where the case is of importance—or, what amounts to the same thing in the political eyes, when the reward is of magnitude,—the qualities in question have *never* been known to fail. You will now understand what I meant in suggesting that, had the purloined letter been hidden any where within the limits of the Prefect's examination—in other words, had the principle of its concealment been comprehended within the principles of the Prefect—its discovery would have been a matter altogether beyond question. This functionary, however, has been thoroughly mystified; and the remote source of his defeat lies in the supposition that the Minister is a fool, because he has acquired renown as a poet. All fools are poets; this the Prefect *feels;* and he is merely guilty of a *non distributio medii** in thence inferring that all poets are fools."

"But is this really the poet?" I asked. "There are two brothers, I know; and both have attained reputation in letters. The Minister I believe has written learnedly on the Differential Calculus. He is a mathematician, and no poet."

"You are mistaken; I know him well; he is both. As poet *and* mathematician, he would reason well; as mere mathematician, he could not have reasoned at all, and thus would have been at the mercy of the Prefect."

"You surprise me," I said, "by these opinions, which have been contradicted by the voice of the world. You do not mean to set at naught the well-digested idea of centuries. The mathematical reason has long been regarded as *the* reason *par excellence.*"

* undistributed middle. A flaw in logical reasoning that leads to a false conclusion.

" '*Il y a à parier,*' " replied Dupin, quoting from Chamfort, " '*que toute idée publique, toute convention reçue, est une sottise, car elle a convenu au plus grand nombre.*'* The mathematicians, I grant you, have done their best to promulgate the popular error to which you allude, and which is none the less an error for its promulgation as truth. With an art worthy a better cause, for example, they have insinuated the term 'analysis' into application to algebra. The French are the originators of this particular deception; but if a term is of any importance—if words derive any value from applicability—then 'analysis' conveys 'algebra' about as much as, in Latin, '*ambitus*' implies 'ambition,' '*religio*' 'religion,' or '*homines honesti,*' a set of *honorable* men."

"You have a quarrel on hand, I see," said I, "with some of the algebraists of Paris; but proceed."

"I dispute the availability, and thus the value, of that reason which is cultivated in any especial form other than the abstractly logical. I dispute, in particular, the reason educed by mathematical study. The mathematics are the science of form and quantity; mathematical reasoning is merely logic applied to observation upon form and quantity. The great error lies in supposing that even the truths of what is called *pure* algebra, are abstract or general truths. And this error is so egregious that I am confounded at the universality with which it has been received. Mathematical axioms are *not* axioms of general truth. What is true of *relation*—of form and quantity—is often grossly false in regard to morals, for example. In this latter science it is very usually *un*true that the aggregated parts are equal to the whole. In chemistry also the axiom fails. In the consideration of motive it fails; for two motives, each of a given value, have not, necessarily, a value when united, equal to the sum of their values apart. There are numerous other mathematical truths which are only truths within the limits of *relation.* But the mathematician argues, from his *finite truths,* through habit, as if they were of an absolutely general applicability—as the world indeed imagines them to be. Bryant, in his very learned 'Mythology,' mentions an analogous source of error, when he says that 'although the Pagan fables are not believed, yet we forget ourselves continually, and make inferences from them as existing realities.' With the algebraists, however, who are Pagans themselves, the 'Pagan fables' *are* believed, and the inferences are made, not so much through lapse of memory, as through an unaccountable addling of the brains. In

* "It's a good bet that every popular idea, every accepted convention, is a stupidity, for it is suited to the masses."

short, I never yet encountered the mere mathematician who could be trusted out of equal roots, or one who did not clandestinely hold it as a point of his faith that $x^2 + px$ was absolutely and unconditionally equal to q. Say to one of these gentlemen, by way of experiment, if you please, that you believe occasions may occur where $x^2 + px$ is *not* altogether equal to q, and, having made him understand what you mean, get out of his reach as speedily as convenient, for, beyond doubt, he will endeavor to knock you down.

"I mean to say," continued Dupin, while I merely laughed at his last observations, "that if the Minister had been no more than a mathematician, the Prefect would have been under no necessity of giving me this check. I knew him, however, as both mathematician and poet, and my measures were adapted to his capacity, with reference to the circumstances by which he was surrounded. I knew him as a courtier, too, and as a bold *intriguant.* Such a man, I considered, could not fail to be aware of the ordinary political modes of action. He could not have failed to anticipate—and events have proved that he did not fail to anticipate—the waylayings to which he was subjected. He must have foreseen, I reflected, the secret investigations of his premises. His frequent absences from home at night, which were hailed by the Prefect as certain aids to his success, I regarded only as *ruses,* to afford opportunity for thorough search to the police, and thus the sooner to impress them with the conviction to which G——, in fact, did finally arrive—the conviction that the letter was not upon the premises. I felt, also, that the whole train of thought, which I was at some pains in detailing to you just now, concerning the invariable principle of political action in searches for articles concealed—I felt that this whole train of thought would necessarily pass through the mind of the Minister. It would imperatively lead him to despise all the ordinary *nooks* of concealment. *He* could not, I reflected, be so weak as not to see that the most intricate and remote recess of his hotel would be as open as his commonest closets to the eyes, to the probes, to the gimlets, and to the microscopes of the Prefect. I saw, in fine, that he would be driven, as a matter of course, to *simplicity,* if not deliberately induced to it as a matter of choice. You will remember, perhaps, how desperately the Prefect laughed when I suggested, upon our first interview, that it was just possible this mystery troubled him so much on account of its being so *very* self-evident."

"Yes," said I, "I remember his merriment well. I really thought he would have fallen into convulsions."

"The material world," continued Dupin, "abounds with very strict analogies to the immaterial; and thus some color of truth has been given to the rhetorical dogma, that metaphor, or simile, may be made to strengthen an argument, as well as to embellish a description. The principle of the *vis inertia*, * for example, seems to be identical in physics and metaphysics. It is not more true in the former, that a large body is with more difficulty set in motion than a smaller one, and that its subsequent *momentum* is commensurate with this difficulty, than it is, in the latter, that intellects of the vaster capacity, while more forcible, more constant, and more eventful in their movements than those of inferior grade, are yet the less readily moved, and more embarrassed and full of hesitation in the first few steps of their progress. Again: have you ever noticed which of the street signs, over the shop doors, are the most attractive of attention?"

"I have never given the matter a thought," I said.

"There is a game of puzzles," he resumed, "which is played upon a map. One party playing requires another to find a given word—the name of town, river, state or empire—any word, in short, upon the motley and perplexed surface of the chart. A novice in the game generally seeks to embarrass his opponents by giving them the most minutely lettered names; but the adept selects such words as stretch, in large characters, from one end of the chart to the other. These, like the over-largely lettered signs and placards of the street, escape observation by dint of being excessively obvious; and here the physical oversight is precisely analogous with the moral inapprehension by which the intellect suffers to pass unnoticed these considerations which are too obtrusively and too palpably self-evident. But this is a point, it appears, somewhat above or beneath the understanding of the Prefect. He never once thought it probable, or possible, that the Minister had deposited the letter immediately beneath the nose of the whole world, by way of best preventing any portion of that world from perceiving it.

"But the more I reflected upon the daring, dashing, and discriminating ingenuity of D——; upon the fact that the document must always have been *at hand*, if he intended to use it to good purpose; and upon the decisive evidence, obtained by the Prefect, that it was not hidden within the limits of that dignitary's ordinary search—the more satisfied I became that, to conceal this letter, the Minister had

* force of inertia.

resorted to the comprehensive and sagacious expedient of not attempting to conceal it at all.

"Full of these ideas, I prepared myself with a pair of green spectacles, and called one fine morning, quite by accident, at the Ministerial hotel. I found D—— at home, yawning, lounging, and dawdling, as usual, and pretending to be in the last extremity of *ennui.* He is, perhaps, the most really energetic human being now alive—but that is only when nobody sees him.

"To be even with him, I complained of my weak eyes, and lamented the necessity of the spectacles, under cover of which I cautiously and thoroughly surveyed the apartment, while seemingly intent only upon the conversation of my host.

"I paid special attention to a large writing-table near which he sat, and upon which lay confusedly, some miscellaneous letters and other papers, with one or two musical instruments and a few books. Here, however, after a long and very deliberate scrutiny, I saw nothing to excite particular suspicion.

"At length my eyes, in going the circuit of the room, fell upon a trumpery fillagree card-rack of paste-board, that hung dangling by a dirty blue ribbon, from a little brass knob just beneath the middle of the mantelpiece. In this rack, which had three or four compartments, were five or six visiting cards and a solitary letter. This last was much soiled and crumpled. It was torn nearly in two, across the middle—as if a design, in the first instance, to tear it entirely up as worthless, had been altered, or stayed, in the second. It had a large black seal, bearing the D—— cipher *very* conspicuously, and was addressed, in a diminutive female hand, to D——, the minister, himself. It was thrust carelessly, and even, as it seemed, contemptuously, into one of the upper divisions of the rack.

"No sooner had I glanced at this letter, than I concluded it to be that of which I was in search. To be sure, it was, to all appearance, radically different from the one which the Prefect had read us so minute a description. Here the seal was large and black, with the D—— cipher; there it was small and red, with the ducal arms of the S—— family. Here, the address, to the Minister, was diminutive and feminine; there the superscription, to a certain royal personage, was markedly bold and decided; the size alone formed a point of correspondence. But, then, the *radicalness* of these differences, which was excessive; the dirt; the soiled and torn condition of the paper, so inconsistent with the *true* methodical habits of D——, and so suggestive of a design to delude the beholder into an idea of the worthlessness of the document; these things, together with the hyperobtrusive situation of this document, full in the view of every visitor, and thus exactly in accordance with the conclusions to which I had previously arrived; these things, I say, were strongly corroborative of suspicion, in one who came with the intention to suspect.

"I protracted my visit as long as possible, and, while I maintained a most animated discussion with the Minister, on a topic which I knew well had never failed to interest and excite him, I kept my attention really riveted upon the letter. In this examination, I committed to memory its external appearance and arrangement in the rack; and also fell, at length, upon a discovery which set at rest whatever trivial doubt I might have entertained. In scrutinizing the edges of the paper, I observed them to be more *chafed* than seemed necessary. They presented the *broken* appearance which is manifested when a stiff paper, having been once folded and pressed with a folder, is refolded in a reversed direction, in the same creases or edges which had formed the original fold. This discovery was sufficient. It was clear to me that the letter had been turned, as a glove, inside out, re-directed, and resealed. I bade the Minister good morning, and took my departure at once, leaving a gold snuff-box upon the table.

"The next morning I called for the snuff-box, when we resumed, quite eagerly, the conversation of the preceding day. While thus engaged, however, a loud report, as if of a pistol, was heard immediately beneath the windows of the hotel, and was succeeded by a series of fearful screams, and the shoutings of a mob. D—— rushed to a casement, threw it open, and looked out. In the meantime, I stepped to the card-rack, took the letter, put it in my pocket, and replaced it by a *fac-simile,* (so far as regards externals,) which I had carefully prepared at my lodgings; imitating the D—— cipher, very readily, by means of a seal formed of bread.

"The disturbance in the street had been occasioned by the frantic behavior of a man with a musket. He had fired it among a crowd of women and children. It proved, however, to have been without ball, and the fellow was suffered to go his way as a lunatic or a drunkard. When he had gone, D—— came from the window, whither I had followed him immediately upon securing the object in view. Soon afterwards I bade him farewell. The pretended lunatic was a man in my own pay."

"But what purpose had you," I asked, "in replacing the letter by a *fac-simile.* Would it not have been better, at the first visit, to have seized it openly, and departed?"

"D——," replied Dupin, "is a desperate man, and a man of nerve. His hotel, too, is not without attendants devoted to his interests. Had I made the wild attempt you suggest, I might never have left the Ministerial presence alive. The good people of Paris might have heard of me no more. But I had an object apart from these considerations. In this matter, I act as a partisan of the lady concerned. For eighteen months the Minister has had her in his power. She has now him in hers; since, being unaware that the letter is not in his possession, he will proceed with his exactions as if it was. Thus will he inevitably commit himself, at once, to his political destruction. His downfall, too, will not be more precipitate than awkward. It is all very well to talk about the *facilis descensus Averni,* * but in all kinds of climbing, as Catalini said of singing, it is far more easy to get up than to come down. In the present instance I have no sympathy—at least no pity—for him who descends. He is that *monstrum horrendum,* an unprincipled man of genius. I confess, however, that I should like very well to know the precise character of his thoughts, when, being defied by her whom the Prefect terms 'a certain personage,' he is reduced to opening the letter which I left for him in the card-rack."

"How? did you put any thing particular in it?"

"Why—it did not seem altogether right to leave the interior blank—that would have been insulting. D——, at Vienna once, did me an evil turn, which I told him, quite good-humoredly, that I should remember. So, as I knew he would feel some curiosity in regard to the identity of the person who had outwitted him, I thought it a pity not to give him a clue. He is well acquainted with my MS., and I just copied into the middle of the blank sheet the words—

—Un dessein si funeste,
S'il n'est digne d'Atrée, est digne de Thyeste.†

They are to be found in Crébillon's 'Atrée.' "

* easy descent to Hades.

† "A scheme so deadly, if not worthy of Atreus, is worthy of Thyestes." In Greek myth, Thyestes seduced the wife of Atreus. In revenge, Atreus killed the sons of Thyestes and served them to Thyestes at a banquet.

ARTHUR CONAN DOYLE
(1859–1930)

Arthur Conan Doyle was born in Edinburgh and studied medicine at the University of Edinburgh. To supplement his physician's income, he began writing mystery tales for magazines such as *The Strand.* He drew on memories of his professor Joseph Bell—who could tell a patient's character and occupation, as well as his state of health, from physical observation alone—to create a detective of extraordinary analytic powers. Sherlock Holmes appeared first in *A Study in Scarlet* (1887) and *The Sign of Four* (1890) and then in a series of tales, the first of which were collected in *The Adventures of Sherlock Holmes* (1892). Holmes quickly became the best-known detective, and one of the best-known characters, in all of English literature, instantly recognizable in appearance—the deerstalker cap, cape, and pipe—and in style: "the eagle eye, the misanthropy, the remoteness" that, as Julian Symons says, convince us that Holmes was "a man who genuinely had a genius for his occupation." Doyle was knighted for services in the Boer War and wrote *The White Company* (1890) and other historical novels but remains indelibly associated with the creation of the Great Detective.

"A Scandal in Bohemia" was placed first among the stories in *The Adventures of Sherlock Holmes* apparently because, as the rare example of Holmes's being bested by an opponent, it serves to humanize him and also to set off his brilliance in the following tales. It pays homage, indirectly but clearly, to Poe's "The Purloined Letter" in its central action—uncovering a piece of compromising evidence—and in the detective's ingenuity and resourcefulness in using disguise and diversionary tactics and, especially, in its emphasis on the Dupin Principle of Investigation, implicit in Holmes's rebuke to Watson: "You see, but you do not observe."

"The Adventure of the Speckled Band" shows the influence of Poe's "The Murders in the Rue Morgue" in several aspects, from the locked-room crime to the animal as killer, but it also reveals the imagination with which Doyle reworked the material to produce an atmosphere of menace in the midst of which Holmes's coolness and patience are as important to success as are his powers of observation and analysis.

A SCANDAL IN BOHEMIA

I

To Sherlock Holmes she is always *the* woman. I have seldom heard him mention her under any other name. In his eyes she eclipses and predominates the whole of her sex. It was not that he felt any emotion akin to love for Irene Adler. All emotions, and that one particularly, were abhorrent to his cold, precise, but admirably balanced mind. He was, I take it, the most perfect reasoning and observing machine that the world has seen; but, as a lover he would have placed himself in a false position. He never spoke of the softer passions, save with a gibe and a sneer. They were admirable things for the observer—excellent for drawing the veil from men's motives and actions. But for the trained reasoner to admit such intrusions into his own delicate and finely adjusted temperament was to introduce a distracting factor which might throw a doubt upon all his mental results. Grit in a sensitive instrument, or a crack in one of his own high-power lenses, would not be more disturbing than a strong emotion in a nature such as his. And yet there was but one woman to him, and that woman was the late Irene Adler, of dubious and questionable memory.

I had seen little of Holmes lately. My marriage had drifted us away from each other. My own complete happiness, and the home-centred interests which rise up around the man who first finds himself master of his own establishment, were sufficient to absorb all my attention; while Holmes, who loathed every form of society with his whole Bohemian soul, remained in our lodgings in Baker Street, buried among his old books, and alternating from week to week between cocaine and ambition, the drowsiness of the drug, and the fierce energy of his own keen nature. He was still, as ever, deeply attracted by the study of crime, and occupied his immense faculties and extraordinary powers of observation in following out those clues, and clearing up those mysteries which had been abandoned as hopeless by the official police. From time to time I heard some vague account of his doings: of his summons to Odessa in the case of the Trepoff murder, of his clearing up of the singular tragedy of the Atkinson brothers at Trincomalee, and finally of the mission which he had accomplished so delicately and successfully for the reigning family of Holland. Beyond these signs of his activity, however, which I merely shared with all the readers of the daily press, I knew little of my former friend and companion.

One night—it was on the 20th of March, 1888—I was returning from a journey to a patient (for I had now returned to civil practice), when my way led me through Baker Street. As I passed the well-remembered door, which must always be associated in my mind with my wooing, and with the dark incidents of the *Study in Scarlet,* I was seized with a keen desire to see Holmes again, and to know how he was employing his extraordinary powers. His rooms were brilliantly lit, and, even as I looked up, I saw his tall, spare figure pass twice in a dark silhouette against the blind. He was pacing the room swiftly, eagerly, with his head sunk upon his chest and his hands clasped behind him. To me, who knew his every mood and habit, his attitude and manner told their own story. He was at work again. He had arisen out of his drug-created dreams, and was hot upon the scent of some new problem. I rang the bell, and was shown up to the chamber which had formerly been in part my own.

His manner was not effusive. It seldom was; but he was glad, I think, to see me. With hardly a word spoken, but with a kindly eye, he waved me to an armchair, threw across his case of cigars, and indicated a spirit case and a gasogene in the corner. Then he stood before the fire and looked me over in his singular introspective fashion.

"Wedlock suits you," he remarked. "I think, Watson, that you have put on seven and a half pounds since I saw you."

"Seven!" I answered.

"Indeed, I should have thought a little more. Just a trifle more, I fancy, Watson. And in practice again, I observe. You did not tell me that you intended to go into harness."

"Then, how do you know?"

"I see it, I deduce it. How do I know that you have been getting yourself very wet lately, and that you have a most clumsy and careless servant girl?"

"My dear Holmes," said I, "this is too much. You would certainly have been burned, had you lived a few centuries ago. It is true that I had a country walk on Thursday and came home in a dreadful mess; but as I have changed my clothes, I can't imagine how you deduce it. As to Mary Jane, she is incorrigible, and my wife has given her notice; but there, again, I fail to see how you work it out."

He chuckled to himself and rubbed his long, nervous hands together.

"It is simplicity itself," said he; "my eyes tell me that on the inside of your left shoe, just where the firelight strikes it, the leather is scored by six almost parallel cuts. Obviously they have been caused by some one who has very carelessly scraped round the edges of the sole in order to remove crusted mud from it. Hence, you see, my double deduction that you had been out in vile weather, and that you had a particularly malignant boot-slitting specimen of the London slavey. As to your practice, if a gentleman walks into my rooms smelling of iodoform, with a black mark of nitrate of silver upon his right forefinger, and a bulge on the side of his top-hat to show where he has secreted his stethoscope, I must be dull, indeed, if I do not pronounce him to be an active member of the medical profession."

I could not help laughing at the ease with which he explained his process of deduction. "When I hear you give your reasons," I remarked, "the thing always appears to me to be so ridiculously simple that I could easily do it myself, though at each successive instance of your reasoning I am baffled until you explain your process. And yet I believe that my eyes are as good as yours."

"Quite so," he answered, lighting a cigarette, and throwing himself down into an armchair. "You see, but you do not observe. The distinction is clear. For example, you have frequently seen the steps which lead up from the hall to this room."

"Frequently."

"How often?"

"Well, some hundreds of times."

"Then how many are there?"

"How many? I don't know."

"Quite so! You have not observed. And yet you have seen. That is just my point. Now, I know that there are seventeen steps, because

I have both seen and observed. By the way, since you are interested in these little problems, and since you are good enough to chronicle one or two of my trifling experiences, you may be interested in this." He threw over a sheet of thick, pink-tinted note-paper which had been lying open upon the table. "It came by the last post," said he. "Read it aloud."

The note was undated, and without either signature or address.

"There will call upon you to-night, at a quarter to eight o'clock," it said, "a gentleman who desires to consult you upon a matter of the very deepest moment. Your recent services to one of the royal houses of Europe have shown that you are one who may safely be trusted with matters which are of an importance which can hardly be exaggerated. This account of you we have from all quarters received. Be in your chamber then at that hour, and do not take it amiss if your visitor wears a mask."

"This is indeed a mystery," I remarked. "What do you imagine that it means?"

"I have no data yet. It is a capital mistake to theorize before one has data. Insensibly one begins to twist facts to suit theories, instead of theories to suit facts. But the note itself. What do you deduce from it?"

I carefully examined the writing, and the paper upon which it was written.

"The man who wrote it was presumably well to do," I remarked, endeavouring to imitate my companion's processes. "Such paper could not be bought under half a crown a packet. It is peculiarly strong and stiff."

"Peculiar—that is the very word," said Holmes. "It is not an English paper at all. Hold it up to the light."

I did so, and saw a large "*E*" with a small "*g*," a "*P*," and a large "G" with a small "*t*" woven into the texture of the paper.

"What do you make of that?" asked Holmes.

"The name of the maker, no doubt; or his monogram, rather."

"Not at all. The 'G' with the small '*t*' stands for 'Gesellschaft,' which is the German for 'Company.' It is a customary contraction like our 'Co.' '*P*,' of course, stands for 'Papier.' Now for the '*Eg*.' Let us glance at our Continental Gazetteer." He took down a heavy brown volume from his shelves. "Eglow, Eglonitz—here we are, Egria. It is in a German-speaking country—in Bohemia, not far from Carlsbad. 'Remarkable as being the scene of the death of Wallenstein, and for its numerous glass-factories and paper-mills.' Ha, ha, my boy, what do you make of that?" His eyes sparkled, and he sent up a great blue triumphant cloud from his cigarette.

"The paper was made in Bohemia," I said.

"Precisely. And the man who wrote the note is a German. Do you note the peculiar construction of the sentence—'This account of you we have from all quarters received.' A Frenchman or Russian could not have written that. It is the German who is so uncourteous to his verbs. It only remains, therefore, to discover what is wanted by this German who writes upon Bohemian paper, and prefers wearing a mask to showing his face. And here he comes, if I am not mistaken, to resolve all our doubts."

As he spoke there was the sharp sound of horses' hoofs and grating wheels against the curb, followed by a sharp pull at the bell. Holmes whistled.

"A pair, by the sound," said he. "Yes," he continued, glancing out of the window. "A nice little brougham and a pair of beauties. A hundred and fifty guineas apiece. There's money in this case, Watson, if there is nothing else."

"I think that I had better go, Holmes."

"Not a bit, Doctor. Stay where you are. I am lost without my Boswell. And this promises to be interesting. It would be a pity to miss it."

"But your client—"

"Never mind him. I may want your help, and so may he. Here he comes. Sit down in that armchair, Doctor, and give us your best attention."

A slow and heavy step, which had been heard upon the stairs and in the passage, paused immediately outside the door. Then there was a loud and authoritative tap.

"Come in!" said Holmes.

A man entered who could hardly have been less than six feet six inches in height, with the chest and limbs of a Hercules. His dress was rich with a richness which would, in England, be looked upon as akin to bad taste. Heavy bands of Astrakhan were slashed across the sleeves and fronts of his double-breasted coat, while the deep blue cloak which was thrown over his shoulders was lined with flame-coloured silk, and secured at the neck with a brooch which consisted of a single flaming beryl. Boots which extended halfway up his calves, and which were trimmed at the tops with rich brown fur, completed the impression of barbaric opulence which was suggested by his whole appearance. He carried a broad-brimmed hat in his hand, while he wore across the upper part of his face, extending down past the cheek-bones, a black vizard mask, which he had apparently adjusted that very moment, for his hand was still raised to it as he entered. From the lower part of the face he appeared to be a man of strong character, with a thick, hanging lip, and a long, straight chin, suggestive of resolution pushed to the length of obstinacy.

"You had my note?" he asked, with a deep harsh voice and a strongly marked German accent. "I told you that I would call." He looked from one to the other of us, as if uncertain which to address.

"Pray take a seat," said Holmes. "This is my friend and colleague, Dr. Watson, who is occasionally good enough to help me in my cases. Whom have I the honour to address?"

"You may address me as the Count Von Kramm, a Bohemian nobleman. I understand that this gentleman, your friend, is a man of honor and discretion, whom I may trust with a matter of the most extreme importance. If not, I should much prefer to communicate with you alone."

I rose to go, but Holmes caught me by the wrist and pushed me back into my chair. "It is both, or none," said he. "You may say before this gentleman anything which you may say to me."

The Count shrugged his broad shoulders. "Then I must begin," said he, "by binding you both to absolute secrecy for two years; at the end of that time the matter will be of no importance. At present it is not too much to say that it is of such weight it may have an influence upon European history."

"I promise," said Holmes.

"And I."

"You will excuse this mask," continued our strange visitor. "The august person who employs me wishes his agent to be unknown to you, and I may confess at once that the title by which I have just called myself is not exactly my own."

"I was aware of it," said Holmes, dryly.

"The circumstances are of great delicacy, and every precaution has to be taken to quench what might grow to be an immense scandal and seriously compromise one of the reigning families of Europe. To speak plainly, the matter implicates the great House of Ormstein, hereditary kings of Bohemia."

"I was also aware of that," murmured Holmes, settling himself down in his arm-chair and closing his eyes.

Our visitor glanced with some apparent surprise at the languid, lounging figure of the man who had been no doubt depicted to him as the most incisive reasoner and most energetic agent in Europe. Holmes slowly reopened his eyes and looked impatiently at his gigantic client.

"If your Majesty would condescend to state your case," he remarked, "I should be better able to advise you."

The man sprang from his chair and paced up and down the room in uncontrollable agitation. Then, with a gesture of desperation, he tore the mask from his face and hurled it upon the ground. "You are right," he cried; "I am the King. Why should I attempt to conceal it?"

"Why, indeed?" murmured Holmes. "Your Majesty had not spoken before I was aware that I was addressing Wilhelm Gottsreich Sigismond von Ormstein, Grand Duke of Cassel-Felstein, and hereditary King of Bohemia."

"But you can understand," said our strange visitor, sitting down once more and passing his hand over his high, white forehead, "you can understand that I am not accustomed to doing such business in my own person. Yet the matter was so delicate that I could not confide it to an agent without putting myself in his power. I have come incognito from Prague for the purpose of consulting you."

"Then, pray consult," said Holmes, shutting his eyes once more.

"The facts are briefly these: Some five years ago, during a lengthy visit to Warsaw, I made the acquaintance of the well-known adventuress, Irene Adler. The name is no doubt familiar to you."

"Kindly look her up in my index, Doctor," murmured Holmes, without opening his eyes. For many years he had adopted a system of docketing all paragraphs concerning men and things, so that it was difficult to name a subject or a person on which he could not at once furnish information. In this case I found her biography sandwiched in between that of a Hebrew rabbi and that of a staff-commander who had written a monograph upon the deep-sea fishes.

"Let me see!" said Holmes. "Hum! Born in New Jersey in the year 1858. Contralto—hum! La Scala, hum! Prima donna Imperial Opera of Warsaw—Yes! Retired from operatic stage—ha! Living in London—quite so! Your Majesty, as I understand, became entangled with this young person, wrote her some compromising letters, and is now desirous of getting those letters back."

"Precisely so. But how—"

"Was there a secret marriage?"

"None."

"No legal papers or certificates?"

"None."

"Then I fail to follow your Majesty. If this young person should produce her letters for blackmailing or other purposes, how is she to prove their authenticity?"

"There is the writing."

"Pooh, pooh! Forgery."

"My private note-paper."

"Stolen."

"My own seal."

"Imitated."

"My photograph."

"Bought."

"We were both in the photograph."

"Oh dear! That is very bad! Your Majesty has indeed committed an indiscretion."

"I was mad—insane."

"You have compromised yourself seriously."

"I was only Crown Prince then. I was young. I am but thirty now."

"It must be recovered."

"We have tried and failed."

"Your Majesty must pay. It must be bought."

"She will not sell."

"Stolen, then."

"Five attempts have been made. Twice burglars in my pay ransacked her house. Once we diverted her luggage when she travelled. Twice she has been waylaid. There has been no result."

"No sign of it?"

"Absolutely none."

Holmes laughed. "It is quite a pretty little problem," said he.

"But a very serious one to me," returned the King, reproachfully.

"Very, indeed. And what does she propose to do with the photograph?"

"To ruin me."

"But how?"

"I am about to be married."

"So I have heard."

"To Clotilde Lothman von Saxe-Meningen, second daughter of the King of Scandinavia. You may know the strict principles of her family. She is herself the very soul of delicacy. A shadow of a doubt as to my conduct would bring the matter to an end."

"And Irene Adler?"

"Threatens to send them the photograph. And she will do it. I know that she will do it. You do not know her, but she has a soul of steel. She has the face of the most beautiful of women, and the mind of the most resolute of men. Rather than I should marry another woman, there are no lengths to which she would not go—none."

"You are sure that she has not sent it yet?"

"I am sure."

"And why?"

"Because she has said that she would send it on the day when the betrothal was publicly proclaimed. That will be next Monday."

"Oh, then, we have three days yet," said Holmes, with a yawn. "That is very fortunate, as I have one or two matters of importance to look into just at present. Your Majesty will, of course, stay in London for the present?"

"Certainly. You will find me at the Langham, under the name of the Count Von Kramm."

"Then I shall drop you a line to let you know how we progress."

"Pray do so. I shall be all anxiety."

"Then, as to money?"

"You have carte blanche."

"Absolutely?"

"I tell you that I would give one of the provinces of my kingdom to have that photograph."

"And for present expenses?"

The king took a heavy chamois leather bag from under his cloak and laid it on the table.

"There are three hundred pounds in gold and seven hundred in notes," he said.

Holmes scribbled a receipt upon a sheet of his note-book and handed it to him.

"And Mademoiselle's address?" he asked.

"Is Briony Lodge, Serpentine Avenue, St. John's Wood."

Holmes took a note of it. "One other question," said he. "Was the photograph a cabinet?"

"It was."

"Then, good-night, your Majesty, and I trust that we shall soon have some good news for you. And good-night, Watson," he added, as the wheels of the royal brougham rolled down the street. "If you will be good enough to call to-morrow afternoon, at three o'clock, I should like to chat this little matter over with you."

II

At three o'clock precisely I was at Baker Street, but Holmes had not yet returned. The landlady informed me that he had left the house shortly after eight o'clock in the morning. I sat down beside the fire, however, with the intention of awaiting him, however long he might be. I was already deeply interested in his inquiry, for, though it was surrounded by none of the grim and strange features which were associated with the two crimes which I have already recorded, still, the nature of the case and the exalted station of his client gave it a character of its own. Indeed, apart from the nature of the investigation which my friend had on hand, there was something in his masterly grasp of a situation, and his keen, incisive reasoning, which made it a pleasure to me to study his system of work, and to follow the quick, subtle methods by which he disentangled the most inextricable mysteries. So accustomed was I to his invariable success that the very possibility of his failing had ceased to enter into my head.

It was close upon four before the door opened, and a drunken-looking groom, ill-kempt and side-whiskered, with an inflamed face and disreputable clothes, walked into the room. Accustomed as I was to my friend's amazing powers in the use of disguises, I had to look three times before I was certain that it was indeed he. With a nod he vanished into the bedroom, whence he emerged in five minutes tweed-suited and respectable, as of old. Putting his hands into his pockets, he stretched out his legs in front of the fire, and laughed heartily for some minutes.

"Well, really!" he cried, and then he choked and laughed again until he was obliged to lie back, limp and helpless, in the chair.

"What is it?"

"It's quite too funny. I am sure you could never guess how I employed my morning, or what I ended by doing."

"I can't imagine. I suppose that you have been watching the habits, and perhaps the house, of Miss Irene Adler."

"Quite so; but the sequel was rather unusual. I will tell you, however. I left the house a little after eight o'clock this morning, in the character of a groom out of work. There is a wonderful sympathy and freemasonry among horsy men. Be one of them, and you will know all that there is to know. I soon found Briony Lodge. It is a *bijou* villa, with a garden at the back, but built out in front right up to the road, two stories. Chubb lock to the door. Large sitting-room on the right side, well furnished, with long windows almost to the floor, and those preposterous English window fasteners which a child could open. Behind there was nothing remarkable, save that the passage window could be reached from the top of the coach-house. I walked round it and examined it closely from every point of view, but without noting anything else of interest.

"I then lounged down the street and found, as I expected, that there was a mews in a lane which runs down by one wall of the garden. I lent the ostlers a hand in rubbing down their horses, and I received in exchange twopence, a glass of half-and-half, two fills of shag tobacco, and as much information as I could desire about Miss Adler, to say nothing of half a dozen other people in the neighbourhood in whom I was not in the least interested, but whose biographies I was compelled to listen to."

"And what of Irene Adler?" I asked.

"Oh, she has turned all the men's heads down in that part. She is the daintiest thing under a bonnet on this planet. So says the Serpentine-mews, to a man. She lives quietly, sings at concerts, drives out at five every day, and returns at seven sharp for dinner. Seldom goes out at other times, except when she sings. Has only one male visitor, but a good deal of him. He is dark, handsome, and dashing, never calls less than once a day, and often twice. He is a Mr. Godfrey Norton, of the Inner Temple. See the advantages of a cabman as a confidant. They had driven him home a dozen times from Serpentine-mews, and knew all about him. When I had listened to all that they had to tell, I began to walk up and down near Briony Lodge once more, and to think over my plan of campaign.

"This Godfrey Norton was evidently an important factor in the matter. He was a lawyer. That sounded ominous. What was the relation between them, and what the object of his repeated visits? Was she his client, his friend, or his mistress? If the former, she had probably transferred the photograph to his keeping. If the latter, it was less likely. On the issue of this question depended whether I should continue my work at Briony Lodge, or turn my attention to the gentleman's chambers in the Temple. It was a delicate point, and it widened the field of my inquiry. I fear that I bore you with these details, but I have to let you see my little difficulties, if you are to understand the situation."

"I am following you closely," I answered.

"I was still balancing the matter in my mind, when a hansom cab drove up to Briony Lodge, and a gentleman sprang out. He was a remarkedly handsome man, dark, aquiline, and mustached—evidently the man of whom I had heard. He appeared to be in a great hurry, shouted to the cabman to wait, and brushed past the maid who opened the door with the air of a man who was thoroughly at home.

"He was in the house about half an hour, and I could catch glimpses of him in the windows of the sitting-room, pacing up and down, talking excitedly, and waving his arms. Of her I could see nothing. Presently he emerged, looking even more flurried than before. As he stepped up to the cab, he pulled a gold watch from his pocket and looked at it earnestly. 'Drive like the devil,' he shouted, 'first to Gross & Hankey's in Regent Street, and then to the Church of St. Monica in the Edgware Road. Half a guinea if you do it in twenty minutes!'

"Away they went, and I was just wondering whether I should not do well to follow them, when up the lane came a neat little landau, the coachman with his coat only half-buttoned, and his tie under his ear, while all the tags of his harness were sticking out of the buckles. It hadn't pulled up before she shot out of the hall door and into it. I only caught a glimpse of her at the moment, but she was a lovely woman, with a face that a man might die for.

" 'The Church of St. Monica, John,' she cried, 'and half a sovereign if you reach it in twenty minutes.'

"This was quite too good to lose, Watson. I was just balancing whether I should run for it, or whether I should perch behind her landau, when a cab came through the street. The driver looked twice at such a shabby fare; but I jumped in before he could object. 'The Church of St. Monica,' said I, 'and half a sovereign if you reach it in twenty minutes.' It was twenty-five minutes to twelve, and of course it was clear enough what was in the wind.

"My cabby drove fast. I don't think I ever drove faster, but the others were there before us. The cab and the landau with their steaming horses were in front of the door when I arrived. I paid the man and hurried into the church. There was not a soul there save the two whom I had followed and a surpliced clergyman, who seemed to be expostulating with them. They were all three standing in a knot in front of the altar. I lounged up the side aisle like any other idler who has dropped into a church. Suddenly, to my surprise, the three at the altar faced round to me, and Godfrey Norton came running as hard as he could towards me.

" 'Thank God!' he cried. 'You'll do. Come! Come!'

" 'What then?' I asked.

" 'Come, man, come, only three minutes, or it won't be legal.'

"I was half-dragged up to the altar, and, before I knew where I was, I found myself mumbling responses which were whispered in my ear, and vouching for things of which I knew nothing, and generally assisting in the secure tying up of Irene Adler, spinster, to Godfrey Norton, bachelor. It was all done in an instant, and there was the gentleman thanking me on the one side and the lady on the other, while the clergyman beamed on me in front. It was the most preposterous position in which I ever found myself in my life, and it was the thought of it that started me laughing just now. It seems that there had been some informality about their license, that the clergyman absolutely refused to marry them without a witness of some sort, and that my lucky appearance saved the bridegroom from having to sally out into the streets in search of a best man. The bride gave me a sovereign, and I mean to wear it on my watch-chain in memory of the occasion."

"This is a very unexpected turn of affairs," said I, "and what then?"

"Well, I found my plans very seriously menaced. It looked as if the pair might take an immediate departure, and so necessitate very prompt and energetic measures on my part. At the church door, however, they separated, he driving back to the Temple, and she to her own house. 'I shall drive out in the park at five as usual,' she said, as she left him. I heard no more. They drove away in different directions, and I went off to make my own arrangements."

"Which are?"

"Some cold beef and a glass of beer," he answered, ringing the bell. "I have been too busy to think of food, and I am likely to be busier still this evening. By the way, Doctor, I shall want your co-operation."

"I shall be delighted."

"You don't mind breaking the law?"

"Not in the least."

"Nor running a chance of arrest?"

"Not in a good cause."

"Oh, the cause is excellent!"

"Then I am your man."

"I was sure that I might rely on you."

"But what is it you wish?"

"When Mrs. Turner has brought in the tray I will make it clear to you. Now," he said, as he turned hungrily on the simple fare that our landlady had provided, "I must discuss it while I eat, for I have not much time. It is nearly five now. In two hours we must be on the scene of action. Miss Irene, or Madame, rather, returns from her drive at seven. We must be at Briony Lodge to meet her."

"And what then?"

"You must leave that to me. I have already arranged what is to occur. There is only one point on which I must insist. You must not interfere, come what may. You understand?"

"I am to be neutral?"

"To do nothing whatever. There will probably be some small unpleasantness. Do not join in it. It will end in my being conveyed into the house. Four or five minutes afterwards the sitting-room window will open. You are to station yourself close to that open window."

"Yes."

"You are to watch me, for I will be visible to you."

"Yes."

"And when I raise my hand—so—you will throw into the room what I give you to throw, and will, at the same time, raise the cry of fire. You quite follow me?"

"Entirely."

"It is nothing very formidable," he said, taking a long cigar-shaped roll from his pocket. "It is an ordinary plumber's smoke-rocket, fitted with a cap at either end to make it self-lighting. Your task is confined to that. When you raise your cry of fire, it will be taken up by quite a number of people. You may then walk to the end of the street, and I will rejoin you in ten minutes. I hope that I have made myself clear?"

"I am to remain neutral, to get near the window, to watch you, and at the signal to throw in this object, then to raise the cry of fire, and to await you at the corner of the street."

"Precisely."

"Then you may entirely rely on me."

"That is excellent. I think, perhaps, it is almost time that I prepare for the new role I have to play."

He disappeared into his bedroom, and returned in a few minutes in the character of an amiable and simple-minded Nonconformist clergyman. His broad black hat, his baggy trousers, his white tie, his sympathetic smile, and general look of peering and benevolent curiosity were such as Mr. John Hare alone could have equalled. It was not merely that Holmes changed his costume. His expression, his manner, his very soul seemed to vary with every fresh part that he assumed. The stage lost a fine actor, even as science lost an acute reasoner, when he became a specialist in crime.

It was a quarter-past six when we left Baker Street, and it still wanted ten minutes to the hour when we found ourselves in Serpentine Avenue. It was already dusk, and the lamps were just being lighted as we paced up and down in front of Briony Lodge, waiting for the coming of its occupant. The house was just such as I had pictured it from Sherlock Holmes's succinct description, but the locality appeared to be less private than I expected. On the contrary, for a small street in a quiet neighbourhood, it was remarkably animated. There was a group of shabbily-dressed men smoking and laughing in a corner, a scissors-grinder with his wheel, two guardsmen who were flirting with a nurse-girl, and several well-dressed young men who were lounging up and down with cigars in their mouths.

"You see," remarked Holmes, as we paced to and fro in front of the house, "this marriage rather simplifies matters. The photograph becomes a double-edged weapon now. The chances are that she would be as averse to its being seen by Mr. Godfrey Norton as our client is to its coming to the eyes of his princess. Now the question is, Where are we to find the photograph?"

"Where, indeed?"

"It is most unlikely that she carries it about with her. It is cabinet size. Too large for easy concealment about a woman's dress. She knows that the King is capable of having her waylaid and searched. Two attempts of the sort have already been made. We may take it, then, that she does not carry it about with her."

"Where, then?"

"Her banker or her lawyer. There is that double possibility. But I am inclined to think neither. Women are naturally secretive, and they like to do their own secreting. Why should she hand it over to anyone else? She could trust her own guardianship, but she could not tell what indirect or political influence might be brought to bear upon a businessman. Besides, remember that she had resolved to use it within a few days. It must be where she can lay her hands upon it. It must be in her own house."

"But it has twice been burgled."

"Pshaw! They did not know how to look."

"But how will you look?"

"I will not look."

"What then?"

"I will get her to show me."

"But she will refuse."

"She will not be able to. But I hear the rumble of wheels. It is her carriage. Now carry out my orders to the letter."

As he spoke the gleam of the side-lights of a carriage came round the curve of the avenue. It was a smart little landau which rattled up to the door of Briony Lodge. As it pulled up, one of the loafing men at the corner dashed forward to open the door in the hope of earning a copper, but was elbowed away by another loafer, who had rushed up with the same intention. A fierce quarrel broke out, which was increased by the two guardsmen, who took sides with one of the loungers, and by the scissors-grinder, who was equally hot upon the other side. A blow was struck, and in an instant the lady, who had stepped from her carriage, was the centre of a little knot of flushed and struggling men, who struck savagely at each other with their fists and sticks. Holmes dashed into the crowd to protect the lady; but just as he reached her he gave a cry and dropped to the ground, with the blood running freely down his face. At his fall the guardsmen took to their heels in one direction and the loungers in the other, while a number of better dressed people, who had watched the scuffle without taking part in it, crowded in to help the lady and to attend to the injured man. Irene Adler, as I will still call her, had hurried up the steps; but she stood at the top with her superb figure outlined against the lights of the hall, looking back into the street.

"Is the poor gentleman much hurt?" she asked.

"He is dead," cried several voices.

"No, no, there's life in him!" shouted another. "But he'll be gone before you can get him to hospital."

"He's a brave fellow," said a woman. "They would have had the lady's purse and watch if it hadn't been for him. They were a gang, and a rough one, too. Ah, he's breathing now."

"He can't lie in the street. May we bring him in, marm?"

"Surely. Bring him into the sitting-room. There is a comfortable sofa. This way, please!"

Slowly and solemnly he was borne into Briony Lodge and laid out in the principal room, while I still observed the proceedings from my post by the window. The lamps had been lit, but the blinds had not been drawn, so that I could see Holmes as he lay upon the couch. I do not know whether he was seized with compunction at that moment for the part he was playing, but I know that I never felt more heartily ashamed of myself in my life than when I saw the beautiful creature against whom I was conspiring, or the grace and kindliness with which she waited upon the injured man. And yet it would be the blackest treachery to Holmes to draw back now from the part which he had intrusted to me. I hardened my heart, and took the smoke-rocket from under my ulster. After all, I thought, we are not injuring her. We are but preventing her from injuring another.

Holmes had sat up upon the couch, and I saw him motion like a man who is in need of air. A maid rushed across and threw open the window. At the same instant I saw him raise his hand, and at the signal I tossed my rocket into the room with a cry of "Fire!" The word was no sooner out of my mouth than the whole crowd of spectators, well dressed and ill—gentlemen, ostlers, and servant-maids—joined in a general shriek of "Fire!" Thick clouds of smoke curled through the room and out at the open window. I caught a glimpse of rushing figures, and a moment later the voice of Holmes from within assuring them that it was a false alarm. Slipping through the shouting crowd I made my way to the corner of the street, and in ten minutes was rejoiced to find my friend's arm in mine, and to get away from the scene of uproar. He walked swiftly and in silence for some few minutes, until we had turned down one of the quiet streets which lead towards the Edgware Road.

"You did it very nicely, doctor," he remarked. "Nothing could have been better. It is all right."

"You have the photograph?"

"I know where it is."

"And how did you find out?"

"She showed me, as I told you that she would."

"I am still in the dark."

"I do not wish to make a mystery," said he, laughing. "The matter was perfectly simple. You, of course, saw that every one in the street was an accomplice. They were all engaged for the evening."

"I guessed as much."

"Then, when the row broke out, I had a little moist red paint in the palm of my hand. I rushed forward, fell down, clapped my hand to my face, and became a piteous spectacle. It is an old trick."

"That also I could fathom."

"Then they carried me in. She was bound to have me in. What else could she do? And into her sitting-room, which was the very room which I suspected. It lay between that and her bedroom, and I was determined to see which. They laid me on a couch, I motioned for air, they were compelled to open the window, and you had your chance."

"How did that help you?"

"It was all-important. When a woman thinks that her house is on fire, her instinct is at once to rush to the thing which she values most. It is a perfectly overpowering impulse, and I have more than once taken advantage of it. In the case of the Darlington substitution scandal it was of use to me, and also in the Arnsworth Castle business. A married woman grabs at her baby; an unmarried one reaches for her jewel-box. Now it was clear to me that our lady of to-day had nothing in the house more precious to her than what we are in quest of. She would rush to secure it. The alarm of fire was admirably done. The smoke and shouting were enough to shake nerves of steel. She responded beautifully. The photograph is in a recess behind a sliding panel just above the right bell-pull. She was there in an instant, and I caught a glimpse of it as she half-drew it out. When I cried out that it was a false alarm, she replaced it, glanced at the rocket, rushed from the room, and I have not seen her since. I rose, and, making my excuses, escaped from the house. I hesitated whether to attempt to secure the photograph at once; but the coachman had come in, and as he was watching me narrowly, it seemed safer to wait. A little over-precipitance may ruin all."

"And now?" I asked.

"Our quest is practically finished. I shall call with the King to-morrow, and with you, if you care to come with us. We will be shown into the sitting-room to wait for the lady, but it is probable that when she comes she may find neither us nor the photograph. It might be a satisfaction to His Majesty to regain it with his own hands."

"And when will you call?"

"At eight in the morning. She will not be up, so that we shall have a clear field. Besides, we must be prompt, for this marriage may mean a complete change in her life and habits. I must wire to the King without delay."

We had reached Baker Street, and had stopped at the door. He was searching his pockets for the key, when some one passing said:

"Good-night, Mister Sherlock Holmes."

There were several people on the pavement at the time, but the greeting appeared to come from a slim youth in an ulster who had hurried by.

"I've heard that voice before," said Holmes, staring down the dimly lit street. "Now, I wonder who the deuce that could have been."

III

I slept at Baker Street that night, and we were engaged upon our toast and coffee in the morning when the King of Bohemia rushed into the room.

"You have really got it!" he cried, grasping Sherlock Holmes by either shoulder, and looking eagerly into his face.

"Not yet."

"But you have hopes?"

"I have hopes."

"Then, come. I am all impatience to be gone."

"We must have a cab."

"No, my brougham is waiting."

"Then that will simplify matters." We descended, and started off once more for Briony Lodge.

"Irene Adler is married," remarked Holmes.

"Married! When?"

"Yesterday."

"But to whom?"

"To an English lawyer named Norton."

"But she could not love him?"

"I am in hopes that she does."

"And why in hopes?"

"Because it would spare your Majesty all fear of future annoyance. If the lady loves her husband, she does not love your Majesty. If she does not love your Majesty, there is no reason why she should interfere with your Majesty's plan."

"It is true. And yet—Well! I wish she had been of my own station! What a queen she would have made!" He relapsed into a moody silence, which was not broken until we drew up in Serpentine Avenue.

The door of Briony Lodge was open, and an elderly woman stood upon the steps. She watched us with a sardonic eye as we stepped from the brougham.

"Mr. Sherlock Holmes, I believe?" said she.

"I am Mr. Holmes," answered my companion, looking at her with a questioning and rather startled gaze.

"Indeed! My mistress told me that you were likely to call. She left this morning with her husband by the 5:15 train from Charing Cross for the Continent."

"What!" Sherlock Holmes staggered back, white with chagrin and surprise. "Do you mean that she has left England?"

"Never to return."

"And the papers?" asked the King hoarsely. "All is lost."

"We shall see." He pushed past the servant and rushed into the drawing-room, followed by the King and myself. The furniture was scattered about in every direction, with dismantled shelves and open drawers, as if the lady had hurriedly ransacked them before her flight. Holmes rushed at the bell-pull, tore back a small sliding shutter, and plunging in his hand, pulled out a photograph and a letter. The photograph was of Irene Adler herself in evening dress, the letter was superscribed to "Sherlock Holmes, Esq. To be left till called for." My friend tore it open, and we all three read it together. It was dated at midnight of the preceding night, and ran in this way:

> My Dear Mr. Sherlock Holmes—You really did it very well. You took me in completely. Until after the alarm of fire, I had not a suspicion. But then, when I found how I had betrayed myself, I began to think. I had been warned against you months ago. I had been told that, if the King employed an agent, it would certainly be you. And your

address had been given me. Yet, with all this, you made me reveal what you wanted to know. Even after I became suspicious, I found it hard to think evil of such a dear, kind old clergyman. But, you know, I have been trained as an actress myself. Male costume is nothing new to me. I often take advantage of the freedom which it gives. I sent John, the coachman, to watch you, ran up-stairs, got into my walking-clothes, as I call them, and came down just as you departed.

Well, I followed you to your door, and so made sure that I was really an object of interest to the celebrated Mr. Sherlock Holmes. Then I, rather imprudently, wished you good-night, and started for the Temple to see my husband.

We both thought the best resource was flight, when pursued by so formidable an antagonist; so you will find the nest empty when you call to-morrow. As to the photograph, your client may rest in peace. I love and am loved by a better man than he. The King may do what he will without hindrance from one whom he has cruelly wronged. I keep it only to safeguard myself, and to preserve a weapon which will always secure me from any steps which he might take in the future. I leave a photograph which he might care to possess; and I remain, dear Mr. Sherlock Holmes, very truly yours,

IRENE NORTON, *née* ADLER

"What a woman—oh, what a woman!" cried the King of Bohemia, when we had all three read this epistle. "Did I not tell you how quick and resolute she was? Would she not have made an admirable queen? Is it not a pity that she was not on my level?"

"From what I have seen of the lady she seems indeed to be on a very different level to your Majesty," said Holmes coldly. "I am sorry that I have not been able to bring your Majesty's business to a more successful conclusion."

"On the contrary, my dear sir," cried the King; "nothing could be more successful. I know that her word is inviolate. The photograph is now as safe as if it were in the fire."

"I am glad to hear your Majesty say so."

"I am immensely indebted to you. Pray tell me in what way I can reward you. This ring—" He slipped an emerald snake ring from his finger and held it out upon the palm of his hand.

"Your Majesty has something which I should value even more highly," said Holmes.

"You have but to name it."

"This photograph!"

The King stared at him in amazement.

"Irene's photograph!" he cried. "Certainly, if you wish it."

"I thank your Majesty. Then there is no more to be done in the matter. I have the honor to wish you a very good-morning." He bowed, and, turning away without observing the hand which the King had stretched out to him, he set off in my company for his chambers.

And that was how a great scandal threatened to affect the kingdom of Bohemia, and how the best plans of Mr. Sherlock Holmes were beaten by a woman's wit. He used to make merry over the cleverness of women, but I have not heard him do it of late. And when he speaks of Irene Adler, or when he refers to her photograph, it is always under the honourable title of *the* woman.

THE ADVENTURE OF THE SPECKLED BAND

On glancing over my notes of the seventy odd cases in which I have during the last eight years studied the methods of my friend Sherlock Holmes, I find many tragic, some comic, a large number merely strange, but none commonplace; for, working as he did rather for the love of his art than for the acquirement of wealth, he refused to associate himself with any investigation which did not tend towards the unusual, and even the fantastic. Of all these varied cases, however, I cannot recall any which presented more singular features than that which was associated with the well-known Surrey family of the Roylotts of Stoke Moran. The events in question occurred in the early days of my association with Holmes, when we were sharing rooms as bachelors in Baker Street. It is possible that I might have placed them upon record before, but a promise of secrecy was made at the time, from which I have only been freed during the last month by the untimely death of the lady to whom the pledge was given. It is perhaps as well that the facts should now come to light, for I have reasons to know that there are wide-spread rumors as to the death of Dr. Grimesby Roylott which tend to make the matter even more terrible than the truth.

It was early in April in the year '83 that I woke one morning to find Sherlock Holmes standing, fully dressed, by the side of my bed. He was a late riser, as a rule, and as the clock on the mantelpiece showed me that it was only a quarter-past seven, I blinked up at him in some surprise, and perhaps just a little resentment, for I was myself regular in my habits.

"Very sorry to knock you up, Watson," said he, "but it's the common lot this morning. Mrs. Hudson has been knocked up, she retorted upon me, and I on you."

"What is it, then—a fire?"

"No; a client. It seems that a young lady has arrived in a considerable state of excitement, who insists upon seeing me. She is waiting now in the sitting-room. Now, when young ladies wander about the metropolis at this hour of the morning, and knock sleepy people up out of their beds, I presume that it is something very pressing which they have to communicate. Should it prove to be an interesting case, you would, I am sure, wish to follow it from the outset. I thought, at any rate, that I should call you and give you the chance."

"My dear fellow, I would not miss it for anything."

I had no keener pleasure than in following Holmes in his professional investigations, and in admiring the rapid deductions, as swift as intuitions, and yet always founded on a logical basis, with which he unravelled the problems which were submitted to him. I rapidly threw on my clothes and was ready in a few minutes to accompany my friend down to the sitting-room. A lady dressed in black and heavily veiled, who had been sitting in the window, rose as we entered.

"Good-morning, madam," said Holmes, cheerily. "My name is Sherlock Holmes. This is my intimate friend and associate, Dr. Watson, before whom you can speak as freely as before myself. Ha! I am glad to see that Mrs. Hudson has had the good sense to light the fire. Pray draw up to it, and I shall order you a cup of hot coffee, for I observe that you are shivering."

"It is not cold which makes me shiver," said the woman in a low voice, changing her seat as requested.

"What, then?"

"It is fear, Mr. Holmes. It is terror." She raised her veil as she spoke, and we could see that she was indeed in a pitiable state of agitation, her face all drawn and gray, with restless, frightened eyes, like those of some hunted animal. Her features and figure were those of a woman of thirty, but her hair was shot with premature gray, and her expression was weary and haggard. Sherlock Holmes ran her over with one of his quick, all-comprehensive glances.

"You must not fear," said he, soothingly, bending forward and patting her forearm. "We shall soon set matters right, I have no doubt. You have come in by train this morning, I see."

"You know me, then?"

"No, but I observe the second half of a return ticket in the palm of your left glove. You must have started early, and yet you had a good drive in a dog-cart, along heavy roads, before you reached the station."

The lady gave a violent start, and stared in bewilderment at my companion.

"There is no mystery, my dear madam," said he, smiling. "The left arm of your jacket is spattered with mud in no less than seven places. The marks are perfectly fresh. There is no vehicle save a dog-cart which throws up mud in that way, and then only when you sit on the left-hand side of the driver."

"Whatever your reasons may be, you are perfectly correct," said she. "I started from home before six, reached Leatherhead at twenty past, and came in by the first train to Waterloo. Sir, I can stand this strain no longer; I shall go mad if it continues. I have no one to turn to—none, save only one, who cares for me, and he, poor fellow, can be of little aid. I have heard of you, Mr. Holmes; I have heard of you from Mrs. Farintosh, whom you helped in the hour of her sore need. It was from her that I had your address. Oh, sir, do you not think that you could help me, too, and at least throw a little light through the dense darkness which surrounds me? At present it is out of my power to reward you for your services, but in a month or six weeks I shall be married, with the control of my own income, and then at least you shall not find me ungrateful."

Holmes turned to his desk, and unlocking it, drew out a small casebook, which he consulted.

"Farintosh," said he. "Ah yes, I recall the case; it was concerned with an opal tiara. I think it was before your time, Watson. I can only say, madam, that I shall be happy to devote the same care to your case as I did to that of your friend. As to reward, my profession is its own reward; but you are at liberty to defray whatever expenses I may be put to, at the time which suits you best. And now I beg that you will lay before us everything that may help us in forming an opinion upon the matter."

"Alas!" replied our visitor, "the very horror of my situation lies in the fact that my fears are so vague, and my suspicions depend so entirely upon small points, which might seem trivial to another, that even he to whom of all others I have a right to look for help and advice looks upon all that I tell him about it as the fancies of a nervous woman. He does not say so, but I can read it from his soothing answers and averted eyes. But I have heard, Mr. Holmes, that you can see deeply into the manifold wickedness of the human heart. You may advise me how to walk amid the dangers which encompass me."

"I am all attention, madam."

"My name is Helen Stoner, and I am living with my stepfather, who is the last survivor of one of the oldest Saxon families in England, the Roylotts of Stoke Moran, on the western border of Surrey."

Holmes nodded his head. "The name is familiar to me," said he.

"The family was at one time among the richest in England, and the estates extended over the borders into Berkshire in the north, and Hampshire in the west. In the last century, however, four successive heirs were of a dissolute and wasteful disposition, and the family ruin was eventually completed by a gambler in the days of the Regency. Nothing was left save a few acres of ground, and the two-hundred-year-old house, which is itself crushed under a heavy mortgage. The last squire dragged out his existence there, living the horrible life of an aristocratic pauper; but his only son, my stepfather, seeing that he must adapt himself to the new conditions, obtained an advance from a relative, which enabled him to take a medical degree and went out to Calcutta, where, by his professional skill and his force of character, he established a large practice. In a fit of anger, however, caused by some robberies which had been perpetrated in the house, he beat his native butler to death and narrowly escaped a capital sentence. As it was, he suffered a long term of imprisonment, and afterwards returned to England a morose and disappointed man.

"When Dr. Roylott was in India he married my mother, Mrs. Stoner, the young widow of Major-General Stoner of the Bengal Artillery. My sister Julia and I were twins, and we were only two years old at the time of my mother's re-marriage. She had a considerable sum of money—not less than £1000 a year—and this she bequeathed to Dr. Roylott entirely while we resided with him, with a provision that a certain annual sum should be allowed to each of us in the event of our marriage. Shortly after our return to England my mother died—she was killed eight years ago in a railway accident near Crewe. Dr. Roylott then abandoned his attempts to establish himself in practice in London and took us to live with him in the old ancestral house at Stoke Moran. The money which my mother had left was enough for all our wants, and there seemed to be no obstacle to our happiness.

"But a terrible change came over our stepfather about this time. Instead of making friends and exchanging visits with our neighbours, who had at first been overjoyed to see a Roylott of Stoke Moran back in the old family seat, he shut himself up in his house and seldom came out save to indulge in ferocious quarrels with whoever might cross his path. Violence of temper approaching to mania has been hereditary in the men of the family, and in my stepfather's case it had, I believe, been intensified by his long residence in the tropics. A series of disgraceful brawls took place, two of which ended in the police-court, until at last he became the terror of the village, and the folks would fly at his approach, for he is a man of immense strength, and absolutely uncontrollable in his anger.

"Last week he hurled the local blacksmith over a parapet into a stream, and it was only by paying over all the money which I could gather together that I was able to avert another public exposure. He had no friends at all save the wandering gypsies, and he would give these vagabonds leave to encamp upon the few acres of bramble-covered land which represent the family estate, and would accept in return the hospitality of their tents, wandering away with them sometimes for weeks on end. He has a passion also for Indian animals, which are sent over to him by a correspondent, and he has at this moment a cheetah and a baboon, which wander freely over his grounds, and are feared by the villagers almost as much as their master.

"You can imagine from what I say that my poor sister Julia and I had no great pleasure in our lives. No servant would stay with us, and for a long time we did all the work of the house. She was but thirty at the time of her death, and yet her hair had already begun to whiten, even as mine has."

"Your sister is dead, then?"

"She died just two years ago, and it is of her death that I wish to speak to you. You can understand that, living the life which I have described, we were little likely to see any one of our own age and position. We had, however, an aunt, my mother's maiden sister, Miss Honoria Westphail, who lives near Harrow, and we were occasionally allowed to pay short visits at this lady's house. Julia went there at Christmas two years ago, and met there a half-pay major of marines, to whom she became engaged. My stepfather learned of the engagement when my sister returned, and offered no objection to the marriage; but within a fortnight of the day which had been fixed for the wedding, the terrible event occurred which has deprived me of my only companion."

Sherlock Holmes had been leaning back in his chair with his eyes closed and his head sunk in a cushion, but he half opened his lids now and glanced across at his visitor.

"Pray be precise as to details," said he.

"It is easy for me to do so, for every event of that dreadful time is seared into my memory. The manor-house is, as I have already said, very old, and only one wing is now inhabited. The bedrooms in this wing are on the ground floor, the sitting-rooms being in the central block of the buildings. Of these bedrooms the first is Dr. Roylott's, the second my sister's, and the third my own. There is no communication between them, but they all open out into the same corridor. Do I make myself plain?"

"Perfectly so."

"The windows of the three rooms open out upon the lawn. That fatal night Dr. Roylott had gone to his room early, though we knew that he had not retired to rest, for my sister was troubled by the smell of the strong Indian cigars which it was his custom to smoke. She left her room, therefore, and came into mine, where she sat for some time, chatting about her approaching wedding. At eleven o'clock she rose to leave me but she paused at the door and looked back.

" 'Tell me, Helen,' said she, 'have you ever heard any one whistle in the dead of the night?'

" 'Never,' said I.

" 'I suppose that you could not possibly whistle, yourself, in your sleep?'

" 'Certainly not. But why?'

" 'Because during the last few nights I have always, about three in the morning, heard a low, clear whistle. I am a light sleeper, and it has awakened me. I cannot tell where it came from—perhaps from the next room, perhaps from the lawn. I thought that I would just ask you whether you had heard it.'

" 'No, I have not. It must be those wretched gypsies in the plantation.'

" 'Very likely. And yet if it were on the lawn, I wonder that you did not hear it also.'

" 'Ah, but I sleep more heavily than you.'

" 'Well, it is of no great consequence, at any rate.' She smiled back at me, closed my door, and a few moments later I heard her key turn in the lock."

"Indeed," said Holmes. "Was it your custom always to lock yourselves in at night?"

"Always."

"And why?"

"I think that I mentioned to you that the doctor kept a cheetah and a baboon. We had no feeling of security unless our doors were locked."

"Quite so. Pray proceed with your statement."

"I could not sleep that night. A vague feeling of impending misfortune impressed me. My sister and I, you will recollect, were twins, and you know how subtle are the links which bind two souls which are so closely allied. It was a wild night. The wind was howling outside, and the rain was beating and splashing against the windows. Suddenly, amid all the hubbub of the gale, there burst forth the wild scream of a terrified woman. I knew that it was my sister's voice. I sprang from my bed, wrapped a shawl round me, and rushed into the corridor. As I opened my door I seemed to hear a low whistle, such as my sister described, and a few moments later a clanging sound, as if a mass of metal had fallen. As I ran down the passage, my sister's door was unlocked, and revolved slowly upon its hinges. I stared at it horror-stricken, not knowing what was about to issue from it. By the light of the corridor-lamp I saw my sister appear at the opening, her face blanched with terror, her hands groping for help, her whole figure swaying to and fro like that of a drunkard. I ran to her and threw my arms round her, but at that moment her knees seemed to give way and she fell to the ground. She writhed as one who is in terrible pain, and her limbs were dreadfully convulsed. At first I thought that she had not recognized me, but as I bent over her she suddenly shrieked out in a voice which I shall never forget, 'Oh, my God! Helen! It was the band! The speckled band!' There was something else which she would fain have said, and she stabbed with her finger into the air in the direction of the doctor's room, but a fresh convulsion seized her and choked her words. I rushed out, calling loudly for my stepfather, and I met him hastening from his room in his dressing-gown. When he reached my sister's side she was unconscious, and though he poured brandy down her throat and sent for medical aid from the village, all efforts were in vain, for she slowly sank and died without having recovered her consciousness. Such was the dreadful end of my beloved sister."

"One moment," said Holmes; "are you sure about this whistle and metallic sound? Could you swear to it?"

"That was what the county coroner asked me at the inquiry. It is my strong impression that I heard it, and yet, among the crash of the gale and the creaking of an old house, I may possibly have been deceived."

"Was your sister dressed?"

"No, she was in her night-dress. In her right hand was found the charred stump of a match, and in her left a match-box."

"Showing that she had struck a light and looked about her when the alarm took place. That is important. And what conclusions did the coroner come to?"

"He investigated the case with great care, for Dr. Roylott's conduct had long been notorious in the county, but he was unable to find any satisfactory cause of death. My evidence showed that the door had been fastened upon the inner side, and the windows were blocked by old-fashioned shutters with broad iron bars, which were secured every night. The walls were carefully sounded and were shown to be quite solid all round, and the flooring was also thoroughly examined, with the same result. The chimney is wide, but is barred up by four large staples. It is certain, therefore, that my sister was quite alone when she met her end. Besides, there were no marks of any violence upon her."

"How about poison?"

"The doctors examined her for it, but without success."

"What do you think that this unfortunate lady died of, then?"

"It is my belief that she died of pure fear and nervous shock, though what it was that frightened her I cannot imagine."

"Were there gypsies in the plantation at the time?"

"Yes, there are nearly always some there."

"Ah, and what did you gather from this allusion to a band—a speckled band?"

"Sometimes I have thought that it was merely the wild talk of delirium, sometimes that it may have referred to some band of people, perhaps to these very gypsies in the plantation. I do not know whether the spotted handkerchiefs which so many of them wear over their heads might have suggested the strange adjective which she used."

Holmes shook his head like a man who is far from being satisfied.

"These are very deep waters," said he; "pray go on with your narrative."

"Two years have passed since then, and my life has been until lately lonelier than ever. A month ago, however, a dear friend, whom I have known for many years, has done me the honor to ask my hand in marriage. His name is Armitage—Percy Armitage—the second son of Mr. Armitage, of Crane Water, near Reading. My stepfather has offered no opposition to the match, and we are to be married in the course of the spring. Two days ago some repairs were started in the west wing of the building, and my bedroom wall has been pierced, so that I have had to move into the chamber in which my sister died, and to sleep in the very bed in which she slept. Imagine, then, my thrill of terror when last night, as I lay awake, thinking over her terrible fate, I suddenly heard in the silence of the night the low whistle which had been the herald of her own death. I sprang up and lit the lamp, but nothing was to be seen in the room. I was too shaken to go to bed again, however, so I dressed, and as soon as it was daylight I slipped down, got a dog-cart at the Crown Inn, which is opposite, and drove to Leatherhead, from whence I have come on this morning with the one object of seeing you and asking your advice."

"You have done wisely," said my friend. "But have you told me all?"

"Yes, all."

"Miss Stoner, you have not. You are screening your stepfather."

"Why, what do you mean?"

For answer Holmes pushed back the frill of black lace which fringed the hand that lay upon our visitor's knee. Five little livid spots, the marks of four fingers and a thumb, were printed upon the white wrist.

"You have been cruelly used," said Holmes.

The lady coloured deeply and covered over her injured wrist. "He is a hard man," she said, "and perhaps he hardly knows his own strength."

There was a long silence, during which Holmes leaned his chin upon his hands and stared into the crackling fire.

"This is a very deep business," he said, at last. "There are a thousand details which I should desire to know before I decide upon our course of action. Yet we have not a moment to lose. If we were to come to Stoke Moran to-day, would it be possible for us to see over these rooms without the knowledge of your stepfather?"

"As it happens, he spoke of coming into town to-day upon some most important business. It is probable that he will be away all day, and that there would be nothing to disturb you. We have a housekeeper now, but she is old and foolish, and I could easily get her out of the way."

"Excellent. You are not adverse to this trip, Watson?"

"By no means."

"Then we shall both come. What are you going to do yourself?"

"I have one or two things which I would wish to do now that I am in town. But I shall return by the twelve o'clock train, so as to be there in time for your coming."

"And you may expect us early in the afternoon. I have myself some small business matters to attend to. Will you not wait and breakfast?"

"No, I must go. My heart is lightened already since I have confided my trouble to you. I shall look forward to seeing you again this afternoon." She dropped her thick black veil over her face and glided from the room.

"And what do you think of it all, Watson?" asked Sherlock Holmes, leaning back in his chair.

"It seems to me to be a most dark and sinister business."

"Dark enough and sinister enough."

"Yet if the lady is correct in saying that the flooring and walls are sound, and that the door, window, and chimney are impassable, then her sister must have been undoubtedly alone when she met her mysterious end."

"What becomes, then, of these nocturnal whistles, and what of the very peculiar words of the dying woman?"

"I cannot think."

"When you combine the ideas of whistles at night, the presence of a band of gypsies who are on intimate terms with this old doctor, the fact that we have every reason to believe that the doctor has an interest in preventing his stepdaughter's marriage, the dying allusion to a band, and, finally, the fact that Miss Helen Stoner heard a metallic clang, which might have been caused by one of those metal bars which secured the shutters falling back into its place, I think that there is good ground to think that the mystery may be cleared along those lines."

"But what, then, did the gypsies do?"

"I cannot imagine."

"I see many objections to any such theory."

"And so do I. It is precisely for that reason that we are going to Stoke Moran this day. I want to see whether the objections are fatal, or if they may be explained away. But what in the name of the devil!"

The ejaculation had been drawn from my companion by the fact that our door had been suddenly dashed open, and that a huge man had framed himself in the aperture. His costume was a peculiar mixture of the professional and of the agricultural, having a black top-hat, a long frock-coat, and a pair of high gaiters, with a hunting-crop swinging in his hand. So tall was he that his hat actually brushed the cross bar of the doorway, and his breadth seemed to span it across from side to side. A large face, seared with a thousand wrinkles, burned yellow with the sun, and marked with every evil passion, was turned from one to the other of us, while his deep-set, bile-shot eyes, and his high, thin, fleshless nose, gave him somewhat the resemblance to a fierce old bird of prey.

"Which of you is Holmes?" asked this apparition.

"My name, sir; but you have the advantage of me," said my companion, quietly.

"I am Dr. Grimesby Roylott, of Stoke Moran."

"Indeed, doctor," said Holmes, blandly. "Pray take a seat."

"I will do nothing of the kind. My stepdaughter has been here. I have traced her. What has she been saying to you?"

"It is a little cold for the time of the year," said Holmes.

"What has she been saying to you?" screamed the old man, furiously.

"But I have heard that the crocuses promise well," continued my companion, imperturbably.

"Ha! You put me off, do you?" said our new visitor, taking a step forward and shaking his hunting-crop. "I know you, you scoundrel! I have heard of you before. You are Holmes, the meddler."

My friend smiled.

"Holmes, the busybody!"

His smile broadened.

"Holmes, the Scotland Yard Jack-in-office!"

Holmes chuckled heartily. "Your conversation is most entertaining," said he. "When you go out close the door, for there is a decided draught."

"I will go when I have said my say. Don't you dare to meddle with my affairs. I know that Miss Stoner has been here. I traced her! I am a dangerous man to fall foul of! See here." He stepped swiftly forward, seized the poker, and bent it into a curve with his huge brown hands.

"See that you keep yourself out of my grip," he snarled, and hurling the twisted poker into the fireplace, he strode out of the room.

"He seems a very amiable person," said Holmes, laughing. "I am not quite so bulky, but if he had remained I might have shown him that my grip was not much more feeble than his own." As he spoke he picked up the steel poker, and with a sudden effort, straightened it out again.

"Fancy his having the insolence to confound me with the official detective force! This incident gives zest to our investigation, however, and I only trust that our little friend will not suffer from her imprudence in allowing this brute to trace her. And now, Watson, we shall order breakfast, and afterwards I shall walk down to Doctors' Commons, where I hope to get some data which may help us in this matter."

It was nearly one o'clock when Sherlock Holmes returned from his excursion. He held in his hand a sheet of blue paper, scrawled over with notes and figures.

"I have seen the will of the deceased wife," said he. "To determine its exact meaning I have been obliged to work out the present prices of the investments with which it is concerned. The total income, which at the time of the wife's death was little short of £1100, is now, through the fall in agricultural prices, not more than £750. Each daughter can claim an income of £250, in case of marriage. It is evident, therefore, that if both girls had married, this beauty would have had a mere pittance, while even one of them would cripple him to a very serious extent. My morning's work has not been wasted, since it has proved that he has the very strongest motives for standing in the way of anything of the sort. And now, Watson, this is too serious for dawdling, especially as the old man is aware that we are interesting ourselves in his affairs; so if you are ready, we shall call a cab and drive to Waterloo. I should be very much obliged if you would slip your revolver into your pocket. An Eley's No. 2 is an excellent argument with gentlemen who can twist steel pokers into knots. That and a tooth-brush are, I think, all that we need."

At Waterloo we were fortunate in catching a train for Leatherhead, where we hired a trap at the station inn, and drove for four or five miles through the lovely Surrey lanes. It was a perfect day, with a bright sun and a few fleecy clouds in the heavens. The trees and wayside hedges were just throwing out their first green shoots, and the air was full of the pleasant smell of the moist earth. To me at least there was a strange contrast between the sweet promise of the spring and this sinister quest upon which we were engaged. My companion sat in the front of the trap, his arms folded, his hat pulled down over his eyes, and his chin sunk upon his breast, buried in the deepest thought. Suddenly, however, he started, tapped me on the shoulder, and pointed over the meadows.

"Look there!" said he.

A heavily-timbered park stretched up in a gentle slope, thickening into a grove at the highest point. From amid the branches there jutted out the gray gables and high roof-tree of a very old mansion.

"Stoke Moran?" said he.

"Yes, sir, that be the house of Dr. Grimesby Roylott," remarked the driver.

"There is some building going on there," said Holmes; "that is where we are going."

"There's the village," said the driver, pointing to a cluster of roofs some distance to the left; "but if you want to get to the house, you'll find it shorter to get over this stile, and so by the foot-path over the fields. There it is, where the lady is walking."

"And the lady, I fancy, is Miss Stoner," observed Holmes, shading his eyes. "Yes, I think we had better do as you suggest."

We got off, paid our fare, and the trap rattled back on its way to Leatherhead.

"I thought it as well," said Holmes, as we climbed the stile, "that this fellow should think we had come here as architects, or on some definite business. It may stop his gossip. Good-afternoon, Miss Stoner. You see that we have been as good as our word."

Our client of the morning had hurried forward to meet us with a face which spoke her joy. "I have been waiting so eagerly for you," she cried, shaking hands with us warmly. "All has turned out splendidly. Dr. Roylott has gone to town, and it is unlikely that he will be back before evening."

"We have had the pleasure of making the doctor's acquaintance," said Holmes, and in a few words he sketched out what had occurred. Miss Stoner turned white to the lips as she listened.

"Good heavens!" she cried, "he has followed me, then."

"So it appears."

"He is so cunning that I never know when I am safe from him. What will he say when he returns?"

"He must guard himself, for he may find that there is some one more cunning than himself upon his track. You must lock yourself up from him to-night. If he is violent, we shall take you away to your aunt's at Harrow. Now, we must make the best use of our time, so kindly take us at once to the rooms which we are to examine."

The building was of gray, lichen-blotched stone, with a high central portion, and two curving wings, like the claws of a crab, thrown out on each side. In one of these wings the windows were broken, and blocked with wooden boards, while the roof was partly caved in, a picture of ruin. The central portion was in little better repair, but the right-hand block was comparatively modern, and the blinds in the windows, with the blue smoke curling up from the chimneys, showed that this was where the family resided. Some scaffolding had been erected against the end wall, and the stonework had been broken into, but there were no signs of any workmen at the moment of our visit. Holmes walked slowly up and down the ill-trimmed lawn, and examined with deep attention the outsides of the windows.

"This, I take it, belongs to the room in which you used to sleep, the centre one to your sister's, and the one next to the main building to Dr. Roylott's chamber?"

"Exactly so. But I am now sleeping in the middle one."

"Pending the alterations, as I understand. By-the-way, there does not seem to be any very pressing need for repairs at that end wall."

"There were none. I believe that it was an excuse to move me from my room."

"Ah! that is suggestive. Now, on the other side of this narrow wing runs the corridor from which these three rooms open. There are windows in it, of course?"

"Yes, but very small ones. Too narrow for any one to pass through."

"As you both locked your doors at night, your rooms were unapproachable from that side. Now, would you have the kindness to go into your room and bar your shutters."

Miss Stoner did so, and Holmes, after a careful examination through the open window, endeavoured in every way to force the shutter open, but without success. There was no slit through which a knife could be passed to raise the bar. Then with his lens he tested the hinges, but they were of solid iron, built firmly into the massive masonry. "Hum!" said he, scratching his chin in some perplexity; "my theory certainly presents some difficulties. No one could pass these shutters if they were bolted. Well, we shall see if the inside throws any light upon the matter."

A small side door led into the whitewashed corridor from which the three bedrooms opened. Holmes refused to examine the third chamber, so we passed at once to the second, that in which Miss Stoner was now sleeping, and in which her sister had met with her fate. It was a homely little room, with a low ceiling and a gaping fireplace, after the fashion of old country-houses. A brown chest of drawers stood in one corner, a narrow white-counterpaned bed in another, and a dressing-table on the left-hand side of the window. These articles, with two small wicker-work chairs, made up all the furniture in the room, save for a square of Wilton carpet in the centre. The boards round and the panelling of the walls were of brown, worm-eaten oak, so old and discolored that it may have dated from the original building of the house. Holmes drew one of the chairs into a corner and sat silent, while his eyes travelled round and round and up and down, taking in every detail of the apartment.

"Where does that bell communicate with?" he asked at last, pointing to a thick bell-rope which hung down beside the bed, the tassel actually lying upon the pillow.

"It goes to the house-keeper's room."

"It looks newer than the other things?"

"Yes, it was only put there a couple of years ago."

"Your sister asked for it, I suppose?"

"No, I never heard of her using it. We used always to get what we wanted for ourselves."

"Indeed, it seemed unnecessary to put so nice a bell-pull there. You will excuse me for a few minutes while I satisfy myself as to this floor." He threw himself down upon his face with his lens in his hand, and crawled swiftly backward and forward, examining minutely the cracks between the boards. Then he did the same with the wood-work with which the chamber was panelled. Finally he walked over to the bed, and spent some time in staring at it, and in running his eye up and down the wall. Finally he took the bell-rope in his hand and gave it a brisk tug.

"Why, it's a dummy," said he.

"Won't it ring?"

"No, it is not even attached to a wire. This is very interesting. You can see now that it is fastened to a hook just above where the little opening for the ventilator is."

"How very absurd! I never noticed that before."

"Very strange!" muttered Holmes, pulling at the rope. "There are one or two very singular points about this room. For example, what a fool a builder must be to open a ventilator into another room, when, with the same trouble, he might have communicated with the outside air!"

"That is also quite modern," said the lady.

"Done about the same time as the bell-rope?" remarked Holmes.

"Yes, there were several little changes carried out about that time."

"They seem to have been of a most interesting character—dummy bell-ropes, and ventilators which do not ventilate. With your permission, Miss Stoner, we shall now carry our researches into the inner apartment."

Dr. Grimesby Roylott's chamber was larger than that of his stepdaughter, but was as plainly furnished. A camp-bed, a small wooden shelf full of books, mostly of a technical character, an armchair beside the bed, a plain wooden chair against the wall, a round table, and a large iron safe were the principal things which met the eye. Holmes walked slowly round and examined each and all of them with the keenest interest.

"What's in here?" he asked, tapping the safe.

"My stepfather's business papers."

"Oh! you have seen inside, then?"

"Only once, some years ago. I remember that it was full of papers."

"There isn't a cat in it, for example?"

"No. What a strange idea!"

"Well, look at this!" He took up a small saucer of milk which stood on the top of it.

"No; we don't keep a cat. But there is a cheetah and a baboon."

"Ah, yes, of course! Well, a cheetah is just a big cat, and yet a saucer of milk does not go very far in satisfying its wants, I dare say. There is one point which I should wish to determine." He squatted down in front of the wooden chair, and examined the seat of it with the greatest attention.

"Thank you. That is quite settled," said he, rising and putting his lens in his pocket. "Hello! Here is something interesting!"

The object which had caught his eye was a small dog-lash hung on one corner of the bed. That lash, however, was curled upon itself, and tied so as to make a loop of whipcord.

"What do you make of that, Watson?"

"It's a common enough lash. But I don't know why it should be tied."

"That is not quite so common, is it? Ah, me! it's a wicked world, and when a clever man turns his brains to crime it is the worst of all. I think that I have seen enough now, Miss Stoner, and with your permission we shall walk out upon the lawn."

I had never seen my friend's face so grim or his brow so dark as it was when we turned from the scene of this investigation. We had walked several times up and down the lawn, neither Miss Stoner nor myself liking to break in upon his thoughts before he roused himself from his reverie.

"It is very essential, Miss Stoner," said he, "that you should absolutely follow my advice in every respect."

"I shall most certainly do so."

"The matter is too serious for any hesitation. Your life may depend upon your compliance."

"I assure you that I am in your hands."

"In the first place, both my friend and I must spend the night in your room."

Both Miss Stoner and I gazed at him in astonishment.

"Yes, it must be so. Let me explain. I believe that that is the village inn over there?"

"Yes, that is the Crown."

"Very good. Your windows would be visible from there?"

"Certainly."

"You must confine yourself to your room, on pretence of a headache, when your stepfather comes back. Then when you hear him retire for the night, you must open the shutters of your window, undo the hasp, put your lamp there as a signal to us, and then withdraw quietly with everything which you are likely to want into the room which you used to occupy. I have no doubt that, in spite of the repairs, you could manage there for one night."

"Oh yes, easily."

"The rest you will leave in our hands."

"But what will you do?"

"We shall spend the night in your room, and we shall investigate the cause of this noise which has disturbed you."

"I believe, Mr. Holmes, that you have already made up your mind," said Miss Stoner, laying her hand upon my companion's sleeve.

"Perhaps I have."

"Then, for pity's sake, tell me what was the cause of my sister's death."

"I should prefer to have clearer proofs before I speak."

"You can at least tell me whether my own thought is correct, and if she died from some sudden fright."

"No, I do not think so. I think that there was probably some more tangible cause. And now, Miss Stoner, we must leave you, for if Dr. Roylott returned and saw us, our journey would be in vain. Good-bye, and be brave, for if you will do what I have told you, you may rest assured that we shall soon drive away the dangers that threaten you."

Sherlock Holmes and I had no difficulty in engaging a bed-room and sitting-room at the Crown Inn. They were on the upper floor, and from our window we could command a view of the avenue gate, and of the inhabited wing of Stoke Moran Manor House. At dusk we saw Dr. Grimesby Roylott drive past, his huge form looming up beside the little figure of the lad who drove him. The boy had some slight difficulty in undoing the heavy iron gates, and we heard the hoarse roar of the doctor's voice, and saw the fury with which he shook his clenched fists at him. The trap drove on, and a few minutes later we saw a sudden light spring up among the trees as the lamp was lit in one of the sitting-rooms.

"Do you know, Watson," said Holmes, as we sat together in the gathering darkness, "I have really some scruples as to taking you to-night. There is a distinct element of danger."

"Can I be of assistance?"

"Your presence might be invaluable."

"Then I shall certainly come."

"It is very kind of you."

"You speak of danger. You have evidently seen more in these rooms than was visible to me."

"No, but I fancy that I may have deduced a little more. I imagine that you saw all that I did."

"I saw nothing remarkable save the bell-rope, and what purpose that could answer I confess is more than I can imagine."

"You saw the ventilator, too?"

"Yes, but I do not think that it is such a very unusual thing to have a small opening between two rooms. It was so small that a rat could hardly pass through."

"I knew that we should find a ventilator before ever we came to Stoke Moran."

"My dear Holmes!"

"Oh yes, I did. You remember in her statement she said that her sister could smell Dr. Roylott's cigar. Now, of course that suggested at once that there must be a communication between the two rooms. It could only be a small one, or it would have been remarked upon at the coroner's inquiry. I deduced a ventilator."

"But what harm can there be in that?"

"Well, there is at least a curious coincidence of dates. A ventilator is made, a cord is hung, and a lady who sleeps in the bed dies. Does not that strike you?"

"I cannot as yet see any connection."

"Did you observe anything very peculiar about that bed?"

"No."

"It was clamped to the floor. Did you ever see a bed fastened like that before?"

"I cannot say that I have."

"The lady could not move her bed. It must always be in the same relative position to the ventilator and to the rope—for so we may call it, since it was clearly never meant for a bell-pull."

"Holmes," I cried, "I seem to see dimly what you are hinting at. We are only just in time to prevent some subtle and horrible crime."

"Subtle enough and horrible enough. When a doctor does go wrong, he is the first of criminals. He has nerve and he has knowledge. Palmer and Pritchard were among the heads of their profession. This man strikes even deeper, but I think, Watson, that we shall be able to strike deeper still. But we shall have horrors enough before the night is over; for goodness' sake let us have a quiet pipe, and turn our minds for a few hours to something more cheerful."

About nine o'clock the light among the trees was extinguished, and all was dark in the direction of the Manor House. Two hours passed slowly away, and then, suddenly, just at the stroke of eleven, a single bright light shone out right in front of us.

"That is our signal," said Holmes, springing to his feet; "it comes from the middle window."

As we passed out he exchanged a few words with the landlord, explaining that we were going on a late visit to an acquaintance, and that it was possible that we might spend the night there. A moment later we were out on the dark road, a chill wind blowing in our faces, and one yellow light twinkling in front of us through the gloom to guide us on our sombre errand.

There was little difficulty in entering the grounds, for unrepaired breaches gaped in the old park wall. Making our way among the trees, we reached the lawn, crossed it, and were about to enter through the window when out from a clump of laurel bushes there darted what seemed to be a hideous and distorted child, who threw itself upon the grass with writhing limbs and then ran swiftly across the lawn into the darkness.

"My God!" I whispered; "did you see it?"

Holmes was for the moment as startled as I. His hand closed like a vice upon my wrist in his agitation. Then he broke into a low laugh, and put his lips to my ear.

"It is a nice household," he murmured. "That is the baboon."

I had forgotten the strange pets which the doctor affected. There was a cheetah, too; perhaps we might find it upon our shoulders at any moment. I confess that I felt easier in my mind when, after following Holmes's example and slipping off my shoes, I found myself inside the bedroom. My companion noiselessly closed the shutters, moved the lamp onto the table, and cast his eyes round the room. All was as we had seen it in the daytime. Then creeping up to me and making a trumpet of his hand, he whispered into my ear again so gently that it was all that I could do to distinguish the words:

"The least sound would be fatal to our plans."

I nodded to show that I had heard.

"We must sit without light. He would see it through the ventilator."

I nodded again.

"Do not go asleep; your very life may depend upon it. Have your pistol ready in case we should need it. I will sit on the side of the bed, and you in that chair."

I took out my revolver and laid it on the corner of the table.

Holmes had brought up a long thin cane, and this he placed upon the bed beside him. By it he laid the box of matches and the stump of a candle. Then he turned down the lamp, and we were left in darkness.

How shall I ever forget that dreadful vigil? I could not hear a sound, not even the drawing of a breath, and yet I knew that my companion sat open-eyed, within a few feet of me, in the same state of nervous tension in which I was myself. The shutters cut off the least ray of light, and we waited in absolute darkness. From outside came the occasional cry of a night-bird, and once at our very window a long drawn catlike whine, which told us that the cheetah was indeed at liberty. Far away we could hear the deep tones of the parish clock, which boomed out every quarter of an hour. How long they seemed, those quarters! Twelve struck, and one and two and three, and still we sat waiting silently for whatever might befall.

Suddenly there was the momentary gleam of a light up in the direction of the ventilator, which vanished immediately, but was succeeded by a strong smell of burning oil and heated metal. Some one in the next room had lit a dark-lantern. I heard a gentle sound of movement, and then all was silent once more, though the smell grew stronger. For half an hour I sat with straining ears. Then suddenly another sound became audible—a very gentle, soothing sound, like that of a small jet of steam escaping continually from a kettle. The instant that we heard it, Holmes sprang from the bed, struck a match, and lashed furiously with his cane at the bell-pull.

"You see it, Watson?" he yelled. "You see it?"

But I saw nothing. At the moment when Holmes struck the light I heard a low, clear whistle, but the sudden glare flashing into my weary eyes made it impossible for me to tell what it was at which my friend lashed so savagely. I could, however, see that his face was deadly pale and filled with horror and loathing.

He had ceased to strike, and was gazing up at the ventilator, when suddenly there broke from the silence of the night the most horrible cry to which I have ever listened. It swelled up louder and louder, a hoarse yell of pain and fear and anger all mingled in the one dreadful shriek. They say that away down in the village, and even in the distant parsonage, that cry raised the sleepers from their beds. It struck cold to our hearts, and I stood gazing at Holmes, and he at me, until the last echoes of it had died away into the silence from which it rose.

"What can it mean?" I gasped.

"It means that it is all over," Holmes answered. "And perhaps, after all, it is for the best. Take your pistol, and we will enter Dr. Roylott's room."

With a grave face he lit the lamp and led the way down the corridor. Twice he struck at the chamber door without any reply from within. Then he turned the handle and entered, I at his heels, with the cocked pistol in my hand.

It was a singular sight which met our eyes. On the table stood a dark-lantern with the shutter half open, throwing a brilliant beam of light upon the iron safe, the door of which was ajar. Beside this table, on the wooden chair, sat Dr. Grimesby Roylott, clad in a long gray dressing-gown, his bare ankles protruding beneath, and his feet thrust into red heelless Turkish slippers. Across his lap lay the short stock with the long lash which we had noticed during the day. His chin was cocked upward and his eyes were fixed in a dreadful, rigid stare at the corner of the ceiling. Round his brow he had a peculiar yellow band, with brownish speckles, which seemed to be bound tightly round his head. As we entered he made neither sound nor motion.

"The band! the speckled band!" whispered Holmes.

I took a step forward. In an instant his strange head-gear began to move, and there reared itself from among his hair the squat diamond-shaped head and puffed neck of a loathsome serpent.

"It is a swamp adder!" cried Holmes; "the deadliest snake in India. He has died within ten seconds of being bitten. Violence does, in truth, recoil upon the violent, and the schemer falls into the pit which he digs for another. Let us thrust this creature back into its den, and we can then remove Miss Stoner to some place of shelter, and let the county police know what has happened."

As he spoke he drew the dog-whip swiftly from the dead man's lap, and throwing the noose round the reptile's neck, he drew it from its horrid perch and, carrying it at arm's length, threw it into the iron safe, which he closed upon it.

Such are the true facts of the death of Dr. Grimesby Roylott, of Stoke Moran. It is not necessary that I should prolong a narrative which has already run to too great a length, by telling how we broke the sad news to the terrified girl, how we conveyed her by the morning train to the care of her good aunt at Harrow, of how the slow process of official inquiry came to the conclusion that the doctor met his fate while indiscreetly playing with a dangerous pet. The little which I had yet to learn of the case was told me by Sherlock Holmes as we travelled back next day.

"I had," said he, "come to an entirely erroneous conclusion which shows, my dear Watson, how dangerous it always is to reason from insufficient data. The presence of the gypsies, and the use of the word 'band,' which was used by the poor girl, no doubt to explain the appearance which she had caught a hurried glimpse of by the light of her match, were sufficient to put me upon an entirely wrong scent. I can only claim the merit that I instantly reconsidered my position when, however, it became clear to me that whatever danger threatened an occupant of the room could not come either from the window or the door. My attention was speedily drawn, as I have already remarked to you, to this ventilator, and to the bell-rope which hung down the bed. The discovery that this was a dummy, and that the bed was clamped to the floor, instantly gave rise to the suspicion that the rope was there as bridge for something passing through the hole, and coming to the bed. The idea of a snake instantly occurred to me, and when I coupled it with my knowledge that the doctor was furnished with a supply of creatures from India, I felt that I was probably on the right track. The idea of using a form of poison which could not possibly be discovered by any chemical test was just such a one as would occur to a clever and ruthless man who had had an Eastern training. The rapidity with which such a poison would take effect would also, from his point of view, be an advantage. It would be a sharp-eyed coroner, indeed, who could distinguish the two little dark punctures which would show where the poison fangs had done their work. Then I thought of the whistle. Of course he must recall the snake before the morning light revealed it to the victim. He had trained it, probably by the use of the milk which we saw, to return to him when summoned. He would put it through this ventilator at the hour that he thought best, with the certainty that it would crawl down the rope and land on the bed. It might or might not bite the occupant, perhaps she might escape every night for a week, but sooner or later she must fall a victim.

"I had come to these conclusions before ever I had entered his room. An inspection of his chair showed me that he had been in the habit of standing on it, which of course would be necessary in order that he should reach the ventilator. The sight of the safe, the saucer of milk, and the loop of whipcord were enough to finally dispel any doubts which may have remained. The metallic clang heard by Miss Stoner was obviously caused by her stepfather hastily closing the door of his safe upon its terrible occupant. Having once made up my mind, you know the steps which I took in order to put the matter to the proof. I heard the creature hiss, as I have no doubt that you did also, and I instantly lit the light and attacked it."

"With the result of driving it through the ventilator."

"And also with the result of causing it to turn upon its master at the other side. Some of the blows of my cane came home, and roused its snakish temper, so that it flew upon the first person it saw. In this way I am no doubt indirectly responsible for Dr. Grimesby Roylott's death, and I cannot say that it is likely to weigh very heavily upon my conscience."

JACQUES FUTRELLE
(1875-1912)

Jacques Futrelle was born in Pike County, Georgia, and worked as a theatrical manager and newspaperman. He was writing for the *Boston American* in 1905 when it serialized, as part of a contest for readers, his story about the eccentric genius Professor Augustus S. F. X. Van Dusen who wagered that he could "think" himself out of prison. Futrelle also used the professor in an adventure novel, *The Chase of the Golden Plate* (1906) and in collections of short stories, *The Thinking Machine* (1907) and *The Thinking Machine on the Case* (1908). Except for one other work, *The Diamond Master* (1909), Futrelle's remaining stories were mainly Edwardian romances. He died in the sinking of the *Titanic*. His wife, L. May Peel Futrelle, also a writer of mysteries, survived him and edited some of his last works. A few of the uncollected tales were published in *Ellery Queen's Mystery Magazine* in 1949 and 1950.

"The Problem of Cell 13," one of the most frequently anthologized mystery pieces of all time, owes its popularity to the way it epitomizes the "locked-room" format of "The Murders in the Rue Morgue" by directly challenging the reader to anticipate the protagonist's mode of escape. Despite the implausibility of the basic situation and some use of coincidence, it "plays fair" in that the reader is supplied with all the clues—and a welter of red herrings besides—necessary to arrive at the professor's solution before he reveals it.

THE PROBLEM OF CELL 13

I

Practically all those letters remaining in the alphabet after Augustus S. F. X. Van Dusen was named were afterward acquired by that gentleman in the course of a brilliant scientific career, and, being honorably acquired, were tacked on to the other end. His name, therefore, taken with all that belonged to it, was a wonderfully imposing structure. He was a Ph.D., an LL.D., an F.R.S., an M.D., and an M.D.S. He was also some other things—just what he himself couldn't say—through recognition of his ability by various foreign educational and scientific institutions.

In appearance he was no less striking than in nomenclature. He was slender with the droop of the student in his thin shoulders and the pallor of a close, sedentary life on his clean-shaven face. His eyes wore a perpetual, forbidding squint—of a man who studies little things—and when they could be seen at all through his thick spectacles, were mere slits of watery blue. But above his eyes was his most striking feature. This was a tall, broad brow, almost abnormal in height and width, crowned by a heavy shock of bushy, yellow hair. All these things conspired to give him a peculiar, almost grotesque, personality.

Professor Van Dusen was remotely German. For generations his ancestors had been noted in the sciences; he was the logical result, the master mind. First and above all he was a logician. At least thirty-five years of the half-century or so of his existence had been devoted exclusively to proving that two and two always equal four, except in unusual cases, where they equal three or five, as the case may be. He stood broadly on the general proposition that all things that start must go somewhere, and was able to bring the concentrated mental force of his forefathers to bear on a given problem. Incidentally it may be remarked that Professor Van Dusen wore a No. 8 hat.

The world at large had heard vaguely of Professor Van Dusen as The Thinking Machine. It was a newspaper catch-phrase applied to him at the time of a remarkable exhibition at chess; he had demonstrated then that a stranger to the game might, by the force of inevitable logic, defeat a champion who had devoted a lifetime to its study. The Thinking Machine! Perhaps that more nearly described him than all his honorary initials, for he spent week after week, month after month, in the seclusion of his small laboratory from which had gone forth thoughts that staggered scientific associates and deeply stirred the world at large.

It was only occasionally that The Thinking Machine had visitors, and these were usually men who, themselves high in the sciences, dropped in to argue a point and perhaps convince themselves. Two of these men, Dr. Charles Ransome and Alfred Fielding, called one evening to discuss some theory which is not of consequence here.

"Such a thing is impossible," declared Dr. Ransome emphatically, in the course of the conversation.

"Nothing is impossible," declared The Thinking Machine with equal emphasis. He always spoke petulantly. "The mind is master of all things. When science fully recognizes that fact a great advance will have been made."

"How about the airship?" asked Dr. Ransome.

"That's not impossible at all," asserted The Thinking Machine. "It will be invented some time. I'd do it myself, but I'm busy."

Dr. Ransome laughed tolerantly.

"I've heard you say such things before," he said. "But they mean nothing. Mind may be master of matter, but it hasn't yet found a way to apply itself. There are some things that can't be *thought* out of existence, or rather which would not yield to any amount of thinking."

"What, for instance?" demanded The Thinking Machine.

Dr. Ransome was thoughtful for a moment as he smoked. "Well, say prison walls," he replied. "No man can *think* himself out of a cell. If he could, there would be no prisoners."

"A man can so apply his brain and ingenuity that he can leave a cell, which is the same thing," snapped The Thinking Machine.

Dr. Ransome was slightly amused.

"Let's suppose a case," he said, after a moment. "Take a cell where prisoners under sentence of death are confined—men who are desperate and, maddened by fear, would take any chance to escape—suppose you were locked in such a cell. Could you escape?"

"Certainly," declared The Thinking Machine.

"Of course," said Mr. Fielding, who entered the conversation for the first time, "you might wreck the cell with an explosive—but inside, a prisoner, you couldn't have that."

"There would be nothing of that kind," said The Thinking Machine. "You might treat me precisely as you treated prisoners under sentence of death, and I would leave the cell."

"Not unless you entered it with tools prepared to get out," said Dr. Ransome.

The Thinking Machine was visibly annoyed and his blue eyes snapped.

"Lock me in any cell in any prison anywhere at any time, wearing only what is necessary, and I'll escape in a week," he declared, sharply.

Dr. Ransome sat up straight in the chair, interested. Mr. Fielding lighted a new cigar.

"You mean you could actually *think* yourself out?" asked Dr. Ransome.

"I would get out," was the response.

"Are you serious?"

"Certainly I am serious."

Dr. Ransome and Mr. Fielding were silent for a long time.

"Would you be willing to try it?" asked Mr. Fielding, finally.

"Certainly," said Professor Van Dusen, and there was a trace of irony in his voice. "I have done more asinine things than that to convince other men of less important truths."

The tone was offensive and there was an undercurrent strongly resembling anger on both sides. Of course it was an absurd thing, but Professor Van Dusen reiterated his willingness to undertake the escape and it was decided upon.

"To begin now," added Dr. Ransome.

"I'd prefer that it begin tomorrow," said The Thinking Machine, "because—"

"No, now," said Mr. Fielding, flatly. "You are arrested, figuratively, of course, without any warning locked in a cell with no chance to communicate with friends, and left there with identically the same care and attention that would be given to a man under sentence of death. Are you willing?"

"All right, now, then," said The Thinking Machine, and he arose.

"Say, the death-cell in Chisholm Prison."

"The death-cell in Chisholm Prison."

"And what will you wear?"

"As little as possible," said The Thinking Machine. "Shoes, stockings, trousers and a shirt."

"You will permit yourself to be searched, of course?"

"I am to be treated precisely as all prisoners are treated," said The Thinking Machine. "No more attention and no less."

There were some preliminaries to be arranged in the matter of obtaining permission for the test, but all three were influential men and everything was done satisfactorily by telephone, albeit the prison commissioners, to whom the experiment was explained on purely scientific grounds, were sadly bewildered. Professor Van Dusen would be the most distinguished prisoner they had ever entertained.

When The Thinking Machine had donned those things which he was to wear during his incarceration he called the little old woman who was his housekeeper, cook and maidservant all in one.

"Martha," he said, "it is now twenty-seven minutes past nine o'clock. I am going away. One week from to-night, at half-past nine, these gentlemen and one, possibly two, others will take supper with me here. Remember Dr. Ransome is very fond of artichokes."

The three men were driven to Chisholm Prison, where the warden was awaiting them, having been informed of the matter by telephone. He understood merely that the eminent Professor Van Dusen was to be his prisoner, if he could keep him, for one week; that he had committed no crime, but that he was to be treated as all other prisoners were treated.

"Search him," instructed Dr. Ransome.

The Thinking Machine was searched. Nothing was found on him; the pockets of the trousers were empty; the white, stiff-bosomed shirt had no pocket. The shoes and stockings were removed, examined, then replaced. As he watched all these preliminaries—the rigid search and noted the pitiful, childlike physical weakness of the man, the colorless face, and the thin, white hands—Dr. Ransome almost regretted his part in the affair.

"Are you sure you want to do this?" he asked.

"Would you be convinced if I did not?" inquired The Thinking Machine in turn.

"No."

"All right. I'll do it."

What sympathy Dr. Ransome had was dissipated by the tone. It nettled him, and he resolved to see the experiment to the end; it would be a stinging reproof to egotism.

"It will be impossible for him to communicate with any one outside?" he asked.

"Absolutely impossible," replied the warden. "He will not be permitted writing materials of any sort."

"And your jailers, would they deliver a message from him?"

"Not one word, directly or indirectly," said the warden. "You may rest assured of that. They will report anything he might say or turn over to me anything he might give them."

"That seems entirely satisfactory," said Mr. Fielding, who was frankly interested in the problem.

"Of course, in the event he fails," said Dr. Ransome, "and asks for his liberty, you understand you are to set him free?"

"I understand," replied the warden.

The Thinking Machine stood listening, but had nothing to say until this was all ended, then:

"I should like to make three small requests. You may grant them or not, as you wish."

"No special favors, now," warned Mr. Fielding.

"I am asking none," was the stiff response. "I would like to have some tooth powder—buy it yourself to see that it is tooth powder—and I should like to have one five-dollar and two ten-dollar bills."

Dr. Ransome, Mr. Fielding and the warden exchanged astonished glances. They were not surprised at the request for tooth powder, but were at the request for money.

"Is there any man with whom our friend would come in contact that he could bribe with twenty-five dollars?" asked Dr. Ransome of the warden.

"Not for twenty-five hundred dollars," was the positive reply.

"Well, let him have them," said Mr. Fielding. "I think they are harmless enough."

"And what is the third request?" asked Dr. Ransome.

"I should like to have my shoes polished."

Again the astonished glances were exchanged. This last request was the height of absurdity, so they agreed to it. These things all being attended to, The Thinking Machine was led back into the prison from which he had undertaken to escape.

"Here is Cell 13," said the warden, stopping three doors down the steel corridor. "This is where we keep condemned murderers. No one can leave it without my permission; and no one in it can communicate with the outside. I'll stake my reputation on that. It's only three doors back of my office and I can readily hear any unusual noise."

"Will this cell do, gentlemen?" asked The Thinking Machine. There was a touch of irony in his voice.

"Admirably," was the reply.

The heavy steel door was thrown open, there was a great scurrying and scampering of tiny feet, and The Thinking Machine passed into the gloom of the cell. Then the door was closed and double locked by the warden.

"What is that noise in there?" asked Dr. Ransome, through the bars.

"Rats—dozens of them," replied The Thinking Machine, tersely.

The three men, with final good nights, were turning away when The Thinking Machine called:

"What time is it exactly, warden?"

"Eleven seventeen," replied the warden.

"Thanks. I will join you gentlemen in your office at half-past eight o'clock one week from to-night," said The Thinking Machine.

"And if you do not?"

"There is no 'if' about it."

II

Chisholm Prison was a great, spreading structure of granite, four stories in all, which stood in the center of acres of open space. It was surrounded by a wall of solid masonry eighteen feet high, and so smoothly finished inside and out as to offer no foothold to a climber, no matter how expert. Atop of this fence, as a further precaution, was a five-foot fence of steel rods, each terminating in a keen point. This fence in itself marked an absolute deadline between freedom and imprisonment, for, even if a man escaped from his cell, it would seem impossible for him to pass the wall.

The yard, which on all sides of the prison building was twenty-five feet wide, that being the distance from the building to the wall, was by day an exercise ground for those prisoners to whom was granted the boon of occasional semiliberty. But that was not for those in Cell 13.

At all times of the day there were armed guards in the yard, four of them, one patrolling each side of the prison building.

By night the yard was almost as brilliantly lighted as by day. On each of the four sides was a great arc light which rose above the prison wall and gave to the guards a clear sight. The lights, too, brightly illuminated the spiked top of the wall. The wires which fed the arc lights ran up the side of the prison building on insulators and from the top story led out to the poles supporting the arc lights.

All these things were seen and comprehended by The Thinking Machine, who was only enabled to see out his closely barred cell window by standing on his bed. This was on the morning following his incarceration. He gathered, too, that the river lay over there beyond the wall somewhere, because he heard faintly the pulsation of a motor boat and high up in the air saw a river bird. From that same direction came the shouts of boys at play and the occasional crack of a batted ball. He knew then that between the prison wall and the river was an open space, a playground.

Chisholm Prison was regarded as absolutely safe. No man had ever escaped from it. The Thinking Machine, from his perch on the bed, seeing what he saw, could readily understand why. The walls of the cell, though built he judged twenty years before, were perfectly solid, and the window bars of new iron had not a shadow of rust on them. The window itself, even with the bars out, would be a difficult mode of egress because it was small.

Yet, seeing these things, The Thinking Machine was not discouraged. Instead, he thoughtfully squinted at the great arc light—there was bright sunlight now—and traced with his eyes the wire which led from it to the building. That electric wire, he reasoned, must come down the side of the building not a great distance from his cell. That might be worth knowing.

Cell 13 was on the same floor with the offices of the prison—that is, not in the basement, nor yet upstairs. There were only four steps up to the office floor, therefore the level of the floor must be only three or four feet above the ground. He couldn't see the ground directly beneath his window, but he could see it further out toward the wall. It would be an easy drop from the window. Well and good.

Then The Thinking Machine fell to remembering how he had come to the cell. First, there was the outside guard's booth, a part of the wall. There were two heavily barred gates there, both of steel. At this gate was one man always on guard. He admitted persons to the prison after much clanking of keys and locks, and let them out when ordered to do so. The warden's office was in the prison building, and in order to reach that official from the prison yard one had to pass a gate of solid steel with only a peep-hole in it. Then coming from that inner office to Cell 13, where he was now, one must pass a heavy wooden door and two steel doors into the corridors of the prison; and always there was the double-locked door to Cell 13 to reckon with.

There were then, The Thinking Machine recalled, seven doors to be overcome before one could pass from Cell 13 into the outer world, a free man. But against this was the fact that he was rarely interrupted. A jailer appeared at his cell door at six in the morning with a breakfast of prison fare; he would come again at noon, and again at six in the afternoon. At nine o'clock at night would come the inspection tour. That would be all.

"It's admirably arranged, this prison system," was the mental tribute paid by The Thinking Machine. "I'll have to study it a little when I get out. I had no idea there was such great care exercised in the prisons."

There was nothing, positively nothing, in his cell, except his iron bed, so firmly put together that no man could tear it to pieces save with sledges or a file. He had neither of these. There was not even a chair, or a small table, or a bit of tin or crockery. Nothing! The jailer stood by when he ate, then took away the wooden spoon and bowl which he had used.

One by one these things sank into the brain of The Thinking Machine. When the last possibility had been considered he began an examination of his cell. From the roof, down the walls on all sides, he examined the stones and the cement between them. He stamped over the floor carefully time after time, but it was cement, perfectly solid. After the examination he sat on the edge of the iron bed and was lost in thought for a long time. For Professor Augustus S. F. X. Van Dusen, The Thinking Machine, had something to think about.

He was disturbed by a rat, which ran across his foot, then scampered away into a dark corner of the cell, frightened at its own daring. After a while The Thinking Machine, squinting steadily into the darkness of the corner where the rat had gone, was able to make out in the gloom many little beady eyes staring at him. He counted six pair, and there were perhaps others; he didn't see very well.

Then The Thinking Machine, from his seat on the bed, noticed for the first time the bottom of his cell door. There was an opening there of two inches between the steel bar and the floor. Still looking steadily at this opening, The Thinking Machine backed suddenly into the corner where he had seen the beady eyes. There was a great scampering of tiny feet, several squeaks of frightened rodents, and then silence.

None of the rats had gone out the door, yet there were none in the cell. Therefore there must be another way out of the cell, however small. The Thinking Machine, on hands and knees, started a search for this spot, feeling in the darkness with his long, slender fingers.

At last his search was rewarded. He came upon a small opening in the floor, level with the cement. It was perfectly round and somewhat larger than a silver dollar. This was the way the rats had gone. He put his fingers deep into the opening; it seemed to be a disused drainage pipe and was dry and dusty.

Having satisfied himself on this point, he sat on the bed again for an hour, then made another inspection of his surroundings through the small cell window. One of the outside guards stood directly opposite, beside the wall, and happened to be looking at the window of Cell 13 when the head of The Thinking Machine appeared. But the scientist didn't notice the guard.

Noon came and the jailer appeared with the prison dinner of repulsively plain food. At home The Thinking Machine merely ate to live; here he took what was offered without comment. Occasionally he spoke to the jailer who stood outside the door watching him.

"Any improvements made here in the last few years?" he asked.

"Nothing particularly," replied the jailer. "New wall was built four years ago."

"Anything done to the prison proper?"

"Painted the woodwork outside, and I believe about seven years ago a new system of plumbing was put in."

"Ah!" said the prisoner. "How far is the river over there?"

"About three hundred feet. The boys have a baseball ground between the wall and the river."

The Thinking Machine had nothing further to say just then, but when the jailer was ready to go he asked for some water.

"I get very thirsty here," he explained. "Would it be possible for you to leave a little water in a bowl for me?"

"I'll ask the warden," replied the jailer, and he went away.

Half an hour later he returned with water in a small earthen bowl.

"The warden says you may keep this bowl," he informed the prisoner. "But you must show it to me when I ask for it. If it is broken, it will be the last."

"Thank you," said The Thinking Machine. "I shan't break it."

The jailer went on about his duties. For just the fraction of a second it seemed that The Thinking Machine wanted to ask a question, but he didn't.

Two hours later this same jailer, in passing the door of Cell No. 13, heard a noise inside and stopped. The Thinking Machine was down on his hands and knees in a corner of the cell, and from that same corner came several frightened squeaks. The jailer looked on interestedly.

"Ah, I've got you," he heard the prisoner say.

"Got what?" he asked, sharply.

"One of these rats," was the reply. "See?" And between the scientist's long fingers the jailer saw a small gray rat struggling. The prisoner brought it over to the light and looked at it closely. "It's a water rat," he said.

"Ain't you got anything better to do than to catch rats?" asked the jailer.

"It's disgraceful that they should be here at all," was the irritated reply. "Take this one away and kill it. There are dozens more where it came from."

The jailer took the wriggling, squirmy rodent and flung it down on the floor violently. It gave one squeak and lay still. Later he reported the incident to the warden, who only smiled.

Still later that afternoon the outside armed guard on Cell 13 side of the prison looked up again at the window and saw the prisoner looking out. He saw a hand raised to the barred window and then something white fluttered to the ground, directly under the window of Cell 13. It was a little roll of linen, evidently of white shirting material, and tied around it was a five-dollar bill. The guard looked up at the window again, but the face had disappeared.

With a grim smile he took the little linen roll and the five-dollar bill to the warden's office. There together they deciphered something which was written on it with a queer sort of ink, frequently blurred. On the outside was this:

"Finder of this please deliver to Dr. Charles Ransome."

"Ah," said the warden, with a chuckle. "Plan of escape number one has gone wrong." Then, as an afterthought: "But why did he address it to Dr. Ransome?"

"And where did he get the pen and ink to write with?" asked the guard.

The warden looked at the guard and the guard looked at the warden. There was no apparent solution of that mystery. The warden studied the writing carefully, then shook his head.

"Well, let's see what he was going to say to Dr. Ransome," he said at length, still puzzled, and he unrolled the inner piece of linen.

"Well, if that—what—what do you think of that?" he asked, dazed.

The guard took the bit of linen and read this:

"*Epa cseot d'net niiy awe htto n'si sih. T.*"

III

The warden spent an hour wondering what sort of a cipher it was, and half an hour wondering why his prisoner should attempt to communicate with Dr. Ransome, who was the cause of him being there. After this the warden devoted some thought to the question of where the prisoner got writing materials, and what sort of writing materials he had. With the idea of illuminating this point, he examined the linen again. It was a torn part of a white shirt and had ragged edges.

Now it was possible to account for the linen, but what the prisoner had used to write with was another matter. The warden knew it would have been impossible for him to have either pen or pencil, and, besides, neither pen nor pencil had been used in this writing. What, then? The warden decided to personally investigate. The Thinking Machine was his prisoner; he had orders to hold his prisoners; if this one sought to escape by sending cipher messages to persons outside, he would stop it, as he would have stopped it in the case of any other prisoner.

The warden went back to Cell 13 and found The Thinking Machine on his hands and knees on the floor, engaged in nothing more alarming than catching rats. The prisoner heard the warden's step and turned to him quickly.

"It's disgraceful," he snapped, "these rats. There are scores of them."

"Other men have been able to stand them," said the warden. "Here is another shirt for you—let me have the one you have on."

"Why?" demanded The Thinking Machine, quickly. His tone was hardly natural, his manner suggested actual perturbation.

"You have attempted to communicate with Dr. Ransome," said the warden severely. "As my prisoner, it is my duty to put a stop to it."

The Thinking Machine was silent for a moment.

"All right," he said, finally. "Do your duty."

The warden smiled grimly. The prisoner arose from the floor and removed the white shirt, putting on instead a striped convict shirt the warden had brought. The warden took the white shirt eagerly, and then and there compared the pieces of linen on which was written the cipher with certain torn places in the shirt. The Thinking Machine looked on curiously.

"The guard brought *you* those, then?" he asked.

"He certainly did," replied the warden triumphantly. "And that ends your first attempt to escape."

The Thinking Machine watched the warden as he, by comparison, established to his own satisfaction that only two pieces of linen had been torn from the white shirt.

"What did you write this with?" demanded the warden.

"I should think it a part of your duty to find out," said The Thinking Machine, irritably.

The warden started to say some harsh things, then restrained himself and made a minute search of the cell and of the prisoner instead. He found absolutely nothing; not even a match or toothpick which might have been used for a pen. The same mystery surrounded the fluid with which the cipher had been written. Although the warden left Cell 13 visibly annoyed, he took the torn shirt in triumph.

"Well, writing notes on a shirt won't get him out, that's certain," he told himself with some complacency. He put the linen scraps into his desk to await developments. "If that man escapes from that cell I'll—hang it—I'll resign."

On the third day of his incarceration The Thinking Machine openly attempted to bribe his way out. The jailer had brought his dinner and was leaning against the barred door, waiting, when The Thinking Machine began the conversation.

"The drainage pipes of the prison lead to the river, don't they?" he asked.

"Yes," said the jailer.

"I suppose they are very small?"

"Too small to crawl through, if that's what you're thinking about," was the grinning response.

There was silence until The Thinking Machine finished his meal. Then:

"You know I'm not a criminal, don't you?"

"Yes."

"And that I've a perfect right to be freed if I demand it?"

"Yes."

"Well, I came here believing that I could make my escape," said the prisoner, and his squint eyes studied the face of the jailer. "Would you consider a financial reward for aiding me to escape?"

The jailer, who happened to be an honest man, looked at the slender, weak figure of the prisoner, at the large head with its mass of yellow hair, and was almost sorry.

"I guess prisons like these were not built for the likes of you to get out of," he said, at last.

"But would you consider a proposition to help me get out?" the prisoner insisted, almost beseechingly.

"No," said the jailer, shortly.

"Five hundred dollars," urged The Thinking Machine. "I am not a criminal."

"No," said the jailer.

"A thousand?"

"No," again said the jailer, and he started away hurriedly to escape further temptation. Then he turned back. "If you should give me ten thousand dollars I couldn't get you out. You'd have to pass through seven doors, and I only have the keys to two."

Then he told the warden all about it.

"Plan number two fails," said the warden, smiling grimly. "First a cipher, then bribery."

When the jailer was on his way to Cell 13 at six o'clock, again bearing food to The Thinking Machine, he paused, startled by the unmistakable scrape, scrape of steel against steel. It stopped at the sound of his steps, then craftily the jailer, who was beyond the prisoner's range of vision, resumed his tramping, the sound being apparently that of a man going away from Cell 13. As a matter of fact he was in the same spot.

After a moment there came again the steady scrape, scrape, and the jailer crept cautiously on tiptoes to the door and peered between the bars. The Thinking Machine was standing on the iron bed working at the bars of the little window. He was using a file, judging from the backward and forward swing of his arms.

Cautiously the jailer crept back to the office, summoned the warden in person, and they returned to Cell 13 on tiptoes. The steady scrape was still audible. The warden listened to satisfy himself and then suddenly appeared at the door.

"Well?" he demanded, and there was a smile on his face.

The Thinking Machine glanced back from his perch on the bed and leaped suddenly to the floor, making frantic efforts to hide something. The warden went in, with hand extended.

"Give it up," he said.

"No," said the prisoner sharply.

"Come, give it up," urged the warden. "I don't want to have to search you again."

"No," repeated the prisoner.

"What was it, a file?" asked the warden.

The Thinking Machine was silent and stood squinting at the warden with something very nearly approaching disappointment on his face—nearly, but not quite. The warden was almost sympathetic.

"Plan number three fails, eh?" he asked, good-naturedly. "Too bad, isn't it?"

The prisoner didn't say.

"Search him," instructed the warden.

The jailer searched the prisoner carefully. At last, artfully concealed in the waistband of the trousers, he found a piece of steel about two inches long, with one side curved like a half moon.

"Ah," said the warden, as he received it from the jailer. "From your shoe heel," and he smiled pleasantly.

The jailer continued his search and on the other side of the trousers waistband was another piece of steel identical with the first. The edges showed where they had been worn against the bars of the window.

"You couldn't saw a way through those bars with these," said the warden.

"I could have," said The Thinking Machine firmly.

"In six months, perhaps," said the warden, good-naturedly.

The warden shook his head slowly as he gazed into the slightly flushed face of his prisoner.

"Ready to give it up?" he asked.

"I haven't started yet," was the prompt reply.

Then came another exhaustive search of the cell. Carefully the two men went over it, finally turning out the bed and searching that. Nothing. The warden in person climbed upon the bed and examined the bars of the window where the prisoner had been sawing. When he looked he was amused.

"Just made it a little bright by hard rubbing," he said to the prisoner, who stood looking on with a somewhat crestfallen air. The warden grasped the iron bars in his strong hands and tried to shake them. They were immovable, set firmly in the solid granite. He examined each in turn and found them all satisfactory. Finally he climbed down from the bed.

"Give it up, professor," he advised.

The Thinking Machine shook his head and the warden and jailer passed on again. As they disappeared down the corridor The Thinking Machine sat on the edge of the bed with his head in his hands.

"He's crazy to try to get out of that cell," commented the jailer.

"Of course he can't get out," said the warden. "But he's clever. I would like to know what he wrote that cipher with."

It was four o'clock next morning when an awful, heart-racking shriek of terror resounded through the great prison. It came from a cell, somewhere about the center, and its tone told a tale of horror, agony, terrible fear. The warden heard and with three of his men rushed into the long corridor leading to Cell 13.

IV

As they ran there came again that awful cry. It died away in a sort of wail. The white faces of prisoners appeared at cell doors upstairs and down, staring out wonderingly, frightened.

"It's that fool in Cell 13," grumbled the warden.

He stopped and stared in as one of the jailers flashed a lantern. "That fool in Cell 13" lay comfortably on his cot, flat on his back with his mouth open, snoring. Even as they looked there came again the piercing cry, from somewhere above. The warden's face blanched a little as he started up the stairs. There on the top floor he found a man in Cell 43, directly above Cell 13, but two floors higher, cowering in a corner of his cell.

"What's the matter?" demanded the warden.

"Thank God you've come," exclaimed the prisoner, and he cast himself against the bars of his cell.

"What is it?" demanded the warden again.

He threw open the door and went in. The prisoner dropped on his knees and clasped the warden about the body. His face was white with terror, his eyes were widely distended, and he was shuddering. His hands, icy cold, clutched at the warden's.

"Take me out of this cell, please take me out," he pleaded.

"What's the matter with you, anyhow?" insisted the warden, impatiently.

"I heard something—something," said the prisoner, and his eyes roved nervously around the cell.

"What did you hear?"

"I—I can't tell you," stammered the prisoner. Then, in a sudden burst of terror: "Take me out of this cell—put me anywhere—but take me out of here."

The warden and the three jailers exchanged glances.

"Who is this fellow? What's he accused of?" asked the warden.

"Joseph Ballard," said one of the jailers. "He's accused of throwing acid in a woman's face. She died from it."

"But they can't prove it," gasped the prisoner. "They can't prove it. Please put me in some other cell."

He was still clinging to the warden, and that official threw his arms off roughly. Then for a time he stood looking at the cowering wretch, who seemed possessed of all the wild, unreasoning terror of a child.

"Look here, Ballard," said the warden, finally, "if you heard anything, I want to know what it was. Now tell me."

"I can't, I can't," was the reply. He was sobbing.

"Where did it come from?"

"I don't know. Everywhere—nowhere. I just heard it."

"What was it—a voice?"

"Please don't make me answer," pleaded the prisoner.

"You must answer," said the warden, sharply.

"It was a voice—but—but it wasn't human," was the sobbing reply.

"Voice, but not human?" repeated the warden, puzzled.

"It sounded muffled and—and far away—and ghostly," explained the man.

"Did it come from inside or outside the prison?"

"It didn't seem to come from anywhere—it was just here, here, everywhere. I heard it. I heard it."

For an hour the warden tried to get the story, but Ballard had become suddenly obstinate and would say nothing—only pleaded to be placed in another cell, or to have one of the jailers remain near him until daylight. These requests were gruffly refused.

"And see here," said the warden, in conclusion, "if there's any more of this screaming I'll put you in the padded cell."

Then the warden went his way, a sadly puzzled man. Ballard sat at his cell door until daylight, his face, drawn and white with terror, pressed against the bars, and looked out into the prison with wide, staring eyes.

That day, the fourth since the incarceration of The Thinking Machine, was enlivened considerably by the volunteer prisoner, who spent most of his time at the little window of his cell. He began proceedings by throwing another piece of linen down to the guard, who picked it up dutifully and took it to the warden. On it was written:

"Only three days more."

The warden was in no way surprised at what he read; he understood that The Thinking Machine meant only three days more of his imprisonment, and he regarded the note as a boast. But how was the thing written? Where had The Thinking Machine found this new piece of linen? Where? How? He carefully examined the linen. It was white, of fine texture, shirting material. He took the shirt which he had taken and carefully fitted the two original pieces of the linen to the torn places. This third piece was entirely superfluous; it didn't fit anywhere, and yet it was unmistakably the same goods.

"And where—where does he get anything to write with?" demanded the warden of the world at large.

Still later on the fourth day The Thinking Machine, through the window of his cell, spoke to the armed guard outside.

"What day of the month is it?" he asked.

"The fifteenth," was the answer.

The Thinking Machine made a mental astronomical calculation and satisfied himself that the moon would not rise until after nine o'clock that night. Then he asked another question:

"Who attends to those arc lights?"

"Man from the company."

"You have no electricians in the building?"

"No."

"I should think you could save money if you had your own man."

"None of my business," replied the guard.

The guard noticed The Thinking Machine at the cell window frequently during that day, but always the face seemed listless and there was a certain wistfulness in the squint eyes behind the glasses. After a while he accepted the presence of the leonine head as a matter of course. He had seen other prisoners do the same thing; it was the longing for the outside world.

That afternoon, just before the day guard was relieved, the head appeared at the window again, and The Thinking Machine's hand held something out between the bars. It fluttered to the ground and the guard picked it up. It was a five-dollar bill.

"That's for you," called the prisoner.

As usual, the guard took it to the warden. That gentleman looked at it suspiciously; he looked at everything that came from Cell 13 with suspicion.

"He said it was for me," explained the guard.

"It's a sort of a tip, I suppose," said the warden. "I see no particular reason why you shouldn't accept—"

Suddenly he stopped. He had remembered that The Thinking Machine had gone into Cell 13 with one five-dollar bill and two ten-dollar bills; twenty-five dollars in all. Now a five-dollar bill had been tied around the first pieces of linen that came from the cell. The warden still had it, and to convince himself he took it out and looked at it. It was five dollars; yet here was another five dollars, and The Thinking Machine had only had ten-dollar bills.

"Perhaps somebody changed one of the bills for him," he thought at last, with a sigh of relief.

But then and there he made up his mind. He would search Cell 13 as a cell was never before searched in this world. When a man could write at will, and change money, and do other wholly inexplicable things, there was something radically wrong with his prison. He planned to enter the cell at night—three o'clock would be an excellent time. The Thinking Machine must do all the weird things he did some time. Night seemed the most reasonable.

Thus it happened that the warden stealthily descended upon Cell 13 that night at three o'clock. He paused at the door and listened. There was no sound save the steady, regular breathing of the prisoner. The keys unfastened the double locks with scarcely a clank, and the warden entered, locking the door behind him. Suddenly he flashed his dark-lantern in the face of the recumbent figure.

If the warden had planned to startle The Thinking Machine he was mistaken, for that individual merely opened his eyes quietly, reached for his glasses and inquired, in a most matter-of-fact tone:

"Who is it?"

It would be useless to describe the search that the warden made. It was minute. Not one inch of the cell or the bed was overlooked. He found the round hole in the floor, and with a flash of inspiration thrust his thick fingers into it. After a moment of fumbling there he drew up something and looked at it in the light of his lantern.

"Ugh!" he exclaimed.

The thing he had taken out was a rat—a dead rat. His inspiration fled as a mist before the sun. But he continued the search.

The Thinking Machine, without a word, arose and kicked the rat out of the cell into the corridor.

The warden climbed on the bed and tried the steel bars in the tiny window. They were perfectly rigid; every bar of the door was the same.

Then the warden searched the prisoner's clothing, beginning at the shoes. Nothing hidden in them! Then the trousers waistband. Still nothing! Then the pockets of the trousers. From one side he drew out some paper money and examined it.

"Five one-dollar bills," he gasped.

"That's right," said the prisoner.

"But the—you had two tens and a five—what the—how do you do it?"

"That's my business," said The Thinking Machine.

"Did any of my men change this money for you—on your word of honor?"

The Thinking Machine paused just a fraction of a second.

"No," he said.

"Well, do you make it?" asked the warden. He was prepared to believe anything.

"That's my business," again said the prisoner.

The warden glared at the eminent scientist fiercely. He felt—he knew—that this man was making a fool of him, yet he didn't know how. If he were a real prisoner he would get the truth—but, then, perhaps, those inexplicable things which had happened would not have been brought before him so sharply. Neither of the men spoke for a long time, then suddenly the warden turned fiercely and left the cell, slamming the door behind him. He didn't dare to speak, then.

He glanced at the clock. It was ten minutes to four. He had hardly settled himself in bed when again came that heart-breaking shriek through the prison. With a few muttered words, which, while not elegant, were highly expressive, he relighted his lantern and rushed through the prison again to the cell on the upper floor.

Again Ballard was crushing himself against the steel door, shrieking, shrieking at the top of his voice. He stopped only when the warden flashed his lamp in the cell.

"Take me out, take me out," he screamed. "I did it, I did it, I killed her. Take it away."

"Take what away?" asked the warden.

"I threw the acid in her face—I did it—I confess. Take me out of here."

Ballard's condition was pitiable; it was only an act of mercy to let him out into the corridor. There he crouched in a corner, like an animal at bay, and clasped his hands to his ears. It took half an hour to calm him sufficiently for him to speak. Then he told incoherently what had happened. On the night before at four o'clock he had heard a voice—a sepulchral voice, muffled and wailing in tone.

"What did it say?" asked the warden, curiously.

"Acid—acid—acid!" gasped the prisoner. "It accused me. Acid! I threw the acid, and the woman died. Oh!" It was a long, shuddering wail of terror.

"Acid?" echoed the warden, puzzled. The case was beyond him.

"Acid. That's all I heard—that one word, repeated several times. There were other things, too, but I didn't hear them."

"That was last night, eh?" asked the warden. "What happened to-night—what frightened you just now?"

"It was the same thing," gasped the prisoner. "Acid—acid—acid." He covered his face with his hands and sat shivering. "It was acid I used on her, but I didn't mean to kill her. I just heard the words. It was something accusing me—accusing me." He mumbled, and was silent.

"Did you hear anything else?"

"Yes—but I couldn't understand—only a little bit—just a word or two."

"Well, what was it?"

"I heard 'acid' three times, then I heard a long, moaning sound, then—then—I heard 'No. 8 hat.' I heard that voice."

"No. 8 hat," repeated the warden. "What the devil—No. 8 hat? Accusing voices of conscience have never talked about No. 8 hats, so far as I ever heard."

"He's insane," said one of the jailers, with an air of finality.

"I believe you," said the warden. "He must be. He probably heard something and got frightened. He's trembling now. No. 8 hat! What the—"

V

When the fifth day of The Thinking Machine's imprisonment rolled around the warden was wearing a hunted look. He was anxious for the end of the thing. He could not help but feel that his distinguished prisoner had been amusing himself. And if this were so, The Thinking Machine had lost none of his sense of humor. For on this fifth day he flung down another linen note to the outside guard, bearing the words: "Only two days more." Also he flung down half a dollar.

Now the warden knew—he *knew*—that the man in Cell 13 didn't have any half dollars—he *couldn't* have any half dollars, no more than he could have pen and ink and linen, and yet he did have them. It was a condition, not a theory; that is one reason why the warden was wearing a hunted look.

That ghastly, uncanny thing, too, about "Acid" and "No. 8 hat" clung to him tenaciously. They didn't mean anything, of course, merely the ravings of an insane murderer who had been driven by fear to confess his crime, still there were so many things that "didn't mean anything" happening in the prison now since The Thinking Machine was there.

On the sixth day the warden received a postal stating that Dr. Ransome and Mr. Fielding would be at Chisholm Prison on the following evening, Thursday, and in the event Professor Van Dusen had not yet escaped—and they presumed he had not because they had not heard from him—they would meet him there.

"In the event he had not yet escaped!" The warden smiled grimly. Escaped!

The Thinking Machine enlivened this day for the warden with three notes. They were on the usual linen and bore generally on the appointment at half-past eight o'clock Thursday night, which appointment the scientist had made at the time of his imprisonment.

On the afternoon of the seventh day the warden passed Cell 13 and glanced in. The Thinking Machine was lying on the iron bed, apparently sleeping lightly. The cell appeared precisely as it always did from a casual glance. The warden would swear that no man was going to leave it between that hour—it was then four o'clock—and half-past eight o'clock that evening.

On his way back past the cell the warden heard the steady breathing again, and coming close to the door looked in. He wouldn't have done so if The Thinking Machine had been looking, but now—well, it was different.

A ray of light came through the high window and fell on the face of the sleeping man. It occurred to the warden for the first time that his prisoner appeared haggard and weary. Just then The Thinking Machine stirred slightly and the warden hurried on up the corridor guiltily. That evening after six o'clock he saw the jailer.

"Everything all right in Cell 13?" he asked.

"Yes, sir," replied the jailer. "He didn't eat much, though."

It was with a feeling of having done his duty that the warden received Dr. Ransome and Mr. Fielding shortly after seven o'clock. He intended to show them the linen notes and lay before them the full story of his woes, which was a long one. But before this came to pass the guard from the river side of the prison yard entered the office.

"The arc light in my side of the yard won't light," he informed the warden.

"Confound it, that man's a hoodoo," thundered the official. "Everything has happened since he's been here."

The guard went back to his post in the darkness, and the warden phoned to the electric light company.

"This is Chisholm Prison," he said through the 'phone. "Send three or four men down here quick, to fix an arc light."

The reply was evidently satisfactory, for the warden hung up the receiver and passed out into the yard. While Dr. Ransome and Mr. Fielding sat waiting, the guard at the outer gate came in with a special delivery letter. Dr. Ransome happened to notice the address, and, when the guard went out, looked at the letter more closely.

"By George!" he exclaimed.

"What is it?" asked Mr. Fielding.

Silently the doctor offered the letter. Mr. Fielding examined it closely.

"Coincidence," he said. "It must be."

It was nearly eight o'clock when the warden returned to his office. The electricians had arrived in a wagon, and were now at work. The warden pressed the buzz-button communicating with the man at the outer gate in the wall.

"How many electricians came in?" he asked, over the short 'phone. "Four? Three workmen in jumpers and overalls and the manager? Frock coat and silk hat? All right. Be certain that only four go out. That's all."

He turned to Dr. Ransome and Mr. Fielding. "We have to be careful here—particularly," and there was broad sarcasm in his tone, "since we have scientists locked up."

The warden picked up the special delivery letter carelessly, and then began to open it.

"When I read this I want to tell you gentlemen something about how—Great Caesar!" he ended, suddenly, as he glanced at the letter. He sat with mouth open, motionless, from astonishment.

"What is it?" asked Mr. Fielding.

"A special delivery letter from Cell 13," gasped the warden. "An invitation to supper."

"What?" and the two others arose, unanimously.

The warden sat dazed, staring at the letter for a moment, then called sharply to a guard outside in the corridor.

"Run down to Cell 13 and see if that man's in there."

The guard went as directed, while Dr. Ransome and Mr. Fielding examined the letter.

"It's Van Dusen's handwriting; there's no question of that," said Dr. Ransome. "I've seen too much of it."

Just then the buzz on the telephone from the outer gate sounded, and the warden, in a semi-trance, picked up the receiver.

"Hello! Two reporters, eh? Let 'em come in." He turned suddenly to the doctor and Mr. Fielding. "Why, the man *can't* be out. He must be in his cell."

Just at that moment the guard returned.

"He's still in his cell, sir," he reported. "I saw him. He's lying down."

"There, I told you so," said the warden, and he breathed freely again. "But how did he mail that letter?"

There was a rap on the steel door which led from the jail yard into the warden's office.

"It's the reporters," said the warden. "Let them in," he instructed the guard; then to the two other gentlemen: "Don't say anything about this before them, because I'd never hear the last of it."

The door opened, and the two men from the front gate entered.

"Good-evening, gentlemen," said one. That was Hutchinson Hatch; the warden knew him well.

"Well?" demanded the other, irritably. "I'm here."

That was The Thinking Machine.

He squinted belligerently at the warden, who sat with mouth agape. For the moment that official had nothing to say. Dr. Ransome and Mr. Fielding were amazed, but they didn't know what the warden knew. They were only amazed; he was paralyzed. Hutchinson Hatch, the reporter, took in the scene with greedy eyes.

"How—how—how did you do it?" gasped the warden, finally.

"Come back to the cell," said The Thinking Machine, in the irritated voice which his scientific associates knew so well.

The warden, still in a condition bordering on trance, led the way.

"Flash your light in there," directed The Thinking Machine.

The warden did so. There was nothing unusual in the appearance of the cell, and there—there on the bed lay the figure of The Thinking Machine. Certainly! There was the yellow hair! Again the warden looked at the man beside him and wondered at the strangeness of his own dreams.

With trembling hands he unlocked the cell door and The Thinking Machine passed inside.

"See here," he said.

He kicked at the steel bars in the bottom of the cell door and three of them were pushed out of place. A fourth broke off and rolled away in the corridor.

"And here, too," directed the erstwhile prisoner as he stood on the bed to reach the small window. He swept his hand across the opening and every bar came out.

"What's this in the bed?" demanded the warden, who was slowly recovering.

"A wig," was the reply. "Turn down the cover."

The warden did so. Beneath it lay a large coil of strong rope, thirty feet or more, a dagger, three files, ten feet of electric wire, a thin, powerful pair of steel pliers, a small tack hammer with its handle, and—and a Derringer pistol.

"How did you do it?" demanded the warden.

"You gentlemen have an engagement to supper with me at half-past nine o'clock," said The Thinking Machine. "Come on, or we shall be late."

"But how did you do it?" insisted the warden.

"Don't ever think you can hold any man who can use his brain," said The Thinking Machine. "Come on; we shall be late."

VI

It was an impatient supper party in the rooms of Professor Van Dusen and a somewhat silent one. The guests were Dr. Ransome, Albert Fielding, the warden, and Hutchinson Hatch, reporter. The meal was served to the minute, in accordance with Professor Van Dusen's instructions of one week before; Dr. Ransome found the artichokes delicious. At last the supper was finished and The Thinking Machine turned full on Dr. Ransome and squinted at him fiercely.

"Do you believe it now?" he demanded.

"I do," replied Dr. Ransome.

"Do you admit that it was a fair test?"

"I do."

With the others, particularly the warden, he was waiting anxiously for the explanation.

"Suppose you tell us how—" began Mr. Fielding.

"Yes, tell us how," said the warden.

The Thinking Machine readjusted his glasses, took a couple of preparatory squints at his audience, and began the story. He told it from the beginning logically; and no man ever talked to more interested listeners.

"My agreement was," he began, "to go into a cell, carrying nothing except what was necessary to wear, and to leave that cell within a week. I had never seen Chisholm Prison. When I went into the cell I asked for tooth powder, two ten and one five-dollar bills, and also to have my shoes blacked. Even if these requests had been refused it would not have mattered seriously. But you agreed to them.

"I knew there would be nothing in the cell which you thought I might use to advantage. So when the warden locked the door on me I was apparently helpless, unless I could turn three seemingly innocent things to use. They were things which would have been permitted any prisoner under sentence of death, were they not, warden?"

"Tooth powder and polished shoes, yes, but not money," replied the warden.

"Anything is dangerous in the hands of a man who knows how to use it," went on The Thinking Machine. "I did nothing that first night but sleep and chase rats." He glared at the warden. "When the matter was broached I knew I could do nothing that night, so suggested next day. You gentlemen thought I wanted time to arrange an escape with outside assistance, but this was not true. I knew I could communicate with whom I pleased, when I pleased."

The warden stared at him a moment, then went on smoking solemnly.

"I was aroused next morning at six o'clock by the jailer with my breakfast," continued the scientist. "He told me dinner was at twelve and supper at six. Between these times, I gathered, I would be pretty much to myself. So immediately after breakfast I examined my outside surroundings from my cell window. One look told me it would be useless to try to scale the wall, even should I decide to leave my cell by the window, for my purpose was to leave not only the cell, but the prison. Of course, I could have gone over the wall, but it would have taken me longer to lay my plans that way. Therefore, for the moment, I dismissed all idea of that.

"From this first observation I knew the river was on that side of the prison, and that there was also a playground there. Subsequently these surmises were verified by a keeper. I knew then one important thing—that any one might approach the prison wall from that side if necessary without attracting any particular attention. That was well to remember. I remembered it.

"But the outside thing which most attracted my attention was the feed wire to the arc light which ran within a few feet—probably three or four—of my cell window. I knew that would be valuable in the event I found it necessary to cut off that arc light."

"Oh, you shut it off to-night, then?" asked the warden.

"Having learned all I could from that window," resumed The Thinking Machine, without heeding the interruption, "I considered the idea of escaping through the prison proper. I recalled just how I had come into the cell, which I knew would be the only way. Seven doors lay between me and the outside. So, also for the time being, I gave up the idea of escaping that way. And I couldn't go through the solid granite walls of the cell."

The Thinking Machine paused for a moment and Dr. Ransome lighted a new cigar. For several minutes there was silence, then the scientific jail-breaker went on:

"While I was thinking about these things a rat ran across my foot. It suggested a new line of thought. There were at least half a dozen rats in the cell—I could see their beady eyes. Yet I had noticed none come under the cell door. I frightened them purposely and watched the cell door to see if they went out that way. They did not, but they were gone. Obviously they went another way. Another way meant another opening.

"I searched for this opening and found it. It was an old drain pipe, long unused and partly choked with dirt and dust. But this was the way the rats had come. They came from somewhere. Where? Drain pipes usually lead outside prison grounds. This one probably led to the river, or near it. The rats must therefore come from that direction. If they came a part of the way, I reasoned that they came all the way, because it was extremely unlikely that a solid iron or lead pipe would have any hole in it except at the exit.

"When the jailer came with my luncheon he told me two important things, although he didn't know it. One was that a new system of plumbing had been put in the prison seven years before; another that the river was only three hundred feet away. Then I knew positively that the pipe was a part of an old system; I knew, too, that it slanted generally toward the river. But did the pipe end in the water or on land?

"This was the next question to be decided. I decided it by catching several of the rats in the cell. My jailer was surprised to see me engaged in this work. I examined at least a dozen of them. They were perfectly dry; they had come through the pipe, and, most important of all, they were *not house rats, but field rats.* The other end of the pipe was on land, then, outside the prison walls. So far, so good.

"Then, I knew that if I worked freely from this point I must attract the warden's attention in another direction. You see, by telling the warden that I had come there to escape you made the test more severe, because I had to trick him by false scents."

The warden looked up with a sad expression in his eyes.

"The first thing was to make him think I was trying to communicate with you, Dr. Ransome. So I wrote a note on a piece of linen I tore from my shirt, addressed it to Dr. Ransome, tied a five-dollar bill around it and threw it out the window. I knew the guard would take it to the warden, but I rather hoped the warden would send it as addressed. Have you that first linen note, warden?"

The warden produced the cipher.

"What the deuce does it mean, anyhow?" he asked.

"Read it backward, beginning with the 'T' signature and disregard the division into words," instructed The Thinking Machine.

The warden did so.

"T-h-i-s, this," he spelled, studied it a moment, then read it off, grinning:

"This is not the way I intend to escape."

"Well, now what do you think o' that?" he demanded, still grinning.

"I knew that would attract your attention, just as it did," said The Thinking Machine, "and if you really found out what it was it would be a sort of gentle rebuke."

"What did you write it with?" asked Dr. Ransome, after he had examined the linen and passed it to Mr. Fielding.

"This," said the erstwhile prisoner, and he extended his foot. On it was the shoe he had worn in prison, though the polish was gone—scraped off clean. "The shoe blacking, moistened with water, was my ink; the metal tip of the shoe lace made a fairly good pen."

The warden looked up and suddenly burst into a laugh, half of relief, half of amusement.

"You're a wonder," he said, admiringly. "Go on."

"That precipitated a search of my cell by the warden, as I had intended," continued The Thinking Machine. "I was anxious to get the warden into the habit of searching my cell, so that finally, constantly finding nothing, he would get disgusted and quit. This at last happened, practically."

The warden blushed.

"He then took my white shirt away and gave me a prison shirt. He was satisfied that those two pieces of the shirt were all that was missing. But while he was searching my cell I had another piece of that same shirt, about nine inches square, rolled into a small ball in my mouth."

"Nine inches of that shirt?" demanded the warden. "Where did it come from?"

"The bosoms of all stiff white shirts are of triple thickness," was the explanation. "I tore out the inside thickness, leaving the bosom only two thicknesses. I knew you wouldn't see it. So much for that."

There was a little pause, and the warden looked from one to another of the men with a sheepish grin.

"Having disposed of the warden for the time being by giving him something else to think about, I took my first serious step toward freedom," said Professor Van Dusen. "I knew, within reason, that the pipe led somewhere to the playground outside; I knew a great many boys played there; I knew that rats came into my cell from out there. Could I communicate with some one outside with these things at hand?

"First was necessary, I saw, a long and fairly reliable thread, so —but here," he pulled up his trousers legs and showed that the tops of both stockings, of fine, strong lisle, were gone. "I unraveled those—after I got them started it wasn't difficult—and I had easily a quarter of a mile of thread that I could depend on.

"Then on half of my remaining linen I wrote, laboriously enough, I assure you, a letter explaining my situation to this gentleman here," and he indicated Hutchinson Hatch. "I knew he would assist me—for the value of the newspaper story. I tied firmly to this linen letter a ten-dollar bill—there is no surer way of attracting the eye of any one—and wrote on the linen: 'Finder of this deliver to Hutchinson Hatch, *Daily American,* who will give another ten dollars for the information.'

"The next thing was to get this note outside on that playground where a boy might find it. There were two ways, but I chose the best. I took one of the rats—I became adept in catching them—tied the linen and money firmly to one leg, fastened my lisle thread to another, and turned him loose in the drain pipe. I reasoned that the natural fright of the rodent would make him run until he was outside the pipe and then out on earth he would probably stop to gnaw off the linen and money.

"From the moment the rat disappeared into that dusty pipe I

became anxious. I was taking so many chances. The rat might gnaw the string, of which I held one end; other rats might gnaw it; the rat might run out of the pipe and leave the linen and money where they would never be found; a thousand other things might have happened. So began some nervous hours, but the fact that the rat ran on until only a few feet of the string remained in my cell made me think he was outside the pipe. I had carefully instructed Mr. Hatch what to do in case the note reached him. The question was: Would it reach him?

"This done, I could only wait and make other plans in case this one failed. I openly attempted to bribe my jailer, and learned from him that he held the keys to only two of seven doors between me and freedom. Then I did something else to make the warden nervous. I took the steel supports out of the heels of my shoes and made a pretense of sawing the bars of my cell window. The warden raised a pretty row about that. He developed, too, the habit of shaking the bars of my cell window to see if they were solid. They were—then."

Again the warden grinned. He had ceased being astonished.

"With this one plan I had done all I could and could only wait to see what happened," the scientist went on. "I couldn't know whether my note had been delivered or even found, or whether the rat had gnawed it up. And I didn't dare to draw back through the pipe that one slender thread which connected me with the outside.

"When I went to bed that night I didn't sleep, for fear there would come the slight signal twitch at the thread which was to tell me that Mr. Hatch had received the note. At half-past three o'clock, I judge, I felt this twitch, and no prisoner actually under sentence of death ever welcomed a thing more heartily."

The Thinking Machine stopped and turned to the reporter.

"You'd better explain just what you did," he said.

"The linen note was brought to me by a small boy who had been playing baseball," said Mr. Hatch. "I immediately saw a big story in it, so I gave the boy another ten dollars, and got several spools of silk, some twine, and a roll of light, pliable wire. The professor's note suggested that I have the finder of the note show me just where it was picked up, and told me to make my search from there, beginning at two o'clock in the morning. If I found the other end of the thread I was to twitch it gently three times, then a fourth.

"I began to search with a small bulb electric light. It was an hour and twenty minutes before I found the end of the drain pipe, half hidden in weeds. The pipe was very large there, say twelve inches across. Then I found the end of the lisle thread, twitched it as directed and immediately I got an answering twitch.

"Then I fastened the silk to this and Professor Van Dusen began to pull it into his cell. I nearly had heart disease for fear the string would break. To the end of the silk I fastened the twine, and when that had been pulled in I tied on the wire. Then that was drawn into the pipe and we had a substantial line, which the rats couldn't gnaw, from the mouth of the drain into the cell."

The Thinking Machine raised his hand and Hatch stopped.

"All this was done in absolute silence," said the scientist. "But when the wire reached my hand I could have shouted. Then we tried another experiment, which Mr. Hatch was prepared for. I tested the pipe as a speaking tube. Neither of us could hear very clearly, but I dared not speak loud for fear of attracting attention in the prison. At last I made him understand what I wanted immediately. He seemed to have great difficulty in understanding when I asked for nitric acid, and I repeated the word 'acid' several times.

"Then I heard a shriek from a cell above me. I knew instantly that someone had overheard, and when I heard you coming, Mr. Warden, I feigned sleep. If you had entered my cell at that moment that whole plan of escape would have ended there. But you passed on. That was the nearest I ever came to being caught.

"Having established this improvised trolley it is easy to see how I got things in the cell and made them disappear at will. I merely dropped them back into the pipe. You, Mr. Warden, could not have reached the connecting wire with your fingers; they are too large. My fingers, you see, are longer and more slender. In addition I guarded the top of that pipe with a rat—you remember how."

"I remember," said the warden, with a grimace.

"I thought that if any one were tempted to investigate that hole the rat would dampen his ardor. Mr. Hatch could not send me anything useful through the pipe until next night, although he did send me change for ten dollars as a test, so I proceeded with other parts of my plan. Then I evolved the method of escape, which I finally employed.

"In order to carry this out successfully it was necessary for the guard in the yard to get accustomed to seeing me at the cell window. I arranged this by dropping linen notes to him, boastful in tone, to make the warden believe, if possible, one of his assistants was communicating with the outside for me. I would stand at my window for hours gazing out, so the guard could see, and occasionally I spoke to him. In that way I learned that the prison had no electricians of its own, but was dependent upon the lighting company if anything should go wrong.

"That cleared the way to freedom perfectly. Early in the evening of the last day of my imprisonment, when it was dark, I planned to cut the feed wire which was only a few feet from my window, reaching it with an acid-tipped wire I had. That would make that side of the prison perfectly dark while the electricians were searching for the break. That would also bring Mr. Hatch into the prison yard.

"There was only one more thing to do before I actually began the work of setting myself free. This was to arrange final details with Mr. Hatch through our speaking tube. I did this within half an hour after the warden left my cell on the fourth night of my imprisonment. Mr. Hatch again had serious difficulty in understanding me, and I repeated the word 'acid' to him several times, and later the words: 'Number eight hat'—that's my size—and these were the things which made a prisoner upstairs confess to murder, so one of the jailers told me next day. This prisoner heard our voices, confused of course, through the pipe, which also went to his cell. The cell directly over me was not occupied, hence no one else heard.

"Of course the actual work of cutting the steel bars out of the window and door was comparatively easy with nitric acid, which I got through the pipe in thin bottles, but it took time. Hour after hour on the fifth and sixth and seventh days the guard below was looking at me as I worked on the bars of the window with the acid on a piece of wire. I used the tooth powder to prevent the acid spreading. I looked away abstractedly as I worked and each minute the acid cut deeper into the metal. I noticed that the jailers always tried the door by shaking the upper part, never the lower bars, therefore I cut the lower bars, leaving them hanging in place by thin strips of metal. But that was a bit of dare-deviltry. I could not have gone that way so easily."

The Thinking Machine sat silent for several minutes.

"I think that makes everything clear," he went on. "Whatever points I have not explained were merely to confuse the warden and jailers. These things in my bed I brought in to please Mr. Hatch, who wanted to improve the story. Of course, the wig was necessary in my plan. The special delivery letter I wrote and directed in my cell with

Mr. Hatch's fountain pen, then sent it out to him and he mailed it. That's all, I think."

"But your actually leaving the prison grounds and then coming in through the outer gate to my office?" asked the warden.

"Perfectly simple," said the scientist. "I cut the electric light wire with acid, as I said, when the current was off. Therefore when the current was turned on the arc didn't light. I knew it would take some time to find out what was the matter and make the repairs. When the guard went to report to you the yard was dark. I crept out the window—it was a tight fit, too—replaced the bars by standing on a narrow ledge and remained in a shadow until the force of electricians arrived. Mr. Hatch was one of them.

"When I saw him I spoke and he handed me a cap, a jumper and overalls, which I put on within ten feet of you, Mr. Warden, while you were in the yard. Later Mr. Hatch called me, presumably as a workman, and together we went out the gate to get something out of the wagon. The gate guard let us pass out readily as two workmen who had just passed in. We changed our clothing and reappeared, asking to see you. We saw you. That's all."

There was silence for several minutes. Dr. Ransome was first to speak.

"Wonderful!" he exclaimed. "Perfectly amazing."

"How did Mr. Hatch happen to come with the electricians?" asked Mr. Fielding.

"His father is manager of the company," replied The Thinking Machine.

"But what if there had been no Mr. Hatch outside to help?"

"Every prisoner has one friend outside who would help him escape if he could."

"Suppose—just suppose—there had been no old plumbing system there?" asked the warden, curiously.

"There were two other ways out," said The Thinking Machine, enigmatically.

Ten minutes later the telephone bell rang. It was a request for the warden.

"Light all right, eh?" the warden asked, through the 'phone. "Good. Wire cut beside Cell 13? Yes, I know. One electrician too many? What's that? Two came out?"

The warden turned to the others with a puzzled expression.

"He only let in four electricians, he has let out two and says there are three left."

"I was the odd one," said The Thinking Machine.

"Oh," said the warden. "I see." Then through the 'phone: "Let the fifth man go. He's all right."

G. K. CHESTERTON
(1874–1936)

Gilbert Keith Chesterton was born in London and educated at St. Paul's and the Slade School of Art before beginning a career as a writer of fiction, poetry, history, biography, and theology. After his first (and only) mystery novel, *The Man Who Was Thursday* (1908), he began a series of stories, collected as *The Innocence of Father Brown* (1911), about an unassuming but wise priest adept at solving mysteries. Father Brown, modeled on Chesterton's priest-friend John O'Connor, proved immensely popular, and over the next twenty-five years Chesterton brought out four more collections of stories featuring him. Although he himself did not become a Roman Catholic until 1922, Chesterton was always interested in the morality of an action, rather than its criminality or the detection process itself; his plots, clothed in wit and paradox, are allegories about what he sees as the real mystery of life, humankind's relationship to God.

"The Invisible Man" reflects not only Chesterton's debt to "The Purloined Letter" in its central thesis but also his own view of detective fiction as romance or fairy tale; the opening description of a city street-scene is intended to evoke a feeling of the wondrous beneath everyday reality. Chesterton's sense of allegory and his penchant for using it for social criticism is apparent in touches such as the automata in the murderer's apartment that suggest the robotization of human beings in a materialist world.

THE INVISIBLE MAN

In the cool blue twilight of two steep streets in Camden Town, the shop at the corner, a confectioner's, glowed like the butt of a cigar. One should rather say, perhaps, like the butt of a firework, for the light was of many colours and some complexity, broken up by many mirrors and dancing on many gilt and gaily-coloured cakes and sweetmeats. Against this one fiery glass were glued the noses of many guttersnipes, for the chocolates were all wrapped in those red and gold and green metallic colours which are almost better than chocolate itself; and the huge white wedding-cake in the window was somehow at once remote and satisfying, just as if the whole North Pole were good to eat. Such rainbow provocations could naturally collect the youth of the neighbourhood up to the ages of ten or twelve. But this corner was also attractive to youth at a later stage; and a young man, not less than twenty-four, was staring into the same shop window. To him, also, the shop was of fiery charm, but this attraction was not wholly to be explained by chocolates; which, however, he was far from despising.

He was a tall, burly, red-haired young man, with a resolute face but a listless manner. He carried under his arm a flat, grey portfolio of black-and-white sketches, which he had sold with more or less success to publishers ever since his uncle (who was an admiral) had disinherited him for Socialism, because of a lecture which he had delivered against that economic theory. His name was John Turnbull Angus.

Entering at last, he walked through the confectioner's shop to the back room, which was a sort of pastry-cook restaurant, merely raising his hat to the young lady who was serving there. She was a dark, elegant, alert girl in black, with a high colour and very quick, dark eyes; and after the ordinary interval she followed him into the inner room to take his order.

His order was evidently a usual one. "I want, please," he said with precision, "one halfpenny bun and a small cup of black coffee." An instant before the girl could turn away he added, "Also, I want you to marry me."

The young lady of the shop stiffened suddenly and said, "Those are jokes I don't allow."

The red-haired young man lifted grey eyes of an unexpected gravity.

"Really and truly," he said, "it's as serious—as serious as the halfpenny bun. It is expensive, like the bun; one pays for it. It is indigestible, like the bun. It hurts."

The dark young lady had never taken her dark eyes off him, but seemed to be studying him with almost tragic exactitude. At the end of her scrutiny she had something like the shadow of a smile, and she sat down in a chair.

"Don't you think," observed Angus, absently, "that it's rather cruel to eat these halfpenny buns? They might grow up into penny buns. I shall give up these brutal sports when we are married."

The dark young lady rose from her chair and walked to the window, evidently in a state of strong but not unsympathetic cogitation. When at last she swung round again with an air of resolution she was bewildered to observe that the young man was carefully laying out on the table various objects from the shop-window. They included a pyramid of highly coloured sweets, several plates of sandwiches, and the two decanters containing that mysterious port and sherry which are peculiar to pastry-cooks. In the middle of this neat arrangement he had carefully let down the enormous load of white sugared cake which had been the huge ornament of the window.

"What on earth are you doing?" she asked.

"Duty, my dear Laura," he began.

"Oh, for the Lord's sake, stop a minute," she cried, "and don't talk to me in that way. I mean, what is all that?"

"A ceremonial meal, Miss Hope."

"And what is *that?*" she asked impatiently, pointing to the mountain of sugar.

"The wedding-cake, Mrs. Angus," he said.

The girl marched to that article, removed it with some clatter, and put it back in the shop window; she then returned, and, putting her elegant elbows on the table, regarded the young man not unfavourably but with considerable exasperation.

"You don't give me any time to think," she said.

"I'm not such a fool," he answered; "that's my Christian humility."

She was still looking at him; but she had grown considerably graver behind the smile.

"Mr. Angus," she said steadily, "before there is a minute more of this nonsense I must tell you something about myself as shortly as I can."

"Delighted," replied Angus gravely. "You might tell me something about myself, too, while you are about it."

"Oh, do hold your tongue and listen," she said. "It's nothing that I'm ashamed of, and it isn't even anything that I'm specially sorry about. But what would you say if there were something that is no business of mine and yet is my nightmare?"

"In that case," said the man seriously, "I should suggest that you bring back the cake."

"Well, you must listen to the story first," said Laura, persistently. "To begin with, I must tell you that my father owned the inn called the 'Red Fish' at Ludbury, and I used to serve people in the bar."

"I have often wondered," he said, "why there was a kind of a Christian air about this one confectioner's shop."

"Ludbury is a sleepy, grassy little hole in the Eastern Counties, and the only kind of people who ever came to the 'Red Fish' were occasional commercial travellers, and for the rest, the most awful people you can see, only you've never seen them. I mean little, loungy men, who had just enough to live on and had nothing to do but lean about in bar-rooms and bet on horses, in bad clothes that were just too good for them. Even these wretched young rotters were not very common at our house; but there were two of them that were a lot too common—common in every sort of way. They both lived on money of their own, and were wearisomely idle and over-dressed. But yet I was a bit sorry for them, because I half believe they slunk into our little empty bar because each of them had a slight deformity; the sort of thing that some yokels laugh at. It wasn't exactly a deformity either; it was more an oddity. One of them was a surprisingly small man, something like a dwarf, or at least like a jockey. He was not at all jockeyish to look at, though; he had a round black head and a well-trimmed black beard, bright eyes like a bird's; he jingled money in his pockets; he jangled a great gold watch chain; and he never turned up except dressed just too much like a gentleman to be one. He was no fool though, though a futile idler; he was curiously clever at all kinds of things that couldn't be the slightest use; a sort of impromptu conjuring; making fifteen matches set fire to each other like a regular firework; or cutting a banana or some such thing into a dancing doll. His name was Isidore Smythe; and I can see him still, with his little dark face, just coming up to the counter, making a jumping kangaroo out of five cigars.

"The other fellow was more silent and more ordinary; but somehow he alarmed me much more than poor little Smythe. He was very tall and slight, and light-haired; his nose had a high bridge, and he might almost have been handsome in a spectral sort of way; but he had one of the most appalling squints I have ever seen or heard of. When he looked straight at you, you didn't know where you were yourself, let alone what he was looking at. I fancy this sort of disfigurement embittered the poor chap a little; for while Smythe was ready to show off his monkey tricks anywhere, James Welkin (that was the squinting man's name) never did anything except soak in our bar parlour, and go for great walks by himself in the flat, grey country all round. All the same, I think Smythe, too, was a little sensitive about being so small, though he carried it off more smartly. And so it was that I was really puzzled, as well as startled, and very sorry, when they both offered to marry me in the same week.

"Well, I did what I've since thought was perhaps a silly thing. But, after all, these freaks were my friends in a way; and I had a horror of their thinking I refused them for the real reason, which was that they were so impossibly ugly. So I made up some gas of another sort, about never meaning to marry anyone who hadn't carved his way in the world. I said it was a point of principle with me not to live on money that was just inherited like theirs. Two days after I had talked in this well-meaning sort of way, the whole trouble began. The first thing I heard was that both of them had gone off to seek their fortunes, as if they were in some silly fairy tale.

"Well, I've never seen either of them from that day to this. But I've had two letters from the little man called Smythe, and really they were rather exciting."

"Ever heard of the other man?" asked Angus.

"No, he never wrote," said the girl, after an instant's hesitation.

"Smythe's first letter was simply to say that he had started out walking with Welkin to London; but Welkin was such a good walker that the little man dropped out of it, and took a rest by the roadside. He happened to be picked up by some travelling show, and, partly because he was nearly a dwarf, and partly because he was really a clever little wretch, he got on quite well in the show business, and was soon sent up to the Aquarium, to do some tricks that I forget. That was his first letter. His second was much more of a startler, and I only got it last week."

The man called Angus emptied his coffee-cup and regarded her with mild and patient eyes. Her own mouth took a slight twist of laughter as she resumed, "I suppose you've seen on the hoardings all about this 'Smythe's Silent Service'? Or you must be the only person that hasn't. Oh, I don't know much about it, it's some clockwork invention for doing all the housework by machinery. You know the sort of thing: 'Press a button—A Butler who Never Drinks.' 'Turn a Handle—Ten Housemaids who Never Flirt.' You must have seen the advertisements. Well, whatever these machines are, they are making pots of money; and they are making it all for that little imp whom I knew down in Ludbury. I can't help feeling pleased the poor little chap has fallen on his feet; but the plain fact is, I'm in terror of his turning up any minute and telling me he's carved his way in the world—as he certainly has."

"And the other man?" repeated Angus with a sort of obstinate quietude.

Laura Hope got to her feet suddenly. "My friend," she said, "I think you are a witch. Yes, you are quite right. I have not seen a line of the other man's writing; and I have no more notion than the dead of what or where he is. But it is of him that I am frightened. It is he who is all about my path. It is he who has half driven me mad. Indeed, I think he has driven me mad; for I have felt him where he could not have been, and I have heard his voice when he could not have spoken."

"Well, my dear," said the young man, cheerfully, "if he were Satan himself, he is done for now you have told somebody. One goes mad all alone, old girl. But when was it you fancied you felt and heard our squinting friend?"

"I heard James Welkin laugh as plainly as I hear you speak," said the girl, steadily. "There was nobody there, for I stood just outside the shop at the corner, and could see down both streets at once. I had forgotten how he laughed, though his laugh was as odd as his squint.

I had not thought of him for nearly a year. But it's a solemn truth that a few seconds later the first letter came from his rival."

"Did you ever make the spectre speak or squeak, or anything?" asked Angus, with some interest.

Laura suddenly shuddered, and then said, with an unshaken voice, "Yes. Just when I had finished reading the second letter from Isidore Smythe announcing his success, just then, I heard Welkin say, 'He shan't have you, though.' It was quite plain, as if he were in the room. It is awful; I think I must be mad."

"If you really were mad," said the young man, "you would think you must be sane. But certainly there seems to me to be something a little rum about this unseen gentleman. Two heads are better than one—I spare you allusions to any other organs—and really, if you would allow me, as a sturdy, practical man, to bring back the wedding-cake out of the window—"

Even as he spoke, there was a sort of steely shriek in the street outside, and a small motor, driven at devilish speed, shot up to the door of the shop and stuck there. In the same flash of time a small man in a shiny top hat stood stamping in the outer room.

Angus, who had hitherto maintained hilarious ease from motives of mental hygiene, revealed the strain of his soul by striding abruptly out of the inner room and confronting the new-comer. A glance at him was quite sufficient to confirm the savage guesswork of a man in love. This very dapper but dwarfish figure, with the spike of black beard carried insolently forward, the clever unrestful eyes, the neat but very nervous fingers, could be none other than the man just described to him: Isidore Smythe, who made dolls out of banana skins and match-boxes; Isidore Smythe, who made millions out of undrinking butlers and unflirting housemaids of metal. For a moment the two men, instinctively understanding each other's air of possession, looked at each other with that curious cold generosity which is the soul of rivalry.

Mr. Smythe, however, made no allusion to the ultimate ground of their antagonism, but said simply and explosively: "Has Miss Hope seen that thing on the window?"

"On the window?" repeated the staring Angus.

"There's no time to explain other things," said the small millionaire shortly. "There's some tomfoolery going on here that has to be investigated."

He pointed his polished walking-stick at the window, recently depleted by the bridal preparations of Mr. Angus; and that gentleman was astonished to see along the front of the glass a long strip of paper pasted, which had certainly not been on the window when he had looked through it some time before. Following the energetic Smythe outside into the street, he found that some yard and a half of stamp paper had been carefully gummed along the glass outside, and on this was written in straggly characters, "If you marry Smythe, he will die."

"Laura," said Angus, putting his big red head into the shop, "you're not mad."

"It's the writing of that fellow Welkin," said Smythe gruffly. "I haven't seen him for years, but he's always bothering me. Five times in the last fortnight he's had threatening letters left at my flat, and I can't even find out who leaves them, let alone if it is Welkin himself. The porter of the flats swears that no suspicious characters have been seen, and here he has pasted up a sort of dado on a public shop window, while the people in the shop—"

"Quite so," said Angus modestly, "while the people in the shop were having tea. Well, sir, I can assure you I appreciate your common sense in dealing so directly with the matter. We can talk about other things afterwards. The fellow cannot be very far off yet, for I swear there was no paper there when I went last to the window, ten or fifteen minutes ago. On the other hand, he's too far off to be chased, as we don't even know the direction. If you'll take my advice, Mr. Smythe, you'll put this at once in the hands of some energetic inquiry man, private rather than public. I know an extremely clever fellow, who has set up in business five minutes from here in your car. His name's Flambeau, and though his youth was a bit stormy, he's a strictly honest man now, and his brains are worth money. He lives in Lucknow Mansions, Hampstead."

"That is odd," said the little man, arching his black eyebrows. "I live, myself, in Himylaya Mansions, round the corner. Perhaps you might care to come with me; I can go to my rooms and sort out these queer Welkin documents, while you run round and get your friend the detective."

"You are very good," said Angus politely. "Well, the sooner we act the better."

Both men, with a queer kind of impromptu fairness, took the same sort of formal farewell of the lady, and both jumped into the brisk little car. As Smythe took the handles and they turned the great corner of the street, Angus was amused to see a gigantesque poster of "Smythe's Silent Service," with a picture of a huge headless iron doll, carrying a saucepan with the legend, "A Cook Who Is Never Cross."

"I use them in my own flat," said the little black-bearded man, laughing, "partly for advertisements, and partly for real convenience. Honestly, and all above board, those big clockwork dolls of mine do bring you coals or claret or a timetable quicker than any live servants I've ever known, if you know which knob to press. But I'll never deny, between ourselves, that such servants have their disadvantages, too."

"Indeed?" said Angus; "is there something they can't do?"

"Yes," replied Smythe coolly; "they can't tell me who left those threatening letters at my flat."

The man's motor was small and swift like himself; in fact, like his domestic service, it was of his own invention. If he was an advertising quack, he was one who believed in his own wares. The sense of something tiny and flying was accentuated as they swept up long white curves of road in the dead but open daylight of evening. Soon the white curves came sharper and dizzier; they were upon ascending spirals, as they say in the modern religions. For, indeed, they were cresting a corner of London which is almost as precipitous as Edinburgh, if not quite so picturesque. Terrace rose above terrace, and the special tower of flats they sought, rose above them all to almost Egyptian height, gilt by the level sunset. The change, as they turned the corner and entered the crescent known as Himylaya Mansions, was as abrupt as the opening of a window; for they found that pile of flats sitting above London as above a green sea of slate. Opposite to the mansions, on the other side of the gravel crescent, was a bushy enclosure more like a steep hedge or dyke than a garden, and some way below that ran a strip of artificial water, a sort of canal, like the moat of that embowered fortress. As the car swept round the crescent it passed, at one corner, the stray stall of a man selling chestnuts; and right away at the other end of the curve, Angus could see a dim blue policeman walking slowly. These were the only human shapes in that high suburban solitude; but he had an irrational sense that they expressed the speechless poetry of London. He felt as if they were figures in a story.

The little car shot up to the right house like a bullet, and shot out its owner like a bomb shell. He was immediately inquiring of a tall commissionaire in shining braid, and a short porter in shirt sleeves, whether anybody or anything had been seeking his apartments. He was assured that nobody and nothing had passed these officials since his last inquiries; whereupon he and the slightly bewildered Angus were shot up in the lift like a rocket, till they reached the top floor.

"Just come in for a minute," said the breathless Smythe. "I want to show you those Welkin letters. Then you might run round the corner and fetch your friend." He pressed a button concealed in the wall, and the door opened of itself.

It opened on a long, commodious ante-room, of which the only arresting features, ordinarily speaking, were the rows of tall half-human mechanical figures that stood up on both sides like tailors' dummies. Like tailors' dummies they were headless; and like tailors' dummies they had a handsome unnecessary humpiness in the shoulders, and a pigeon-breasted protuberance of chest; but barring this, they were not much more like a human figure than any automatic machine at a station that is about the human height. They had two great hooks like arms, for carrying trays; and they were painted pea-green, or vermillion, or black for convenience of distinction; in every other way they were only automatic machines and nobody would have looked twice at them. On this occasion, at least, nobody did. For between the two rows of these domestic dummies lay something more interesting than most of the mechanics of the world. It was a white, tattered scrap of paper scrawled with red ink; and the agile inventor had snatched it up almost as soon as the door flew open. He handed it to Angus without a word. The red ink on it actually was not dry, and the message ran, "If you have been to see her today, I shall kill you."

There was a short silence, and then Isidore Smythe said quietly, "Would you like a little whiskey? I rather feel as if I should."

"Thank you; I should like a little Flambeau," said Angus, gloomily. "This business seems to me to be getting rather grave. I'm going round at once to fetch him."

"Right you are," said the other, with admirable cheerfulness. "Bring him round here as quick as you can."

But as Angus closed the front door behind him he saw Smythe push back a button, and one of the clockwork images glided from its place and slid along a groove in the floor carrying a tray with syphon and decanter. There did seem something a trifle weird about leaving the little man alone among those dead servants, who were coming to life as the door closed.

Six steps down from Smythe's landing the man in shirt sleeves was doing something with a pail. Angus stopped to extract a promise, fortified with a prospective bribe, that he would remain in that place until the return with the detective, and would keep count of any kind of stranger coming up those stairs. Dashing down to the front hall he then laid similar charges of vigilance on the commissionaire at the front door, from whom he learned the simplifying circumstances that there was no back door. Not content with this, he captured the floating policeman and induced him to stand opposite the entrance and watch it; and finally paused an instant for a pennyworth of chestnuts, and an inquiry as to the probable length of the merchant's stay in the neighbourhood.

The chestnut seller, turning up the collar of his coat, told him he should probably be moving shortly, as he thought it was going to snow. Indeed, the evening was growing grey and bitter, but Angus, with all his eloquence, proceeded to nail the chestnut man to his post.

"Keep yourself warm on your own chestnuts," he said earnestly. "Eat up your whole stock; I'll make it worth your while. I'll give you a sovereign if you'll wait here till I come back, and then tell me whether any man, woman, or child has gone into that house where the commissionaire is standing."

He then walked away smartly, with a last look at the besieged tower.

"I've made a ring round that room, anyhow," he said. "They can't all four of them be Mr. Welkin's accomplices."

Lucknow Mansions were, so to speak, on a lower platform of that hill of houses, of which Himylaya Mansions might be called the peak. Mr. Flambeau's semi-official flat was on the ground floor, and presented in every way a marked contrast to the American machinery and cold hotel-like luxury of the flat of the Silent Service. Flambeau, who was a friend of Angus, received him in a rococo artistic den behind his office, of which the ornaments were sabres, harquebuses, Eastern curiosities, flasks of Italian wine, savage cooking-pots, a plumy Persian cat, and a small dusty-looking Roman Catholic priest, who looked particularly out of place.

"This is my friend Father Brown," said Flambeau. "I've often wanted you to meet him. Splendid weather, this; a little cold for Southerners like me."

"Yes, I think it will keep clear," said Angus, sitting down on a violet-striped Eastern ottoman.

"No," said the priest quietly, "it has begun to snow."

And, indeed, as he spoke, the first few flakes, foreseen by the man of chestnuts, began to drift across the darkening window-pane.

"Well," said Angus heavily. "I'm afraid I've come on business, and rather jumpy business at that. The fact is, Flambeau, within a stone's throw of your house is a fellow who badly wants your help; he's perpetually being haunted and threatened by an invisible enemy—a scoundrel whom nobody has even seen." As Angus proceeded to tell the whole tale of Smythe and Welkin, beginning with Laura's story, and going on with his own, the supernatural laugh at the corner of two empty streets, the strange distinct words spoken in an empty room, Flambeau grew more and more vividly concerned, and the little priest seemed to be left out of it, like a piece of furniture. When it came to the scribbled stamp-paper pasted on the window, Flambeau rose, seeming to fill the room with his huge shoulders.

"If you don't mind," he said, "I think you had better tell me the rest on the nearest road to this man's house. It strikes me, somehow, that there is no time to be lost."

"Delighted," said Angus, rising also, "though he's safe enough for the present, for I've set four men to watch the only hole to his burrow."

They turned out into the street, the small priest trundling after them with the docility of a small dog. He merely said, in a cheerful way, like one making conversation, "How quick the snow gets thick on the ground."

As they threaded the steep side streets already powdered with silver, Angus finished his story; and by the time they reached the crescent with the towering flats, he had leisure to turn his attention to the four sentinels. The chestnut seller, both before and after receiving a sovereign, swore stubbornly that he had watched the door and seen no visitor enter. The policeman was even more emphatic. He said he had had experience of crooks of all kinds, in top hats and in rags; he wasn't so green as to expect suspicious characters to look suspicious; he looked out for anybody, and, so help him, there had been nobody. And when all three men gathered round the gilded commissionaire, who still stood smiling astride of the porch, the verdict was more final still.

"I've got a right to ask any man, duke or dustman, what he wants in these flats," said the genial and gold-laced giant, "and I'll swear there's been nobody to ask since this gentleman went away."

The unimportant Father Brown, who stood back, looking modestly at the pavement, here ventured to say meekly, "Has nobody been up and down stairs, then, since the snow began to fall? It began while we were all round at Flambeau's."

"Nobody's been in here, sir, you can take it from me," said the official, with beaming authority.

"Then I wonder what that is?" said the priest, and stared at the ground blankly like a fish.

The others all looked down also; and Flambeau used a fierce exclamation and a French gesture. For it was unquestionably true that down the middle of the entrance guarded by the man in gold lace, actually between the arrogant, stretched legs of that colossus, ran a stringy pattern of grey footprints stamped upon the white snow.

"God!" cried Angus involuntarily, "the Invisible Man!"

Without another word he turned and dashed up the stairs, with Flambeau following; but Father Brown still stood looking about him in the snowclad street as if he had lost interest in his query.

Flambeau was plainly in a mood to break down the door with his big shoulders; but the Scotchman, with more reason, if less intuition, fumbled about on the frame of the door till he found the invisible button; and the door swung slowly open.

It showed substantially the same serried interior; the hall had grown darker, though it was still struck here and there with the last crimson shafts of sunset, and one or two of the headless machines had been moved from their places for this or that purpose, and stood here and there about the twilit place. The green and red of their coats were all darkened in the dusk; and their likeness to human shapes slightly increased by their very shapelessness. But in the middle of them all, exactly where the paper with the red ink had lain, there lay something that looked like red ink spilt out of its bottle. But it was not red ink.

With a French combination of reason and violence Flambeau simply said "Murder!" and, plunging into the flat, had explored every corner and cupboard of it in five minutes. But if he expected to find a corpse he found none. Isidore Smythe was not in the place, either dead or alive. After the most tearing search the two men met each other in the outer hall, with streaming faces and staring eyes. "My friend," said Flambeau, talking French in his excitement, "not only is your murderer invisible, but he makes invisible also the murdered man."

Angus looked round at the dim room full of dummies, and in some Celtic corner of his Scotch soul a shudder started. One of the life-size dolls stood immediately overshadowing the blood stain, summoned, perhaps, by the slain man an instant before he fell. One of the high-shouldered hooks that served the thing for arms, was a little lifted, and Angus had suddenly the horrid fancy that poor Smythe's own iron child had struck him down. Matter had rebelled, and these machines had killed their master. But even so, what had they done with him?

"Eaten him?" said the nightmare at his ear; and he sickened for an instant at the idea of rent, human remains absorbed and crushed into all that acephalous clockwork.

He recovered his mental health by an emphatic effort, and said to Flambeau, "Well, there it is. The poor fellow has evaporated like a cloud and left a red streak on the floor. The tale does not belong to this world."

"There is only one thing to be done," said Flambeau, "whether it belongs to this world or the other, I must go down and talk to my friend."

They descended, passing the man with the pail, who again asseverated that he had let no intruder pass, down to the commissionaire and the hovering chestnut man, who rigidly reasserted their own watchfulness. But when Angus looked round for his fourth confirmation he could not see it, and called out with some nervousness, "Where is the policeman?"

"I beg your pardon," said Father Brown; "that is my fault. I just sent him down the road to investigate something—that I just thought worth investigating."

"Well, we want him back pretty soon," said Angus abruptly, "for the wretched man upstairs has not only been murdered, but wiped out."

"How?" asked the priest.

"Father," said Flambeau, after a pause, "upon my soul I believe it is more in your department than mine. No friend or foe has entered the house, but Smythe is gone, as if stolen by the fairies. If that is not supernatural, I—"

As he spoke they were all checked by an unusual sight; the big blue policeman came round the corner of the crescent, running. He came straight up to Brown.

"You're right, sir," he panted, "they've just found poor Mr. Smythe's body in the canal down below."

Angus put his hand wildly to his head. "Did he run down and drown himself?" he asked.

"He never came down, I'll swear," said the constable, "and he wasn't drowned either, for he died of a great stab over the heart."

"And yet you saw no one enter?" said Flambeau in a grave voice.

"Let us walk down the road a little," said the priest.

As they reached the other end of the crescent he observed abruptly, "Stupid of me! I forgot to ask the policeman something. I wonder if they found a light brown sack."

"Why a light brown sack?" asked Angus, astonished.

"Because if it was any other coloured sack, the case must begin over again," said Father Brown; "but if it was a light brown sack, why, the case is finished."

"I am pleased to hear it," said Angus with hearty irony. "It hasn't begun, so far as I am concerned."

"You must tell us all about it," said Flambeau with a strange heavy simplicity, like a child.

Unconsciously they were walking with quickening steps down the long sweep of road on the other side of the high crescent, Father Brown leading briskly, though in silence. At last he said with an almost touching vagueness, "Well, I'm afraid you'll think it so prosy. We always begin at the abstract end of things, and you can't begin this story anywhere else.

"Have you ever noticed this—that people never answer what you say? They answer what you mean—or what they think you mean. Suppose one lady says to another in a country house, 'Is anybody staying with you?' the lady doesn't answer 'Yes; the butler, the three footmen, the parlourmaid, and so on,' though the parlourmaid may be in the room, or the butler behind her chair. She says 'There is *nobody* staying with us,' meaning nobody of the sort you mean. But suppose a doctor inquiring into an epidemic asks, 'Who is staying in the house?' then the lady will remember the butler, parlourmaid, and the rest. All language is used like that; you never get a question answered literally, even when you get it answered truly. When those four quite honest men said that no man had gone into the Mansions, they did not really mean that *no man* had gone into them. They meant no man whom they could suspect of being your man. A man did go into the house, and did come out of it, but they never noticed him."

"An invisible man?" inquired Angus, raising his red eyebrows.

"A mentally invisible man," said Father Brown.

A minute or two after he resumed in the same unassuming voice, like a man thinking his way. "Of course you can't think of such a man, until you do think of him. That's where his cleverness comes in. But I came to think of him through two or three little things in the tale Mr. Angus told us. First, there was the fact that this Welkin went for long walks. And then there was the vast lot of stamp paper on the window. And then, most of all, there were the two things the young lady said—things that couldn't be true. Don't get annoyed," he added hastily, noting a sudden movement of the Scotchman's head; "she thought they were true. A person *can't* be quite alone in a street a second before she receives a letter. She can't be quite alone in a street when she starts reading a letter just received. There must be somebody pretty near her; he must be mentally invisible."

"Why must there be somebody near her?" asked Angus.

"Because," said Father Brown, "barring carrier-pigeons, somebody must have brought her the letter."

"Do you really mean to say," asked Flambeau, with energy, "that Welkin carried his rival's letters to his lady?"

"Yes," said the priest. "Welkin carried his rival's letters to his lady. You see, he had to."

"Oh, I can't stand much more of this," exploded Flambeau. "Who is this fellow? What does he look like? What is the usual get-up of a mentally invisible man?"

"He is dressed rather handsomely in red, blue and gold," replied the priest promptly with precision, "and in this striking, and even showy, costume he entered Himylaya Mansions under eight human eyes; he killed Smythe in cold blood, and came down into the street again carrying the dead body in his arms—"

"Reverend sir," cried Angus, standing still, "are you raving mad, or am I?"

"You are not mad," said Brown, "only a little unobservant. You have not noticed such a man as this, for example."

He took three quick strides forward, and put his hand on the shoulder of an ordinary passing postman who had bustled by them unnoticed under the shade of the trees.

"Nobody ever notices postmen somehow," he said thoughtfully; "yet they have passions like other men, and even carry large bags where a small corpse can be stowed quite easily."

The postman, instead of turning naturally, had ducked and tumbled against the garden fence. He was a lean fair-bearded man of very ordinary appearance, but as he turned an alarmed face over his shoulder, all three men were fixed with an almost fiendish squint.

Flambeau went back to his sabres, purple rugs and Persian cat, having many things to attend to. John Turnbull Angus went back to the lady at the shop, with whom that imprudent young man contrives to be extremely comfortable. But Father Brown walked those snow-covered hills under the stars for many hours with a murderer, and what they said to each other will never be known.

SUSAN GLASPELL
(1882–1948)

Susan Glaspell, fiction writer and playwright, was born in Davenport, Iowa. Her desire to portray in her art the special characteristics of America's Midwest places her among the local color writers of the late nineteenth and early twentieth centuries. Though she stopped writing short stories by 1922, "A Jury of Her Peers," published in *Everyweek*, 5 March 1917, reveals her unsentimental approach to local color writing as well as the period's feminist concerns. The story appeared first in dramatic form as the one-act play *Trifles*, produced in 1917, and was based on an actual case Glaspell covered while working as a journalist in Des Moines.

"A Jury of Her Peers" reflects a feminist approach to crime and detection, coming as it does from a period in which women's legal rights, including the right to serve on juries, were still only partially recognized. Glaspell emphasizes not only the limitations of "official" detection (which dismisses women's concerns as "trifles") but also the psychological aspects of the process by which the two women "detectives" resolve the case, ranging from their own sympathy, guilt, and resentment to their grasp of the extenuating circumstances of the murder.

A JURY OF HER PEERS

When Martha Hale opened the storm-door and got a cut of the north wind, she ran back for her big woolen scarf. As she hurriedly wound that round her head her eye made a scandalized sweep of her kitchen. It was no ordinary thing that called her away—it was probably farther from ordinary than anything that had ever happened in Dickson County. But what her eye took in was that her kitchen was in no shape for leaving: her bread all ready for mixing, half the flour sifted and half unsifted.

She hated to see things half done; but she had been at that when the team from town stopped to get Mr. Hale, and then the sheriff came running in to say his wife wished Mrs. Hale would come too—adding, with a grin, that he guessed she was getting scarey and wanted another woman along. So she had dropped everything right where it was.

"Martha!" now came her husband's impatient voice. "Don't keep folks waiting out here in the cold."

She again opened the storm-door, and this time joined the three men and the one woman waiting for her in the big two-seated buggy.

After she had the robes tucked around her she took another look at the woman who sat beside her on the back seat. She had met Mrs. Peters the year before at the county fair, and the thing she remembered about her was that she didn't seem like a sheriff's wife. She was small and thin and didn't have a strong voice. Mrs. Gorman, sheriff's wife before Gorman went out and Peters came in, had a voice that somehow seemed to be backing up the law with every word. But if Mrs. Peters didn't look like a sheriff's wife, Peters made it up in looking like a sheriff. He was to a dot the kind of man who could get himself elected sheriff—a heavy man with a big voice, who was particularly genial with the law-abiding, as if to make it plain that he knew the difference between criminals and non-criminals. And right there it came into Mrs. Hale's mind, with a stab, that this man who was so pleasant and lively with all of them was going to the Wrights' now as a sheriff.

"The country's not very pleasant this time of year," Mrs. Peters at last ventured, as if she felt they ought to be talking as well as the men.

Mrs. Hale scarcely finished her reply, for they had gone up a little hill and could see the Wright place now, and seeing it did not make her feel like talking. It looked very lonesome this cold March morning. It had always been a lonesome-looking place. It was down in a hollow, and the poplar trees around it were lonesome-looking trees. The men were looking at it and talking about what had happened. The county attorney was bending to one side of the buggy, and kept looking steadily at the place as they drew up to it.

"I'm glad you came with me," Mrs. Peters said nervously, as the two women were about to follow the men in through the kitchen door.

Even after she had her foot on the door-step, her hand on the knob, Martha Hale had a moment of feeling she could not cross the threshold. And the reason it seemed she couldn't cross it now was simply because she hadn't crossed it before. Time and time again it had been in her mind, "I ought to go over and see Minnie Foster"—she still thought of her as Minnie Foster, though for twenty years she had been Mrs. Wright. And then there was always something to do and Minnie Foster would go from her mind. But *now* she could come.

The men went over to the stove. The women stood close together by the door. Young Henderson, the county attorney, turned around and said, "Come up to the fire, ladies."

Mrs. Peters took a step forward, then stopped. "I'm not—cold," she said.

And so the two women stood by the door, at first not even so much as looking around the kitchen.

The men talked for a minute about what a good thing it was the sheriff had sent his deputy out that morning to make a fire for them, and then Sheriff Peters stepped back from the stove, unbuttoned his outer coat, and leaned his hands on the kitchen table in a way that seemed to mark the beginning of official business. "Now, Mr. Hale," he said in a sort of semi-official voice, "before we move things about, you tell Mr. Henderson just what it was you saw when you came here yesterday morning."

The county attorney was looking around the kitchen.

"By the way," he said, "has anything been moved?" He turned to the sheriff. "Are things just as you left them yesterday?"

Peters looked from cupboard to sink; from that to a small worn rocker a little to one side of the kitchen table.

"It's just the same."

"Somebody should have been left here yesterday," said the county attorney.

"Oh—yesterday," returned the sheriff, with a little gesture as of yesterday having been more than he could bear to think of. "When I had to send Frank to Morris Center for that man who went crazy—let me tell you, I had my hands full *yesterday*. I knew you could get back from Omaha by to-day, George, and as long as I went over everything here myself—"

"Well, Mr. Hale," said the county attorney, in a way of letting what was past and gone go, "tell just what happened when you came here yesterday morning."

Mrs. Hale, still leaning against the door, had that sinking feeling of the mother whose child is about to speak a piece. Lewis often wandered along and got things mixed up in a story. She hoped he would tell this straight and plain, and not say unnecessary things that would just make things harder for Minnie Foster. He didn't begin at once, and she noticed that he looked queer—as if standing in that kitchen and having to tell what he had seen there yesterday morning made him almost sick.

"Yes, Mr. Hale?" the county attorney reminded.

"Harry and I had started to town with a load of potatoes," Mrs. Hale's husband began.

Harry was Mrs. Hale's oldest boy. He wasn't with them now, for the very good reason that those potatoes never got to town yesterday and he was taking them this morning, so he hadn't been home when the sheriff stopped to say he wanted Mr. Hale to come over to the Wright place and tell the county attorney his story there, where he could point it all out. With all Mrs. Hale's other emotions came the fear that maybe Harry wasn't dressed warm enough—they hadn't any of them realized how that north wind did bite.

"We come along this road," Hale was going on, with a motion of his hand to the road over which they had just come, "and as we got in sight of the house I says to Harry, 'I'm goin' to see if I can't get John Wright to take a telephone.' You see," he explained to Henderson, "unless I can get somebody to go in with me they won't come out this branch road except for a price *I* can't pay. I'd spoke to Wright about it once before; but he put me off, saying folks talked too much anyway, and all he asked was peace and quiet—guess you know about how much he talked himself. But I thought maybe if I went to the house and talked about it before his wife, and said all the women-folks liked the telephones, and that in this lonesome stretch of road it would be a good thing—well, I said to Harry that that was what I was going to say—though I said at the same time that I didn't know as what his wife wanted made much difference to John—"

Now, there he was!—saying things he didn't need to say. Mrs. Hale tried to catch her husband's eye, but fortunately the county attorney interrupted with:

"Let's talk about that a little later, Mr. Hale. I do want to talk about that, but I'm anxious now to get along to just what happened when you got here."

When he began this time, it was very deliberately and carefully:

"I didn't see or hear anything. I knocked at the door. And still it was all quiet inside. I knew they must be up—it was past eight o'clock. So I knocked again, louder, and I thought I heard somebody say 'Come in.' I wasn't sure—I'm not sure yet. But I opened the door—this door," jerking a hand toward the door by which the two women stood, "and there, in that rocker"—pointing to it—"sat Mrs. Wright."

Every one in the kitchen looked at the rocker. It came into Mrs. Hale's mind that that rocker didn't look in the least like Minnie Foster—the Minnie Foster of twenty years before. It was a dingy red, with wooden rungs up the back, and the middle rung was gone, and the chair sagged to one side.

"How did she—look?" the county attorney was inquiring.

"Well," said Hale, "she looked—queer."

"How do you mean—queer?"

As he asked it he took out a note-book and pencil. Mrs. Hale did not like the sight of that pencil. She kept her eye fixed on her husband, as if to keep him from saying unnecessary things that would go into that note-book and make trouble.

Hale did speak guardedly, as if the pencil had affected him too.

"Well, as if she didn't know what she was going to do next. And kind of—done up."

"How did she seem to feel about your coming?"

"Why, I don't think she minded—one way or other. She didn't pay much attention. I said, 'Ho' do, Mrs. Wright? It's cold, ain't it?' And she said, 'Is it?'—and went on pleatin' at her apron.

"Well, I was surprised. She didn't ask me to come up to the stove, or to sit down, but just set there, not even lookin' at me. And so I said: 'I want to see John.'

"And then she—laughed. I guess you would call it a laugh.

"I thought of Harry and the team outside, so I said, a little sharp, 'Can I see John?' 'No,' says she—kind of dull like. 'Ain't he home?' says I. Then she looked at me. 'Yes,' says she, 'he's home.' 'Then why can't I see him?' I asked her, out of patience with her now. ' 'Cause he's dead.' says she, just as quiet and dull—and fell to pleatin' her apron. 'Dead?' says I, like you do when you can't take in what you've heard.

"She just nodded her head, not getting a bit excited, but rockin' back and forth.

" 'Why—where is he?' says I, not knowing *what* to say.

"She just pointed upstairs—like this"—pointing to the room above.

"I got up, with the idea of going up there myself. By this time I—didn't know what to do. I walked from there to here; then I says: 'Why, what did he die of?'

" 'He died of a rope around his neck,' says she; and just went on pleatin' at her apron."

Hale stopped speaking, and stood staring at the rocker, as if he were still seeing the woman who had sat there the morning before. Nobody spoke; it was as if every one were seeing the woman who had sat there the morning before.

"And what did you do then?" the county attorney at last broke the silence.

"I went out and called Harry. I thought I might—need help. I got Harry in, and we went upstairs." His voice fell almost to a whisper. "There he was—lying over the—"

"I think I'd rather have you go into that upstairs," the county attorney interrupted, "where you can point it all out. Just go on now with the rest of the story."

"Well, my first thought was to get that rope off. It looked—"

He stopped, his face twitching.

"But Harry, he went up to him, and he said, 'No, he's dead all right, and we'd better not touch anything.' So we went downstairs.

"She was still sitting that same way. 'Has anybody been notified?' I asked. 'No,' says she, unconcerned.

" 'Who did this, Mrs. Wright?' said Harry. He said it business-like, and she stopped pleatin' at her apron. 'I don't know,' she says. 'You don't *know?*' says Harry. 'Weren't you sleepin' in the bed with him?' 'Yes,' says she, 'but I was on the inside.' 'Somebody slipped a rope round his neck and strangled him, and you didn't wake up?' says Harry. 'I didn't wake up,' she said after him.

"We may have looked as if we didn't see how that could be, for after a minute she said, 'I sleep sound.'

"Harry was going to ask her more questions, but I said maybe that weren't our business; maybe we ought to let her tell her story first to the coroner or the sheriff. So Harry went fast as he could over to High Road—the Rivers' place, where there's a telephone."

"And what did she do when she knew you had gone for the coroner?" The attorney got his pencil in his hand all ready for writing.

"She moved from that chair to this one over here"—Hale pointed to a small chair in the corner—"and just sat there with her hands held together and looking down. I got a feeling that I ought to make some conversation, so I said I had come in to see if John wanted to put in a telephone; and at that she started to laugh, and then she stopped and looked at me—scared."

At the sound of a moving pencil the man who was telling the story looked up.

"I dunno—maybe it wasn't scared," he hastened; "I wouldn't like to say it was. Soon Harry got back, and then Dr. Lloyd came, and you, Mr. Peters, and so I guess that's all I know that you don't."

He said that last with relief, and moved a little, as if relaxing. Every one moved a little. The county attorney walked toward the stair door.

"I guess we'll go upstairs first—then out to the barn and around there."

He paused and looked around the kitchen.

"You're convinced there was nothing important here?" he asked the sheriff. "Nothing that would—point to any motive?"

The sheriff too looked all around, as if to re-convince himself.

"Nothing here but kitchen things," he said, with a little laugh for the insignificance of kitchen things.

The county attorney was looking at the cupboard—a peculiar,

ungainly structure, half closet and half cupboard, the upper part of it being built in the wall, and the lower part just the old-fashioned kitchen cupboard. As if its queerness attracted him, he got a chair and opened the upper part and looked in. After a moment he drew his hand away sticky.

"Here's a nice mess," he said resentfully.

The two women had drawn nearer, and now the sheriff's wife spoke.

"Oh—her fruit," she said, looking to Mrs. Hale for sympathetic understanding. She turned back to the county attorney and explained: "She worried about that when it turned so cold last night. She said the fire would go out and her jars might burst."

Mrs. Peters's husband broke into a laugh.

"Well, can you beat the women! Held for murder, and worrying about her preserves!"

The young attorney set his lips.

"I guess before we're through with her she may have something more serious than preserves to worry about."

"Oh, well," said Mrs. Hale's husband, with good-natured superiority, "women are used to worrying over trifles."

The two women moved a little closer together. Neither of them spoke. The county attorney seemed suddenly to remember his manners—and think of his future.

"And yet," said he, with the gallantry of a young politician, "for all their worries, what would we do without the ladies?"

The women did not speak, did not unbend. He went to the sink and began washing his hands. He turned to wipe them on the roller towel—whirled it for a cleaner place.

"Dirty towels! Not much of a housekeeper, would you say, ladies?"

He kicked his foot against some dirty pans under the sink.

"There's a great deal of work to be done on a farm," said Mrs. Hale stiffly.

"To be sure. And yet"—with a little bow to her—"I know there are some Dickson County farm-houses that do not have such roller towels." He gave it a pull to expose its full length again.

"Those towels get dirty awful quick. Men's hands aren't always as clean as they might be."

"Ah, loyal to your sex, I see," he laughed. He stopped and gave her a keen look. "But you and Mrs. Wright were neighbors. I suppose you were friends, too."

Martha Hale shook her head.

"I've seen little enough of her of late years. I've not been in this house—it's more than a year."

"And why was that? You didn't like her?"

"I liked her well enough," she replied with spirit. "Farmers' wives have their hands full, Mr. Henderson. And then"—She looked around the kitchen.

"Yes?" he encouraged.

"It never seemed a very cheerful place," said she, more to herself than to him.

"No," he agreed; "I don't think any one would call it cheerful. I shouldn't say she had the home-making instinct."

"Well, I don't know as Wright had, either," she muttered.

"You mean they didn't get on very well?" he was quick to ask.

"No; I don't mean anything," she answered, with decision. As she turned a little away from him, she added: "But I don't think a place would be any the cheerfuler for John Wright's bein' in it."

"I'd like to talk to you about that a little later, Mrs. Hale," he said. "I'm anxious to get the lay of things upstairs now."

He moved toward the stair door, followed by the two men.

"I suppose anything Mrs. Peters does'll be all right?" the sheriff inquired. "She was to take in some clothes for her, you know—and a few little things. We left in such a hurry yesterday."

The county attorney looked at the two women whom they were leaving alone there among the kitchen things.

"Yes—Mrs. Peters," he said, his glance resting on the woman who was not Mrs. Peters, the big farmer woman who stood behind the sheriff's wife. "Of course Mrs. Peters is one of us," he said, in a manner of entrusting responsibility. "And keep your eye out, Mrs. Peters, for anything that might be of use. No telling; you women might come upon a clue to the motive—and that's the thing we need."

Mr. Hale rubbed his face after the fashion of a show man getting ready for a pleasantry.

"But would the women know a clue if they did come upon it?" he said; and, having delivered himself of this, he followed the others through the stair door.

The women stood motionless and silent, listening to the footsteps, first upon the stairs, then in the room above them.

Then, as if releasing herself from something strange, Mrs. Hale began to arrange the dirty pans under the sink, which the county attorney's disdainful push of the foot had deranged.

"I'd hate to have men comin' into my kitchen," she said testily—"snoopin' round and criticizin'."

"Of course it's no more than their duty," said the sheriff's wife, in her manner of timid acquiescence.

"Duty's all right," replied Mrs. Hale bluffly; "but I guess that deputy sheriff that come out to make the fire might have got a little of this on." She gave the roller towel a pull. "Wish I'd thought of that sooner! Seems mean to talk about her for not having things slicked up, when she had to come away in such a hurry."

She looked around the kitchen. Certainly it was not "slicked up." Her eye was held by a bucket of sugar on a low shelf. The cover was off the wooden bucket, and beside it was a paper bag—half full.

Mrs. Hale moved toward it.

"She was putting this in here," she said to herself—slowly.

She thought of the flour in her kitchen at home—half sifted, half not sifted. She had been interrupted, and had left things half done. What had interrupted Minnie Foster? Why had that work been left half done? She made a move as if to finish it,—unfinished things always bothered her,—and then she glanced around and saw that Mrs. Peters was watching her—and she didn't want Mrs. Peters to get that feeling she had got of work begun and then—for some reason—not finished.

"It's a shame about her fruit," she said, and walked toward the cupboard that the county attorney had opened, and got on the chair, murmuring: "I wonder if it's all gone."

It was a sorry enough looking sight, but "Here's one that's all right," she said at last. She held it toward the light. "This is cherries, too." She looked again. "I declare I believe that's the only one."

With a sigh, she got down from the chair, went to the sink, and wiped off the bottle.

"She'll feel awful bad, after all her hard work in the hot weather. I remember the afternoon I put up my cherries last summer."

She set the bottle on the table, and, with another sigh, started to sit down in the rocker. But she did not sit down. Something kept her from sitting down in that chair. She straightened—stepped back, and, half turned away, stood looking at it, seeing the woman who sat there "pleatin' at her apron."

The thin voice of the sheriff's wife broke in upon her: "I must be getting those things from the front room closet." She opened the door into the other room, started in, stepped back. "You coming with me, Mrs. Hale?" she asked nervously. "You—you could help me get them."

They were soon back—the stark coldness of that shut-up room was not a thing to linger in.

"My!" said Mrs. Peters, dropping the things on the table and hurrying to the stove.

Mrs. Hale stood examining the clothes the woman who was being detained in town had said she wanted.

"Wright was close!" she exclaimed, holding up a shabby black skirt that bore the marks of much making over. "I think maybe that's why she kept so much to herself. I s'pose she felt she couldn't do her part; and then, you don't enjoy things when you feel shabby. She used to wear pretty clothes and be lively—when she was Minnie Foster, one of the town girls, singing in the choir. But that—oh, that was twenty years ago."

With a carefulness in which there was something tender, she folded the shabby clothes and piled them at one corner of the table. She looked at Mrs. Peters, and there was something in the other woman's look that irritated her.

"She don't care," she said to herself. "Much difference it makes to her whether Minnie Foster had pretty clothes when she was a girl."

Then she looked again, and she wasn't so sure; in fact, she hadn't at any time been perfectly sure about Mrs. Peters. She had that shrinking manner, and yet her eyes looked as if they could see a long way into things.

"This all you was to take in?" asked Mrs. Hale.

"No," said the sheriff's wife; "she said she wanted an apron. Funny thing to want," she ventured in her nervous little way, "for there's not much to get you dirty in jail, goodness knows. But I suppose just to make her feel more natural. If you're used to wearing an apron—. She said they were in the bottom drawer of this cupboard. Yes—here they are. And then her little shawl that always hung on the stair door."

She took the small gray shawl from behind the door leading upstairs, and stood a minute looking at it.

Suddenly Mrs. Hale took a quick step toward the other woman.

"Mrs. Peters!"

"Yes, Mrs. Hale?"

"Do you think she—did it?"

A frightened look blurred the other things in Mrs. Peters's eyes.

"Oh, I don't know," she said, in a voice that seemed to shrink away from the subject.

"Well, I don't think she did," affirmed Mrs. Hale stoutly. "Asking for an apron, and her little shawl. Worryin' about her fruit."

"Mr. Peters says—." Footsteps were heard in the room above; she stopped, looked up, then went on in a lowered voice: "Mr. Peters says—it looks bad for her. Mr. Henderson is awful sarcastic in a speech, and he's going to make fun of her saying she didn't—wake up."

For a moment Mrs. Hale had no answer. Then, "Well, I guess John Wright didn't wake up—when they was slippin' that rope under his neck," she muttered.

"No, it's *strange,*" breathed Mrs. Peters. "They think it was such a—funny way to kill a man."

She began to laugh; at the sound of the laugh, abruptly stopped.

"That's just what Mr. Hale said," said Mrs. Hale, in a resolutely natural voice. "There was a gun in the house. He says that's what he can't understand."

"Mr. Henderson said, coming out, that what was needed for the case was a motive. Something to show anger—or sudden feeling."

"Well, I don't see any signs of anger around here," said Mrs. Hale. "I don't—"

She stopped. It was as if her mind tripped on something. Her eye was caught by a dish-towel in the middle of the kitchen table. Slowly she moved toward the table. One half of it was wiped clean, the other half messy. Her eyes made a slow, almost unwilling turn to the bucket of sugar and the half empty bag beside it. Things begun—and not finished.

After a moment she stepped back, and said, in that manner of releasing herself:

"Wonder how they're finding things upstairs? I hope she had it a little more red up up there. You know,"—she paused, and feeling gathered,—"it seems kind of *sneaking;* locking her up in town and coming out here to get her own house to turn against her!"

"But, Mrs. Hale," said the sheriff's wife, "the law is the law."

"I s'pose 'tis," answered Mrs. Hale shortly.

She turned to the stove, saying something about that fire not being much to brag of. She worked with it a minute, and when she straightened up she said aggressively:

"The law is the law—and a bad stove is a bad stove. How'd you like to cook on this?"—pointing with the poker to the broken lining. She opened the oven door and started to express her opinion of the oven; but she was swept into her own thoughts, thinking of what it would mean, year after year, to have that stove to wrestle with. The thought of Minnie Foster trying to bake in that oven—and the thought of her never going over to see Minnie Foster—.

She was startled by hearing Mrs. Peters say: "A person gets discouraged—and loses heart."

The sheriff's wife had looked from the stove to the sink—to the pail of water which had been carried in from outside. The two women stood there silent, above them the footsteps of the men who were looking for evidence against the woman who had worked in that kitchen. That look of seeing into things, of seeing through a thing to something else, was in the eyes of the sheriff's wife now. When Mrs. Hale next spoke to her, it was gently:

"Better loosen up your things, Mrs. Peters. We'll not feel them when we go out."

Mrs. Peters went to the back of the room to hang up the fur tippet she was wearing. A moment later she exclaimed, "Why, she was piecing a quilt," and held up a large sewing basket piled high with quilt pieces.

Mrs. Hale spread some of the blocks on the table.

"It's log-cabin pattern," she said, putting several of them together. "Pretty, isn't it?"

They were so engaged with the quilt that they did not hear the footsteps on the stairs. Just as the stair door opened Mrs. Hale was saying:

"Do you suppose she was going to quilt it or just knot it?"

The sheriff threw up his hands.

"They wonder whether she was going to quilt it or just knot it!"

There was a laugh for the ways of women, a warming of hands over the stove, and then the county attorney said briskly:

"Well, let's go right out to the barn and get that cleared up."

"I don't see as there's anything so strange," Mrs. Hale said resentfully, after the outside door had closed on the three men—"our taking up our time with little things while we're waiting for them to get the evidence. I don't see as it's anything to laugh about."

"Of course they've got awful important things on their minds," said the sheriff's wife apologetically.

They returned to an inspection of the blocks for the quilt. Mrs.

Hale was looking at the fine, even sewing, and preoccupied with thoughts of the woman who had done that sewing, when she heard the sheriff's wife say, in a queer tone:

"Why, look at this one."

She turned to take the block held out to her.

"The sewing," said Mrs. Peters, in a troubled way. "All the rest of them have been so nice and even—but—this one. Why, it looks as if she didn't know what she was about!"

Their eyes met—something flashed to life, passed between them; then, as if with an effort, they seemed to pull away from each other. A moment Mrs. Hale sat there, her hands folded over that sewing which was so unlike all the rest of the sewing. Then she had pulled a knot and drawn the threads.

"Oh, what are you doing, Mrs. Hale?" asked the sheriff's wife, startled.

"Just pulling out a stitch or two that's not sewed very good," said Mrs. Hale mildly.

"I don't think we ought to touch things," Mrs. Peters said, a little helplessly.

"I'll just finish up this end," answered Mrs. Hale, still in that mild, matter-of-fact fashion.

She threaded a needle and started to replace bad sewing with good. For a little while she sewed in silence. Then, in that thin, timid voice, she heard:

"Mrs. Hale!"

"Yes, Mrs. Peters?"

"What do you suppose she was so—nervous about?"

"Oh, *I* don't know," said Mrs. Hale, as if dismissing a thing not important enough to spend much time on. "I don't know as she was—nervous. I sew awful queer sometimes when I'm just tired."

She cut a thread, and out of the corner of her eye looked up at Mrs. Peters. The small, lean face of the sheriff's wife seemed to have tightened up. Her eyes had that look of peering into something. But the next moment she moved, and said in her thin, indecisive way:

"Well, I must get those clothes wrapped. They may be through sooner than we think. I wonder where I could find a piece of paper—and string."

"In that cupboard, maybe," suggested Mrs. Hale, after a glance around.

One piece of the crazy sewing remained unripped. Mrs. Peters's back turned, Martha Hale now scrutinized that piece, compared it with the dainty, accurate sewing of the other blocks. The difference was startling. Holding this block made her feel queer, as if the distracted thoughts of the woman who had perhaps turned to it to try and quiet herself were communicating themselves to her.

Mrs. Peters's voice roused her.

"Here's a bird-cage," she said. "Did she have a bird, Mrs. Hale?"

"Why, I don't know whether she did or not." She turned to look at the cage Mrs. Peters was holding up. "I've not been here in so long." She sighed. "There was a man round last year selling canaries cheap—but I don't know as she took one. Maybe she did. She used to sing real pretty herself."

Mrs. Peters looked around the kitchen.

"Seems kind of funny to think of a bird here." She half laughed—an attempt to put up a barrier. "But she must have had one—or why would she have a cage? I wonder what happened to it."

"I suppose maybe the cat got it," suggested Mrs. Hale, resuming her sewing.

"No, she didn't have a cat. She's got that feeling some people have about cats—being afraid of them. When they brought her to our house yesterday, my cat got in the room, and she was real upset and asked me to take it out."

"My sister Bessie was like that," laughed Mrs. Hale.

The sheriff's wife did not reply. The silence made Mrs. Hale turn around. Mrs. Peters was examining the bird-cage.

"Look at this door," she said slowly. "It's broke. One hinge has been pulled apart."

Mrs. Hale came nearer.

"Looks as if some one must have been—rough with it."

Again their eyes met—startled, questioning, apprehensive. For a moment neither spoke nor stirred. Then Mrs. Hale, turning away, said brusquely:

"If they're going to find any evidence, I wish they'd be about it. I don't like this place."

"But I'm awful glad you came with me, Mrs. Hale." Mrs. Peters put the bird-cage on the table and sat down. "It would be lonesome for me—sitting here alone."

"Yes, it would, wouldn't it?" agreed Mrs. Hale, a certain determined naturalness in her voice. She picked up the sewing, but now it dropped in her lap, and she murmured in a different voice: "But I tell you what I *do* wish, Mrs. Peters. I wish I had come over sometimes when she was here. I wish—I had."

"But of course you were awful busy, Mrs. Hale. Your house—and your children."

"I could've come," retorted Mrs. Hale shortly. "I stayed away because it weren't cheerful—and that's why I ought to have come. I"—she looked around—"I've never liked this place. Maybe because it's down in a hollow and you don't see the road. I don't know what it is, but it's a lonesome place, and always was. I wish I had come over to see Minnie Foster sometimes. I can see now—" She did not put it into words.

"Well, you mustn't reproach yourself," counseled Mrs. Peters. "Somehow, we just don't see how it is with other folks till—something comes up."

"Not having children makes less work," mused Mrs. Hale, after a silence, "but it makes a quiet house—and Wright out to work all day—and no company when he did come in. Did you know John Wright, Mrs. Peters?"

"Not to know him. I've seen him in town. They say he was a good man."

"Yes—good," conceded John Wright's neighbor grimly. "He didn't drink, and kept his word as well as most, I guess, and paid his debts. But he was a hard man, Mrs. Peters. Just to pass the time of day with him—." She stopped, shivered a little. "Like a raw wind that gets to the bone." Her eye fell upon the cage on the table before her, and she added, almost bitterly: "I should think she would've wanted a bird!"

Suddenly she leaned forward, looking intently at the cage. "But what do you s'pose went wrong with it?"

"I don't know," returned Mrs. Peters; "unless it got sick and died."

But after she said it she reached over and swung the broken door. Both women watched it as if somehow held by it.

"You didn't know—her?" Mrs. Hale asked, a gentler note in her voice.

"Not till they brought her yesterday," said the sheriff's wife.

"She—come to think of it, she was kind of like a bird herself. Real sweet and pretty, but kind of timid and—fluttery. How—she—did—change."

That held her for a long time. Finally, as if struck with a happy thought and relieved to get back to everyday things, she exclaimed:

"Tell you what, Mrs. Peters, why don't you take the quilt in with you? It might take up her mind."

"Why, I think that's a real nice idea, Mrs. Hale," agreed the sheriff's wife, as if she too were glad to come into the atmosphere of a simple kindness. "There couldn't possibly be any objection to that, could there? Now, just what will I take? I wonder if her patches are in here—and her things."

They turned to the sewing basket.

"Here's some red," said Mrs. Hale, bringing out a roll of cloth. Underneath that was a box. "Here, maybe her scissors are in here—and her things." She held it up. "What a pretty box! I'll warrant that was something she had a long time ago—when she was a girl."

She held it in her hand a moment; then, with a little sigh, opened it.

Instantly her hand went to her nose.

"Why—!"

Mrs. Peters drew nearer—then turned away.

"There's something wrapped up in this piece of silk," faltered Mrs. Hale.

"This isn't her scissors," said Mrs. Peters in a shrinking voice.

Her hand not steady, Mrs. Hale raised the piece of silk. "Oh, Mrs. Peters!" she cried. "It's—"

Mrs. Peters bent closer.

"It's the bird," she whispered.

"But, Mrs. Peters!" cried Mrs. Hale. "*Look* at it! Its neck—look at its neck! It's all—other side *to*."

She held the box away from her.

The sheriff's wife again bent closer.

"Somebody wrung its neck," said she, in a voice that was slow and deep.

And then again the eyes of the two women met—this time clung together in a look of dawning comprehension, of growing horror. Mrs. Peters looked from the dead bird to the broken door of the cage. Again their eyes met. And just then there was a sound at the outside door.

Mrs. Hale slipped the box under the quilt pieces in the basket, and sank into the chair before it. Mrs. Peters stood holding to the table. The county attorney and the sheriff came in from outside.

"Well, ladies," said the county attorney, as one turning from serious things to little pleasantries, "have you decided whether she was going to quilt it or knot it?"

"We think," began the sheriff's wife in a flurried voice, "that she was going to—knot it."

He was too preoccupied to notice the change that came in her voice on that last.

"Well, that's very interesting, I'm sure," he said tolerantly. He caught sight of the bird-cage. "Has the bird flown?"

"We think the cat got it," said Mrs. Hale in a voice curiously even.

He was walking up and down, as if thinking something out.

"Is there a cat?" he asked absently.

Mrs. Hale shot a look up at the sheriff's wife.

"Well, not *now*," said Mrs. Peters. "They're superstitious, you know; they leave."

She sank into her chair.

The county attorney did not heed her. "No sign at all of any one having come in from the outside," he said to Peters, in the manner of continuing an interrupted conversation. "Their own rope. Now let's go upstairs again and go over it, piece by piece. It would have to have been some one who knew just the—"

The stair door closed behind them and their voices were lost.

The two women sat motionless, not looking at each other, but as if peering into something and at the same time holding back. When they spoke now it was as if they were afraid of what they were saying, but as if they could not help saying it.

"She liked the bird," said Martha Hale, low and slowly. "She was going to bury it in that pretty box."

"When I was a girl," said Mrs. Peters, under her breath, "my kitten—there was a boy took a hatchet, and before my eyes—before I could get there—" She covered her face an instant. "If they hadn't held me back I would have"—she caught herself, looked upstairs where footsteps were heard, and finished weakly—"hurt him."

Then they sat without speaking or moving.

"I wonder how it would seem," Mrs. Hale at last began, as if feeling her way over strange ground—"never to have had any children around?" Her eyes made a slow sweep of the kitchen, as if seeing what that kitchen had meant through all the years. "No, Wright wouldn't like the bird," she said after that—"a thing that sang. She used to sing. He killed that too." Her voice tightened.

Mrs. Peters moved uneasily.

"Of course we don't know who killed the bird."

"I knew John Wright," was Mrs. Hale's answer.

"It was an awful thing was done in this house that night, Mrs. Hale," said the sheriff's wife. "Killing a man while he slept—slipping a thing round his neck that choked the life out of him."

Mrs. Hale's hand went out to the bird-cage.

"His neck. Choked the life out of him."

"We don't *know* who killed him," whispered Mrs. Peters wildly. "We don't *know.*"

Mrs. Hale had not moved. "If there had been years and years of—nothing, then a bird to sing to you, it would be awful—still—after the bird was still."

It was as if something within her not herself had spoken, and it found in Mrs. Peters something she did not know as herself.

"I know what stillness is," she said, in a queer, monotonous voice. "When we homesteaded in Dakota, and my first baby died—after he was two years old—and me with no other then—"

Mrs. Hale stirred.

"How soon do you suppose they'll be through looking for evidence?"

"I know what stillness is," repeated Mrs. Peters, in just that same way. Then she too pulled back. "The law has got to punish crime, Mrs. Hale," she said in her tight little way.

"I wish you'd seen Minnie Foster," was the answer, "when she wore a white dress with blue ribbons, and stood up there in the choir and sang."

The picture of that girl, the fact that she had lived neighbor to that girl for twenty years, and had let her die for lack of life, was suddenly more than she could bear.

"Oh, I *wish* I'd come over here once in a while!" she cried. "That was a crime! That was a crime! Who's going to punish that?"

"We mustn't take on," said Mrs. Peters, with a frightened look toward the stairs.

"I might 'a' *known* she needed help! I tell you, it's *queer,* Mrs. Peters. We live close together, and we live far apart. We all go through the same things—it's all just a different kind of the same thing! If it weren't—why do you and I *understand?* Why do we *know*—what we know this minute?"

She dashed her hand across her eyes. Then, seeing the jar of fruit on the table, she reached for it and choked out:

"If I was you I wouldn't *tell* her her fruit was gone! Tell her it *ain't.* Tell her it's all right—all of it. Here—take this in to prove it to her! She—she may never know whether it was broke or not."

She turned away.

Mrs. Peters reached out for the bottle of fruit as if she were glad to take it—as if touching a familiar thing, having something to do, could keep her from something else. She got up, looked about for something to wrap the fruit in, took a petticoat from the pile of clothes she had brought from the front room, and nervously started winding that round the bottle.

"My!" she began, in a high, false voice, "it's a good thing the men couldn't hear us! Getting all stirred up over a little thing like a—dead canary." She hurried over that. "As if that could have anything to do with—with—My, wouldn't they *laugh?*"

Footsteps were heard on the stairs.

"Maybe they would," muttered Mrs. Hale—"maybe they wouldn't."

"No, Peters," said the county attorney incisively; "it's all perfectly clear, except the reason for doing it. But you know juries when it comes to women. If there was some definite thing—something to show. Something to make a story about. A thing that would connect up with this clumsy way of doing it."

In a covert way Mrs. Hale looked at Mrs. Peters. Mrs. Peters was looking at her. Quickly they looked away from each other. The outer door opened and Mr. Hale came in.

"I've got the team round now," he said. "Pretty cold out there."

"I'm going to stay here awhile by myself," the county attorney suddenly announced. "You can send Frank out for me, can't you?" he asked the sheriff. "I want to go over everything. I'm not satisfied we can't do better."

Again, for one brief moment, the two women's eyes found one another.

The sheriff came up to the table.

"Did you want to see what Mrs. Peters was going to take in?"

The county attorney picked up the apron. He laughed.

"Oh, I guess they're not very dangerous things the ladies have picked out."

Mrs. Hale's hand was on the sewing basket in which the box was concealed. She felt that she ought to take her hand off the basket. She did not seem able to. He picked up one of the quilt blocks which she had piled on to cover the box. Her eyes felt like fire. She had a feeling that if he took up the basket she would snatch it from him.

But he did not take it up. With another little laugh, he turned away, saying:

"No; Mrs. Peters doesn't need supervising. For that matter, a sheriff's wife is married to the law. Ever think of it that way, Mrs. Peters?"

Mrs. Peters was standing beside the table. Mrs. Hale shot a look up at her; but she could not see her face. Mrs. Peters had turned away. When she spoke, her voice was muffled.

"Not—just that way," she said.

"Married to the law!" chuckled Mrs. Peters's husband. He moved toward the door into the front room, and said to the county attorney:

"I just want you to come in here a minute, George. We ought to take a look at these windows."

"Oh—windows," said the county attorney scoffingly.

"We'll be right out, Mr. Hale," said the sheriff to the farmer, who was still waiting by the door.

Hale went to look after the horses. The sheriff followed the county attorney into the other room. Again—for one moment—the two women were alone in that kitchen.

Martha Hale sprang up, her hands tight together, looking at that other woman, with whom it rested. At first she could not see her eyes, for the sheriff's wife had not turned back since she turned away at that suggestion of being married to the law. But now Mrs. Hale made her turn back. Her eyes made her turn back. Slowly, unwillingly, Mrs. Peters turned her head until her eyes met the eyes of the other woman. There was a moment when they held each other in a steady, burning look in which there was no evasion nor flinching. Then Martha Hale's eyes pointed the way to the basket in which was hidden the thing that would make certain the conviction of the other woman—that woman who was not there and yet who had been there with them all through the hour.

For a moment Mrs. Peters did not move. And then she did it. With a rush forward, she threw back the quilt pieces, got the box, tried to put it in her handbag. It was too big. Desperately she opened it, started to take the bird out. But there she broke—she could not touch the bird. She stood helpless, foolish.

There was the sound of a knob turning in the inner door. Martha Hale snatched the box from the sheriff's wife, and got it in the pocket of her big coat just as the sheriff and the county attorney came back into the kitchen.

"Well, Henry," said the county attorney facetiously, "at least we found out that she was not going to quilt it. She was going to—what is it you call it, ladies?"

Mrs. Hale's hand was against the pocket of her coat.

"We call it—knot it, Mr. Henderson."

DASHIELL HAMMETT
(1894–1961)

(Samuel) Dashiell Hammett was born in St. Mary's County, Maryland. He left school early to work as a newsboy, stevedore, and private investigator for the Pinkerton Detective Agency. In the early 1920s he began writing stories about the nameless Continental Op, an investigator for the Continental Detective Agency. He wrote for pulp magazines, particularly *Black Mask,* which then serialized his novels: *Red Harvest* and *The Dain Curse* (both 1929). His most famous detective is Sam Spade, who became a prototype of the hard-boiled private investigator. He appears in *The Maltese Falcon* (1930) and in short stories collected in 1944 as *The Adventures of Sam Spade.* Hammett was a master of the form that emphasized violence and suspense rather than ingeniously plotted crime. Most of his creative work was done by the mid-1930s; he later wrote some screenplays and became involved in leftist politics but suffered in his last decades from ill health, an aftereffect of a World War I lung injury.

"The House in Turk Street" foreshadows in abbreviated form much that characterizes Hammett's classic novel, *The Maltese Falcon:* rapid action, constant violence, colloquial dialogue, and a tone that Julian Symons describes as "wistful cynicism." The mundane setting contrasts with the atmosphere of treachery, greed, and lust and the unheroic detective—fat, middle-aged, and beleaguered—provides another touch of realism.

THE HOUSE IN TURK STREET

I had been told that the man for whom I was hunting lived in a certain Turk Street block, but my informant hadn't been able to give me his house number. Thus it came about that late one rainy afternoon I was canvassing this certain block, ringing each bell, and reciting a myth that went like this:

"I'm from the law office of Wellington and Berkeley. One of our clients—an elderly lady—was thrown from the rear platform of a street car last week and severely injured. Among those who witnessed the accident was a young man whose name we don't know. But we have been told that he lives in this neighborhood." Then I would describe the man I wanted, and wind up: "Do you know of anyone who looks like that?"

All down one side of the block the answers were: "No," "No," "No."

I crossed the street and started on the other side. The first house: "No." The second: "No." The third. The fourth. The fifth—

No one came to the door in answer to my first ring. After a while, I rang again. I had just decided that no one was at home, when the knob turned slowly and a little old woman opened the door. She was a very fragile little old woman, with a piece of gray knitting in one hand, and faded eyes that twinkled pleasantly behind goldrimmed spectacles. She wore a stiffly starched apron over a black dress.

"Good evening," she said in a thin friendly voice. "I hope you didn't mind waiting. I always have to peep out to see who's there before I open the door—an old woman's timidity."

"Sorry to disturb you," I apologized. "But—"

"Won't you come in, please?"

"No; I just want a little information. I won't take much time."

"I wish you would come in," she said, and then added with mock severity, "I'm sure my tea is getting cold."

She took my damp hat and coat, and I followed her down a narrow hall to a dim room, where a man got up as we entered. He was old too, and stout, with a thin white beard that fell upon a white vest that was as stiffly starched as the woman's apron.

"Thomas," the little fragile woman told him; "this is Mr.—"

"Tracy," I said, because that was the name I had given the other residents of the block; but I came as near blushing when I said it as I have in fifteen years. These folks weren't made to be lied to.

Their name, I learned, was Quarre; and they were an affectionate old couple. She called him "Thomas" every time she spoke to him, rolling the name around in her mouth as if she liked the taste of it. He called her "my dear" just as frequently, and twice he got up to adjust a cushion more comfortably to her frail back.

I had to drink a cup of tea with them and eat some little spiced cookies before I could get them to listen to a question. Then Mrs. Quarre made little sympathetic clicking sounds with her tongue and teeth, while I told about the elderly lady who had fallen off a street car. The old man rumbled in his beard that it was "a damn shame," and gave me a fat cigar.

Finally I got away from the accident, and described the man I wanted.

"Thomas," Mrs. Quarre said, "isn't that the young man who lives in the house with the railing—the one who always looks so worried?"

The old man stroked his snowy beard and pondered for a moment.

"But, my dear," he rumbled at last, "hasn't he got dark hair?"

She beamed upon her husband. "Thomas is *so* observant," she said with pride. "I had forgotten; but the young man I spoke of does have dark hair, so he couldn't be the one."

The old man then suggested that one who lived in the block below might be my man. They discussed this one at some length before they decided that he was too tall and too old. Mrs. Quarre suggested another. They discussed that one, and voted against him. Thomas offered a candidate; he was weighed and discarded. They chattered on.

Darkness settled. The old man turned on a light in a tall lamp that threw a soft yellow circle upon us, and left the rest of the room dim. The room was a large one, and heavy with the thick hangings and bulky horsehair furniture of a generation ago. I didn't expect to get any information here; but I was comfortable, and the cigar was a good one. Time enough to go out into the drizzle when I had finished my smoke.

Something cold touched the nape of my neck.

"Stand up!"

I didn't stand up: I couldn't. I was paralyzed. I sat and blinked at the Quarres.

And looking at them, I knew that something cold *couldn't* be against the back of my neck; a harsh voice *couldn't* have ordered me to stand up. It wasn't possible!

Mrs. Quarre still sat primly upright against the cushions her husband had adjusted to her back; her eyes still twinkled with friendliness behind her glasses. The old man still stroked his white beard, and let cigar smoke drift unhurriedly from his nostrils.

They would go on talking about the young men in the neighborhood who might be the man I wanted. Nothing had happened. I had dozed.

"Get up!" The cold thing against my neck jabbed deep into the flesh.

I stood up. "Frisk him," the harsh voice came from behind.

The old man carefully laid his cigar down, came to me, and ran his hands over my body. Satisfied that I was unarmed, he emptied my pockets, dropping the contents upon the chair that I had just left.

"That's all," he told the man behind me, and returned to his chair.

"Turn around, you!" the harsh voice ordered.

I turned and faced a tall, gaunt, raw-boned man of about my own age, which is thirty-five. He had an ugly face—hollow-cheeked, bony, and spattered with big pale freckles. His eyes were of a watery blue, and his nose and chin stuck out abruptly. "Know me?" he asked.

"No."

"You're a liar!"

I didn't argue the point; he was holding a gun in one big freckled hand.

"You're going to know me pretty well before you're through with me," this big ugly man threatened. "You're going to—"

"Hook!" a voice came from a portièred doorway—the doorway through which the ugly man had no doubt crept up behind me. "Hook, come here!" The voice was feminine—young, clear, and musical.

"What do you want?" the ugly man called over his shoulder.

"*He's* here."

"All right!" He turned to Thomas Quarre. "Keep this joker safe."

From somewhere among his whiskers, his coat, and his stiff white vest, the old man brought out a big black revolver, which he handled with no signs of unfamiliarity.

The ugly man swept up the things that had been taken from my pockets, and carried them through the portières with him.

Mrs. Quarre smiled up at me. "Do sit down, Mr. Tracy," she said.

I sat.

Through the portières a new voice came from the next room; a drawling baritone voice whose accent was unmistakably British; cultured British. "What's up, Hook?" this voice was asking.

The harsh voice of the ugly man:

"Plenty's up, I'm telling you! They're on to us! I started out a while ago; and as soon as I got to the street, I seen a man I knowed on the other side. He was pointed out to me in Philly five–six years ago. I don't know his name, but I remember his mug—he's a Continental Detective Agency man. I came back in right away, and me and Elvira watched him out of the window. He went to every house on the other side of the street, asking questions or something. Then he came over and started to give this side a whirl, and after a while he rings the bell. I tell the old woman and her husband to get him in, stall him along, and see what he says for himself. He's got a song and dance about looking for a guy what seen an old woman bumped by a street car—but that's the bunk! He's gunning for us. I went in and stuck him up just now. I meant to wait till you come, but I was scared he'd get nervous and beat it."

The British voice: "You shouldn't have shown yourself to him. The others could have taken care of him."

Hook: "What's the diff? Chances is he knows us all anyway. But supposing he didn't, what diff does it make?"

The drawling British voice: "It may make a deal of difference. It was stupid."

Hook, blustering: "Stupid, huh? You're always bellyaching about other people being stupid. To hell with you, I say! Who does all the work? Who's the guy that swings all the jobs? Huh? Where—"

The young feminine voice: "Now, Hook, for God's sake don't make that speech again. I've listened to it until I know it by heart!"

A rustle of papers, and the British voice: "I say, Hook, you're correct about his being a detective. Here is an identification card."

The feminine voice from the next room: "Well, what's to be done? What's our play?"

Hook: "That's easy to answer. We're going to knock this sleuth off!"

The feminine voice: "And put our necks in the noose?"

Hook, scornfully: "As if they ain't there if we don't! You don't think this guy ain't after us for the L.A. job, do you?"

The British voice: "You're an ass, Hook, and a quite hopeless one. Suppose this chap is interested in the Los Angeles affair, as is probable; what then? He is a Continental operative. Is it likely that his organization doesn't know where he is? Don't you think they know he was coming up here? And don't they know as much about us—chances are—as he does? There's no use killing him. That would only make matters worse. The thing to do is to tie him up and leave him here. His associates will hardly come looking for him until tomorrow."

My gratitude went out to the British voice! Somebody was in my favor, at least to the extent of letting me live. I hadn't been feeling very cheerful these last few minutes. Somehow, the fact that I couldn't see these people who were deciding whether I was to live or die, made my plight seem all the more desperate. I felt better now, though far from gay; I had confidence in the drawling British voice; it was the voice of a man who habitually carries his point.

Hook, bellowing: "Let me tell you something, brother: that guy's going to be knocked off! That's flat! I'm taking no chances. You can jaw all you want to about it, but I'm looking out for my own neck and it'll be a lot safer with that guy where he can't talk. That's flat."

The feminine voice, disgustedly: "Aw, Hook, be reasonable!"

The British voice, still drawling, but dead cold: "There's no use reasoning with you, Hook, you've the instincts and the intellect of a troglodyte. There is only one sort of language that you understand; and I'm going to talk that language to you, my son. If you are tempted to do anything silly between now and the time of our departure, just say this to yourself two or three times: 'If he dies, I die.' Say it as if it were out of the Bible—because it's that true."

There followed a long space of silence, with a tenseness that made my not particularly sensitive scalp tingle.

When, at last, a voice cut the silence, I jumped as if a gun had been fired; though the voice was low and smooth enough.

It was the British voice, confidently victorious, and I breathed again.

"We'll get the old people away first," the voice was saying. "You take charge of our guest, Hook. Tie him up while I get the bonds, and we'll be gone in less than half an hour."

The portières parted and Hook came into the room—a scowling Hook whose freckles had a greenish tinge against the sallowness of his face. He pointed a revolver at me, and spoke to the Quarres, short and harsh:

"He wants you." They got up and went into the next room.

Hook, meanwhile, had stepped back to the doorway, still menacing me with his revolver; and pulled loose the plush ropes that were around the heavy curtains. Then he came around behind me, and tied me securely to the highbacked chair; my arms to the chair's arms, my legs to the chair's legs, my body to the chair's back and seat; and he wound up by gagging me with the corner of a cushion that was too well-stuffed.

As he finished lashing me into place, and stepped back to scowl at me, I heard the street door close softly, and then light footsteps ran back and forth overhead.

Hook looked in the direction of those footsteps, and his little watery blue eyes grew cunning. "Elvira!" he called softly.

The portières bulged as if someone had touched them, and the musical feminine voice came through. "What?"

"Come here."

"I'd better not. He wouldn't—"

"Damn him!" Hook flared up. "Come here!"

She came into the room and into the circle of light from the tall lamp; a girl in her early twenties, slender and lithe, and dressed for the street, except that she carried her hat in one hand. A white face beneath a bobbed mass of flame-colored hair. Smoke-gray eyes that were set too far apart for trustworthiness—though not for beauty—laughed at me; and her red mouth laughed at me, exposing the edges of little sharp animal-teeth. She was as beautiful as the devil, and twice as dangerous.

She laughed at me—a fat man, all trussed up with red plush rope, and with the corner of a green cushion in my mouth—and she turned to the ugly man. "What do you want?"

He spoke in an undertone, with a furtive glance at the ceiling, above which soft steps still padded back and forth.

"What say we shake him?"

Her smoke-gray eyes lost their merriment and became calculating.

"There's a hundred thousand he's holding—a third of it's mine. You don't think I'm going to take a Mickey Finn on that, do you?"

"Course not! Supposing we get the hundred-grand?"

"How?"

"Leave it to me, kid; leave it to me! If I swing it, will you go with me? You know I'll be good to you."

She smiled contemptuously, I thought—but he seemed to like it.

"You're whooping right you'll be good to me," she said. "But listen, Hook: we couldn't get away with it—not unless you *get him.* I know him! I'm not running away with anything that belongs to him unless he is fixed so that he can't come after it."

Hook moistened his lips and looked around the room at nothing. Apparently he didn't like the thought of tangling with the owner of the British drawl. But his desire for the girl was too strong for his fear.

"I'll do it!" he blurted. "I'll get him! Do you mean it, kid? If I get him, you'll go with me?"

She held out her hand. "It's a bet," she said and he believed her.

His ugly face grew warm and red and utterly happy, and he took a deep breath and straightened his shoulders. In his place, I might have believed her myself—all of us have fallen for that sort of thing at one time or another—but sitting tied up on the side-lines, I knew that he'd have been better off playing with a gallon of nitro than with this baby. She was dangerous! There was a rough time ahead for Hook!

"This is the lay—" Hook began, and stopped, tongue-tied.

A step had sounded in the next room.

Immediately the British voice came through the portières, and there was exasperation to the drawl now:

"This is really too much! I can't"—he said *reahly* and *cawnt*—"leave for a moment without having things done all wrong. Now just what got into you, Elvira, that you must go in and exhibit yourself to our detective?"

Fear flashed into her smoke-gray eyes, and out again, and she spoke airily. "Don't be altogether yellow," she said. "Your precious neck can get along all right without so much guarding."

The portières parted, and I twisted my head around as far as I could get it for my first look at this man who was responsible for my still being alive. I saw a short fat man, hatted and coated for the street, and carrying a tan traveling bag in one hand.

Then his face came into the yellow circle of light, and I saw that it was a Chinese face. A short fat Chinese, immaculately clothed in garments that were as British as his accent.

"It isn't a matter of color," he told the girl—and I understood now the full sting of her jibe; "it's simply a matter of ordinary wisdom."

His face was a round yellow mask, and his voice was the same emotionless drawl that I had heard before; but I knew that he was as surely under the girl's sway as the ugly man—or he wouldn't have let her taunt bring him into the room. But I doubted that she'd find this Anglicized Oriental as easily handled as Hook.

"There was no particular need," the Chinese was still talking, "for this chap to have seen any of us." He looked at me now for the first time, with little opaque eyes that were like two black seeds. "It's quite possible that he didn't know any of us, even by description. This showing ourselves to him is the most arrant sort of nonsense."

"Aw, hell, Tai!" Hook blustered. "Quit your bellyaching, will you? What's the diff? I'll knock him off, and that takes care of that!"

The Chinese set down his tan bag and shook his head.

"There will be no killing," he drawled, "or there will be quite a bit of killing. You don't mistake my meaning, do you, Hook?"

Hook didn't. His Adam's apple ran up and down with the effort of his swallowing and behind the cushion that was choking me, I thanked the yellow man again.

Then this red-haired she-devil put her spoon in the dish.

"Hook's always offering to do things that he has no intention of doing," she told the Chinese.

Hook's ugly face blazed red at this reminder of his promise to *get* the Chinese, and he swallowed again, and his eyes looked as if nothing would have suited him better than an opportunity to crawl under something. But the girl had him; her influence was stronger than his cowardice.

He suddenly stepped close to the Chinese, and from his advantage of a full head in height scowled down into the round yellow face.

"Tai," the ugly man snarled; "you're done. I'm sick and tired of all this dog you put on—acting like you was a king or something. I'm going to—"

He faltered, and his words faded away into silence. Tai looked up at him with eyes that were as hard and black and inhuman as two pieces of coal. Hook's lips twitched and he flinched away a little.

I stopped sweating. The yellow man had won again. But I had forgotten the red-haired she-devil. She laughed now—a mocking laugh that must have been like a knife to the ugly man.

A bellow came from deep in his chest, and he hurled one big fist into the round blank face of the yellow man.

The force of the punch carried Tai all the way across the room, and threw him on his side in one corner.

But he had twisted his body around to face the ugly man even as he went hurtling across the room—a gun was in his hand before he went down—and he was speaking before his legs had settled upon the floor—and his voice was a cultured British drawl.

"Later," he was saying; "we will settle this thing that is between us. Just now you will drop your pistol and stand very still while I get up."

Hook's revolver—only half out of his pocket when the Oriental had covered him—thudded to the rug. He stood rigidly still while Tai got to his feet, and Hook's breath came out noisily, and each freckle stood ghastlily out against the dirty scared white of his face.

I looked at the girl. There was contempt in the eyes with which she looked at Hook, but no disappointment.

Then I made a discovery: *something had changed in the room near her!*

I shut my eyes and tried to picture that part of the room as it had been before the two men had clashed. Opening my eyes suddenly, I had the answer.

On the table beside the girl had been a book and some magazines. They were gone now. Not two feet from the girl was the tan bag that Tai had brought into the room. Suppose the bag had held the bonds from the Los Angeles job that they had mentioned. It probably had. What then? It probably now held the book and magazines that had been on the table. The girl had stirred up the trouble between the two men to distract their attention while she made a switch. Where would the loot be, then? I didn't know, but I suspected that it was too bulky to be on the girl's slender person.

Just beyond the table was a couch, with a wide red cover that went all the way down to the floor. I looked from the couch to the girl. She was watching me, and her eyes twinkled with a flash of mirth as they met mine coming from the couch. The couch it was!

By now the Chinese had pocketed Hook's revolver, and was talking to him: "If I hadn't a dislike for murder, and didn't think that you will perhaps be of some value to Elvira and me in effecting our departure, I should certainly relieve us of the handicap of your stupidity now. But I'll give you one more chance. I would suggest, however, that you think carefully before you give way to any more of your violent impulses." He turned to the girl. "Have you been putting foolish ideas in our Hook's head?"

She laughed. "Nobody could put any kind in it."

"Perhaps you're right," he said, and then came over to test the lashings about my arms and body.

Finding them satisfactory, he picked up the tan bag, and held out the gun he had taken from the ugly man a few minutes before.

"Here's your revolver, Hook, now try to be sensible. We may as well go now. The old man and his wife will do as they were told. They are on their way to a city that we needn't mention by name in front of our friend here, to wait for us and their share of the bonds. Needless to say, they will wait a long while—they are out of it now. But between ourselves there must be no more treachery. If we're to get clear, we must help each other."

According to the best dramatic rules, these folks should have made sarcastic speeches to me before they left, but they didn't. They passed me without even a farewell look, and went out of sight into the darkness of the hall.

Suddenly the Chinese was in the room again, running tiptoe—an open knife in one hand, a gun in the other. This was the man I had been thanking for saving my life! He bent over me.

The knife moved on my right side, and the rope that held that arm slackened its grip. I breathed again, and my heart went back to beating.

"Hook will be back," Tai whispered, and was gone.

On the carpet, three feet in front of me, lay a revolver.

The street door closed, and I was alone in the house for a while.

You may believe that I spent that while struggling with the red plush ropes that bound me. Tai had cut one length, loosening my right arm somewhat and giving my body more play, but I was far from free. And his whispered "Hook will be back" was all the spur I needed to throw my strength against my bonds.

I understood now why the Chinese had insisted so strongly upon my life being spared. *I was the weapon with which Hook was to be removed!*

The Chinese figured that Hook would make some excuse as soon as they reached the street, slip back into the house, knock me off, and rejoin his confederates. If he didn't do it on his own initiative, I suppose the Chinese would suggest it.

So he had put a gun within reach and had loosened my ropes as much as he could, not to have me free before he himself got away.

This thinking was a side-issue. I didn't let it slow up my efforts to get loose. The *why* wasn't important to me just now—the important thing was to have that revolver in my hand when the ugly man came back.

Just as the front door opened, I got my right arm completely free, and plucked the strangling cushion from my mouth. The rest of my body was still held by the ropes—held loosely—but held.

I threw myself, chair and all, forward, breaking the fall with my free arm. The carpet was thick. I went down on my face, with the heavy chair atop me, all doubled up, but my right arm was free of the tangle, and my right hand grasped the gun. The dim light hit upon a man hurrying into the room—a glint of metal in his hand.

I fired.

He caught both hands to his belly, bent double, and slid out across the carpet.

That was over. But that was far from being all. I wrenched at the plush ropes that held me, while my mind tried to sketch what lay ahead.

The girl had switched the bonds, hiding them under the couch—there was no question of that. She had intended coming back for them before I had time to get free. But Hook had come back first, and she would have to change her plan. What more likely than that she would now tell the Chinese that Hook had made the switch? What then? There was only one answer: Tai would come back for the bonds—both of them would come. Tai knew that I was armed now, but they had said that the bonds represented a hundred thousand dollars. That would be enough to bring them back!

I kicked the last rope loose and scrambled to the couch. The bonds were beneath it: four thick bundles, done up with heavy rubber bands. I tucked them under one arm, and went over to the man who was dying near the door. His gun was under one of his legs. I pulled it out, stepped over him, and went into the dark hall. Then I stopped to consider.

The girl and the Chinese would split to tackle me. One would come in the front door and the other in the rear. That would be the safest way for them to handle me. My play, obviously, was to wait just inside one of those doors for them. It would be foolish for me to leave the house. That's exactly what they would be expecting at first—and they would be lying in ambush.

Decidedly, my play was to lie low within sight of this front door and wait until one of them came through it—as one of them surely would, when they had tired of waiting for me to come out.

Toward the street door, the hall was lighted with the glow that filtered through the glass from the street lights. The stairway leading to the second-story threw a triangular shadow across part of the hall—a shadow that was black enough for any purpose. I crouched low in this three-cornered slice of night, and waited.

I had two guns: the one the Chinese had given me, and the one I had taken from Hook. I had fired one shot; that would leave me eleven still to use—unless one of the weapons had been used since it was loaded. I broke the gun Tai had given me, and in the dark ran my fingers across the back of the cylinder. My fingers touched *one* shell—under the hammer. Tai had taken no chances; he had given me one bullet—the bullet with which I had dropped Hook.

I put that gun down on the floor, and examined the one I had taken from Hook. It was *empty.* The Chinese had taken no chances at all! He had emptied Hook's gun before returning it to him after their quarrel.

I was in a hole! Alone, unarmed, in a strange house that would presently hold two who were hunting me—and that one of them was a woman didn't soothe me any—she was none the less deadly on that account.

For a moment I was tempted to make a dash for it; the thought of being out in the street again was pleasant; but I put the idea away. That would be foolishness, and plenty of it. Then I remembered the bonds under my arm. They would have to be my weapon; and if they were to serve me, they would have to be concealed.

I slipped out of my triangular shadow and went up the stairs. Thanks to the street lights, the upstairs rooms were not too dark for me to move around. Around and around I went through the rooms, hunting for a place to hide the bonds. But when suddenly a window rattled, as if from the draught created by the opening of an outside door somewhere, I still had the loot in my hands.

There was nothing to do now but to chuck them out of a window and trust to luck. I grabbed a pillow from a bed, stripped off the white case, and dumped the bonds into it. Then I leaned out of an already open window and looked down into the night, searching for a desirable dumping place: I didn't want the bonds to land on anything that would make a racket.

And, looking out of the window, I found a better hiding place. The window opened into a narrow court, on the other side of which was a house of the same sort as the one I was in. That house was of the same height as this one, with a flat tin roof that sloped down the other way. The roof wasn't far from me—not too far to chuck the pillow case. I chucked it. It disappeared over the edge of the roof and crackled softly on the tin.

Then I turned on all the lights in the room, lighted a cigarette (we all like to pose a little now and then), and sat down on the bed to await my capture. I might have stalked my enemies through the dark house, and possibly have nabbed them; but most likely I would simply have succeeded in getting myself shot. And I don't like to be shot.

The girl found me.

She came creeping up the hall, an automatic in each hand, hesitated for an instant outside the door, and then came in on the jump. And when she saw me sitting peacefully on the side of the bed, her eyes snapped scornfully at me, as if I had done something mean. I suppose she thought I should have given her an opportunity to shoot.

"I got him, Tai," she called, and the Chinese joined us.

"What did Hook do with the bonds?" he asked point blank.

I grinned into his round yellow face and led my ace.

"Why don't you ask the girl?"

His face showed nothing, but I imagined that his fat body stiffened a little within its fashionable British clothing. That encouraged me, and I went on with my little lie that was meant to stir things up.

"Haven't you rapped to it," I asked, "that they were fixing up to ditch you?"

"You dirty liar!" the girl screamed, and took a step toward me.

Tai halted her with an imperative gesture. He stared through her with his opaque black eyes, and as he stared the blood slid out of his face. She had this fat yellow man on her string, right enough, but he wasn't exactly a harmless toy.

"So that's how it is?" he said slowly, to no one in particular. Then to me: "Where did they put the bonds?"

The girl went close to him and her words came out tumbling over each other:

"Here's the truth of it, Tai, so help me God! I switched the stuff myself. Hook wasn't in it. I was going to run out on both of you. I stuck them under the couch downstairs, but they're not there now. That's the God's truth!"

He was eager to believe her, and her words had the ring of truth to them. And I knew that—in love with her as he was—he'd more readily forgive her treachery with the bonds than he would forgive her for planning to run off with Hook; so I made haste to stir things up again.

"Part of that is right enough," I said. "She did stick the bonds under the couch—but Hook was in on it. They fixed it up between them while you were upstairs. He was to pick a fight with you, and during the argument she was to make the switch, and that is exactly what they did."

I had him! As she wheeled savagely toward me, he stuck the muzzle of an automatic in her side—a smart jab that checked the angry words she was hurling at me.

"I'll take your guns, Elvira," he said, and took them.

"Where are the bonds now?" he asked me.

I grinned. "I'm not with you, Tai. I'm against you."

"I don't like violence," he said slowly, "and I believe you are a sensible person. Let us traffic, my friend."

"You name it," I suggested.

"Gladly! As a basis for our bargaining, we will stipulate that you have hidden the bonds where they cannot be found by anyone else; and that I have you completely in my power, as the shilling shockers used to have it."

"Reasonable enough," I said; "go on."

"The situation, then, is what gamblers call a standoff. Neither of us has the advantage. As a detective, you want us; but we have you. As thieves, we want the bonds; but you have them. I offer you the girl in exchange for the bonds, and that seems to me an equitable offer. It will give me the bonds and a chance to get away. It will give you no small degree of success in your task as a detective. Hook is dead. You will have the girl. All that will remain is to find me and the bonds again—by no means a hopeless task. You will have turned a defeat into half a victory, with an excellent chance to make it a complete one."

"How do I know that you'll give me the girl?"

He shrugged. "Naturally, there can be no guarantee. But, knowing that she planned to desert me for the swine who lies dead below, you can't imagine that my feelings for her are the most friendly. Too, if I take her with me, she will want a share in the loot."

I turned the lay-out over in my mind.

"This is the way it looks to me," I told him at last. "You aren't a killer. I'll come through alive no matter what happens. All right, why should I swap? You and the girl will be easier to find again than the bonds, and they are the most important part of the job anyway. I'll hold on to them, and take my chances on finding you folks again. Yes, I'm playing it safe."

"No, I'm not a killer," he said, very softly; and he smiled the first smile I had seen on his face. It wasn't a pleasant smile: and there was something in it that made you want to shudder. "But I am other things, perhaps, of which you haven't thought. But this talking is to no purpose. Elvira!"

The girl came obediently forward.

"You will find sheets in one of the bureau drawers," he told her. "Tear one or two of them into strips strong enough to tie up our friend securely."

The girl went to the bureau. I wrinkled my head, trying to find a not too disagreeable answer to the question in my mind. The answer that came first wasn't nice: *torture.*

Then a faint sound brought us all into tense motionlessness.

The room we were in had two doors: one leading into the hall, the other into another bedroom. It was through the hall door that the faint sound had come—the sound of creeping feet.

Swiftly, silently, Tai moved backward to a position from which he could watch the hall door without losing sight of the girl and me—and the gun poised like a live thing in his fat hand was all the warning we needed to make no noise.

The faint sound again, just outside the door.

The gun in Tai's hand seemed to quiver with eagerness.

Through the other door—the door that gave to the next room—popped Mrs. Quarre, an enormous cocked revolver in her thin hand.

"Let it go, you nasty heathen," she screeched.

Tai dropped his pistol before he turned to face her, and he held his hands up high—all of which was very wise.

Thomas Quarre came through the hall door then; he also held a cocked revolver—the mate of his wife's—though, in front of his bulk, his didn't look so enormously large.

I looked at the old woman again, and found little of the friendly fragile one who had poured tea and chatted about the neighbors. This was a witch if there ever was one—a witch of the blackest, most malignant sort. Her little faded eyes were sharp with ferocity, her withered lips were taut in a wolfish snarl, and her thin body fairly quivered with hate.

"I knew it," she was shrilling. "I told Tom as soon as we got far enough away to think things over. I knew it was a frame-up! I knew this supposed detective was a pal of yours! I knew it was just a scheme to beat Thomas and me out of our shares! Well, I'll show you, you yellow monkey! Where are them bonds? Where are they?"

The Chinese had recovered his poise, if he had ever lost it.

"Our stout friend can tell you perhaps," he said. "I was about to extract the information from him when you so—ah—dramatically arrived."

"Thomas, for goodness sakes don't stand there dreaming," she snapped at her husband, who to all appearances was still the same mild old man who had given me an excellent cigar. "Tie up this Chinaman! I don't trust him an inch, and I won't feel easy until he's tied up."

I got up from my seat on the side of the bed, and moved cautiously to a spot that I thought would be out of the line of fire if the thing I expected happened.

Tai had dropped the gun that had been in his hand, but he hadn't been searched. The Chinese are a thorough people; if one of them carries a gun at all, he usually carries two or three or more. One gun had been taken from Tai, and if they tried to truss him up without frisking him, there was likely to be fireworks. So I moved to one side.

Fat Thomas Quarre went phlegmatically up to the Chinese to carry out his wife's orders—and bungled the job perfectly.

He put his bulk between Tai and the old woman's gun.

Tai's hands moved. An automatic was in each.

Once more Tai ran true to racial form. When a Chinese shoots he keeps on until his gun is empty.

When I yanked Tai over backward by his fat throat, and slammed him to the floor, his guns were still barking metal; and they clicked empty as I got a knee on one of his arms. I didn't take any chances. I worked on his throat until his eyes and tongue told me that he was out of things for a while. Then I looked around.

Thomas Quarre was against the bed, plainly dead, with three round holes in his starched white vest.

Across the room, Mrs. Quarre lay on her back. Her clothes had somehow settled in place around her fragile body, and death had given her once more the gentle friendly look she had worn when I first saw her.

The red-haired girl Elvira was gone.

Presently Tai stirred, and after taking another gun from his clothes, I helped him sit up. He stroked his bruised throat with one fat hand and looked coolly around the room.

"Where's Elvira?" he asked.

"Got away—for the time being."

He shrugged. "Well, you can call it a decidedly successful operation. The Quarres and Hook dead; the bonds and I in your hands."

"Not so bad," I admitted, "but will you do me a favor?"

"If I may."

"Tell me what the hell this is all about!"

"All about?" he asked.

"Exactly! From what you people have let me overhear, I gather that you pulled some sort of job in Los Angeles that netted you a hundred-thousand-dollars' worth of bonds; but I can't remember any recent job of that size down there."

"Why, that's preposterous!" he said with what, for him, was almost wild-eyed amazement. "Preposterous! Of course you know all about it!"

"I do not! I was trying to find a young fellow named Fisher who left his Tacoma home in anger a week or two ago. His father wants him found on the quiet, so that he can come down and try to talk him into going home again. I was told that I might find Fisher in this block of Turk Street, and that's what brought me here."

He didn't believe me. He never believed me. He went to the gallows thinking me a liar.

When I got out into the street again (and Turk Street was a lovely place when I came free into it after my evening in that house!) I bought a newspaper that told me most of what I wanted to know.

A boy of twenty—a messenger in the employ of a Los Angeles stock and bond house—had disappeared two days before, while on his way to a bank with a wad of bonds. That same night this boy and a slender girl with bobbed red hair had registered at a hotel in Fresno as *J. M. Riordan and wife.* The next morning the boy had been found in his room—murdered. The girl was gone. The bonds were gone.

That much the paper told me. During the next few days, digging up a little here and a little there, I succeeded in piecing together most of the story.

The Chinese—whose full name was Tai Choon Tau—had been the brains of the mob. Their game had been a variation of the always-reliable badger game. Tai would pick out some youth who was messenger or runner for a banker or broker—one who carried either cash or negotiable securities in large quantities.

The girl Elvira would then *make* this lad, get him all fussed up over her—which shouldn't have been very hard for her—and then lead him gently around to running away with her and whatever he could grab in the way of his employer's bonds or currency.

Wherever they spent the first night of their flight, there Hook would appear—foaming at the mouth and loaded for bear. The girl would plead and tear her hair and so forth, trying to keep Hook—in his rôle of irate husband—from butchering the youth. Finally she would succeed, and in the end the youth would find himself without either girl or the fruits of his thievery.

Sometimes he had surrendered to the police. Two we found had committed suicide. The Los Angeles lad had been built of tougher stuff than the others. He had put up a fight, and Hook had had to kill him. You can measure the girl's skill in her end of the game by the fact that not one of the half dozen youths who had been trimmed had said the least thing to implicate her; and some of them had gone to great trouble to keep her out of it.

The house in Turk Street had been the mob's retreat, and, that it might be always a safe one, they had not worked their game in San Francisco. Hook and the girl were supposed by the neighbors to be the Quarres' son and daughter—and Tai was the Chinese cook. The Quarres' benign and respectable appearances had also come in handy when the mob had securities to be disposed of.

The Chinese went to the gallows. We threw out the widest and finest-meshed of dragnets for the red-haired girl; and we turned up girls with bobbed red hair by the scores. But the girl Elvira was not among them.

I promised myself that some day . . .

DOROTHY L. SAYERS
(1893-1957)

Dorothy Leigh Sayers was born in England, in East Anglia, and was one of the first women to obtain a degree at Oxford, where she studied medieval literature. She became an advertising copywriter and, in 1923, began writing mystery novels about a gentleman-scholar, Lord Peter Wimsey, who is called upon to solve crimes taking place within his aristocratic set. *Whose Body?* was followed by *Clouds of Witness* (1926), in which Wimsey clears his brother's name, and *Strong Poison* (1930), in which he saves from the gallows a young detective-fiction writer named Harriet Vane, whom he then woos and wins in *Gaudy Night* (1935) as she works to solve a series of crimes at the fictional Shrewsbury College, Oxford, which is her alma mater. The debonair Lord Peter, complete with monocle and trusty valet Bunter, also appeared in seven other novels as well as in several volumes of short stories before Sayers gave up mysteries to return to medieval studies. Her other contribution to detective fiction was the editing of several collections of detective stories, under the general title of *The Omnibus of Crime,* with an influential introductory essay on the theory and history of the genre.

"The Adventurous Exploit of the Cave of Ali Baba" is typical Sayers in its playful treatment of the detective process (the far-fetched premise, for example) and literary allusions (as in the title) and in its considerable narrative verve and the suspense created by bizarre juxtapositions (the danse macabre as fox trot, the communications by carrier pigeon and voice-activated machine).

THE ADVENTUROUS EXPLOIT OF THE CAVE OF ALI BABA

In the front room of a grim and narrow house in Lambeth a man sat eating kippers and glancing through the *Morning Post.* He was smallish and spare, with brown hair rather too regularly waved and a strong, brown beard, cut to a point. His double-breasted suit of navy-blue and his socks, tie, and handkerchief, all scrupulously matched, were a trifle more point-device than the best taste approves, and his boots were slightly too bright a brown. He did not look a gentleman, not even a gentleman's gentleman, yet there was something about his appearance which suggested that he was accustomed to the manner of life in good families. The breakfast-table, which he had set with his own hands, was arrayed with the attention to detail which is exacted of good-class servants. His action, as he walked over to a little side-table and carved himself a plate of ham, was the action of a superior butler; yet he was not old enough to be a retired butler; a footman, perhaps, who had come into a legacy.

He finished the ham with good appetite, and, as he sipped his coffee, read through attentively a paragraph which he had already noticed and put aside for consideration.

> "LORD PETER WIMSEY'S WILL
> BEQUEST TO VALET
> £10,000 TO CHARITIES
>
> "The will of Lord Peter Wimsey, who was killed last December while shooting big game in Tanganyika, was proved yesterday at £500,000. A sum of £10,000 was left to various

charities, including [here followed a list of bequests]. To his valet, Mervyn Bunter, was left an annuity of £500 and the lease of the testator's flat in Piccadilly. [Then followed a number of personal bequests.] The remainder of the estate, including the valuable collection of books and pictures at 110a Piccadilly, was left to the testator's mother, the Dowager Duchess of Denver.

"Lord Peter Wimsey was thirty-seven at the time of his death. He was the younger brother of the present Duke of Denver, who is the wealthiest peer in the United Kingdom. Lord Peter was distinguished as a criminologist and took an active part in the solution of several famous mysteries. He was a well-known book collector and man-about-town."

The man gave a sigh of relief.

"No doubt about that," he said aloud. "People don't give their money away if they're going to come back again. The blighter's dead and buried right enough. I'm free."

He finished his coffee, cleared the table, and washed up the crockery, took his bowler hat from the hall-stand, and went out.

A bus took him to Bermondsey. He alighted, and plunged into a network of gloomy streets, arriving after a quarter of an hour's walk at a seedy-looking public-house in a low quarter. He entered and called for a double whisky.

The house had only just opened, but a number of customers, who had apparently been waiting on the doorstep for this desirable event, were already clustered about the bar. The man who might have been a footman reached for his glass, and in doing so jostled the elbow of a flash person in a check suit and regrettable tie.

"Here!" expostulated the flash person, "What d'yer mean by it? We don't want your sort here. Get out!"

He emphasised his remarks with a few highly coloured words, and a violent push in the chest.

"Bar's free to everybody, isn't it?" said the other, returning the shove with interest.

"Now then!" said the barmaid, "none o' that. The gentleman didn't do it intentional, Mr. Jukes."

"Didn't he?" said Mr. Jukes. "Well, I *did.*"

"And you ought to be ashamed of yourself," retorted the young lady, with a toss of the head. "I'll have no quarrelling in my bar—not this time in the morning."

"It was quite an accident," said the man from Lambeth. "I'm not one to make a disturbance, having always been used to the best houses. But if any gentleman *wants* to make trouble—"

"All right, all right," said Mr. Jukes, more pacifically. "I'm not keen to give you a new face. Not but what any alteration wouldn't be for the better. Mind your manners another time, that's all. What'll you have?"

"No, no," protested the other, "this one must be on me. Sorry I pushed you. I didn't mean it. But I didn't like to be taken up so short."

"Say no more about it," said Mr. Jukes generously. "I'm standing this. Another double whisky, miss, and one of the usual. Come over here where there isn't so much of a crowd, or you'll be getting yourself into trouble again."

He led the way to a small table in the corner of the room.

"That's all right," said Mr. Jukes. "Very nicely done. I don't think there's any danger here, but you can't be too careful. Now, what about it, Rogers. Have you made up your mind to come in with us?"

"Yes," said Rogers, with a glance over his shoulder, "yes, I have. That is, mind you, if everything seems all right. I'm not looking for trouble, and I don't want to get let in for any dangerous games. I don't mind giving you information, but it's understood as I take no active part in whatever goes on. Is that straight?"

"You wouldn't be allowed to take an active part if you wanted to," said Mr. Jukes. "Why, you poor fish. Number One wouldn't have anybody but experts on his jobs. All you have to do is let us know where the stuff is and how to get it. The Society does the rest. It's some organisation, I can tell you. You won't even know who's doing it, or how it's done. You won't know anybody, and nobody will know you—except Number One, of course. He knows everybody."

"And you," said Rogers.

"And me, of course. But I shall be transferred to another district. We shan't meet again after to-day, except at the general meetings, and then we shall all be masked."

"Go on!" said Rogers incredulously.

"Fact. You'll be taken to Number One—he'll see you, but you won't see him. Then, if he thinks you're any good, you'll be put on the roll, and after that you'll be told where to make your reports to. There is a divisional meeting called once a fortnight, and every three months there's a general meeting and share-out. Each member is called up by number and has his whack handed over to him. That's all."

"Well, but suppose two members are put on the same job together?"

"If it's a daylight job, they'll be so disguised their mothers wouldn't know 'em. But it's mostly night work."

"I see. But, look here—what's to prevent somebody following me home and giving me away to the police?"

"Nothing, of course. Only I wouldn't advise him to try it, that's all. The last man who had that bright idea was fished out of the river down Rotherhithe way, before he had time to get his precious report in. Number One knows everybody, you see."

"Oh!—and who is this Number One?"

"There's lots of people would give a good bit to know that."

"Does nobody know?"

"Nobody. He's a fair marvel, is Number One. He's a gentleman, I can tell you that, and a pretty high-up one, from his ways. *And* he's got eyes all round his head. *And* he's got an arm as long as from here to Australia. *But* nobody knows anything about him, unless it's Number Two, and I'm not even sure about her."

"There are women in it, then?"

"You can bet your boots there are. You can't do a job without 'em nowadays. But that needn't worry you. The women are safe enough. They don't want to come to a sticky end, no more than you and me."

"But, look here, Jukes—how about the money? It's a big risk to take. Is it worth it?"

"Worth it?" Jukes leant across the little marble-topped table and whispered.

"Coo!" gasped Rogers. "And how much of that would I get, now?"

"You'd share and share alike with the rest, whether you'd been in that particular job or not. There's fifty members, and you'd get one-fiftieth, same as Number One and same as me."

"Really? No kidding?"

"See that wet, see that dry!" Jukes laughed. "Say, can you beat it? There's never been anything like it. It's the biggest thing ever been known. He's a great man, is Number One."

"And do you pull off many jobs?"

"Many? Listen. You remember the Carruthers necklace, and the Gorleston Bank robbery? And the Faversham burglary? And the big

Rubens that disappeared from the National Gallery? And the Frensham pearls? All done by the Society. And never one of them cleared up."

Rogers licked his lips.

"But now, look here," he said cautiously. "Supposing I was a spy, as you might say, and supposing I was to go straight off and tell the police about what you've been saying?"

"Ah," said Jukes, "suppose you did, eh? Well, supposing something nasty didn't happen to you on the way there—which I wouldn't answer for, mind—"

"Do you mean to say you've got me watched?"

"You can bet your sweet life we have. Yes. Well, *supposing* nothing happened on the way there, and you was to bring the slops to this pub, looking for yours truly—"

"Yes?"

"You wouldn't find me, that's all. I should have gone to Number Five."

"Who's Number Five?"

"Ah! I don't know. But he's the man that makes you a new face while you wait. Plastic surgery, they call it. And new finger-prints. New everything. We go in for up-to-date methods in our show."

Rogers whistled.

"Well, how about it?" asked Jukes, eyeing his acquaintance over the rim of his tumbler.

"Look here—you've told me a lot of things. Shall I be safe if I say 'no'?"

"Oh yes—if you behave yourself and don't make trouble for us."

"H'm, I see. And if I say 'yes'?"

"Then you'll be a rich man in less than no time, with money in your pocket to live like a gentleman. And nothing to do for it, except to tell us what you know about the houses you've been to when you were in service. It's money for jam if you act straight by the Society."

Rogers was silent, thinking it over.

"I'll do it!" he said at last.

"Good for you. Miss! The same again, please. Here's to it, Rogers! I knew you were one of the right sort the minute I set eyes on you. Here's to money for jam, and take care of Number One! Talking of Number One, you'd better come round and see him to-night. No time like the present."

"Right you are. Where'll I come to? Here?"

"Nix. No more of this little pub for us. It's a pity, because it's nice and comfortable, but it can't be helped. Now, what you've got to do is this. At ten o'clock to-night exactly, you walk north across Lambeth Bridge" (Rogers winced at this intimation that his abode was known), "and you'll see a yellow taxi standing there, with the driver doing something to his engine. You'll say to him, 'Is your bus fit to go?' and he'll say, 'Depends where you want to go to.' And you'll say, 'Take me to Number One, London.' There's a shop called that, by the way, but he won't take you there. You won't know where he *is* taking you, because the taxi-windows will be covered up, but you mustn't mind that. It's the rule for the first visit. Afterwards, when you're regularly one of us, you'll be told the name of the place. And when you get there, do as you're told and speak the truth, because, if you don't, Number One will deal with you. See?"

"I see."

"Are you game? You're not afraid?"

"Of course I'm not afraid."

"Good man! Well, we'd better be moving now. And I'll say good-bye, because we shan't see each other again. Good-bye—and good luck!"

"Good-bye."

They passed through the swing-doors, and out into the mean and dirty street.

The two years subsequent to the enrolment of the ex-footman Rogers in a crook society were marked by a number of startling and successful raids on the houses of distinguished people. There was the theft of the great diamond tiara from the Dowager Duchess of Denver; the burglary at the flat formerly occupied by the late Lord Peter Wimsey, resulting in the disappearance of £7,000 worth of silver and gold plate; the burglary at the country mansion of Theodore Winthrop, the millionaire—which, incidentally, exposed that thriving gentleman as a confirmed Society blackmailer and caused a reverberating scandal in Mayfair; and the snatching of the famous eight-string necklace of pearls from the neck of the Marchioness of Dinglewood during the singing of the Jewel Song in *Faust* at Covent Garden. It is true that the pearls turned out to be imitation, the original string having been pawned by the noble lady under circumstances highly painful to the Marquis, but the coup was nevertheless a sensational one.

On a Saturday afternoon in January, Rogers was sitting in his room in Lambeth, when a slight noise at the front door caught his ear. He sprang up almost before it had ceased, dashed through the small hallway, and flung the door open. The street was deserted. Nevertheless, as he turned back to the sitting-room, he saw an envelope lying on the hat-stand. It was addressed briefly to "Number Twenty-one." Accustomed by this time to the somewhat dramatic methods used by the Society to deliver its correspondence, he merely shrugged his shoulders, and opened the note.

It was written in cipher, and, when transcribed, ran thus:

> "Number Twenty-one,—An Extraordinary General Meeting will be held to-night at the house of Number One at 11:30. You will be absent at your peril. The word is FINALITY."

Rogers stood for a little time considering this. Then he made his way to a room at the back of the house, in which there was a tall safe, built into the wall. He manipulated the combination and walked into the safe, which ran back for some distance, forming, indeed, a small strongroom. He pulled out a drawer marked "Correspondence," and added the paper he had just received to the contents.

After a few moments he emerged, re-set the lock to a new combination, and returned to the sitting-room.

"Finality," he said. "Yes—I think so." He stretched out his hand to the telephone—then appeared to alter his mind.

He went upstairs to an attic, and thence climbed into a loft close under the roof. Crawling among the rafters, he made his way into the farthest corner: then carefully pressed a knot on the timber-work. A concealed trap-door swung open. He crept through it, and found himself in the corresponding loft of the next house. A soft cooing noise greeted him as he entered. Under the skylight stood three cages, each containing a carrier pigeon.

He glanced cautiously out of the skylight, which looked out upon a high blank wall at the back of some factory or other. There was nobody in the dim little courtyard, and no window within sight. He drew his head in again, and, taking a small fragment of thin paper from his pocketbook, wrote a few letters and numbers upon it. Going to the nearest cage, he took out the pigeon and attached the message to its wing. Then he carefully set the bird on the window-ledge. It hesitated a moment, shifted its pink feet a few times, lifted its wings, and was gone. He saw it tower up into the already darkening sky over the factory roof and vanish into the distance.

He glanced at his watch and returned downstairs. An hour later he released the second pigeon, and in another hour the third. Then he sat down to wait.

At half-past nine he went up to the attic again. It was dark, but a few frosty stars were shining, and a cold air blew through the open window. Something pale gleamed faintly on the floor. He picked it up—it was warm and feathery. The answer had come.

He ruffled the soft plumes and found the paper. Before reading it, he fed the pigeon and put it into one of the cages. As he was about to fasten the door, he checked himself.

"If anything happens to me," he said, "there's no need for you to starve to death, my child."

He pushed the window a little wider open and went downstairs again. The paper in his hand bore only the two letters, "O.K." It seemed to have been written hurriedly, for there was a long smear of ink in the upper left-hand corner. He noted this with a smile, put the paper in the fire, and, going out into the kitchen, prepared and ate a hearty meal of eggs and corned beef from a new tin. He ate it without bread, though there was a loaf on the shelf near at hand, and washed it down with water from the tap, which he let run for some time before venturing to drink it. Even then he carefully wiped the tap, both inside and outside, before drinking.

When he had finished, he took a revolver from a locked drawer, inspecting the mechanism with attention to see that it was in working order, and loaded it with new cartridges from an unbroken packet. Then he sat down to wait again.

At a quarter before eleven, he rose and went out into the street. He walked briskly, keeping well away from the wall, till he came out into a well-lighted thoroughfare. Here he took a bus, securing the corner seat next the conductor, from which he could see everybody who got on and off. A succession of buses eventually brought him to a respectable residential quarter of Hampstead. Here he alighted and, still keeping well away from the walls, made his way up to the Heath.

The night was moonless, but not altogether black, and, as he crossed a deserted part of the Heath, he observed one or two other dark forms closing in upon him from various directions. He paused in the shelter of a large tree, and adjusted to his face a black velvet mask, which covered him from brow to chin. At its base the number 21 was clearly embroidered in white thread.

At length a slight dip in the ground disclosed one of those agreeable villas which stand, somewhat isolated, among the rural surroundings of the Heath. One of the windows was lighted. As he made his way to the door, other dark figures, masked like himself, pressed forward and surrounded him. He counted six of them.

The foremost man knocked on the door of the solitary house. After a moment, it was opened slightly. The man advanced his head to the opening; there was a murmur, and the door opened wide. The man stepped in, and the door was shut.

When three of the men had entered, Rogers found himself to be the next in turn. He knocked, three times loudly, then twice faintly. The door opened to the extent of two or three inches, and an ear was presented to the chink. Rogers whispered "Finality." The ear was withdrawn, the door opened, and he passed in.

Without any further word of greeting, Number Twenty-one passed into a small room on the left, which was furnished like an office, with a desk, a safe, and a couple of chairs. At the desk sat a massive man in evening dress, with a ledger before him. The new arrival shut the door carefully after him; it clicked to, on a spring lock. Advancing to the desk, he announced, "Number Twenty-one, sir," and stood respectfully waiting. The big man looked up, showing the number 1 startingly white on his velvet mask. His eyes, of a curious hard blue, scanned Rogers attentively. At a sign from him, Rogers removed his mask. Having verified his identity with care, the President said, "Very well, Number Twenty-one," and made an entry in the ledger. The voice was hard and metallic, like his eyes. The close scrutiny from behind the immovable black mask seemed to make Rogers uneasy; he shifted his feet, and his eyes fell. Number One made a sign of dismissal, and Rogers, with a faint sigh as though of relief, replaced his mask and left the room. As he came out, the next comer passed in in his place.

The room in which the Society met was a large one, made by knocking the two largest of the first-floor rooms into one. It was furnished in the standardised taste of twentieth-century suburbia and brilliantly lighted. A gramophone in one corner blared out a jazz tune, to which about ten couples of masked men and women were dancing, some in evening dress and others in tweeds and jumpers.

In one corner of the room was an American bar. Rogers went up and asked the masked man in charge for a double whisky. He consumed it slowly, leaning on the bar. The room filled. Presently somebody moved across to the gramophone and stopped it. He looked round. Number One had appeared on the threshold. A tall woman in black stood beside him. The mask, embroidered with a white 2, covered hair and face completely; only her fine bearing and her white arms and bosom and the dark eyes shining through the eye-slits proclaimed her a woman of power and physical attraction.

"Ladies and gentlemen." Number One was standing at the upper end of the room. The woman sat beside him; her eyes were cast down and betrayed nothing, but her hands were clenched on the arms of the chair and her whole figure seemed tensely aware.

"Ladies and gentlemen. Our numbers are two short to-night." The masks moved; eyes were turned, seeking and counting. "I need not inform you of the disastrous failure of our plan for securing the plans of the Court-Windlesham helicopter. Our courageous and devoted comrades, Number Fifteen and Number Forty-eight, were betrayed and taken by the police."

An uneasy murmur arose among the company.

"It may have occurred to some of you that even the well-known steadfastness of these comrades might give way under examination. There is no cause for alarm. The usual orders have been issued, and I have this evening received the report that their tongues have been effectually silenced. You will, I am sure, be glad to know that these two brave men have been spared the ordeal of so great a temptation to dishonour, and that they will not be called upon to face a public trial and the rigours of a long imprisonment."

A hiss of intaken breath moved across the assembled members like the wind over a barley-field.

"Their dependants will be discreetly compensated in the usual manner. I call upon Numbers Twelve and Thirty-four to undertake this agreeable task. They will attend me in my office for their instructions after the meeting. Will the Numbers I have named kindly signify that they are able and willing to perform this duty?"

Two hands were raised in salute. The President continued, looking at his watch:

"Ladies and gentlemen, please take your partners for the next dance."

The gramophone struck up again. Rogers turned to a girl near him in a red dress. She nodded, and they slipped into the movement of a fox-trot. The couples gyrated solemnly and in silence. Their shadows were flung against the blinds as they turned and stepped to and fro.

"What has happened?" breathed the girl in a whisper, scarcely moving her lips. "I'm frightened, aren't you? I feel as if something awful was going to happen."

"It does take one a bit short, the President's way of doing things," agreed Rogers, "but it's safer like that."

"Those poor men—"

A dancer, turning and following on their heels, touched Rogers on the shoulder.

"No talking, please," he said. His eyes gleamed sternly; he twirled his partner into the middle of the crowd and was gone. The girl shuddered.

The gramophone stopped. There was a burst of clapping. The dancers again clustered before the President's seat.

"Ladies and gentlemen. You may wonder why this extraordinary meeting has been called. The reason is a serious one. The failure of our recent attempt was no accident. The police were not on the premises that night by chance. We have a traitor among us."

Partners who had been standing close together fell distrustfully apart. Each member seemed to shrink, as a snail shrinks from the touch of a finger.

"You will remember the disappointing outcome of the Dinglewood affair," went on the President, in his harsh voice. "You may recall other smaller matters which have not turned out satisfactorily. All these troubles have been traced to their origin. I am happy to say that our minds can now be easy. The offender has been discovered and will be removed. There will be no more mistakes. The misguided member who introduced the traitor to our Society will be placed in a position where his lack of caution will have no further ill-effects. There is no cause for alarm."

Every eye roved about the company, searching for the traitor and his unfortunate sponsor. Somewhere beneath the black masks a face must have turned white; somewhere under the stifling velvet there must have been a brow sweating, not with the heat of the dance. But the masks hid everything.

"Ladies and gentlemen, please take your partners for the next dance."

The gramophone struck into an old and half-forgotten tune: "There ain't nobody loves me." The girl in red was claimed by a tall mask in evening dress. A hand laid on Rogers's arm made him start.

A small, plump woman in a green jumper slipped a cold hand into his. The dance went on.

When it stopped, amid the usual applause, everyone stood, detached, stiffened in expectation. The President's voice was raised again.

"Ladies and gentlemen, please behave naturally. This is a dance, not a public meeting."

Rogers led his partner to a chair and fetched her an ice. As he stopped over her, he noticed the hurried rise and fall of her bosom.

"Ladies and gentlemen." The endless interval was over. "You will no doubt wish to be immediately relieved from suspense. I will name the persons involved. Number Thirty-seven!"

A man sprang up with a fearful, strangled cry.

"Silence!"

The wretch choked and gasped.

"I never—I swear I never—I'm innocent."

"Silence. You have failed in discretion. You will be dealt with. If you have anything to say in defence of your folly, I will hear it later. Sit down."

Number Thirty-seven sank down upon a chair. He pushed his handkerchief under the mask to wipe his face. Two tall men closed in upon him. The rest fell back, feeling the recoil of humanity from one stricken by mortal disease.

The gramophone struck up.

"Ladies and gentlemen, I will now name the traitor. Number Twenty-one, stand forward."

Rogers stepped forward. The concentrated fear and loathing of forty-eight pairs of eyes burned upon him. The miserable Jukes set up a fresh wail.

"Oh, my God! Oh, my God!"

"Silence! Number Twenty-one, take off your mask." The traitor pulled the thick covering from his face. The intense hatred of the eyes devoured him.

"Number Thirty-seven, this man was introduced here by you, under the name of Joseph Rogers, formerly second footman in the service of the Duke of Denver, dismissed for pilfering. Did you take steps to verify that statement?"

"I did—I did! As God's my witness, it was all straight. I had him identified by two of the servants. I made enquiries. The tale was straight—I'll swear it was."

The President consulted a paper before him, then he looked at his watch again.

"Ladies and gentlemen, please take your partners . . ."

Number Twenty-one, his arms twisted behind him and bound, and his wrists handcuffed, stood motionless, while the dance of doom circled about him. The clapping, as it ended, sounded like the clapping of the men and women who sat, thirsty-lipped, beneath the guillotine.

"Number Twenty-one, your name has been given as Joseph Rogers, footman, dismissed for theft. Is that your real name?"

"No."

"What is your name?"

"Peter Death Bredon Wimsey."

"We thought you were dead."

"Naturally. You were intended to think so."

"What has become of the genuine Joseph Rogers?"

"He died abroad. I took his place. I may say that no real blame attaches to your people for not having realised who I was. I not only took Rogers's place; I *was* Rogers. Even when I was alone, I walked like Rogers, I sat like Rogers, I read Rogers's books, and wore Rogers's clothes. In the end, I almost thought Rogers's thoughts. The only way to keep up a successful impersonation is never to relax."

"I see. The robbery of your own flat was arranged?"

"Obviously."

"The robbery of the Dowager Duchess, your mother, was connived at by you?"

"It was. It was a very ugly tiara—no real loss to anybody with decent taste. May I smoke, by the way?"

"You may not. Ladies and gentlemen . . ."

The dance was like the mechanical jigging of puppets. Limbs jerked, feet faltered. The prisoner watched with an air of critical detachment.

"Numbers Fifteen, Twenty-two, and Forty-nine. You have watched the prisoner. Has he made any attempts to communicate with anybody?"

"None." Number Twenty-two was the spokesman. "His letters and parcels have been opened, his telephone tapped, and his movements followed. His water-pipes have been under observation for Morse signals."

"You are sure of what you say?"

"Absolutely."

"Prisoner, have you been alone in this adventure? Speak the truth, or things will be made somewhat more unpleasant for you than they might otherwise be."

"I have been alone. I have taken no unnecessary risks."

"It may be so. It will, however, be as well that steps should be taken to silence the man at Scotland Yard—what is his name?—Parker. Also the prisoner's manservant, Mervyn Bunter, and possibly also his mother and sister. The brother is a stupid oaf, and not, I think, likely to have been taken into the prisoner's confidence. A precautionary watch will, I think, meet the necessities of his case."

The prisoner appeared, for the first time, to be moved.

"Sir, I assure you that my mother and sister know nothing which could possibly bring danger on the Society."

"You should have thought of their situation earlier. Ladies and gentlemen, please take—"

"No—no!" Flesh and blood could endure the mockery no longer. "No! Finish with him. Get it over. Break up the meeting. It's dangerous. The police—"

"Silence!"

The President glanced round at the crowd. It had a dangerous look about it. He gave way.

"Very well. Take the prisoner away and silence him. He will receive Number 4 treatment. And be sure you explain it to him carefully first."

"Ah!"

The eyes expressed a wolfish satisfaction. Strong hands gripped Wimsey's arms.

"One moment—for God's sake, let me die decently."

"You should have thought this over earlier. Take him away. Ladies and gentlemen, be satisfied—he will not die quickly."

"Stop! Wait!" cried Wimsey desperately. "I have something to say. I don't ask for life—only for a quick death. I—I have something to sell."

"To sell?"

"Yes."

"We make no bargains with traitors."

"No—but listen! Do you think I have not thought of this? I am not so mad. I have left a letter."

"Ah! now it is coming. A letter. To whom?"

"To the police. If I do not return to-morrow—"

"Well?"

"The letter will be opened."

"Sir," broke in Number Fifteen. "This is bluff. The prisoner has not sent any letter. He has been strictly watched for many months."

"Ah! but listen. I left the letter before I came to Lambeth."

"Then it can contain no information of value."

"Oh, but it does."

"What?"

"The combination of my safe."

"Indeed? Has this man's safe been searched?"

"Yes, sir."

"What did it contain?"

"No information of importance, sir. An outline of our organisation—the name of this house—nothing that cannot be altered and covered before morning."

Wimsey smiled.

"Did you investigate the inner compartment of the safe?"

There was a pause.

"You hear what he says," snapped the President sharply. "Did you find this inner compartment?"

"There was no inner compartment, sir. He is trying to bluff."

"I hate to contradict you," said Wimsey, with an effort at his ordinary pleasant tone, "but I really think you must have overlooked the inner compartment."

"Well," said the President, "and what do you say is in this inner compartment, if it does exist?"

"The names of every member of this Society, with their addresses, photographs, and finger-prints."

"What?"

The eyes round him now were ugly with fear. Wimsey kept his face steadily turned towards the President.

"How do you say you have contrived to get this information?"

"Well, I have been doing a little detective work on my own, you know."

"But you have been watched."

"True. The finger-prints of my watchers adorn the first page of the collection."

"This statement can be proved?"

"Certainly. I will prove it. The name of Number Fifty, for example—"

A fierce muttering arose. The President silenced it with a gesture.

"If you mention names here, you will certainly have no hope of mercy. There is a fifth treatment—kept specially for people who mention names. Bring the prisoner to my office. Keep the dance going."

The President took an automatic from his hip-pocket and faced his tightly fettered prisoner across the desk.

"Now speak!" he said.

"I should put that thing away, if I were you," said Wimsey contemptuously. "It would be a much pleasanter form of death than treatment Number 5, and I might be tempted to ask for it."

"Ingenious," said the President, "but a little too ingenious. Now, be quick; tell me what you know."

"Will you spare me if I tell you?"

"I make no promises. Be quick."

Wimsey shrugged his bound and aching shoulders.

"Certainly. I will tell you what I know. Stop me when you have heard enough."

He leaned forward and spoke low. Overhead the noise of the gramophone and the shuffling of feet bore witness that the dance was going on. Stray passers-by crossing the Heath noted that the people in the lonely house were making a night of it again.

"Well," said Wimsey, "am I to go on?"

From beneath the mask the President's voice sounded as though he were grimly smiling.

"My lord," he said, "your story fills me with regret that you are not, in fact, a member of our Society. Wit, courage, and industry are valuable to an association like ours. I fear I cannot persuade you? No—I supposed not."

He touched a bell on his desk.

"Ask the members kindly to proceed to the supper-room," he said to the mask who entered.

The "supper-room" was on the ground-floor, shuttered and curtained. Down its centre ran a long, bare table, with chairs set about it.

"A Barmecide feast,* I see," said Wimsey pleasantly. It was the

* In *The Arabian Nights,* a Barmecide feast was an imaginary banquet; a table was lavishly set to torment a hungry man.

first time he had seen this room. At the far end, a trap-door in the floor gaped ominously.

The President took the head of the table.

"Ladies and gentlemen," he began, as usual—and the foolish courtesy had never sounded so sinister—"I will not conceal from you the seriousness of the situation. The prisoner has recited to me more than twenty names and addresses which were thought to be unknown, except to their owners and to me. There has been great carelessness"—his voice rang harshly—"which will have to be looked into. Finger-prints have been obtained—he has shown me the photographs of some of them. How our investigators came to overlook the inner door of this safe is a matter which calls for enquiry."

"Don't blame them," put in Wimsey. "It was meant to be overlooked, you know. I made it like that on purpose."

The President went on, without seeming to notice the interruption.

"The prisoner informs me that the book with the names and addresses is to be found in this inner compartment, together with certain letters and papers stolen from the houses of members, and numerous objects bearing authentic finger-prints. I believe him to be telling the truth. He offers the combination of the safe in exchange for a quick death. I think the offer should be accepted. What is your opinion, ladies and gentlemen?"

"The combination is known already," said Number Twenty-two.

"Imbecile! This man has told us, and has proved to me, that he is Lord Peter Wimsey. Do you think he will have forgotten to alter the combination? And then there is the secret of the inner door. If he disappears to-night and the police enter his house—"

"I say," said a woman's rich voice, "that the promise should be given and the information used—and quickly. Time is getting short."

A murmur of agreement went round the table.

"You hear," said the President, addressing Wimsey. "The Society offers you the privilege of a quick death in return for the combination of the safe and the secret of the inner door."

"I have your word for it?"

"You have."

"Thank you. And my mother and sister?"

"If you in your turn will give us your word—you are a man of honour—that these women know nothing that could harm us, they shall be spared."

"Thank you, sir. You may rest assured, upon my honour, that they know nothing. I should not think of burdening any woman with such dangerous secrets—particularly those who are dear to me."

"Very well. It is agreed—yes?"

The murmur of assent was given, though with less readiness than before.

"Then I am willing to give you the information you want. The word of the combination is UNRELIABILITY."

"And the inner door?"

"In anticipation of the visit of the police, the inner door—which might have presented difficulties—is open."

"Good! You understand that if the police interfere with our messenger—"

"That would not help me, would it?"

"It is a risk," said the President thoughtfully, "but a risk which I think we must take. Carry the prisoner down to the cellar. He can amuse himself by contemplating apparatus Number 5. In the meantime, Numbers Twelve and Forty-six—"

"No, no!"

A sullen mutter of dissent arose and swelled threateningly.

"No," said a tall man with a voice like treacle. "No—why should any members be put in possession of this evidence? We have found one traitor among us to-night and more than one fool. How are we to know that Numbers Twelve and Forty-six are not fools and traitors also?"

The two men turned savagely upon the speaker, but a girl's voice struck into the discussion, high and agitated.

"Hear, hear! That's right, I say. How about us? We ain't going to have our names read by somebody we don't know nothing about. I've had enough of this. They might sell the 'ole lot of us to the narks."

"I agree," said another member. "Nobody ought to be trusted, nobody at all."

The President shrugged his shoulders.

"Then what, ladies and gentlemen, do you suggest?"

There was a pause. Then the same girl shrilled out again:

"I say Mr. President oughter go himself. He's the only one as knows all the names. It won't be no cop to him. Why should we take all the risk and trouble and him sit at home and collar the money? Let him go himself, that's what I say."

A long rustle of approbation went round the table.

"I second that motion," said a stout man who wore a bunch of gold seals at his fob. Wimsey smiled as he looked at the seals; it was that trifling vanity which had led him directly to the name and address of the stout man, and he felt a certain affection for the trinkets on that account.

The President looked round.

"It is the wish of the meeting, then, that I should go?" he said, in an ominous voice.

Forty-five hands were raised in approbation. Only the woman known as Number Two remained motionless and silent, her strong white hands clenched on the arm of the chair.

The President rolled his eyes slowly round the threatening ring till they rested upon her.

"Am I to take it that this vote is unanimous?" he enquired.

The woman raised her head.

"Don't go," she gasped faintly.

"You hear," said the President, in a faintly derisive tone. "This lady says, don't go."

"I submit that what Number Two says is neither here nor there," said the man with the treacly voice. "Our own ladies might not like us to be going, if they were in madam's privileged position." His voice was an insult.

"Hear, hear!" cried another man. "This is a democratic society, this is. We don't want no privileged classes."

"Very well," said the President. "You hear, Number Two. The feeling of the meeting is against you. Have you any reasons to put forward in favour of your opinion?"

"A hundred. The President is the head and soul of our Society. If anything should happen to him—where should we be? You"—she swept the company magnificently with her eyes—"you have all blundered. We have your carelessness to thank for all this. Do you think we should be safe for five minutes if the President were not here to repair your follies?"

"Something in that," said a man who had not hitherto spoken.

"Pardon my suggesting," said Wimsey maliciously, "that, as the lady appears to be in a position peculiarly favourable for the reception of the President's confidences, the contents of my modest volume will probably be no news to her. Why should not Number Two go herself?"

"Because I say she must not," said the President sternly, checking the quick reply that rose to his companion's lips. "If it is the will of the meeting, I will go. Give me the key of the house."

One of the men extracted it from Wimsey's jacket pocket and handed it over.

"Is the house watched?" he demanded of Wimsey.

"No."

"That is the truth?"

"It is the truth."

The President turned at the door.

"If I have not returned in two hours' time," he said, "act for the best to save yourselves, and do what you like with the prisoner. Number Two will give orders in my absence."

He left the room. Number Two rose from her seat with a gesture of command.

"Ladies and gentlemen. Supper is now considered over. Start the dancing again."

Down in the cellar the time passed slowly, in the contemplation of apparatus Number 5. The miserable Jukes, alternately wailing and raving, at length shrieked himself into exhaustion. The four members guarding the prisoners whispered together from time to time.

"An hour and a half since the President left," said one.

Wimsey glanced up. Then he returned to his examination of the room. There were many curious things in it, which he wanted to memorise.

Presently the trap-door was flung open. "Bring him up!" cried a voice. Wimsey rose immediately, and his face was rather pale.

The members of the gang were again seated round the table. Number Two occupied the President's chair, and her eyes fastened on Wimsey's face with a tigerish fury, but when she spoke it was with a self-control which roused his admiration.

"The President has been two hours gone," she said. "What has happened to him? Traitor twice over—what has happened to him?"

"How should I know?" said Wimsey. "Perhaps he has looked after Number One and gone while the going was good!"

She sprang up with a little cry of rage, and came close to him.

"Beast! liar!" she said, and struck him on the mouth. "You know he would never do that. He is faithful to his friends. What have you done with him? Speak—or I will make you speak. You two, there—bring the irons. He *shall* speak!"

"I can only form a guess, Madame," replied Wimsey, "and I shall not guess any the better for being stimulated with hot irons, like Pantaloon at the circus. Calm yourself, and I will tell you what I think. I think—indeed, I greatly fear—that Monsieur le President in his hurry to examine the interesting exhibits in my safe may, quite inadvertently, no doubt, have let the door of the inner compartment close behind him. In which case—"

He raised his eyebrows, his shoulders being too sore for shrugging, and gazed at her with a limpid and innocent regret.

"What do you mean?"

Wimsey glanced round the circle.

"I think," he said, "I had better begin from the beginning by explaining to you the mechanism of my safe. It is rather a nice safe," he added plaintively. "I invented the idea myself—not the principle of its working, of course; that is a matter for scientists—but just the idea of the thing.

"The combination I gave you is perfectly correct as far as it goes. It is a three-alphabet thirteen-letter lock by Bunn & Fishett—a very good one of its kind. It opens the outer door, leading into the ordinary strong-room, where I keep my cash and my Froth Blower's cuff-links and all that. But there is an inner compartment with two doors, which open in a quite different manner. The outermost of these two inner doors is merely a thin steel skin, painted to look like the back of the safe and fitting closely, so as not to betray any join. It lies in the same plane as the wall of the room, you understand, so that if you were to measure the outside and the inside of the safe you would discover no discrepancy. It opens outwards with an ordinary key, and, as I truly assured the President, it was left open when I quitted my flat."

"Do you think," said the woman sneeringly, "that the President is so simple as to be caught in a so obvious trap? He will have wedged open that inner door undoubtedly."

"Undoubtedly, madame. But the sole purpose of that outer inner door, if I may so express myself, is to appear to be the only inner door. But hidden behind the hinge of that door is another door, a sliding panel, set so closely in the thickness of the wall that you would hardly see it unless you knew it was there. This door was also left open. Our revered Number One had nothing to do but to walk straight through into the inner compartment of the safe, which, by the way, is built into the chimney of the old basement kitchen, which runs up the house at that point. I hope I make myself clear?"

"Yes, yes—get on. Make your story short."

Wimsey bowed, and, speaking with even greater deliberation than ever, resumed:

"Now, this interesting list of the Society's activities, which I have had the honour of compiling, is written in a very large book—bigger, even, than Monsieur le President's ledger which he uses downstairs. (I trust, by the way, madame, that you have borne in mind the necessity of putting that ledger in a safe place. Apart from the risk of investigation by some officious policeman, it would be inadvisable that any junior member of the Society should get hold of it. The feeling of the meeting would, I fancy, be opposed to such an occurrence.)"

"It is secure," she answered hastily. "*Mon dieu!* get on with your story."

"Thank you—you have relieved my mind. Very good. This big book lies on a steel shelf at the back of the inner compartment. Just a moment. I have not described this inner compartment to you. It is six feet high, three feet wide, and three feet deep. One can stand up in it quite comfortably, unless one is very tall. It suits me nicely—as you may see, I am not more than five feet eight and a half. The President has the advantage of me in height; he might be a little cramped, but there would be room for him to squat if he grew tired of standing. By the way, I don't know if you know it, but you have tied me up rather tightly."

"I would have you tied till your bones were locked together. Beat him, you! He is trying to gain time."

"If you beat me," said Wimsey, "I'm damned if I'll speak at all. Control yourself, madame; it does not do to move hastily when your king is in check."

"Get on!" she cried again, stamping with rage.

"Where was I? Ah! the inner compartment. As I say, it is a little snug—the more so that it is not ventilated in any way. Did I mention that the book lay on a steel shelf?"

"You did."

"Yes. The steel shelf is balanced on a very delicate concealed spring. When the weight of the book—a heavy one, as I said—is lifted, the shelf rises almost imperceptibly. In rising it makes an electrical contact. Imagine to yourself, madame; our revered President steps in—propping the false door open behind him—he sees the book—quickly he snatches it up. To make sure that it is the right one, he opens it—he studies the pages. He looks about for the other objects I have mentioned, which bear the marks of fingerprints. And silently, but very, very quickly—you can imagine it, can you not?—the secret panel, released by the rising of the shelf, leaps across like a panther behind him. Rather a trite simile, but apt, don't you think?"

"My God! oh, my God!" Her hand went up as though to tear the choking mask from her face. "You—you devil—devil! What is the word that opens the inner door? Quick! I will have it torn out of you—the word!"

"It is not a hard word to remember, madame—though it has been forgotten before now. Do you recollect, when you were a child, being told the tale of 'Ali Baba and the Forty Thieves'? When I had that door made, my mind reverted, with rather a pretty touch of sentimentality, in my opinion, to the happy hours of my childhood. The words that open the door are—'Open Sesame.' "

"Ah! How long can a man live in this devil's trap of yours?"

"Oh," said Wimsey cheerfully, "I should think he might hold out a few hours if he kept cool and didn't use up the available oxygen by shouting and hammering. If we went there at once, I dare say we should find him fairly all right."

"I shall go myself. Take this man and—do your worst with him. Don't finish him till I come back. I want to see him die!"

"One moment," said Wimsey, unmoved by this amiable wish. "I think you had better take me with you."

"Why—why?"

"Because, you see, I'm the only person who can open the door."

"But you have given me the word. Was that a lie?"

"No—the word's all right. But, you see, it's one of these new-style electric doors. In fact, it's really the very latest thing in doors. I'm rather proud of it. It opens to the words 'Open Sesame' all right—*but to my voice only.*"

"Your voice? I will choke your voice with my own hands. What do you mean—your voice only?"

"Just what I say. Don't clutch my throat like that, or you may alter my voice so that the door won't recognise it. That's better. It's apt to be rather pernickety about voices. It got stuck up for a week once, when I had a cold and could only implore it in a hoarse whisper. Even in the ordinary way, I sometimes have to try several times before I hit on the exact right intonation."

She turned and appealed to a short, thick-set man standing beside her.

"Is this true? Is it possible?"

"Perfectly, ma'am, I'm afraid," said the man civilly. From his voice Wimsey took him to be a superior workman of some kind—probably an engineer.

"Is it an electrical device? Do you understand it?"

"Yes, ma'am. It will have a microphone arrangement somewhere, which converts the sound into a series of vibrations controlling an electric needle. When the needle has traced the correct pattern, the circuit is completed and the door opens. The same thing can be done by light vibrations equally easily."

"Couldn't you open it with tools?"

"In time, yes, ma'am. But only by smashing the mechanism, which is probably well protected."

"You may take that for granted," interjected Wimsey reassuringly.

She put her hands to her head.

"I'm afraid we're done in," said the engineer, with a kind of respect in his tone for a good job of work.

"No—wait! Somebody must know—the workmen who made this thing?"

"In Germany," said Wimsey briefly.

"Or—yes, yes, I have it—a gramophone. This—this—*he*—shall be made to say the word for us. Quick—how can it be done?"

"Not possible, ma'am. Where should we get the apparatus at half-past three on a Sunday morning? The poor gentleman would be dead long before—"

There was a silence, during which the sounds of the awakening day came through the shuttered windows. A motor-horn sounded distantly.

"I give in," she said. "We must let him go. Take the ropes off him. You will free him, won't you?" she went on, turning piteously to Wimsey. "Devil as you are, you are not such a devil as that! You will go straight back and save him!"

"Let him go, nothing!" broke in one of the men. "He doesn't go to preach to the police, my lady, don't you think it. The President's done in, that's all, and we'd all better make tracks while we can. It's all up, boys. Chuck this fellow down the cellar and fasten him in, so he can't make a row and wake the place up. I'm going to destroy the ledgers. You can see it done if you don't trust me. And you, Thirty, you know where the switch is. Give us a quarter of an hour to clear, and then you can blow the place to glory."

"No! You can't go—you can't leave him to die—your President—your leader—my—I won't let it happen. Set this devil free. Help me, one of you, with the ropes—"

"None of that, now," said the man who had spoken before. He caught her by the wrists, and she twisted, shrieking, in his arms, biting and struggling to get free.

"Think, think," said the man with the treacly voice. "It's getting on to morning. It'll be light in an hour or two. The police may be here any minute."

"The police!" She seemed to control herself by a violent effort. "Yes, yes, you are right. We must not imperil the safety of all for the sake of one man. *He* himself would not wish it. That is so. We will put this carrion in the cellar where it cannot harm us, and depart, every one to his own place, while there is time."

"And the other prisoner?"

"He? Poor fool—he can do no harm. He knows nothing. Let him go," she answered contemptuously.

In a few minutes' time Wimsey found himself bundled unceremoniously into the depths of the cellar. He was a little puzzled. That they should refuse to let him go, even at the price of Number One's life, he could understand. He had taken the risk with his eyes open. But that they should leave him as a witness against them seemed incredible.

The men who had taken him down strapped his ankles together and departed, switching the lights out as they went.

"Hi! Kamerad!" said Wimsey. "It's a bit lonely sitting here. You might leave the light on."

"It's all right, my friend," was the reply. "You will not be in the dark long. They have set the time-fuse."

The other man laughed with rich enjoyment, and they went out together. So that was it. He was to be blown up with the house. In that case the President would certainly be dead before he was extricated. This worried Wimsey; he would rather have been able to bring the big crook to justice. After all, Scotland Yard had been waiting six years to break up this gang.

He waited, straining his ears. It seemed to him that he heard footsteps over his head. The gang had all crept out by this time. . . .

There was certainly a creak. The trap-door had opened; he felt, rather than heard, somebody creeping into the cellar.

"Hush!" said a voice in his ear. Soft hands passed over his face, and went fumbling about his body. There came the cold touch of steel on his wrists. The ropes slackened and dropped off. A key clicked in the handcuffs. The strap about his ankles was unbuckled.

"Quick! quick! they have set the time-switch. The house is mined. Follow me as fast as you can. I stole back—I said I had left my jewelry. It was true. I left it on purpose. *He* must be saved—only you can do it. Make haste."

Wimsey, staggering with pain, as the blood rushed back into his bound and numbed arms, crawled after her into the room above. A moment, and she had flung back the shutters and thrown the window open.

"Now go! Release him! You promise?"

"I promise. And I warn you, madame, that this house is surrounded. When my safe-door closed it gave a signal which sent my servant to Scotland Yard. Your friends are all taken—"

"Ah! But you go—never mind me—quick! The time is almost up."

"Come away from this!"

He caught her by the arm, and they went running and stumbling across the little garden. An electric torch shone suddenly in the bushes.

"That you, Parker?" cried Wimsey. "Get your fellows away. Quick! the house is going up in a minute."

The garden seemed suddenly full of shouting, hurrying men. Wimsey, floundering in the darkness, was brought up violently against the wall. He made a leap at the coping, caught it, and hoisted himself up. His hands groped for the woman; he swung her up beside him. They jumped; everyone was jumping; the woman caught her foot and fell with a gasping cry. Wimsey tried to stop himself, tripped over a stone, and came down headlong. Then, with a flash and a roar, the night went up in fire.

Wimsey picked himself painfully out from among the débris of the garden wall. A faint moaning near him proclaimed that his companion was still alive. A lantern was turned suddenly upon them.

"Here you are!" said a cheerful voice. "Are you all right, old thing? Good lord! What a hairy monster!"

"All right," said Wimsey. "Only a bit winded. Is the lady safe? H'm—arm broken, apparently—otherwise sound. What's happened?"

"About half a dozen of 'em got blown up; the rest we've bagged." Wimsey became aware of a circle of dark forms in the wintry dawn. "Good Lord, what a day! What a come-back for a public character! You old stinker—to let us go on for two years thinking you were dead! I bought a bit of black for an arm-band. I did, really. Did anybody know, besides Bunter?"

"Only my mother and sister. I put it in a secret trust—you know, the thing you send to executors and people. We shall have an awful time with the lawyers, I'm afraid, proving I'm me. Hullo! Is that friend Sugg?"

"Yes, my lord," said Inspector Sugg, grinning and nearly weeping with excitement. "Damned glad to see your lordship again. Fine piece of work, your lordship. They're all wanting to shake hands with you, sir."

"Oh, Lord! I wish I could get washed and shaved first. Awfully glad to see you all again, after two years' exile in Lambeth. Been a good little show, hasn't it?"

"Is he safe?"

Wimsey started at the agonised cry.

"Good Lord!" he cried. "I forgot the gentleman in the safe. Here, fetch a car, quickly. I've got the great big top Moriarty of the whole bunch quietly asphyxiating at home. Here—hop in, and put the lady in too. I promised we'd get back and save him—though" (he finished the sentence in Parker's ear) "there may be murder charges too, and I wouldn't give much for his chance at the Old Bailey. Whack her up. He can't last much longer shut up there. He's the bloke you've been wanting, the man at the back of the Morrison case and the Hope-Wilmington case, and hundreds of others."

The cold morning had turned the streets grey when they drew up before the door of the house in Lambeth. Wimsey took the woman by the arm and helped her out. The mask was off now, and showed her face, haggard and desperate, and white with fear and pain.

"Russian, eh?" whispered Parker in Wimsey's ear.

"Something of the sort. Damn! the front door's blown shut, and the blighter's got the key with him in the safe. Hop through the window, will you?"

Parker bundled obligingly in, and in a few seconds threw open the door to them. The house seemed very still. Wimsey led the way to the back room, where the strong-room stood. The outer door and the second door stood propped open with chairs. The inner door faced them like a blank green wall.

"Only hope he hasn't upset the adjustment with thumping at it," muttered Wimsey. The anxious hand on his arm clutched feverishly. He pulled himself together, forcing his tone to one of cheerful commonplace.

"Come on, old thing," he said, addressing himself conversationally to the door. "Show us your paces. Open Sesame, confound you. Open Sesame!"

The green door slid suddenly away into the wall. The woman sprang forward and caught in her arms the humped and senseless thing that rolled out from the safe. Its clothes were torn to ribbons, and its battered hands dripped blood.

"It's all right," said Wimsey, "it's all right! He'll live—to stand his trial."

AGATHA CHRISTIE
(1890–1976)

Agatha Christie, née Miller was born in Devon, England, studied to be a singer, and took up writing mysteries between hospital duties in World War I. Her first novel, *The Mysterious Affair at Styles* (1920), featured the diminutive Belgian detective Hercule Poirot, of the waxed mustache and busy "little grey cells," who appeared in dozens of novels—most notably *The Murder of Roger Ackroyd* (1926) and *Murder on the Orient Express* (1934)—before his last performance in *Curtain* (1975). A second detective, the village spinster Jane Marple, was introduced in *The Murder at the Vicarage* (1930) and appeared in a number of short stories and novels over the next decades. Most of Christie's stories are set in English country houses but some have exotic settings that reflect her travels with her second husband, archaeologist Max Mallowan, on Mideastern expeditions. No other detective story writer has approached her in worldwide popularity; her books, which number over eighty, are said to be second in sales only to the Bible, and her mystery play *The Mousetrap* (1952) has had a run of three decades. She was made a Dame Commander, Order of the British Empire, in 1971.

"The Blue Geranium," which illustrates "armchair detection" in that the detective arrives at the solution entirely on the basis of reported information, is typical of Golden Age fiction in its "cozy" setting (it is from a series called *The Tuesday Club Murders* in which a group of friends meet regularly to match wits at solving murder cases), its unusual murder, its playful tone (Miss Marple described as "the typical old maid of fiction"), and, above all, its observance of "fair play" in giving the reader the key clue pointing to the murderer before the final revelation.

THE BLUE GERANIUM

"When I was down here last year—" said Sir Henry Clithering, and stopped.

His hostess, Mrs. Bantry, looked at him curiously.

The ex-Commissioner of Scotland Yard was staying with old friends of his, Colonel and Mrs. Bantry, who lived near St. Mary Mead.

Mrs. Bantry, pen in hand, had just asked his advice as to who should be invited to make a sixth guest at dinner that evening.

"Yes?" said Mrs. Bantry encouragingly. "When you were here last year?"

"Tell me," said Sir Henry, "do you know a Miss Marple?"

Mrs. Bantry was surprised. It was the last thing she had expected.

"Know Miss Marple? Who doesn't! The typical old maid of fiction. Quite a dear, but hopelessly behind the times. Do you mean you would like me to ask her to dinner?"

"You are surprised?"

"A little, I must confess. I should hardly have thought you—but perhaps there's an explanation?"

"The explanation is simple enough. When I was down here last year we got into the habit of discussing unsolved mysteries—there were five or six of us. We each supplied a story to which we knew the answer, but nobody else did. It was supposed to be an exercise in the deductive faculties—to see who could get nearest the truth."

"Well?"

"Like in the old story—we hardly realized that Miss Marple was playing; but we were very polite about it—didn't want to hurt the old dear's feelings. And now comes the cream of the jest. The old lady outdid us every time!"

"But how extraordinary! Why, dear old Miss Marple has hardly ever been out of St. Mary Mead."

"Ah! But according to her, that has given her unlimited opportunities of observing human nature—under the microscope, as it were."

"I suppose there's something in that," conceded Mrs. Bantry. "One would at least know the petty side of people. But I don't think we have any really exciting criminals in our midst. I think we must try her with Arthur's ghost story after dinner. I'd be thankful if she'd find a solution to that."

"I didn't know that Arthur believed in ghosts?"

"Oh, he doesn't. That's what worries him so. And it happened to a friend of his, George Pritchard—a most prosaic person. It's really rather tragic for poor George. Either this extraordinary story is true—or else—"

"Or else what?"

Mrs. Bantry did not answer. After a minute or two she said irrelevantly:

"You know, I like George—everyone does. One can't believe that he—but people do do such extraordinary things."

Sir Henry nodded. He knew, better than Mrs. Bantry, the extraordinary things that people did.

So it came about that that evening Mrs. Bantry looked around her dinner table (shivering a little as she did so, because the dining room, like most English dining rooms, was extremely cold) and fixed her gaze on the very upright old lady sitting on her husband's right. Miss Marple wore black lace mittens; an old lace fichu was draped round her shoulders and another piece of lace surmounted her white hair. She was talking animatedly to the elderly doctor, Dr. Lloyd, about the workhouse and the suspected shortcomings of the district nurse.

Mrs. Bantry marvelled anew. She even wondered whether Sir Henry had been making an elaborate joke—but there seemed no point in that. Incredible that what he had said could be really true.

Her glance went on and rested affectionately on her red-faced broad-shouldered husband as he sat talking horses to Jane Helier, the beautiful and popular actress. Jane, more beautiful (if that were possible) off the stage than on, opened enormous blue eyes and murmured at discreet intervals, "Really?" "Oh, fancy!" "How extraordinary!" She knew nothing whatever about horses and cared less.

"Arthur," said Mrs. Bantry, "you're boring poor Jane to distraction. Leave your horses alone and tell her your ghost story instead. You know . . . George Pritchard."

"Eh, Dolly? Oh, but I don't know—"

"Sir Henry wants to hear it too. I was telling him something about it this morning. It would be interesting to hear what everyone has to say about it."

"Oh, do!" said Jane. "I love ghost stories."

"Well—" Colonel Bantry hesitated. "I've never believed much in the supernatural. But this . . .

"I don't think any of you know George Pritchard. He's one of the best. His wife—well, she's dead now, poor woman. I'll just say this much: she didn't give George any too easy a time when she was alive. She was one of those semi-invalids—I believe she really had something wrong with her, but whatever it was, she played it for all it was worth. She was capricious, exacting, unreasonable. She complained from morning to night. George was expected to wait on her hand and foot, and everything he did was always wrong."

"She was a dreadful woman," said Mrs. Bantry with conviction.

"I don't quite know how this business started. George was rather vague about it. I gather Mrs. Pritchard had always had a weakness for fortunetellers, palmists, clairvoyants—anything of that sort. George didn't mind. If she found amusement in it, well and good. But he refused to go into rhapsodies himself, and that was another grievance.

"A succession of hospital nurses was always passing through the house, Mrs. Pritchard usually becoming dissatisfied with them after a few weeks. One young nurse had been very keen on this fortunetelling stunt, and for a time Mrs. Pritchard had been very fond of her. Then she suddenly fell out with her and insisted on her going. She had back another nurse who had been with her previously—an older woman, experienced and tactful in dealing with a neurotic patient. Nurse Copling, according to George, was a very good sort—a sensible woman to talk to. She put up with Mrs. Pritchard's tantrums and nerve storms with complete indifference.

"Mrs. Pritchard always lunched upstairs, and it was usual at lunch time for George and the nurse to come to some arrangement for the afternoon. Strictly speaking, the nurse went off from two to four, but 'to oblige,' as the phrase goes, she would sometimes take her time off after tea if George wanted to be free for the afternoon. On this occasion she mentioned that she was going to see a sister at Golders Green and might be a little late returning. George's face fell, for he had arranged to play a round of golf. Nurse Copling, however, reassured him.

" 'We'll neither of us be missed, Mr. Pritchard.' A twinkle came into her eye. 'Mrs. Pritchard's going to have more exciting company than ours.'

" 'Who's that?'

" 'Wait a minute.' Nurse Copling's eyes twinkled more than ever. 'Let me get it right. *Zarida, Psychic Reader of the Future.*'

" 'That's a new one, isn't it?' groaned George.

" 'Quite new. I believe my predecessor, Nurse Carstairs, sent her along. Mrs. Pritchard hasn't seen her yet. She made me write, fixing an appointment for this afternoon.'

" 'Well, at any rate, I shall get my golf,' said George, and he went off with the kindliest feelings toward Zarida, the reader of the future.

"On his return to the house, he found Mrs. Pritchard in a state of great agitation. She was, as usual, lying on her invalid couch, and she had a bottle of smelling salts in her hand which she sniffed at frequent intervals.

" 'George,' she exclaimed, 'what did I tell you about this house? The moment I came into it, I felt there was something wrong! Didn't I tell you so at the time?'

"Repressing his desire to reply, 'You always do,' George said, 'No, can't say I remember it.'

" 'You never do remember anything that has to do with me. Men are all extraordinarily callous—but I really believe that you are even more insensitive than most.'

" 'Oh, come now, Mary dear, that's not fair.'

" 'Well, as I was telling you, this woman knew at once! She—she actually blenched—if you know what I mean—as she came in at that door, and she said, "There is evil here—evil and danger. I feel it." '

"Very unwisely George laughed.

" 'Well, you have had your money's worth this afternoon.'

"His wife closed her eyes and took a long sniff from her smelling bottle.

" 'How you hate me! You would jeer and laugh if I were dying.'

"George protested, and after a minute or two she went on.

" 'You may laugh, but I shall tell you the whole thing. This house is definitely dangerous to me—the woman said so.'

"George's formerly kind feeling toward Zarida underwent a change. He knew his wife was perfectly capable of insisting on moving to a new house if the caprice got hold of her.

" 'What else did she say?' he asked.

" 'She couldn't tell me very much. She was so upset. One thing she did say. I had some violets in a glass. She pointed at them and cried out:

" ' "Take those away. No blue flowers—never have blue flowers. Blue flowers are fatal to you—remember that."

" 'And you know,' added Mrs. Pritchard, 'I always have told you that blue as a colour is repellent to me. I feel a natural instinctive sort of warning against it.'

"George was much too wise to remark that he had never heard her say so before. Instead he asked what the mysterious Zarida was like. Mrs. Pritchard entered with gusto upon a description.

" 'Black hair in coiled knobs over her ears—her eyes were half closed—great black rims round them—she had a black veil over her mouth and chin—she spoke in a kind of singing voice with a marked foreign accent—Spanish, I think—'

" 'In fact, all the usual stock in trade,' said George cheerfully.

"His wife immediately closed her eyes.

" 'I feel extremely ill,' she said. 'Ring for Nurse. Unkindness upsets me, as you know only too well.'

"It was two days later that Nurse Copling came to George with a grave face.

" 'Will you come to Mrs. Pritchard, please. She has had a letter which upsets her greatly.'

"He found his wife with the letter in her hand. She held it out to him.

" 'Read it,' she said.

"George read it. It was on heavily scented paper, and the writing was big and black.

> I have seen the Future. Be warned before it is too late. Beware of the full moon. The Blue Primrose means Warning; the Blue Hollyhock means Danger; the Blue Geranium means Death. . . .

"Just about to burst out laughing, George caught Nurse Copling's eye. She made a quick warning gesture. He said rather awkwardly, 'The woman's probably trying to frighten you, Mary. Anyway, there aren't such things as blue primroses and blue geraniums.'

"But Mrs. Pritchard began to cry and say her days were numbered. Nurse Copling came out with George upon the landing.

" 'Of all the silly tomfoolery,' he burst out.

" 'I suppose it is.'

"Something in the nurse's tone struck him, and he stared at her in amazement.

" 'Surely, Nurse, you don't believe—'

" 'No, no, Mr. Pritchard. I don't believe in reading the future—that's nonsense. What puzzles me is the meaning of this. Fortunetellers are usually out for what they can get. But this woman seems to be frightening Mrs. Pritchard with no advantage to herself. I can't see the point. There's another thing—'

" 'Yes?'

" 'Mrs. Pritchard says that something about Zarida was faintly familiar to her.'

" 'Well?'

" 'Well, I don't like it, Mr. Pritchard, that's all.'

" 'I didn't know you were so superstitious, Nurse.'

" 'I'm not superstitious, but I know when a thing is fishy.'

"It was about four days after this that the first incident happened. To explain it to you, I shall have to describe Mrs. Pritchard's room—"

"You'd better let me do that," interrupted Mrs. Bantry. "It was papered with one of these new wallpapers where you apply clumps of flowers to make a kind of herbaceous border. The effect is almost like being in a garden—though, of course, the flowers are all wrong. I mean they simply couldn't be in bloom all at the same time—"

"Don't let a passion for horticultural accuracy run away with you, Dolly," said her husband. "We all know you're an enthusiastic gardener."

"Well, it is absurd," protested Mrs. Bantry. "To have bluebells and daffodils and lupins and hollyhocks and Michaelmas daisies all grouped together."

"Most unscientific," said Sir Henry. "But to proceed with the story . . ."

"Well, among these massed flowers were primroses, clumps of

yellow and pink primroses, and—oh, go on, Arthur, this is your story."

Colonel Bantry took up the tale.

"Mrs. Pritchard rang her bell violently one morning. The household came running—thought she was in extremis; not at all. She was violently excited and pointing at the wallpaper, and there, sure enough, was one blue primrose in the midst of the others . . ."

"Oh!" said Miss Helier, "how creepy!"

"The question was: Hadn't the blue primrose always been there? That was George's suggestion and the nurse's. But Mrs. Pritchard wouldn't have it at any price. She had never noticed it till that very morning, and the night before had been full moon. She was very upset about it."

"I met George Pritchard that same day and he told me about it," said Mrs. Bantry. "I went to see Mrs. Pritchard and did my best to ridicule the whole thing, but without success. I came away really concerned, and I remember I met Jean Instow and told her about it. Jean is a queer girl. She said, 'So she's really upset about it?' I told her that I thought the woman was perfectly capable of dying of fright—she was really abnormally superstitious.

"I remember Jean rather startled me with what she said next. She said, 'Well, that might be all for the best, mightn't it?' And she said it so coolly, in so matter-of-fact a tone, that I was really—well, shocked. Of course I know it's done nowadays—to be brutal and outspoken, but I never get used to it. Jean smiled at me rather oddly and said, 'You don't like my saying that—but it's true. What use is Mrs. Pritchard's life to her? None at all, and it's hell for George Pritchard. To have his wife frightened out of existence would be the best thing that could happen to him.' I said, 'George is most awfully good to her always.' And she said, 'Yes, he deserves a reward, poor dear. He's a very attractive person, George Pritchard. The last nurse thought so—the pretty one—what was her name? Carstairs. That was the cause of the row between her and Mrs. P.'

"Now I didn't like hearing Jean say that. Of course, one had wondered—"

Mrs. Bantry paused significantly.

"Yes, dear," said Miss Marple placidly. "One always does. Is Miss Instow a pretty girl? I suppose she plays golf?"

"Yes. She's good at all games. And she's nice-looking, attractive-looking, very fair with a healthy skin and nice steady blue eyes. Of course, we always have felt that she and George Pritchard—I mean, if things had been different—they are so well suited to one another."

"And they were friends?" asked Miss Marple.

"Oh yes. Great friends."

"Do you think, Dolly," said Colonel Bantry plaintively, "that I might be allowed to go on with my story?"

"Arthur," said Mrs. Bantry resignedly, "wants to get back to his ghosts."

"I had the rest of the story from George himself," went on the colonel. "There's no doubt that Mrs. Pritchard got the wind up badly toward the end of the next month. She marked off on a calendar the day when the moon would be full, and on that night she had both the nurse and then George into her room and made them study the wallpaper carefully. There were pink hollyhocks and red ones, but there were no blue among them. Then when George left the room she locked the door—"

"And in the morning there was a large blue hollyhock," said Miss Helier joyfully.

"Quite right," said Colonel Bantry. "Or at any rate, nearly right. One flower of a hollyhock just above her head had turned blue. It staggered George, and of course, the more it staggered him the more he refused to take the thing seriously. He insisted that the whole thing was some kind of a practical joke. He ignored the evidence of the locked door and the fact that Mrs. Pritchard discovered the change before anyone—even Nurse Copling—was admitted.

"It staggered George, and it made him unreasonable. His wife wanted to leave the house, and he wouldn't let her. He was inclined to believe in the supernatural for the first time, but he wasn't going to admit it. He usually gave in to his wife, but this time he wouldn't. Mary was not to make a fool of herself, he said. The whole thing was the most infernal nonsense.

"And so the next month sped away. Mrs. Pritchard made less protest than one would have imagined. I think she was superstitious enough to believe that she couldn't escape her fate. She repeated again and again: 'The blue primrose—warning. The blue hollyhock—danger. The blue geranium—death.' And she would lie looking at the clump of pinky-red geraniums nearest her bed.

"The whole business was pretty nervy. Even the nurse caught the infection. She came to George two days before full moon and begged him to take Mrs. Pritchard away. George was angry.

" 'If all the flowers on that wall turned into blue devils, it couldn't kill anyone!' he shouted.

" 'It might. Shock has killed people before now.'

" 'Nonsense,' said George.

"George has always been a shade pigheaded. You can't drive him. I believe he had a secret idea that his wife worked the changes herself and that it was all some morbid, hysterical plan of hers.

"Well, the fatal night came. Mrs. Pritchard locked her door as usual. She was very calm—in almost an exalted state of mind. The nurse was worried by her state—and wanted to give her a stimulant, an injection of strychnine, but Mrs. Pritchard refused. In a way, I believe, she was enjoying herself. George said she was."

"I think that's quite possible," said Mrs. Bantry. "There must have been a strange sort of glamour about the whole thing."

"There was no violent ringing of a bell the next morning. Mrs. Pritchard usually woke about eight. When, at eight-thirty, there was no sign from her, Nurse rapped loudly on the door. Getting no reply, she fetched George and insisted on the door being broken open. They did so with the help of a chisel.

"One look at the still figure on the bed was enough for Nurse Copling. She sent George to telephone for the doctor, but it was too late. Mrs. Pritchard, he said, must have been dead at least eight hours. Her smelling salts lay by her hand on the bed, and on the wall beside her one of the pinky-red geraniums was a bright deep blue."

"Horrible," said Miss Helier with a shiver.

Sir Henry was frowning.

"No additional details?"

Colonel Bantry shook his head, but Mrs. Bantry spoke quickly.

"The gas."

"What about the gas?" asked Sir Henry.

"When the doctor arrived there was a slight smell of gas, and sure enough, he found the gas ring in the fireplace very slightly turned on, but so little that it couldn't have mattered."

"Did Mr. Pritchard and the nurse not notice it when they first went in?"

"The nurse said she did notice a slight smell. George said he didn't notice gas, but something made him feel very queer and overcome; but he put that down to shock—and probably it was. At any rate, there was no question of gas poisoning. The smell was scarcely noticeable."

"And that's the end of the story?"

"No, it isn't. One way and another, there was a lot of talk. The servants, you see, had overheard things—had heard, for instance, Mrs. Pritchard telling her husband that he hated her and would jeer if she were dying. And also more recent remarks. She said one day, apropos of his refusing to leave the house, 'Very well. When I am dead, I hope everyone will realize that you have killed me.' And as ill luck would have it, he had been mixing some weed killer for the garden paths the very day before. One of the younger servants had seen him and had afterward seen him taking up a glass of hot milk to his wife.

"The talk spread and grew. The doctor had given a certificate—I don't know exactly in what terms—shock, syncope, heart failure, probably some medical term meaning nothing much. However, the poor lady had not been a month in her grave before an exhumation order was applied for and granted."

"And the result of the autopsy was nil, I remember," said Sir Henry gravely. "A case, for once, of smoke without fire."

"The whole thing is really very curious," said Mrs. Bantry. "That fortuneteller, for instance—Zarida. At the address where she was supposed to be, no one had ever heard of any such person!"

"She appeared once—out of the blue," said her husband, "and then utterly vanished. Out of the blue—that's rather good!"

"And what is more," continued Mrs. Bantry, "little Nurse Carstairs, who was supposed to have recommended her, had never even heard of her."

They looked at each other.

"It's a mysterious story," said Dr. Lloyd. "One can make guesses, but to guess—"

He shook his head.

"Has Mr. Pritchard married Miss Instow?" asked Miss Marple in her gentle voice.

"Now why do you ask that?" inquired Sir Henry.

Miss Marple opened gentle blue eyes.

"It seems to me so important," she said. "Have they married?"

Colonel Bantry shook his head.

"We—well, we expected something of the kind—but it's eighteen months now. I don't believe they even see much of each other."

"That is important," said Miss Marple. "Very important."

"Then you think the same as I do," said Mrs. Bantry. "You think—"

"Now, Dolly," said her husband. "It's unjustifiable—what you're going to say. You can't go about accusing people without a shadow of proof."

"Don't be so—so manly, Arthur. Men are always afraid to say anything. Anyway, this is all between ourselves. It's just a wild, fantastic idea of mine that possibly—only possibly—Jean Instow disguised herself as a fortuneteller. Mind you, she may have done it for a joke. I don't for a minute think that she meant any harm; but if she did do it, and if Mrs. Pritchard was foolish enough to die of fright—well, that's what Miss Marple meant, wasn't it?"

"No, dear, not quite," said Miss Marple. "You see, if I were going to kill anyone—which, of course, I wouldn't dream of doing for a minute, because it would be very wicked, and besides, I don't like killing—not even wasps, though I know it has to be, and I'm sure the gardener does it as humanely as possible. Let me see, what was I saying?"

"If you wished to kill anyone," prompted Sir Henry.

"Oh yes. Well, if I did, I shouldn't be at all satisfied to trust to fright. I know one reads of people dying of it, but it seems a very uncertain sort of thing, and the most nervous people are far more brave than one really thinks they are. I should like something definite and certain and make a thoroughly good plan about it."

"Miss Marple," said Sir Henry, "you frighten me. I hope you will never wish to remove me. Your plans would be too good."

Miss Marple looked at him reproachfully.

"I thought I had made it clear that I would never contemplate such wickedness," she said. "No, I was trying to put myself in the place of—er—a certain person."

"Do you mean George Pritchard?" asked Colonel Bantry. "I'll never believe it of George—though, mind you, even the nurse believes it. I went and saw her about a month afterward, at the time of the exhumation. She didn't know how it was done—in fact, she wouldn't say anything at all—but it was clear enough that she believed George to be in some way responsible for his wife's death. She was convinced of it."

"Well," said Dr. Lloyd, "perhaps she wasn't so far wrong. And mind you, a nurse often knows. She can't say—she's got no proof—but she knows."

Sir Henry leaned forward.

"Come now, Miss Marple," he said persuasively. "You're lost in a daydream. Won't you tell us all about it?"

Miss Marple started and turned pink.

"I beg your pardon," she said. "I was just thinking about our district nurse. A most difficult problem."

"More difficult than the problem of a blue geranium?"

"It really depends on the primroses," said Miss Marple. "I mean, Mrs. Bantry said they were yellow and pink. If it was a pink primrose that turned blue, of course, that fits in perfectly. But if it happened to be a yellow one—"

"It was a pink one," said Mrs. Bantry.

She stared. They all stared at Miss Marple.

"Then that seems to settle it," said Miss Marple. She shook her head regretfully. "And the wasp season and everything. And of course the gas."

"It reminds you, I suppose, of countless village tragedies?" said Sir Henry.

"Not tragedies," said Miss Marple. "And certainly nothing criminal. But it does remind me a little of the trouble we are having with the district nurse. After all, nurses are human beings, and what with having to be so correct in their behaviour and wearing those uncomfortable collars and being so thrown with the family—well, can you wonder that things sometimes happen?"

A glimmer of light broke upon Sir Henry.

"You mean Nurse Carstairs?"

"Oh no. Not Nurse Carstairs. Nurse Copling. You see, she had been there before and very much thrown with Mr. Pritchard, who you say is an attractive man. I daresay she thought, poor thing—well, we needn't go into that. I don't suppose she knew about Miss Instow, and of course afterward, when she found out, it turned her against him and she tried to do all the harm she could. Of course, the letter really gave her away, didn't it?"

"What letter?"

"Well, she wrote to the fortuneteller at Mrs. Pritchard's request, and the fortuneteller came, apparently in answer to the letter. But later it was discovered that there never had been such a person at that address. So that shows that Nurse Copling was in it. She only pretended to write—so what could be more likely than that she was the fortuneteller herself?"

"I never saw the point about the letter," said Sir Henry. "That's a most important point, of course."

"Rather a bold step to take," said Miss Marple, "because Mrs.

Pritchard might have recognized her in spite of the disguise—though of course if she had, the nurse could have pretended it was a joke."

"What did you mean," said Sir Henry, "when you said that if you were a certain person, you would not have trusted to fright?"

"One couldn't be sure that way," said Miss Marple. "No, I think that the warnings and the blue flowers were, if I may use a military term"—she laughed self-consciously—"just camouflage."

"And the real thing?"

"I know," said Miss Marple apologetically, "that I've got wasps on the brain. Poor things, destroyed in their thousands—and usually on such a beautiful summer's day. But I remember thinking, when I saw the gardener shaking up the cyanide of potassium in a bottle with water, how like smelling salts it looked. And if it were put in a smelling-salt bottle and substituted for the real one—well, the poor lady was in the habit of using her smelling salts. Indeed, you said they were found by her hand. Then, of course, while Mr. Pritchard went to telephone to the doctor, the nurse would change it for the real bottle, and she'd just turn on the gas a little bit to mask any smell of almonds and in case anyone felt queer, and I always have heard that cyanide leaves no trace if you wait long enough. But, of course, I may be wrong, and it may have been something entirely different in the bottle, but that doesn't really matter, does it?"

Miss Marple paused, a little out of breath.

Jane Helier leaned forward and said, "But the blue geranium and the other flowers?"

"Nurses always have litmus paper, don't they?" said Miss Marple, "for—well, for testing. Not a very pleasant subject. We won't dwell on it. I have done a little nursing myself." She grew delicately pink. "Blue turns red with acids, and red turns blue with alkalies. So easy to paste some red litmus over a red flower—near the bed, of course. And then, when the poor lady used her smelling salts, the strong ammonia fumes would turn it blue. Really most ingenious. Of course, the geranium wasn't blue when they first broke into the room—nobody noticed it till afterward. When nurse changed the bottles, she held the sal ammoniac against the wallpaper for a minute, I expect."

"You might have been there, Miss Marple," said Sir Henry.

"What worries me," said Miss Marple, "is poor Mr. Pritchard and that nice girl, Miss Instow. Probably both suspecting each other and keeping apart—and life so very short."

She shook her head.

"You needn't worry," said Sir Henry. "As a matter of fact, I have something up my sleeve. A nurse has been arrested on a charge of murdering an elderly patient who had left her a legacy. It was done with cyanide of potassium substituted for smelling salts. Nurse Copling trying the same trick again. Miss Instow and Mr. Pritchard need have no doubts as to the truth."

"Now isn't that nice?" cried Miss Marple. "I don't mean about the new murder, of course. That's very sad and shows how much wickedness there is in the world and that if once you give away—which reminds me, I must finish my little conversation with Dr. Lloyd about the village nurse."

CORNELL WOOLRICH
(1903-1968)

Cornell Woolrich (William Irish) was born in New York City, grew up in South America, and attended Columbia University. A "twentieth-century Poe," Woolrich influenced mystery and suspense fiction with his use of oppressive atmosphere and his fascination with the irrational. Products of a bizarre and claustrophobic life and an imagination that fed on a sense of catastrophic doom, his stories depict a universe of ill-defined threat, despair, and failed love. His shorter works, reflecting the grayness of the Depression era, appeared during the 1930s in pulps such as *Black Mask* and *Detective Fiction Weekly*. His longer fiction, like his first suspense novel, *The Bride Wore Black* (1940), also reflected his grim awareness of the irrational subsurface of life and inspired the French *roman noir* and *film noir*, as well as some of Alfred Hitchcock's finest suspense movies.

"Murder at the Automat" is an example of "Black Mask" fiction in its grimy setting, colloquial language, and atmosphere of greed, treachery, and violence. It is also an early example of the police procedural, as the detective pursues his "private" case at the same time he pursues his "official" case for the department. The detective relies less on technical help, however, than on observation and persistence and, especially, on a grasp of human psychology ("misers seldom commit suicide").

MURDER AT THE AUTOMAT

Nelson pushed through the revolving-door at twenty to one in the morning, his squadmate, Sarecky, in the compartment behind him. They stepped clear and looked around. The place looked funny. Almost all the little white tables had helpings of food on them, but no one was at them eating. There was a big black crowd ganged up over in one corner, thick as bees and sending up a buzz. One or two were standing up on chairs, trying to see over the heads of the ones in front, rubbering like a flock of cranes.

The crowd burst apart, and a cop came through. "Now, stand back. Get away from this table, all of you," he was saying. "There's nothing to see. The man's dead—that's all."

He met the two dicks halfway between the crowd and the door. "Over there in the corner," he said unnecessarily. "Indigestion, I guess." He went back with them.

They split the crowd wide open again, this time from the outside. In the middle of it was one of the little white tables, a dead man in a chair, an ambulance doctor, a pair of stretcher-bearers, and the automat manager.

"He gone?" Nelson asked the interne.

"Yep. We got here too late." He came closer so the mob wouldn't overhear. "Better send him down to the morgue and have him looked at. I think he did the Dutch. There's a white streak on his chin, and a half-eaten sandwich under his face spiked with some more of it, whatever it is. That's why I got in touch with you fellows. Good night," he wound up pleasantly and elbowed his way out of the crowd, the two stretcher-bearers tagging after him. The ambulance clanged dolorously outside, swept its fiery headlights around the corner, and whined off.

Nelson said to the cop: "Go over to the door and keep everyone in here, until we get the three others that were sitting at this table with him."

The manager said: "There's a little balcony upstairs. Couldn't he be taken up there, instead of being left down here in full sight like this?"

"Yeah, pretty soon," Nelson agreed, "but not just yet."

He looked down at the table. There were four servings of food on it, one on each side. Two had barely been touched. One had been finished and only the soiled plates remained. One was hidden by the prone figure sprawled across it, one arm out, the other hanging limply down toward the floor.

"Who was sitting here?" said Nelson, pointing to one of the unconsumed portions. "Kindly step forward and identify yourself." No one made a move. "No one," said Nelson, raising his voice, "gets out of here until we have a chance to question the three people that were at this table with him when it happened."

Someone started to back out of the crowd from behind. The woman who had wanted to go home so badly a minute ago, pointed accusingly. "*He* was—that man there! I remember him distinctly. He bumped into me with his tray just before he sat down."

Sarecky went over, took him by the arm, and brought him forward again. "No one's going to hurt you," Nelson said, at sight of his pale face. "Only don't make it any tougher for yourself than you have to."

"I never even saw the guy before," wailed the man, as if he had already been accused of murder, "I just happened to park my stuff at the first vacant chair I—" Misery liking company, he broke off short and pointed in turn. "*He* was at the table, too. Why doncha hold him, if you're gonna hold me?"

"That's just what we're going to do," said Nelson dryly. "Over here, you," he ordered the new witness. "Now, who was eating spaghetti on the right here? As soon as we find that out, the rest of you can go home."

The crowd looked around indignantly in search of the recalcitrant witness that was the cause of detaining them all. But this time no one was definitely able to single him out. A white-uniformed busman finally edged forward and said to Nelson: "I think he musta got out of the place right after it happened. I looked over at this table a minute before it happened, and he was already through eating, picking his teeth and just holding down the chair."

"Well, he's not as smart as he thinks he is," said Nelson. "We'll catch up with him, whether he got out or didn't. The rest of you clear out of here now. And don't give fake names and addresses to the cop at the door, or you'll be making trouble for yourselves."

The place emptied itself like magic, self-preservation being stronger than curiosity in most people. The two table-mates of the dead man, the manager, the staff, and the two dicks remained inside.

An assistant medical examiner arrived, followed by two men with the usual basket, and made a brief preliminary investigation. While this was going on, Nelson was questioning the two witnesses, the busman, and the manager. He got an illuminating composite picture.

The man was well known to the staff by sight, and was considered an eccentric. He always came in at the same time each night, just before closing time, and always helped himself to the same snack—coffee and a bologna sandwich. It hadn't varied for six months now. The remnants that the busman removed from where the man sat each time were always the same. The manager was able to corroborate this. He, the dead man, had raised a kick one night about a week ago, because the bologna-sandwich slots had all been emptied before he came in. The manager had had to remind him that it's first come, first served, at an automat, and you can't reserve your food ahead of time. The man at the change-booth, questioned by Nelson, added to the old fellow's reputation for eccentricity. Other, well-dressed people came in and changed a half-dollar, or at the most a dollar bill. He, in his battered hat and derelict's overcoat, never failed to produce a ten and sometimes even a twenty.

"One of these misers, eh?" said Nelson. "They always end up behind the eight-ball, one way or another."

The old fellow was removed, also the partly consumed sandwich. The assistant examiner let Nelson know: "I think you've got something here, brother. I may be wrong, but that sandwich was loaded with cyanide."

Sarecky, who had gone through the man's clothes, said: "The name was Leo Avram, and here's the address. Incidentally, he had seven hundred dollars, in C's, in his right shoe and three hundred in his left. Want me to go over there and nose around?"

"Suppose I go," Nelson said. "You stay here and clean up."

"My pal," murmured the other dick dryly.

The waxed paper from the sandwich had been left lying under the chair. Nelson picked it up, wrapped it in a paper-napkin, and put it in his pocket. It was only a short walk from the automat to where Avram lived, an outmoded, walk-up building, falling to pieces with neglect.

Nelson went into the hall and there was no such name listed. He thought at first Sarecky had made a mistake, or at least been misled by whatever memorandum it was he had found that purported to give the old fellow's address. He rang the bell marked *Superintendent,* and went down to the basement-entrance to make sure. A stout blond woman in an old sweater and carpet-slippers came out.

"Is there anyone named Avram living in this building?"

"That's my husband—he's the superintendent. He's out right now, I expect him back any minute."

Nelson couldn't understand, himself, why he didn't break it to her then and there. He wanted to get a line, perhaps, on the old man's surroundings while they still remained normal. "Can I come in and wait a minute?" he said.

"Why not?" she said indifferently.

She led him down a barren, unlit basement-way, stacked with empty ashcans, into a room green-yellow with a tiny bud of gaslight. Old as the building upstairs was, it had been wired for electricity, Nelson had noted. For that matter, so was this basement down here. There was a cord hanging from the ceiling ending in an empty socket. It had been looped up out of reach. "The old bird sure was a miser," thought Nelson. "Walking around on one grand and living like this!" He couldn't help feeling a little sorry for the woman.

He noted to his further surprise that a pot of coffee was boiling on a one-burner gas stove over in the corner. He wondered if she knew that he treated himself away from home each night. "Any idea where he went?" he asked, sitting down in a creaking rocker.

"He goes two blocks down to the automat for a bite to eat every night at this time," she said.

"How is it," he asked curiously, "he'll go out and spend money like that, when he could have coffee right here where he lives with you?"

A spark of resentment showed in her face, but a defeated resentment that had long turned to resignation. She shrugged. "For himself, nothing's too good. He goes there because the light's better, he says. But for me and the kids, he begrudges every penny."

"You've got kids, have you?"

"They're mine, not his," she said dully.

Nelson had already caught sight of a half-grown girl and a little boy peeping shyly out at him from another room. "Well," he said, getting up, "I'm sorry to have to tell you this, but your husband had an accident a little while ago at the automat, Mrs. Avram. He's gone."

The weary stolidity on her face changed very slowly. But it did change—to fright. "Cyanide—what's that?" she breathed, when he'd told her.

"Did he have any enemies?"

She said with utter simplicity, "Nobody loved him. Nobody hated him that much, either."

"Do you know of any reason he'd have to take his own life?"

"Him? Never! He held on tight to life, just like he did to his money."

There was some truth in that, the dick had to admit. Misers seldom commit suicide.

The little girl edged into the room fearfully, holding her hands behind her. "Is—is he dead, Mom?"

The woman just nodded, dry-eyed.

"Then, can we use this now?" She was holding a fly-blown electric bulb in her hands.

Nelson felt touched, hard-boiled dick though he was. "Come down to headquarters tomorrow, Mrs. Avram. There's some money there you can claim. G'night." He went outside and clanged the basement-gate shut after him. The windows alongside him suddenly bloomed feebly with electricity, and the silhouette of a woman standing up on a chair was outlined against them.

"It's a funny world," thought the dick with a shake of his head, as he trudged up to sidewalk-level.

It was now two in the morning. The automat was dark when Nelson returned there, so he went down to headquarters. They were questioning the branch-manager and the unseen counterman who prepared the sandwiches and filled the slots from the inside.

Nelson's captain said: "They've already telephoned from the chem lab that the sandwich is loaded with cyanide crystals. On the other hand, they give the remainder of the loaf that was used, the leftover bologna from which the sandwich was prepared, the breadknife, the cutting-board, and the scraps in the garbage-receptacle—all of which we sent over there—a clean bill of health. There was clearly no slip-up or carelessness in the automat pantry. Which means that cyanide got into that sandwich on the consumer's side of the apparatus. He committed suicide or was deliberately murdered by one of the other customers."

"I was just up there," Nelson said. "It wasn't suicide. People don't worry about keeping their light bills down when they're going to take their own lives."

"Good psychology," the captain nodded. "My experience is that miserliness is simply a perverted form of self-preservation, an exaggerated clinging to life. The choice of method wouldn't be in character, either. Cyanide's expensive, and it wouldn't be sold to a man of Avram's type, just for the asking. It's murder, then. I think it's highly important you men bring in whoever the fourth man at that table was tonight. Do it with the least possible loss of time."

A composite description of him, pieced together from the few scraps that could be obtained from the busman and the other two at the table, was available. He was a heavy-set dark-complected man, wearing a light-tan suit. He had been the first of the four at the table, and already through eating, but had lingered on. Mannerisms—had kept looking back over his shoulder, from time to time, and picking his teeth. He had had a small black satchel, or sample-case, parked at his feet under the table. Both survivors were positive on this point. Both had stubbed their toes against it in sitting down, and both had glanced to the floor to see what it was.

Had he reached down toward it at any time, after their arrival, as if to open it or take anything out of it?

To the best of their united recollections—no.

Had Avram, *after* bringing the sandwich to the table, gotten up again and left it unguarded for a moment?

Again, no. In fact the whole thing had been over with in a flash. He had noisily unwrapped it, taken a huge bite, swallowed without chewing, heaved convulsively once or twice, and fallen prone across the tabletop.

"Then it must have happened right outside the slot—I mean the inserting of the stuff—and not at the table, at all," Sarecky told Nelson privately. "Guess he laid it down for a minute while he was drawing his coffee."

"Absolutely not!" Nelson contradicted. "You're forgetting it was all wrapped up in wax-paper. How could anyone have opened, then closed it again, without attracting his attention? And if we're going to suspect the guy with the satchel—and the cap seems to want us to—he was already *at* the table and all through eating when Avram came over. How could he know ahead of time which table the old guy was going to select?"

"Then how did the stuff get on it? Where did it come from?" the other dick asked helplessly.

"It's little things like that we're paid to find out," Nelson reminded him dryly.

"Pretty large order, isn't it?"

"You talk like a layman. You've been on the squad long enough by now to know how damnably unescapable little habits are, how impossible it is to shake them off, once formed. The public at large thinks detective work is something miraculous like pulling rabbits out of a silk hat. They don't realize that no adult is a free agent—that they're tied hand and foot by tiny, harmless little habits, and held helpless. This man has a habit of taking a snack to eat at midnight in a public place. He has a habit of picking his teeth after he's through, of lingering on at the table, of looking back over his shoulder aimlessly from time to time. Combine that with a stocky build, a dark complexion, and you have him! What more d'ya want—a spotlight trained on him?"

It was Sarecky, himself, in spite of his misgivings, who picked him up forty-eight hours later in another automat, sample-case and all, at nearly the same hour as the first time, and brought him in for questioning! The busman from the former place, and the two customers, called in, identified him unhesitatingly, even if he was now wearing a gray suit.

His name, he said, was Alexander Hill, and he lived at 215 Such-and-such a street.

"What business are you in?" rapped out the captain.

The man's face got livid. His Adam's apple went up and down like an elevator. He could barely articulate the words. "I'm—I'm a salesman for a wholesale drug concern," he gasped terrifiedly.

"Ah!" said two of his three questioners expressively. The sample-case, opened, was found to contain only tooth-powders, aspirins, and headache remedies.

But Nelson, rummaging through it, thought: "Oh, nuts, it's too pat. And he's too scared, too defenseless, to have really done it. Came in here just now without a bit of mental build-up prepared ahead of time. The real culprit would have been all primed, all rehearsed, for just this. Watch him go all to pieces. The innocent ones always do."

The captain's voice rose to a roar. "How is it everyone else stayed in the place that night, but you got out in such a hurry?"

"I—I don't know. It happened so close to me, I guess I—I got nervous."

That wasn't necessarily a sign of guilt; Nelson was thinking. It was his duty to take part in the questioning, so he shot out at him: "You got nervous, eh? What reason d'you have for getting nervous? How'd *you* know it wasn't just a heart attack or malnutrition—unless you were the cause of it?"

He stumbled badly over that one. "No! No! I don't handle that stuff! I don't carry anything like that—"

"So you know what it was? How'd you know? We didn't tell you," Sarecky jumped on him.

"I—I read it in the papers next morning," he wailed.

Well, it had been in all of them, Nelson had to admit.

"You didn't reach out in front of you—toward him—for anything that night? You kept your hands to yourself?" Then, before he could get a word out, "*What about sugar?*"

The suspect went from bad to worse: "I don't use any!" he whimpered.

Sarecky had been just waiting for that. "Don't lie to us!" he yelled, and swung at him. "I watched you for ten full minutes tonight before I went over and tapped your shoulder. You emptied half the container into your cup!" His fist hit him a glancing blow on the side of the jaw, knocked him and the chair he was sitting on both off-balance. Fright was making the guy sew himself up twice as badly as before.

"Aw, we're just barking up the wrong tree," Nelson kept saying to himself. "It's just one of those fluke coincidences. A drug salesman happens to be sitting at the same table where a guy drops from cyanide poisoning!" Still, he knew that more than one guy had been strapped into the chair just on the strength of such a coincidence and nothing more. You couldn't expect a jury not to pounce on it for all it was worth.

The captain took Nelson out of it at this point, somewhat to his relief, took him aside and murmured: "Go over there and give his place a good cleaning while we're holding him here. If you can turn up any of that stuff hidden around there, that's all we need. He'll break down like a stack of cards." He glanced over at the cowering figure in the chair. "We'll have him before morning," he promised.

"That's what I'm afraid of," thought Nelson, easing out. "And then what'll we have? Exactly nothing." He wasn't the kind of a dick that would have rather had a wrong guy than no guy at all, like some of them. He wanted the right guy—or none at all. The last he saw of the captain, he was stripping off his coat for action, more as a moral threat than a physical one, and the unfortunate victim of circumstances was wailing, "I didn't do it, I didn't do it," like a record with a flaw in it.

Hill was a bachelor and lived in a small, one-room flat on the upper West Side. Nelson let himself in with the man's own key, put on the lights, and went to work. In half an hour, he had investigated the place upside-down. There was not a grain of cyanide to be found, nor anything beyond what had already been revealed in the sample-case. This did not mean, of course, that he couldn't have obtained some either through the firm he worked for, or some of the retail druggists whom he canvassed. Nelson found a list of the latter and took it with him to check over the following day.

Instead of returning directly to headquarters, he detoured on an impulse past the Avram house, and, seeing a light shining in the basement windows, went over and rang the bell.

The little girl came out, her brother behind her. "Mom's not in," she announced.

"She's out with Uncle Nick," the boy supplied.

His sister whirled on him. "She told us not to tell anybody that, didn't she!"

Nelson could hear the instructions as clearly as if he'd been in the room at the time, "If that man comes around again, don't you tell him I've gone out with Uncle Nick, now!"

Children are after all very transparent. They told him most of what he wanted to know without realizing they were doing it. "He's not really your uncle, is he?"

A gasp of surprise. "How'd you know that?"

"Your ma gonna marry him?"

They both nodded approvingly. "He's gonna be our new Pop."

"What was the name of your real Pop—the one before the last?"

"Edwards," they chorused proudly.

"What happened to him?"

"He died."

"In Dee-troit," added the little boy.

He only asked them one more question. "Can you tell me his full name?"

"Albert J. Edwards," they recited.

He gave them a friendly push. "All right, kids, go back to bed."

He went back to headquarters, sent a wire to the Bureau of Vital Statistics in Detroit, on his own hook. They were still questioning Hill down to the bone, meanwhile, but he hadn't caved in yet. "Nothing," Nelson reported. "Only this account-sheet of where he places his orders."

"I'm going to try framing him with a handful of bicarb of soda, or something—pretend we got the goods on him. I'll see if that'll open him up," the captain promised wrathfully. "He's not the push-over I expected. You start in at seven this morning and work your way through this list of retail druggists. Find out if he ever tried to contract them for any of that stuff."

Meanwhile, he had Hill smuggled out the back way to an outlying precinct, to evade the statute governing the length of time a prisoner can be held before arraignment. They didn't have enough of a case against him to arraign him, but they weren't going to let him go.

Nelson was even more surprised than the prisoner at what he caught himself doing. As they stood Hill up next to him in the corridor, for a minute, waiting for the Black Maria, he breathed over his shoulder, "Hang on tight, or you're sunk!"

The man acted too far gone even to understand what he was driving at.

Nelson was present the next morning when Mrs. Avram showed up to claim the money, and watched her expression curiously. She had the same air of weary resignation as the night he had broken the news to her. She accepted the money from the captain, signed for it, turned apathetically away, holding it in her hand. The captain, by prearrangement, had pulled another of his little tricks—purposely withheld one of the hundred-dollar bills to see what her reaction would be.

Halfway to the door, she turned in alarm, came hurrying back. "Gentlemen, there must be a mistake! There's—there's a hundred-dollar bill here on top!" She shuffled through the roll hastily. "They're all hundred-dollar bills!" she cried out aghast. "I knew he had a little money in his shoes—he slept with them under his pillow at nights—but I thought maybe, fifty, seventy dollars—"

"There was a thousand in his shoes," said the captain, "and another thousand stitched all along the seams of his overcoat."

She let the money go, caught the edge of the desk he was sitting behind with both hands, and slumped draggingly down it to the floor in a dead faint. They had to hustle in with a pitcher of water to revive her.

Nelson impatiently wondered what the heck was the matter with him, what more he needed to be convinced she hadn't known what she was coming into? And yet, he said to himself, how are you going to tell a real faint from a fake one! They close their eyes and they flop, and which is it?

He slept three hours, and then he went down and checked at the wholesale-drug concern Hill worked for. The firm did not handle cyanide or any other poisonous substance, and the man had a very good record there. He spent the morning working his way down the list of retail druggists who had placed their orders through Hill, and again got nowhere. At noon he quit and went back to the automat where it had happened—not to eat but to talk to the manager. He was really working on two cases simultaneously—an official one for his captain and a private one of his own. The captain would have had a fit if he'd known it.

"Will you lemme have that busman of yours, the one we had down at headquarters the other night? I want to take him out of here with me for about half an hour."

"You're the Police Department," the manager smiled acquiescently.

Nelson took him with him in his streetclothes. "You did a pretty good job of identifying Hill, the fourth man at that table," he told him. "Naturally, I don't expect you to remember every face that was in there that night. Especially with the quick turnover there is in an automat. However, here's what you do. Go down this street here to Number One-twenty-one—you can see it from here. Ring the superintendent's bell. You're looking for an apartment, see? But while you're at it, you take a good look at the woman you'll see, and then come back and tell me if you remember seeing her face in the automat that night or any other night. Don't stare now—just size her up."

It took him a little longer than Nelson had counted on. When he finally rejoined the dick around the corner, where the latter was waiting, he said: "Nope, I've never seen her in our place, that night or any other, to my knowledge. But don't forget—I'm not on the floor every minute of the time. She could have been in and out often without my spotting her."

"But not," thought Nelson, "without Avram seeing her, if she went anywhere near him at all." She hadn't been there, then. That was practically certain. "What took you so long?" he asked him.

"Funny thing. There was a guy there in the place with her that used to work for us. He remembered me right away."

"Oh, yeah?" The dick drew up short. "Was *he* in there that night?"

"Naw, he quit six months ago. I haven't seen him since."

"What was he, sandwich-maker?"

"No, busman like me. He cleaned up the tables."

Just another coincidence, then. But, Nelson reminded himself, if one coincidence was strong enough to put Hill in jeopardy, why should the other be passed over as harmless? Both cases—his and the captain's—now had their coincidences. It remained to be seen which was just that—a coincidence and nothing more—and which was the McCoy.

He went back to headquarters. No wire had yet come from Detroit in answer to his, but he hadn't expected any this soon—it took time. The captain, bulldog-like, wouldn't let Hill go. They had spirited him away to still a third place, were holding him on some technicality or other that had nothing to do with the Avram case. The bicarbonate of soda trick hadn't worked, the captain told Nelson ruefully.

"Why?" the dick wanted to know. "Because he caught on just by looking at it that it wasn't cyanide—is that it? I think that's an important point, right there."

"No, he thought it was the stuff all right. But he hollered blue murder it hadn't come out of his room."

"Then if he doesn't know the difference between cyanide and bicarb of soda at sight, doesn't that prove he didn't put any on that sandwich?"

The captain gave him a look. "Are you for us or against us?" he wanted to know acidly. "You go ahead checking that list of retail druggists until you find out where he got it. And if we can't dig up any other motive, unhealthy scientific curiosity will satisfy me. He wanted to study the effects at first hand, and picked the first stranger who came along."

"Sure, in an automat—the most conspicuous, crowded public eating-place there is. The one place where human handling of the food is reduced to a minimum."

He deliberately disobeyed orders, a thing he had never done before—or rather, postponed carrying them out. He went back and commenced a one-man watch over the basement-entrance of the Avram house.

In about an hour, a squat, foreign-looking man came up the steps and walked down the street. This was undoubtedly "Uncle Nick," Mrs. Avram's husband-to-be, and former employee of the automat. Nelson tailed him effortlessly on the opposite side, boarded the same bus he did a block below, and got off at the same stop. "Uncle Nick" went into a bank, and Nelson into a cigar-store across the way that had transparent telephone booths commanding the street through the glass front.

When he came out again, Nelson didn't bother following him any more. Instead, he went into the bank himself. "What'd that guy do—open an account just now? Lemme see the deposit-slip."

He had deposited a thousand dollars cash under the name of Nicholas Krassin, half of the sum Mrs. Avram had claimed at headquarters only the day before. Nelson didn't have to be told that this by no means indicated Krassin and she had had anything to do with the old man's death. The money was rightfully hers as his widow, and, if she wanted to divide it with her groom-to-be, that was no criminal offense. Still, wasn't there a stronger motive here than the "unhealthy scientific curiosity" the captain had pinned on Hill? The fact remained that she wouldn't have had possession of the money had Avram still been alive. It would have still been in his shoes and coat-seams where she couldn't get at it.

Nelson checked Krassin at the address he had given at the bank, and, somewhat to his surprise, found it to be on the level, not fictitious. Either the two of them weren't very bright, or they were innocent. He went back to headquarters at six, and the answer to his telegram to Detroit had finally come. "Exhumation order obtained as per request stop Albert J. Edwards deceased January 1936 stop death certificate gives cause fall from steel girder while at work building under construction stop—autopsy—"

Nelson read it to the end, folded it, put it in his pocket without changing his expression.

"Well, did you find out anything?" the captain wanted to know.

"No, but I'm on the way to," Nelson assured him, but he may have been thinking of that other case of his own, and not the one they were all steamed up over. He went out again without saying where.

He got to Mrs. Avram's at quarter to seven, and rang the bell. The little girl came out to the basement-entrance. At sight of him, she called out shrilly, but without humorous intent, "Ma, that man's here again."

Nelson smiled a little and walked back to the living-quarters. A sudden hush had fallen thick enough to cut with a knife. Krassin was there again, in his shirt-sleeves, having supper with Mrs. Avram and the two kids. They not only had electricity now but a midget radio as well, he noticed. You can't arrest people for buying a midget radio. It was silent as a tomb, but he let the back of his hand brush it, surreptitiously, and the front of the dial was still warm from recent use.

"I'm not butting in, am I?" he greeted them cheerfully.

"N-no, sit down," said Mrs. Avram nervously. "This is Mr. Krassin, a friend of the family. I don't know your name—"

"Nelson."

Krassin just looked at him watchfully.

The dick said: "Sorry to trouble you. I just wanted to ask you a couple questions about your husband. About what time was it he had the accident?"

"You know better than I," she objected. "You were the one came here and told me."

"I don't mean Avram, I mean Edwards, in Detroit—the riveter that fell off the girder."

Her face went a little gray, as if the memory were painful. Krassin's face didn't change color, but only showed considerable surprise.

"About what time of day?" he repeated.

"Noon," she said almost inaudibly.

"Lunch-time," said the dick softly, as if to himself. "Most workmen carry their lunch from home in a pail—" He looked at her thoughtfully. Then he changed the subject, wrinkled up his nose appreciatively. "That coffee smells good," he remarked.

She gave him a peculiar, strained smile. "Have a cup, Mr. Detective," she offered. He saw her eyes meet Krassin's briefly.

"Thanks, don't mind if I do," drawled Nelson.

She got up. Then, on her way to the stove, she suddenly flared out at the two kids for no apparent reason: "What are you hanging around here for? Go to bed. Get out of here now, I say!" She banged the door shut on them, stood before it with her back to the room for a minute. Nelson's sharp ears caught the faint but unmistakable click of a key.

She turned back again, purred to Krassin: "Nick, go outside and take a look at the furnace, will you, while I'm pouring Mr. Nelson's coffee? If the heat dies down, they'll all start complaining from upstairs right away. Give it a good shaking up."

The hairs at the back of Nelson's neck stood up a little as he watched the man get up and sidle out. But he'd asked for the cup of coffee, himself.

He couldn't see her pouring it—her back was turned toward him again as she stood over the stove. But he could hear the splash of the hot liquid, see her elbow-motions, hear the clink of the pot as she replaced it. She stayed that way a moment longer, after it had been poured, with her back to him—less than a moment, barely thirty seconds. One elbow moved slightly. Nelson's eyes were narrow slits. It was thirty seconds too long, one elbow-motion too many.

She turned, came back, set the cup down before him. "I'll let you put your own sugar in, yes?" she said almost playfully. "Some like a lot, some like a little." There was a disappearing ring of froth in the middle of the black steaming liquid.

Outside somewhere, he could hear Krassin raking up the furnace.

"Drink it while it's still hot," she urged.

He lifted it slowly to his lips. As the cup went up, her eyelids went down. Not all the way, not enough to completely shut out sight, though.

He blew the steam away. "Too hot—burn my mouth. Gotta give it a minute to cool," he said. "How about you—ain't you having any? I couldn't drink alone. Ain't polite."

"I had mine," she breathed heavily, opening her eyes again. "I don't think there's any left."

"Then I'll give you half of this."

Her hospitable alarm was almost overdone. She all but jumped back in protest. "No, no! Wait, I'll look. Yes, there's more, there's plenty!"

He could have had an accident with it while her back was turned a second time, upset it over the floor. Instead, he took a kitchen-match out of his pocket, broke the head off short with his thumbnail. He threw the head, not the stick, over on top of the warm stove in front of which she was standing. It fell to one side of her, without making any noise, and she didn't notice it. If he'd thrown stick and all, it would have clicked as it dropped and attracted her attention.

She came back and sat down opposite him. Krassin's footsteps could be heard shuffling back toward them along the cement corridor outside.

"Go ahead. Don't be bashful—drink up," she encouraged. There was something ghastly about her smile, like a death's-head grinning across the table from him.

The match-head on the stove, heated to the point of combustion, suddenly flared up with a little spitting sound and a momentary gleam. She jumped a little, and her head turned nervously to see what it was. When she looked back again, he already had his cup to his lips. She raised hers, too, watching him over the rim of it. Krassin's footfalls had stopped somewhere just outside the room door, and there wasn't another sound from him, as if he were standing there, waiting.

At the table, the cat-and-mouse play went on a moment longer. Nelson started swallowing with a dry constriction of the throat. The woman's eyes, watching him above her cup, were greedy half-moons of delight. Suddenly, her head and shoulders went down across the table with a bang, like her husband's had at the automat that other night, and the crash of the crushed cup sounded from underneath her.

Nelson jumped up watchfully, throwing his chair over. The door shot open, and Krassin came in, with an ax in one hand and an empty burlap-bag in the other.

"I'm not quite ready for cremation yet," the dick gritted, and threw himself at him.

Krassin dropped the superfluous burlap-bag, the ax flashed up overhead. Nelson dipped his knees, down in under it before it could fall. He caught the shaft with one hand, midway between the blade and Krassin's grip, and held the weapon teetering in mid-air. With his other fist he started imitating a hydraulic drill against his assailant's teeth. Then he lowered his barrage suddenly to solar-plexus level, sent in two bodyblows that caved his opponent in—and that about finished it.

Out in the wilds of Corona, an hour later, in a sub-basement locker-room, Alexander Hill—or at least what was left of him—was saying: "And you'll lemme sleep if I do? And you'll get it over real quick, send me up and put me out of my misery?"

"Yeah, yeah!" said the haggard captain, flicking ink out of a fountain pen and jabbing it at him. "Why dincha do this days ago, make it easier for us all?"

"Never saw such a guy," complained Sarecky, rinsing his mouth with water over in a corner.

"What's that man signing?" exploded Nelson's voice from the stairs.

"Whaddye think he's signing?" snarled the captain. "And where you been all night, incidentally?"

"Getting poisoned by the same party that croaked Avram!" He came the rest of the way down, and Krassin walked down alongside at the end of a short steel link.

"Who's this guy?" they both wanted to know.

Nelson looked at the first prisoner, in the chair. "Take him out of here a few minutes, can't you?" he requested. "He don't have to know all our business."

"Just like in the story-books," muttered Sarecky jealously. "One-Man Nelson walks in at the last minute and cops all the glory."

A cop led Hill upstairs. Another cop brought down a small brown-paper parcel at Nelson's request. Opened, it revealed a small tin that had once contained cocoa. Nelson turned it upside down and a few threads of whitish substance spilled lethargically out, filling the close air of the room with a faint odor of bitter almonds.

"There's your cyanide," he said. "It came off the shelf above Mrs. Avram's kitchen-stove. Her kids, who are being taken care of at headquarters until I can get back there, will tell you it's roach-powder and they were warned never to go near it. She probably got it in Detroit, way back last year."

"She did it?" said the captain. "How could she? It was on the automat-sandwich, not anything he ate at home. *She* wasn't at the automat that night, she was home, you told us that yourself."

"Yeah, she was at home, but she poisoned him at the automat just the same. Look, it goes like this." He unlocked his manacle, refastened his prisoner temporarily to a plumbing-pipe in the corner. He took a paper-napkin out of his pocket, and, from within that, the carefully preserved waxpaper wrapper the death-sandwich had been done in.

Nelson said: "This has been folded over twice, once on one side, once on the other. You can see that, yourself. Every crease in it is double-barreled. Meaning what? The sandwich was taken out, doctored, and rewrapped. Only, in her hurry, Mrs. Avram slipped up and put the paper back the other way around.

"As I told Sarecky already, there's death in little habits. Avram was a miser. Bologna is the cheapest sandwich that automat sells. For six months straight, he never bought any other kind. This guy here used to work there. He knew at what time the slots were refilled for the last time. He knew that that was just when Avram always showed up. And, incidentally, the old man was no fool. He didn't go there because the light was better—he went there to keep from getting poisoned at home. Ate all his meals out.

"All right, so what did they do? They got him, anyway—like this. Krassin, here, went in, bought a bologna sandwich, and took it home to her. She spiked it, rewrapped it, and, at eleven-thirty, he took it back there in his pocket. The sandwich-slots had just been refilled for the last time. They wouldn't put any more in till next morning. There are three bologna-slots. He emptied all three, to make sure the victim wouldn't get any but the lethal sandwich. After they're taken out, the glass slides remain ajar. You can lift them and reach in without inserting a coin. He put his death-sandwich in, stayed by it so no one else would get it. The old man came in. Maybe he's near sighted and didn't recognize Krassin. Maybe he didn't know him at all—I haven't cleared that point up yet. Krassin eased out of the place. The old man is a miser. He sees he can get a sandwich for nothing, thinks something went wrong with the mechanism, maybe. He grabs it up twice as quick as anyone else would have. There you are.

"What was in his shoes is the guy's motive. As for her, that was only partly her motive. She was a congenital killer, anyway, outside of that. He would have married her, and it would have happened to him in his turn some day. She got rid of her first husband, Edwards, in Detroit that way. She got a wonderful break. He ate the poisoned lunch she'd given him way up on the crossbeams of a building under construction, and it looked like he'd lost his balance and toppled to his death. They exhumed the body and performed an autopsy at my request. This telegram says they found traces of cyanide poisoning even after all this time.

"I paid out rope to her tonight, let her know I was onto her. I told her her coffee smelled good. Then I switched cups on her. She's up there now, dead. I can't say that I wanted it that way, but it was me or her. You never would have gotten her to the chair, anyway. She was unbalanced of course, but not the kind that's easily recognizable. She'd have spent a year in an institution, been released, and gone out and done it all over again. It grows on 'em, gives 'em a feeling of power over their fellow human beings.

"This louse, however, is *not* insane. He did it for exactly one thousand dollars and no cents—and he knew what he was doing from first to last. So I think he's entitled to a chicken-and-ice-cream-dinner in the death-house, at the state's expense."

"The Sphinx," growled Sarecky under his breath, shrugging into his coat. "Sees all, knows all, keeps all to himself."

"Who stinks?" corrected the captain, misunderstanding. "If anyone does, it's you and me. He brought home the bacon!"

WILLIAM FAULKNER
(1897-1962)

William Faulkner was born in New Albany, Mississippi, and lived most of his life in the town of Oxford, where he attended the University of Mississippi. With good reason, Faulkner has been called America's greatest modern writer. The range of his literary experimentation, the variety and dimension of his characters, and the depth of engagement with his themes in such classic novels as *Light in August* (1932) and *Absalom, Absalom* (1936) all testify to his achievement. Throughout his works, crime, violence, and retribution form consistent motifs, even when they are not central to a novel. As a professional writer concerned with earning his living, he also wrote popular detective stories. What sets them apart is not only the craft they exhibit, but their ability to bear the weight of Faulkner's familiar themes, settings, and characters. Faulkner's detective stories, like his other fiction, make Yoknapatawpha County a stage for all the world and create figures who grow into mythic stature embodying fundamental traits of humankind.

"Hand Upon the Waters," published originally in the *Saturday Evening Post* and later in a collection called *Knight's Gambit* (1949), shows Faulkner adapting characters, such as Gavin Stevens, and themes, such as the past's refusal to stay buried, from his other works for use in the detective genre. The biblical overtones of the title suggest that he is more concerned with justice than with legality in the detecting process. The detective comes to the solution, not out of arcane knowledge or through brilliant deduction, but from a deep understanding of his place and his people.

HAND UPON THE WATERS

The two men followed the path where it ran between the river and the dense wall of cypress and cane and gum and brier. One of them carried a gunny sack which had been washed and looked as if it had been ironed too. The other was a youth, less than twenty, by his face. The river was low, at mid-July level.

"He ought to been catching fish in this water," the youth said.

"If he happened to feel like fishing," the one with the sack said. "Him and Joe run that line when Lonnie feels like it, not when the fish are biting."

"They'll be on the line, anyway," the youth said. "I don't reckon Lonnie cares who takes them off for him."

Presently the ground rose to a cleared point almost like a headland. Upon it sat a conical hut with a pointed roof, built partly of mildewed canvas and odd-shaped boards and partly of oil tins hammered out flat. A rusted stove pipe projected crazily above it, there was a meager woodpile and an ax, and a bunch of cane poles leaned against it. Then they saw, on the earth before the open door, a dozen or so short lengths of cord just cut from a spool near by, and a rusted can half full of heavy fishhooks, some of which had already been bent onto the cords. But there was nobody there.

"The boat's gone," the man with the sack said. "So he ain't gone to the store." Then he discovered that the youth had gone on, and he drew in his breath and was just about to shout when suddenly a man rushed out of the undergrowth and stopped, facing him and making an urgent whimpering sound—a man not large, but with tremendous arms and shoulders; an adult, yet with something childlike about him, about the way he moved, barefoot, in battered overalls and with the urgent eyes of the deaf and dumb.

"Hi, Joe," the man with the sack said, raising his voice as people will with those who they know cannot understand them. "Where's Lonnie?" He held up the sack. "Got some fish?"

But the other only stared at him, making that rapid whimpering. Then he turned and scuttled on up the path where the youth had disappeared, who, at that moment, shouted: "Just look at this line!"

The older one followed. The youth was leaning eagerly out over the water beside a tree from which a light cotton rope slanted tautly downward into the water. The deaf-and-dumb man stood just behind him, still whimpering and lifting his feet rapidly in turn, though before the older man reached him he turned and scuttled back past him, toward the hut. At this stage of the river the line should have been clear of the water, stretching from bank to bank, between the two trees, with only the hooks on the dependent cords submerged. But now it slanted into the water from either end, with a heavy downstream sag, and even the older man could feel movement on it. "It's big as a man!" the youth cried.

"Yonder's his boat," the older man said. The youth saw it, too —across the stream and below them, floated into a willow clump inside a point. "Cross and get it, and we'll see how big this fish is."

The youth stepped out of his shoes and overalls and removed his shirt and waded out and began to swim, holding straight across to let the current carry him down to the skiff and got the skiff and paddled back, standing erect in it and staring eagerly upstream toward the heavy sag of the line, near the center of which the water, from time to time, roiled heavily with submerged movement. He brought the skiff in below the older man, who, at that moment, discovered the deaf-and-dumb man just behind him again, still making the rapid and urgent sound and trying to enter the skiff.

"Get back!" the older man said, pushing the other back with his arm. "Get back, Joe!"

"Hurry up!" the youth said, staring eagerly toward the submerged line, where, as he watched, something rolled sluggishly to the surface, then sank again. "There's something on there, or there ain't a hog in Georgia. It's big as a man too!"

The older one stepped into the skiff. He still held the rope, and he drew the skiff, hand over hand, along the line itself.

Suddenly, from the bank of the river behind them, the deaf-and-dumb man began to make an actual sound. It was quite loud.

2

"Inquest?" Stevens said.

"Lonnie Grinnup." The coroner was an old country doctor. "Two fellows found him drowned on his own trotline this morning."

"No!" Stevens said. "Poor damned feeb. I'll come out." As county attorney he had no business there, even if it had not been an accident. He knew it. He was going to look at the dead man's face for a sentimental reason. What was now Yoknapatawpha County had been founded not by one pioneer but by three simultaneous ones. They came together on horseback, through the Cumberland Gap from the Carolinas, when Jefferson was still a Chickasaw Agency post, and bought land in the Indian patent and established families and flourished and vanished, so that now, a hundred years afterward, there was in all the county they helped to found but one representative of the three names.

This was Stevens, because the last of the Holston family had died before the end of the last century, and the Louis Grenier, whose dead face Stevens was driving eight miles in the heat of a July afternoon to look at, had never even known he was Louis Grenier. He could not even spell the Lonnie Grinnup he called himself—an orphan, too, like Stevens, a man a little under the medium size and somewhere in his middle thirties, whom the whole county knew—the face which was almost delicate when you looked at it again, equable, constant, always cheerful, with an invariable fuzz of soft golden beard which had never known a razor, and light-colored peaceful eyes—"touched," they said, but whatever it was, had touched him lightly, taking not very much away that need be missed—living, year in and year out, in the hovel he had built himself of an old tent and a few mismatched boards and flattened oil tins, with the deaf-and-dumb orphan he had taken into his hut ten years ago and clothed and fed and raised, and who had not even grown mentally as far as he himself had.

Actually his hut and trotline and fish trap were in almost the exact center of the thousand and more acres his ancestors had once owned. But he never knew it.

Stevens believed he would not have cared, would have declined to accept the idea that any one man could or should own that much of the earth which belongs to all, to every man for his use and pleasure—in his own case, that thirty or forty square feet where his hut sat and the span of river across which his trotline stretched where anyone was welcome at any time, whether he was there or not, to use his gear and eat his food as long as there was food.

And at times he would wedge his door shut against prowling animals and with his deaf-and-dumb companion he would appear without warning or invitation at houses or cabins ten and fifteen miles away, where he would remain for weeks, pleasant, equable, demanding nothing and without servility, sleeping wherever it was convenient for his hosts to have him sleep—in the hay of lofts, or in beds in family or company rooms, while the deaf-and-dumb youth lay on the porch or the ground just outside, where he could hear him who was brother and father both, breathing. It was his one sound out of all the voiceless earth. He was infallibly aware of it.

It was early afternoon. The distances were blue with heat. Then, across the long flat where the highway began to parallel the river bottom, Stevens saw the store. By ordinary it would have been deserted, but now he could already see clotted about it the topless and battered cars, the saddled horses and mules and the wagons, the riders and drivers of which he knew by name. Better still, they knew him, voting for him year after year and calling him by his given name even though they did not quite understand him, just as they did not understand the Harvard Phi Beta Kappa key on his watch chain. He drew in beside the coroner's car.

Apparently it was not to be in the store, but in the grist mill beside it, before the open door of which the clean Saturday overalls and shirts and the bared heads and the sunburned necks striped with the white razor lines of Saturday neck shaves were densest and quietest. They made way for him to enter. There was a table and three chairs where the coroner and two witnesses sat.

Stevens noticed a man of about forty holding a clean gunny sack, folded and refolded until it resembled a book, and a youth whose face wore an expression of weary yet indomitable amazement. The body lay under a quilt on the low platform to which the silent mill was bolted. He crossed to it and raised the corner of the quilt and looked at the face and lowered the quilt and turned, already on his way back to town, and then he did not go back to town. He moved over among the men who stood along the wall, their hats in their hands, and listened to the two witnesses—it was the youth telling it in his amazed, spent, incredulous voice—finish describing the finding of the body. He watched the coroner sign the certificate and return the pen to his pocket, and he knew he was not going back to town.

"I reckon that's all," the coroner said. He glanced toward the door. "All right, Ike," he said. "You can take him now."

Stevens moved aside with the others and watched the four men cross toward the quilt. "You going to take him, Ike?" he said.

The eldest of the four glanced back at him for a moment. "Yes. He had his burying money with Mitchell at the store."

"You, and Pose, and Matthew, and Jim Blake," Stevens said.

This time the other glanced back at him almost with surprise, almost impatiently.

"We can make up the difference," he said.

"I'll help," Stevens said.

"I thank you," the other said. "We got enough."

Then the coroner was among them, speaking testily: "All right, boys. Give them room."

With the others, Stevens moved out into the air, the afternoon again. There was a wagon backed up to the door now which had not been there before. Its tail gate was open, the bed was filled with straw, and with the others Stevens stood bareheaded and watched the four men emerge from the shed, carrying the quilt-wrapped bundle, and approach the wagon. Three or four others moved forward to help, and Stevens moved, too, and touched the youth's shoulder, seeing again that expression of spent and incredulous wild amazement.

"You went and got the boat before you knew anything was wrong," he said.

"That's right," the youth said. He spoke quietly enough at first. "I swum over and got the boat and rowed back. I knowed something was on the line. I could see it swagged—"

"You mean you swam the boat back," Stevens said.

"—down into the—Sir?"

"You swam the boat back. You swam over and got it and swam it back."

"No, sir! I rowed the boat back. I rowed it straight back across! I never suspected nothing! I could see them fish—"

"What with?" Stevens said. The youth glared at him. "What did you row it back with?"

"With the oar! I picked up the oar and rowed it right back, and all the time I could see them flopping around in the water. They didn't want to let go! They held on to him even after we hauled him up, still eating him! Fish were! I knowed turtles would, but these were fish! Eating him! Of course it was fish we thought was there! It was! I won't never eat another one! Never!"

It had not seemed long, yet the afternoon had gone somewhere, taking some of the heat with it. Again in his car, his hand on the switch, Stevens sat looking at the wagon, now about to depart. *And it's not right,* he thought. *It don't add. Something more that I missed, didn't see. Or something that hasn't happened yet.*

The wagon was now moving, crossing the dusty banquette toward the highroad, with two men on the seat and the other two on saddled mules beside it. Stevens' hand turned the switch; the car was already in gear. It passed the wagon, already going fast.

A mile down the road he turned into a dirt lane, back toward the hills. It began to rise, the sun intermittent now, for in places among the ridges sunset had already come. Presently the road forked. In the V of the fork stood a church, white-painted and steepleless, beside an unfenced straggle of cheap marble headstones and other graves outlined only by rows of inverted glass jars and crockery and broken brick.

He did not hesitate. He drove up beside the church and turned and stopped the car facing the fork and the road over which he had just come where it curved away and vanished. Because of the curve, he could hear the wagon for some time before he saw it, then he heard the truck. It was coming down out of the hills behind him, fast, sweeping into sight, already slowing—a cab, a shallow bed with a tarpaulin spread over it.

It drew out of the road at the fork and stopped; then he could hear the wagon again, and then he saw it and the two riders come around the curve in the dusk, and there was a man standing in the road beside the truck now, and Stevens recognized him: Tyler Ballenbaugh—a farmer, married and with a family and a reputation for self-sufficiency and violence, who had been born in the county and went out West and returned, bringing with him, like an effluvium, rumors of sums he had won gambling, who had married and bought land and no longer gambled at cards, but on certain years would mortgage his own crop and buy or sell cotton futures with the money—standing in the road beside the wagon, tall in the dusk, talking to the men in the wagon without raising his voice or making any gesture. Then there was another man beside him, in a white shirt, whom Stevens did not recognize or look at again.

His hand dropped to the switch; again the car was in motion with the sound of the engine. He turned the headlights on and dropped rapidly down out of the churchyard and into the road and up behind the wagon as the man in the white shirt leaped onto the running board, shouting at him, and Stevens recognized him too: A younger brother of Ballenbaugh's, who had gone to Memphis years ago, where it was understood he had been a hired armed guard during a textile strike, but who, for the last two or three years, had been at his brother's, hiding, it was said, not from the police but from some of his Memphis friends or later business associates. From time to time his name made one in reported brawls and fights at country dances and picnics. He was subdued and thrown into jail once by two officers in Jefferson, where, on Saturdays, drunk, he would brag about his past exploits or curse his present luck and the older brother who made him work about the farm.

"Who in hell you spying on?" he shouted.

"Boyd," the other Ballenbaugh said. He did not even raise his voice. "Get back in the truck." He had not moved—a big somber-faced man who stared at Stevens out of pale, cold, absolutely expressionless eyes. "Howdy, Gavin," he said.

"Howdy, Tyler," Stevens said. "You going to take Lonnie?"

"Does anybody here object?"

"I don't," Stevens said, getting out of the car. "I'll help you swamp him."

Then he got back into the car. The wagon moved on. The truck backed and turned, already gaining speed; the two faces fled past—the one which Stevens saw now was not truculent, but frightened; the other, in which there was nothing at all save the still, cold, pale eyes. The cracked tail lamp vanished over the hill. *That was an Okatoba County license number,* he thought.

Lonnie Grinnup was buried the next afternoon, from Tyler Ballenbaugh's house.

Stevens was not there. "Joe wasn't there, either, I suppose," he said. "Lonnie's dummy."

"No. He wasn't there, either. The folks that went in to Lonnie's camp on Sunday morning to look at that trotline said that he was still there, hunting for Lonnie. But he wasn't at the burying. When he finds Lonnie this time, he can lie down by him, but he won't hear him breathing."

3

"No," Stevens said.

He was in Mottstown, the seat of Okatoba County, on that afternoon. And although it was Sunday, and although he would not know until he found it just what he was looking for, he found it before dark—the agent for the company which, eleven years ago, had issued to Lonnie Grinnup a five-thousand-dollar policy, with double indemnity for accidental death, on his life, with Tyler Ballenbaugh as beneficiary.

It was quite correct. The examining doctor had never seen Lonnie Grinnup before, but he had known Tyler Ballenbaugh for years, and Lonnie had made his mark on the application and Ballenbaugh had paid the first premium and kept them up ever since.

There had been no particular secrecy about it other than transacting the business in another town, and Stevens realized that even that was not unduly strange.

Okatoba County was just across the river, three miles from where Ballenbaugh lived, and Stevens knew of more men than Ballenbaugh who owned land in one county and bought their cars and trucks and banked their money in another, obeying the country-bred man's inherent, possibly atavistic, faint distrust, perhaps, not of men in white collars but of paving and electricity.

"Then I'm not to notify the company yet?" the agent asked.

"No. I want you to accept the claim when he comes in to file it, explain to him it will take a week or so to settle it, wait three days and send him word to come in to your office to see you at nine o'clock or ten o'clock the next morning; don't tell him why, what for. Then telephone me at Jefferson when you know he has got the message."

Early the next morning, about daybreak, the heat wave broke. He lay in bed watching and listening to the crash and glare of lightning and the rain's loud fury, thinking of the drumming of it and the fierce channeling of clay-colored water across Lonnie Grinnup's raw and kinless grave in the barren hill beside the steepleless church, and of the sound it would make, above the turmoil of the rising river, on the tin-and-canvas hut where the deaf-and-dumb youth probably still waited for him to come home, knowing that something had happened, but not how, not why. *Not how,* Stevens thought. *They fooled him someway. They didn't even bother to tie him up. They just fooled him.*

On Wednesday night he received a telephone message from the Mottstown agent that Tyler Ballenbaugh had filed his claim.

"All right," Stevens said. "Send him the message Monday, to come in Tuesday. And let me know when you know he has gotten it." He put the phone down. *I am playing stud poker with a man who has proved himself a gambler, which I have not,* he thought. *But at least I have forced him to draw a card. And he knows who is in the pot with him.*

So when the second message came, on the following Monday afternoon, he knew only what he himself was going to do. He had thought once of asking the sheriff for a deputy, or of taking some friend with him. *But even a friend would not believe that what I have is a hold card,* he told himself, *even though I do: That one man, even an amateur at murder, might be satisfied that he had cleaned up after himself. But when there are two of them, neither one is going to be satisfied that the other has left no ravelings.*

So he went alone. He owned a pistol. He looked at it and put it back into its drawer. *At least nobody is going to shoot me with that,* he told himself. He left town just after dusk.

This time he passed the store, dark at the roadside. When he reached the lane into which he had turned nine days ago, this time he turned to the right and drove on for a quarter of a mile and turned into a littered yard, his headlights full upon a dark cabin. He did not turn them off. He walked full in the yellow beam, toward the cabin, shouting: "Nate! Nate!"

After a moment a Negro voice answered, though no light showed.

"I'm going in to Mr. Lonnie Grinnup's camp. If I'm not back by daylight, you better go up to the store and tell them."

There was no answer. Then a woman's voice said: "You come on away from that door!" The man's voice murmured something.

"I can't help it!" the woman cried. "You come away and let them white folks alone!"

So there are others besides me, Stevens thought, thinking how quite often, almost always, there is in Negroes an instinct not for evil but to recognize evil at once when it exists. He went back to the car and snapped off the lights and took his flashlight from the seat.

He found the truck. In the close-held beam of the light he read again the license number which he had watched nine days ago flee over the hill. He snapped off the light and put it into his pocket.

Twenty minutes later he realized he need not have worried about the light. He was in the path, between the black wall of jungle and the river, he saw the faint glow inside the canvas wall of the hut and he could already hear the two voices—the one cold, level and steady, the other harsh and high. He stumbled over the woodpile and then over something else and found the door and flung it back and entered the devastation of the dead man's house—the shuck mattresses dragged out of the wooden bunks, the overturned stove and scattered cooking vessels—where Tyler Ballenbaugh stood facing him with a pistol and the younger one stood half-crouched above an overturned box.

"Stand back, Gavin," Ballenbaugh said.

"Stand back yourself, Tyler," Stevens said. "You're too late."

The younger one stood up. Stevens saw recognition come into his face. "Well, by—" he said.

"Is it all up, Gavin?" Ballenbaugh said. "Don't lie to me."

"I reckon it is," Stevens said. "Put your pistol down."

"Who else is with you?"

"Enough," Stevens said. "Put your pistol down, Tyler."

"Hell," the younger one said. He began to move; Stevens saw his eyes go swiftly from him to the door behind him. "He's lying. There ain't anybody with him. He's just spying around like he was the other day, putting his nose into business he's going to wish he had kept it out of. Because this time it's going to get bit off."

He was moving towards Stevens, stooping a little, his arms held slightly away from his sides.

"Boyd!" Tyler said. The other continued to approach Stevens, not smiling, but with a queer light, a glitter, in his face. "Boyd!" Tyler said. Then he moved, too, with astonishing speed, and overtook the younger and with one sweep of his arm hurled him back into the bunk. They faced each other—the one cold, still, expressionless, the pistol held before him aimed at nothing, the other half-crouched, snarling.

"What the hell you going to do? Let him take us back to town like two damn sheep?"

"That's for me to decide," Tyler said. He looked at Stevens. "I never intended this, Gavin. I insured his life, kept the premiums paid—yes. But it was good business: If he had outlived me, I wouldn't have had any use for the money, and if I had outlived him, I would have collected on my judgment. There was no secret about it. It was done in open daylight. Anybody could have found out about it. Maybe he told about it. I never told him not to. And who's to say against it anyway? I always fed him when he came to my house, he always stayed as long as he wanted to, come when he wanted to. But I never intended this."

Suddenly the younger one began to laugh, half-crouched against the bunk where the other had flung him. "So that's the tune," he said. "That's the way it's going." Then it was not laughter any more, though the transition was so slight or perhaps so swift as to be imperceptible. He was standing now, leaning forward a little, facing his brother. "I never insured him for five thousand dollars! I wasn't going to get—"

"Hush," Tyler said.

"—five thousand dollars when they found him dead on that—"

Tyler walked steadily to the other and slapped him in two motions, palm and back, of the same hand, the pistol still held before him in the other.

"I said, hush, Boyd," he said. He looked at Stevens again. "I never intended this. I don't want that money now, even if they were going to pay it, because this is not the way I aimed for it to be. Not the way I bet. What are you going to do?"

"Do you need to ask that? I want an indictment for murder."

"And then prove it!" the younger one snarled. "Try and prove it! I never insured his life for—"

"Hush," Tyler said. He spoke almost gently, looking at Stevens with the pale eyes in which there was absolutely nothing. "You can't do that. It's a good name. Has been. Maybe nobody's done much for it yet, but nobody's hurt it bad yet, up to now. I have owed no man, I have taken nothing that was not mine. You musn't do that, Gavin."

"I mustn't do anything else, Tyler."

The other looked at him. Stevens heard him draw a long breath and expel it. But his face did not change at all. "You want your eye for an eye and tooth for a tooth."

"Justice wants it. Maybe Lonnie Grinnup wants it. Wouldn't you?"

For a moment longer the other looked at him. Then Ballenbaugh turned and made a quiet gesture at his brother and another toward Stevens, quiet and peremptory.

Then they were out of the hut, standing in the light from the door; a breeze came up from somewhere and rustled in the leaves overhead and died away, ceased.

At first Stevens did not know what Ballenbaugh was about. He watched in mounting surprise as Ballenbaugh turned to face his brother, his hand extended, speaking in a voice which was actually harsh now: "This is the end of the row. I was afraid from that night when you came home and told me. I should have raised you better, but I didn't. Here. Stand up and finish it."

"Look out, Tyler!" Stevens said. "Don't do that!"

"Keep out of this, Gavin. If it's meat for meat you want, you will get it." He still faced his brother, he did not even glance at Stevens. "Here," he said. "Take it and stand up."

Then it was too late. Stevens saw the younger one spring back. He saw Tyler take a step forward and he seemed to hear in the other's voice the surprise, the disbelief, then the realization of the mistake. "Drop the pistol, Boyd," he said. "Drop it."

"So you want it back, do you?" the younger said. "I come to you that night and told you you were worth five thousand dollars as soon as somebody happened to look on that trotline, and asked you to give me ten dollars, and you turned me down. Ten dollars, and you wouldn't. Sure you can have it. Take it." It flashed, low against his side; the orange fire lanced downward again as the other fell.

Now it's my turn, Stevens thought. They faced each other; he heard again that brief wind come from somewhere and shake the leaves overhead and fall still.

"Run while you can, Boyd," he said. "You've done enough. Run, now."

"Sure I'll run. You do all your worrying about me now, because in a minute you won't have any worries. I'll run all right, after I've said a word to smart guys that come sticking their noses where they'll wish to hell they hadn't—"

Now he's going to shoot, Stevens thought, and he sprang. For an instant he had the illusion of watching himself springing, reflected somehow by the faint light from the river, that luminousness which water gives back to the dark, in the air above Boyd Ballenbaugh's head. Then he knew it was not himself he saw, it had not been wind he heard, as the creature, the shape which had no tongue and needed none, which had been waiting nine days now for Lonnie Grinnup to come home, dropped toward the murderer's back with its hands already extended and its body curved and rigid with silent and deadly purpose.

He was in the tree, Stevens thought. The pistol glared. He saw the flash, but he heard no sound.

4

He was sitting on the veranda with his neat surgeon's bandage after supper when the sheriff of the county came up the walk—a big man, too, pleasant, affable, with eyes even paler and colder and more expressionless than Tyler Ballenbaugh's. "It won't take but a minute," he said, "or I wouldn't have bothered you."

"How bothered me?" Stevens said.

The sheriff lowered one thigh to the veranda rail. "Head feel all right?"

"Feels all right," Stevens said.

"That's good, I reckon you heard where we found Boyd."

Stevens looked back at him just as blankly. "I may have," he said pleasantly. "Haven't remembered much today but a headache."

"You told us where to look. You were conscious when I got there. You were trying to give Tyler water. You told us to look on that trotline."

"Did I? Well, well, what won't a man say, drunk or out of his head? Sometimes he's right too."

"You were. We looked on the line, and there was Boyd hung on one of the hooks, dead, just like Lonnie Grinnup was. And Tyler Ballenbaugh with a broken leg and another bullet in his shoulder, and you with a crease in your skull you could hide a cigar in. How did he get on that trotline, Gavin?"

"I don't know," Stevens said.

"All right. I'm not sheriff now. How did Boyd get on that trotline?"

"I don't know."

The sheriff looked at him; they looked at each other. "Is that what you answer any friend that asks?"

"Yes. Because I was shot, you see. I don't know."

The sheriff took a cigar from his pocket and looked at it for a time. "Joe—that deaf-and-dumb boy Lonnie raised—seems to have gone away at last. He was still around there last Sunday, but nobody has seen him since. He could have stayed. Nobody would have bothered him."

"Maybe he missed Lonnie too much to stay," Stevens said.

"Maybe he missed Lonnie." The sheriff rose. He bit the end from the cigar and lit it. "Did that bullet cause you to forget this too? Just what made you suspect something was wrong? What was it the rest of us seem to have missed?"

"It was that paddle," Stevens said.

"Paddle?"

"Didn't you ever run a trotline, a trotline right at your camp? You don't paddle, you pull the boat hand over hand along the line itself from one hook to the next. Lonnie never did use his paddle; he even kept the skiff tied to the same tree his trotline was fastened to, and the paddle stayed in his house. If you had ever been there, you would have seen it. But the paddle was in the skiff when that boy found it."

JORGE LUIS BORGES (1899–1986)

Jorge Luis Borges was born in Buenos Aires to a Spanish-English family, studied in Switzerland, and lived for many years in Spain before returning to his native Argentina, where he became director of the National Library. He first won recognition as a poet and essayist, then international fame as a writer of enigmatic philosophical tales, collected in *Ficciones* (1944), *El Aleph* (1949), and *Labyrinths* (1962). His fiction is marked by concision and by fantastic themes worked out in elaborate verbal and emotional structures that create their own universe divorced from the chaos of the actual world. Borges' fascination with puzzles is revealed in his recurrent images of mazes and mirrors. An avid reader of stories of mystery and detection, he collaborated with his friend Adolfo Bioy-Casares to create an Argentinian private investigator in *Six Problems for Don Isidro Parodí* (1942) and in a novella, *A Model for Death* (1946). Also with Bioy-Casares, he edited and translated two anthologies of largely English and American detective short stories (1943 and 1956). His contribution to the detective genre—revising, parodying, and subverting its formulas—shows the genre's adaptability for new schools of writers who challenge the restrictions and conventions of fiction.

"Death and the Compass" shows the influence of G. K. Chesterton, whom Borges greatly admired, in treating metaphysical concerns with paradox and allegory. It was also influenced by Agatha Christie's *The A B C Murders* (1936) in which a series of murders is committed for the sake of the pattern they create, a pattern intended to mislead the detective. In Borges' hands, this pattern becomes a critique on the limits of detection by showing both the ultimate unknowability of truth and the inexorable power of logic to draw the detective to his destruction.

DEATH AND THE COMPASS

Of the many problems which exercised the daring perspicacity of Lönnrot none was so strange—so harshly strange, we may say—as the staggered series of bloody acts which culminated at the villa of Triste-le-Roy, amid the boundless odor of the eucalypti. It is true that Erik Lönnrot did not succeed in preventing the last crime, but it is indisputable that he foresaw it. Nor did he, of course, guess the identity of Yarmolinsky's unfortunate assassin, but he did divine the secret morphology of the vicious series as well as the participation of Red Scharlach, whose alias is Scharlach the Dandy. This criminal (as so many others) had sworn on his honor to kill Lönnrot, but the latter had never allowed himself to be intimidated. Lönnrot thought of himself as a pure thinker, an Auguste Dupin, but there was something of the adventurer in him, and even of the gamester.

The first crime occurred at the Hôtel du Nord—that high prism that dominates the estuary whose waters are the colors of the desert. To this tower (which most manifestly unites the hateful whiteness of a sanitorium, the numbered divisibility of a prison, and the general appearance of a bawdy house) on the third day of December came the delegate from Podolsk to the Third Talmudic Congress, Doctor Marcel Yarmolinsky, a man of gray beard and gray eyes. We shall never know whether the Hôtel du Nord pleased him: he accepted it with the ancient resignation which had allowed him to endure three years of war in the Carpathians and three thousand years of oppression and pogroms. He was given a sleeping room on floor R, in front of the suite which the Tetrarch of Galilee occupied not without some splendor. Yarmolinsky supped, postponed until the following day an investigation of the unknown city, arranged upon a cupboard his many books and his few possessions, and before midnight turned off the light. (Thus declared the Tetrarch's chauffeur, who slept in an adjoining room.) On the fourth, at 11:03 A.M., there was a telephone call for him from the editor of the *Yiddische Zeitung;* Doctor Yarmolinsky did not reply; he was found in his room, his face already a little dark, and his body, almost nude, beneath a large anachronistic cape. He was lying not far from the door which gave onto the corridor; a deep stab wound had split open his breast. In the same room, a couple of hours later, in the midst of journalists, photographers, and police, Commissioner Treviranus and Lönnrot were discussing the problem with equanimity.

"There's no need to look for a Chimera, or a cat with three legs," Treviranus was saying as he brandished an imperious cigar. "We all know that the Tetrarch of Galilee is the possessor of the finest sapphires in the world. Someone, intending to steal them, came in here by mistake. Yarmolinsky got up; the robber had to kill him. What do you think?"

"It's possible, but not interesting," Lönnrot answered. "You will reply that reality hasn't the slightest need to be of interest. And I'll answer you that reality may avoid the obligation to be interesting, but that hypotheses may not. In the hypothesis you have postulated, chance intervenes largely. Here lies a dead rabbi; I should prefer a purely rabbinical explanation; not the imaginary mischances of an imaginary robber."

Treviranus answered ill-humoredly:

"I am not interested in rabbinical explanations; I am interested in the capture of the man who stabbed this unknown person."

"Not so unknown," corrected Lönnrot. "Here are his complete works." He indicated a line of tall volumes: *A Vindication of the Cabala; An Examination of the Philosophy of Robert Fludd*; a literal translation of the *Sepher Yezirah*; a *Biography of the Baal Shem*; a *History of the Sect of the Hasidim*; a monograph (in German) on the Tetragrammaton; another, on the divine nomenclature of the Pentateuch. The Commissioner gazed at them with suspicion, almost with revulsion. Then he fell to laughing.

"I'm only a poor Christian," he replied. "Carry off all these moth-eaten classics if you like; I haven't got time to lose in Jewish superstitions."

"Maybe this crime belongs to the history of Jewish superstitions," murmured Lönnrot.

"Like Christianity," the editor of the *Yiddische Zeitung* dared to put in. He was a myope, an atheist, and very timid.

No one answered him. One of the agents had found inserted in the small typewriter a piece of paper on which was written the following inconclusive sentence.

The first letter of the Name has been spoken

Lönnrot abstained from smiling. Suddenly become a bibliophile—or Hebraist—he directed that the dead man's books be made into a parcel, and he carried them to his office. Indifferent to the police investigation, he dedicated himself to studying them. A large octavo volume revealed to him the teachings of Israel Baal Shem-Tob, founder of the sect of the Pious; another volume, the virtues and terrors of the Tetragrammaton, which is the ineffable name of God; another, the thesis that God has a secret name, in which is epitomized (as in the crystal sphere which the Persians attribute to Alexander of Macedon) his ninth attribute, eternity—that is to say, the immediate knowledge of everything that will exist, exists, and has existed in the universe. Tradition numbers ninety-nine names of God; the Hebraists attribute this imperfect number to the magical fear of even numbers; the Hasidim reason that this hiatus indicates a hundredth name—the Absolute Name.

From this erudition he was distracted, within a few days, by the appearance of the editor of the *Yiddische Zeitung*. This man wished to talk of the assassination; Lönnrot preferred to speak of the diverse names of God. The journalist declared, in three columns, that the investigator Erik Lönnrot had dedicated himself to studying the names of God in order to "come up with" the name of the assassin. Lönnrot, habituated to the simplifications of journalism, did not become indignant. One of those shopkeepers who have found that there are buyers for every book came out with a popular edition of the *History of the Sect of the Hasidim*.

The second crime occurred on the night of the third of January, in the most deserted and empty corner of the capital's western suburbs. Toward dawn, one of the gendarmes who patrol these lonely places on horseback detected a man in a cape, lying prone in the shadow of an ancient paint shop. The hard visage seemed bathed in blood; a deep stab wound had split open his breast. On the wall, upon the yellow and red rhombs, there were some words written in chalk. The gendarme spelled them out. . . .

That afternoon Treviranus and Lönnrot made their way toward the remote scene of the crime. To the left and right of the automobile, the city disintegrated; the firmament grew larger and the houses meant less and less and a brick kiln or a poplar grove more and more. They reached their miserable destination: a final alley of rose-colored mud walls which in some way seemed to reflect the disordered setting of the sun. The dead man had already been identified. He was Daniel Simon Azevedo, a man of some fame in the ancient northern suburbs, who had risen from wagoner to political tough, only to degenerate later into a thief and even an informer. (The singular style of his death struck them as appropriate: Azevedo was the last representative of a generation of bandits who knew how to handle a dagger, but not a revolver.) The words in chalk were the following:

The second letter of the Name has been spoken

The third crime occurred on the night of the third of February. A little before one o'clock, the telephone rang in the office of Commissioner Treviranus. In avid secretiveness a man with a guttural voice spoke: he said his name was Ginzberg (or Ginsburg) and that he was disposed to communicate, for a reasonable remuneration, an explanation of the two sacrifices of Azevedo and Yarmolinsky. The discordant sound of whistles and horns drowned out the voice of the informer. Then the connection was cut off. Without rejecting the possibility of a hoax (it was carnival time), Treviranus checked and found he had been called from Liverpool House, a tavern on the Rue de Toulon—that dirty street where cheek by jowl are the peepshow and the milk store, the bordello and the women selling Bibles. Treviranus called back and spoke to the owner. This personage (Black Finnegan by name, an old Irish criminal who was crushed, annihilated almost, by respectability) told him that the last person to use the establishment's phone had been a lodger, a certain Gryphius, who had just gone out with some friends. Treviranus immediately went to Liverpool House, where Finnegan related the following facts. Eight days previously, Gryphius had taken a room above the saloon. He was a man of sharp features, a nebulous gray beard, shabbily clothed in black; Finnegan (who put the room to a use which Treviranus guessed) demanded a rent which was undoubtedly excessive; Gryphius immediately paid the stipulated sum. He scarcely ever went out; he dined and lunched in his room; his face was hardly known in the bar. On this particular night, he came down to telephone from Finnegan's office. A closed coupe stopped in front of the tavern. The driver did not move from his seat; several of the patrons recalled that he was wearing a bear mask. Two harlequins descended from the coupe; they were short in stature, and no one could fail to observe that they were very drunk. With a tooting of horns they burst into Finnegan's office; they embraced Gryphius, who seemed to recognize them but who replied to them coldly; they exchanged a few words in Yiddish—he, in a low guttural voice; they, in shrill, falsetto tones—and then the party climbed to the upstairs room. Within a quarter hour the three descended, very joyous; Gryphius, staggering, seemed as drunk as the others. He walked—tall, dazed—in the middle, between the masked harlequins. (One of the women in the bar remembered the yellow, red and green rhombs, the diamond designs.) Twice he stumbled; twice he was held up by the harlequins. Alongside the adjoining dock basin, whose water was rectangular, the trio got into the coupe and disappeared. From the running board, the last of the harlequins had scrawled an obscene figure and a sentence on one of the slates of the outdoor shed.

Treviranus gazed upon the sentence. It was nearly foreknowable. It read:

The last of the letters of the Name has been spoken

He examined, then, the small room of Gryphius-Ginzberg. On the floor was a violent star of blood; in the corners, the remains of some Hungarian-brand cigarettes; in a cabinet, a book in Latin—the *Philologus Hebraeo-Graecus* (1739) of Leusden—along with various manuscript notes. Treviranus studied the book with indignation and had Lönnrot summoned. The latter, without taking off his hat, began to read while the Commissioner questioned the contradictory witnesses to the possible kidnapping. At four in the morning they came out. In the tortuous Rue de Toulon, as they stepped on the dead serpentines of the dawn, Treviranus said:

"And supposing the story of this night were a sham?"

Erik Lönnrot smiled and read him with due gravity a passage (underlined) of the thirty-third dissertation of the *Philologus*:

Dies Judaeorum incipit a solis occasu
usque ad solis occasum diei sequentis.

"This means," he added, "that *the Hebrew day begins at sundown and lasts until the following sundown.*"

Treviranus attempted an irony.

"Is this fact the most worthwhile you've picked up tonight?"

"No. Of even greater value is a word Ginzberg used."

The afternoon dailies did not neglect this series of disappearances. *The Cross and the Sword* contrasted them with the admirable discipline and order of the last Eremitical Congress; Ernest Palast, writing in *The Martyr,* spoke out against "the intolerable delays in this clandestine and frugal pogrom, which has taken three months to liquidate three Jews"; the *Yiddische Zeitung* rejected the terrible hypothesis of an anti-Semitic plot, "even though many discerning intellects do not admit of any other solution to the triple mystery"; the most illustrious gunman in the South, Dandy Red Scharlach, swore that in his district such crimes as these would never occur, and he accused Commissioner Franz Treviranus of criminal negligence.

On the night of March first, the Commissioner received an imposing-looking, sealed envelope. He opened it: the envelope contained a letter signed Baruj Spinoza, and a detailed plan of the city, obviously torn from a Baedeker. The letter prophesied that on the third of March there would *not* be a fourth crime, inasmuch as the paint shop in the West, the Tavern on the Rue de Toulon and the Hôtel du Nord were the "perfect vertices of an equilateral and mystic triangle"; the regularity of this triangle was made clear on the map with red ink. This argument, *more geometrico,* Treviranus read with resignation, and sent the letter and map on to Lönnrot—who deserved such a piece of insanity.

Erik Lönnrot studied the documents. The three sites were in fact equidistant. Symmetry in time (the third of December, the third of January, the third of February); symmetry in space as well. . . . Of a sudden he sensed he was about to decipher the mystery. A set of calipers and a compass completed his sudden intuition. He smiled, pronounced the word "Tetragrammaton" (of recent acquisition), and called the Commissioner on the telephone. He told him:

"Thank you for the equilateral triangle you sent me last night. It has enabled me to solve the problem. Tomorrow, Friday, the criminals will be in jail, we can rest assured."

"In that case, they're not planning a fourth crime?"

"Precisely because they *are* planning a fourth crime can we rest assured."

Lönnrot hung up. An hour later he was traveling in one of the trains of the Southern Railways, en route to the abandoned villa of Triste-le-Roy. South of the city of our story there flows a blind little river filled with muddy water made disgraceful by floating scraps and garbage. On the further side is a manufacturing suburb where, under the protection of a chief from Barcelona, gunmen flourish. Lönnrot smiled to himself to think that the most famous of them—Red Scharlach—would have given anything to know of this clandestine visit. Azevedo had been a comrade of Scharlach's; Lönnrot considered the remote possibility that the fourth victim might be Scharlach himself. Then, he put aside the thought. . . . He had virtually deciphered the problem; the mere circumstances, or the reality (names, prison records, faces, judicial and penal proceedings), scarcely interested him now. Most of all he wanted to take a stroll, to relax from three months of sedentary investigation. He reflected on how the explanation of the crimes lay in an anonymous triangle and a dust-laden Greek word. The mystery seemed to him almost crystalline now; he was mortified to have dedicated a hundred days to it.

The train stopped at a silent loading platform. Lönnrot descended. It was one of those deserted afternoons which seem like dawn. The air over the muddy plain was damp and cold. Lönnrot set off across the fields. He saw dogs, he saw a wagon on a dead road, he saw the horizon, he saw a silvery horse drinking the crapulous water of a puddle. Dusk was falling when he saw the rectangular belvedere of the villa of Triste-le-Roy, almost as tall as the black eucalypti which surrounded it. He thought of the fact that only one more dawn and one more nightfall (an ancient splendor in the east, and another in the west) separated him from the hour so much desired by the seekers of the Name.

A rust colored wrought-iron fence defined the irregular perimeter of the villa. The main gate was closed. Without much expectation of entering, Lönnrot made a complete circuit. In front of the insurmountable gate once again, he put his hand between the bars almost mechanically and chanced upon the bolt. The creaking of the iron surprised him. With laborious passivity the entire gate gave way.

Lönnrot advanced among the eucalypti, stepping amidst confused generations of rigid, broken leaves. Close up, the house on the estate of Triste-le-Roy was seen to abound in superfluous symmetries and in maniacal repetitions: a glacial Diana in one lugubrious niche was complemented by another Diana in another niche; one balcony was repeated by another balcony; double steps of stairs opened into a double balustrade. A two-faced Hermes cast a monstrous shadow. Lönnrot circled the house as he had the estate. He examined everything; beneath the level of the terrace he noticed a narrow shutter door.

He pushed against it: some marble steps descended to a vault. Versed now in the architect's preferences, Lönnrot divined that there would be a set of stairs on the opposite wall. He found them, ascended, raised his hands, and pushed up a trap door.

The diffusion of light guided him to a window. He opened it: a round, yellow moon outlined two stopped-up fountains in the melancholy garden. Lönnrot explored the house. He traveled through antechambers and galleries to emerge upon duplicate patios; several times he emerged upon the same patio. He ascended dust-covered stairways and came out into circular antechambers; he was infinitely reflected in opposing mirrors; he grew weary of opening or half-opening windows which revealed the same desolate garden outside, from various heights and various angles; inside, the furniture was wrapped in yellow covers and the chandeliers bound up with cretonne. A bedroom detained him; in the bedroom, a single rose in a porcelain vase—at the first touch the ancient petals fell apart. On the second floor, on the top story, the house seemed to be infinite and growing. *The house is not this large,* he thought. *It is only made larger by the penumbra, the symmetry, the mirrors, the years, my ignorance, the solitude.*

Going up a spiral staircase he arrived at the observatory. The evening moon shone through the rhomboid diamonds of the windows, which were yellow, red and green. He was brought to a halt by a stunning and dizzying recollection.

Two men of short stature, ferocious and stocky, hurled themselves upon him and took his weapon. Another man, very tall, saluted him gravely, and said:

"You are very thoughtful. You've saved us a night and a day."

It was Red Scharlach. His men manacled Lönnrot's hands. Lönnrot at length found his voice.

"Are you looking for the Secret Name, Scharlach?"

Scharlach remained standing, indifferent. He had not participated in the short struggle; he scarcely stretched out his hand to receive Lönnrot's revolver. He spoke; in his voice Lönnrot detected a fatigued triumph, a hatred the size of the universe, a sadness no smaller than that hatred.

"No," answered Scharlach. "I am looking for something more ephemeral and slippery, I am looking for Erik Lönnrot. Three years ago, in a gambling house on the Rue de Toulon, you arrested my brother and had him sent to prison. In the exchange of shots that night my men got me away in a coupe, with a police bullet in my chest. Nine days and nine nights I lay dying in this desolate, symmetrical villa; I was racked with fever, and the odious double-faced Janus who gazes toward the twilights of dusk and dawn terrorized my dreams and my waking. I learned to abominate my body, I came to feel that two eyes, two hands, two lungs are as monstrous as two faces. An Irishman attempted to convert me to the faith of Jesus; he repeated to me that famous axiom of the *goyim:* All roads lead to Rome. At night, my delirium nurtured itself on this metaphor: I sensed that the world was a labyrinth, from which it was impossible to flee, for all paths, whether they seemed to lead north or south, actually led to Rome, which was also the quadrilateral jail where my brother was dying and the villa of Triste-le-Roy. During those nights I swore by the god who sees from two faces, and by all the gods of fever and of mirrors, to weave a labyrinth around the man who had imprisoned my brother. I have woven it, and it holds: the materials are a dead writer on heresies, a compass, an eighteenth-century sect, a Greek word, a dagger, the rhombs of a paint shop.

"The first objective in the sequence was given me by chance. I had made plans with some colleagues—among them, Daniel Azevedo—to take the Tetrarch's sapphires. Azevedo betrayed us; with the money we advanced him he got himself inebriated and started on the job a day early. In the vastness of the hotel he got lost; at two in the morning he blundered into Yarmolinsky's room. The latter, harassed by insomnia, had set himself to writing. He was editing some notes, apparently, or writing an article on the Name of God; he had just written the words *The first letter of the Name has been spoken.* Azevedo enjoined him to be quiet; Yarmolinsky reached out his hand for the bell which would arouse all the hotel's forces; Azevedo at once stabbed him in the chest. It was almost a reflex action: half a century of violence had taught him that it was easiest and surest to kill. . . . Ten days later, I learned through the *Yiddische Zeitung* that you were perusing the writings of Yarmolinsky for the key to his death. For my part I read the *History of the Sect of the Hasidim*; I learned that the reverent fear of pronouncing the Name of God had given rise to the doctrine that this Name is all-powerful and mystic. I learned that some Hasidim, in search of this secret Name, had gone as far as to offer human sacrifices. . . . I knew you would conjecture that the Hasidim had sacrificed the rabbi; I set myself to justifying this conjecture.

"Marcel Yarmolinsky died on the night of December third; for the second sacrifice I selected the night of January third. Yarmolinsky died in the North; for the second sacrifice a place in the West was preferable. Daniel Azevedo was the inevitable victim. He deserved death: he was an impulsive person, a traitor; his capture could destroy the entire plan. One of our men stabbed him; in order to link his corpse to the other one I wrote on the paint shop diamonds *The second letter of the Name has been spoken.*

"The third 'crime' was produced on the third of February. It was as Treviranus must have guessed, a mere mockery, a simulacrum. I am Gryphius-Ginzberg-Ginsburg; I endured an interminable week (filled out with a tenuous false beard) in that perverse cubicle on the Rue de Toulon, until my friends spirited me away. From the running board one of them wrote on a pillar *The last of the letters of the Name has been spoken.* This sentence revealed that the series of crimes was *triple.* And the public thus understood it; nevertheless, I interspersed repeated signs that would allow you, Erik Lönnrot, the reasoner, to understand that it is *quadruple.* A portent in the North, others in the East and West, demand a fourth portent in the South; the Tetragrammaton—the name of God, JHVH—is made up of *four* letters; the harlequins and the paint shop sign suggested four points. In the manual of Leusden I underlined a certain passage: it manifested that the Hebrews calculate a day counting from dusk to dusk and that therefore the deaths occurred on the *fourth* day of each month. To Treviranus I sent the equilateral triangle. I sensed that you would supply the missing point. The point which would form a perfect rhomb, the point which fixes where death, exactly, awaits you. In order to attract you I have premeditated everything, Erik Lönnrot, so as to draw you to the solitude of Triste-le-Roy."

Lönnrot avoided Scharlach's eyes. He was looking at the trees and the sky divided into rhombs of turbid yellow, green and red. He felt a little cold, and felt, too, an impersonal, almost anonymous sadness. It was already night; from the dusty garden arose the useless cry of a bird. For the last time, Lönnrot considered the problem of symmetrical and periodic death.

"In your labyrinth there are three lines too many," he said at last. "I know of a Greek labyrinth which is a single straight line. Along this line so many philosophers have lost themselves that a mere detective might well do so too. Scharlach, when, in some other incarnation you hunt me, feign to commit (or do commit) a crime at A, then a second crime at B, eight kilometers from A, then a third crime at C, four kilometers from A and B, halfway enroute between the two. Wait for me later at D, two kilometers from A and C, halfway, once again, between both. Kill me at D, as you are now going to kill me at Triste-le-Roy."

"The next time I kill you," said Scharlach, "I promise you the labyrinth made of the single straight line which is invisible and everlasting."

He stepped back a few paces. Then, very carefully, he fired.

—Translated by Anthony Kerrigan

ELLERY QUEEN
FREDERIC DANNAY (1905–1982)
MANFRED BENNINGTON LEE (1905–1971)

Ellery Queen was the creation of two Brooklyn-born cousins, Frederic Dannay and Manfred Bennington Lee, who collaborated on a story about a private investigator named Ellery Queen for a crime novel contest in 1928. Thus began one of the longest mystery-writing careers in literature, as they proceeded over the next four decades to publish stories and novels about their detective, using the joint pseudonym of "Ellery Queen." A thoroughly commercial venture from the start, the Queen collaboration underwent a series of changes in style that provide an index to shifting popular tastes in detective fiction. As characterized by Francis M. Nevins, Jr. in an essay on Queen in *Twentieth-Century Crime and Mystery Writers,* the first stage of Queen's career, inspired by S. S. Van Dine's aristocratic detective Philo Vance, was marked by a brittleness that reflected the 1920s' fascination with wealth and social prominence. In the second period, in response to Hollywood's demands, Queen's character became less priggish and love interests were introduced. In the late 1930s and early 1940s the Queen authors initiated a popular radio series about their detective, as well as the famous *Ellery Queen's Mystery Magazine,* which continues to this day to publish work by some of the most prominent practitioners of the genre. The third Queen period, considered by many to be the best, dates from 1942 when the writers began to explore character in depth and to create evocative settings. The fourth period saw a falling back into the stylized plots and thin characterization of the earliest stage. Nevins notes that "Most of Queen's distinctive story motifs—the negative clue, the dying message, the murderer as Iagoesque manipulator, the patterned series of clues deliberately left at the crime scenes, the false answer followed by the true and devastating solution—originated in [Queen's] early novels" and were used throughout his long career.

"The Adventure of Abraham Lincoln's Clue," from Ellery Queen's best period, reflects the Golden Age style in its central puzzle (the decoding of the message) and in its use of literary allusions and abstruse facts (about historical figures, philately, and the like). It harks back to Poe's "The Purloined Letter" in that the solution rests on the ability of the detective (and the reader) to see the object (in this case the cryptic message) from a, quite literally, different perspective or angle of vision.

THE ADVENTURE OF ABRAHAM LINCOLN'S CLUE

The case began on the outskirts of an upstate New York city with the dreadful name of Eulalia, behind the flaking shutters of a fat and curlicued house with architectural dandruff, recalling for all the world some blowsy ex-Bloomer Girl from the Gay Nineties of its origin.

The owner, a formerly wealthy man named DiCampo, possessed a grandeur not shared by his property, although it was no less fallen into ruin. His falcon's face, more Florentine then Victorian, was—like the house—ravaged by time and the inclemencies of fortune; but haughtily so, and indeed DiCampo wore his scurfy purple velvet house jacket like the prince he was entitled to call himself, but did not. He was proud, and stubborn, and useless; and he had a lovely daughter named Bianca, who taught at a Eulalia grade school and, through marvels of economy, supported them both.

How Lorenzo San Marco Borghese-Ruffo DiCampo came to this decayed estate is no concern of ours. The presence there this day of a man named Harbidger and a man named Tungston, however, is to the point: they had come, Harbidger from Chicago, Tungston from Philadelphia, to buy something each wanted very much, and DiCampo had summoned them in order to sell it. The two visitors were collectors, Harbidger's passion being Lincoln, Tungston's Poe.

The Lincoln collector, an elderly man who looked like a migrant fruit picker, had plucked his fruits well: Harbidger was worth about $40,000,000, every dollar of which was at the beck of his mania for Lincolniana. Tungston, who was almost as rich, had the aging body of a poet and the eyes of a starving panther, armament that had served him well in the wars of Poeana.

"I must say, Mr. DiCampo," remarked Harbidger, "that your letter surprised me." He paused to savor the wine his host had poured from an ancient and honorable bottle (DiCampo had filled it with California claret before their arrival). "May I ask what has finally induced you to offer the book and document for sale?"

"To quote Lincoln in another context, Mr. Harbidger," said DiCampo with a shrug of his wasted shoulders, " 'the dogmas of the quiet past are inadequate to the stormy present.' In short, a hungry man sells his blood."

"Only if it's of the right type," said old Tungston, unmoved. "You've made that book and document less accessible to collectors and historians, DiCampo, than the gold in Fort Knox. Have you got them here? I'd like to examine them."

"No other hand will ever touch them except by right of ownership," Lorenzo DiCampo replied bitterly. He had taken a miser's glee in his lucky finds, vowing never to part with them; now forced by his need to sell them, he was like a suspicion-caked old prospector who, stumbling at last on pay dirt, draws cryptic maps to keep the world from stealing the secret of its location. "As I informed you gentlemen, I represent the book as bearing the signatures of Poe and Lincoln, and the document as being in Lincoln's hand; I am offering them with the customary proviso that they are returnable if they should prove to be not as represented; and if this does not satisfy you," and the old prince actually rose, "let us terminate our business here and now."

"Sit down, sit down, Mr. DiCampo," Harbidger said.

"No one is questioning your integrity," snapped old Tungston. "It's just that I'm not used to buying sight unseen. If there's a money-back guarantee, we'll do it your way."

Lorenzo DiCampo reseated himself stiffly. "Very well, gentlemen. Then I take it you are both prepared to buy?"

"Oh, yes!" said Harbidger. "What is your price?"

"Oh, no," said DiCampo. "What is your bid?"

The Lincoln collector cleared his throat, which was full of slaver. "If the book and document are as represented, Mr. DiCampo, you might hope to get from a dealer or realize at auction—oh—$50,000. I offer you $55,000."

"$56,000," said Tungston.

"$57,000," said Harbidger.

"$58,000," said Tungston.

"$59,000," said Harbidger.

Tungston showed his fangs. "$60,000," he said.

Harbidger fell silent, and DiCampo waited. He did not expect miracles. To these men, five times $60,000 was of less moment than the undistinguished wine they were smacking their lips over; but they were veterans of many a hard auction-room campaign, and a collector's victory tasted very nearly as sweet for the price as for the prize.

So the impoverished prince was not surprised when the Lincoln collector suddenly said, "Would you be good enough to allow Mr. Tungston and me to talk privately for a moment?"

DiCampo rose and strolled out of the room, to gaze somberly through a cracked window at the jungle growth that had once been his Italian formal gardens.

It was the Poe collector who summoned him back. "Harbidger has convinced me that for the two of us to try to outbid each other would simply run the price up out of all reason. We're going to make you a sporting proposition."

"I've proposed to Mr. Tungston, and he has agreed," nodded Harbidger, "that our bid for the book and document be $65,000. Each of us is prepared to pay that sum, and not a penny more."

"So that is how the screws are turned," said DiCampo, smiling. "But I do not understand. If each of you makes the identical bid, which of you gets the book and document?"

"Ah," grinned the Poe man, "that's where the sporting proposition comes in."

"You see, Mr. DiCampo," said the Lincoln man, "we are going to leave that decision to you."

Even the old prince, who had seen more than his share of the astonishing, was astonished. He looked at the two rich men really for the first time. "I must confess," he murmured, "that your compact is an amusement. Permit me?" He sank into thought while the two collectors sat expectantly. When the old man looked up he was smiling like a fox. "The very thing, gentlemen! From the typewritten copies of the document I sent you, you both know that Lincoln himself left a clue to a theoretical hiding place for the book which he never explained. Some time ago I arrived at a possible solution to the President's little mystery. I propose to hide the book and document in accordance with it."

"You mean whichever of us figures out your interpretation of the Lincoln clue and finds the book and document where you will hide them, Mr. DiCampo, gets both for the agreed price?"

"That is it exactly."

The Lincoln collector looked dubious. "I don't know . . ."

"Oh, come, Harbidger," said Tungston, eyes glittering. "A deal is a deal. We accept, DiCampo! Now what?"

"You gentlemen will of course have to give me a little time. Shall we say three days?"

Ellery let himself into the Queen apartment, tossed his suitcase aside, and set about opening windows. He had been out of town for a week on a case, and Inspector Queen was in Atlantic City attending a police convention.

Breathable air having been restored, Ellery sat down to the week's accumulation of mail. One envelope made him pause. It had come by airmail special delivery, it was postmarked four days earlier, and in the lower left corner, in red, flamed the word *URGENT*. The printed return address on the flap said: L.S.M.B.-R DICAMPO, POST OFFICE BOX 69, SOUTHERN DISTRICT, EULALIA, N.Y. The initials of the name had been crossed out and "Bianca" written above them.

The enclosure, in a large agitated female hand on inexpensive notepaper, said:

> Dear Mr. Queen,
>
> The most important detective book in the world has disappeared. Will you please find it for me?
>
> Phone me on arrival at the Eulalia RR station or airport and I will pick you up.
>
> Bianca DiCampo

A yellow envelope then caught his eye. It was a telegram, dated the previous day:

> WHY HAVE I NOT HEARD FROM YOU STOP AM IN DESPERATE NEED YOUR SERVICES
>
> BIANCA DICAMPO

He had no sooner finished reading the telegram than the telephone on his desk trilled. It was a long-distance call.

"Mr. Queen?" throbbed a contralto voice. "Thank heaven I've finally got through to you! I've been calling all day—"

"I've been away," said Ellery, "and you would be Miss Bianca DiCampo of Eulalia. In two words, Miss DiCampo: Why me?"

"In two words, Mr. Queen: Abraham Lincoln."

Ellery was startled. "You plead a persuasive case," he chuckled. "It's true, I'm an incurable Lincoln addict. How did you find out? Well, never mind. Your letter refers to a book, Miss DiCampo. Which book?"

The husky voice told him, and certain other provocative things as well. "So will you come, Mr. Queen?"

"Tonight if I could! Suppose I drive up first thing in the morning. I ought to make Eulalia by noon. Harbidger and Tungston are still around, I take it?"

"Oh, yes. They're staying at a motel downtown."

"Would you ask them to be there?"

The moment he hung up, Ellery leaped to his bookshelves. He snatched out his volume of *Murder for Pleasure,* the historical work on detective stories by his good friend Howard Haycraft, and found what he was looking for on page 26:

> And . . . young William Dean Howells thought it significant praise to assert of a nominee for President of the United States:
>
> The bent of his mind is mathematical and metaphysical, and he is therefore pleased with the absolute and logical method of Poe's tales and sketches, in which the problem of mystery is given, and wrought out into everyday facts by processes of cunning analysis. It is said that he suffers no year to pass without a perusal of this author.
>
> Abraham Lincoln subsequently confirmed this statement, which appeared in his little-known "campaign biography" by Howells in 1860. . . . The instance is chiefly notable, of course, for its revelation of a little-suspected affinity between two great Americans. . . .

Very early the next morning Ellery gathered some papers from his files, stuffed them into his brief case, scribbled a note for his father, and ran for his car, Eulalia-bound.

He was enchanted by the DiCampo house, which looked like something out of Poe by Charles Addams; and, for other reasons, by Bianca, who turned out to be a genetic product supreme of northern Italy, with titian hair and Mediterranean blue eyes and a figure that needed only some solid steaks to qualify her for Miss Universe competition. Also, she was in deep mourning; so her conquest of the Queen heart was immediate and complete.

"He died of a cerebral hemorrhage, Mr. Queen," Bianca said, dabbing at her absurd little nose. "In the middle of the second night after his session with Mr. Harbidger and Mr. Tungston."

So Lorenzo San Marco Borghese-Ruffo DiCampo was unexpectedly dead, bequeathing the lovely Bianca near-destitution and a mystery.

"The only things of value Father really left me are that book and the Lincoln document. The $65,000 they now represent would pay off Father's debts and give me a fresh start. But I can't find them, Mr. Queen, and neither can Mr. Harbidger and Mr. Tungston—who'll be here soon, by the way. Father hid the two things, as he told them he would; but where? We've ransacked the place."

"Tell me more about the book, Miss DiCampo."

"As I said over the phone, it's called *The Gift: 1845*. The Christmas annual that contained the earliest appearance of Edgar Allan Poe's 'The Purloined Letter.' "

"Published in Philadelphia by Carey & Hart? Bound in red?" At Bianca's nod Ellery said, "You understand that an ordinary copy of *The Gift: 1845* isn't worth more than about $50. What makes your father's copy unique is that double autograph you mentioned."

"That's what he said, Mr. Queen. I wish I had the book here to show you—that beautifully handwritten *Edgar Allan Poe* on the flyleaf, and under Poe's signature the signature *Abraham Lincoln*."

"Poe's own copy, once owned, signed and read by Lincoln," Ellery said slowly. "Yes, that would be a collector's item for the ages. By the way, Miss DiCampo, what's the story behind the other piece—the Lincoln document?"

Bianca told him what her father had told her.

One morning in the spring of 1865, Abraham Lincoln opened the rosewood door of his bedroom in the southwest corner of the second floor of the White House and stepped out into the redcarpeted hall at the unusually late hour—for him—of 7:00 a.m.; he was more accustomed to beginning his workday at six.

But (as Lorenzo DiCampo had reconstructed events) Mr. Lincoln that morning had lingered in his bedchamber. He had awakened at his usual hour but, instead of leaving immediately on dressing for his office, he had pulled one of the cane chairs over to the round table, with its gas-fed reading lamp, and sat down to reread Poe's "The Purloined Letter" in his copy of the 1845 annual; it was a dreary morning, and the natural light was poor. The President was alone; the folding doors to Mrs. Lincoln's bedroom remained closed.

Impressed as always with Poe's tale, Mr. Lincoln on this occasion was struck by a whimsical thought; and, apparently finding no paper handy, he took an envelope from his pocket, discarded its enclosure, slit the two short edges so that the envelope opened out into a single sheet, and began to write on the blank side . . .

"Describe it to me, please."

"It's a long envelope, one that must have contained a bulky letter. It is addressed to the White House, but there is no return address, and Father was never able to identify the sender from the handwriting. We do know that the letter came through the regular mails, because there are two Lincoln stamps on it, lightly but unmistakably canceled."

"May I see your father's transcript of what Lincoln wrote out that morning on the inside of the envelope?"

Bianca handed him a typewritten copy and, in spite of himself, Ellery felt goose flesh rise as he read:

> *Apr. 14, 1865*
>
> Mr. Poe's The Purloined Letter is a work of singular originality. Its simplicity is a master-stroke of cunning, which never fails to arouse my wonder.
>
> Reading the tale over this morning has given me a "notion." Suppose I wished to hide a book, this very book, perhaps? Where best to do so? Well, as Mr. Poe in his tale hid a letter *among letters,* might not a book be hidden *among books?* Why, if this very copy of the tale were to be deposited in a library and on purpose not recorded—would not the Library of Congress make a prime depository!—well might it repose there, undiscovered, for a generation.
>
> On the other hand, let us regard Mr. Poe's "notion" turn-about: suppose the book were to be placed, not amongst other books, but *where no book would reasonably be expected?*

(I may follow the example of Mr. Poe, and, myself, compose a tale of "ratiocination"!)

The "notion" beguiles me, it is nearly seven o'clock. Later to-day, if the vultures and my appointments leave me a few moments of leisure, I may write further of my imagined hiding-place.

In self-reminder: the hiding place of the book is in 3od, which

Ellery looked up. "The document ends there?"

"Father said that Mr. Lincoln must have glanced again at his watch, and shamefacedly jumped up to go to his office, leaving the sentence unfinished. Evidently he never found the time to get back to it."

Ellery brooded. Evidently indeed. From the moment when Abraham Lincoln stepped from his bedroom that Good Friday morning, fingering his thick gold watch on its vest chain, to bid the still-unrelieved night guard his customary courteous "Good morning" and make for his office at the other end of the hall, his day was spoken for. The usual patient push through the clutching crowd of favor seekers, many of whom had bedded down all night on the hall carpet; sanctuary in his sprawling office, where he read official correspondence; by 8:00 a.m. having breakfast with his family—Mrs. Lincoln chattering away about plans for the evening, twelve-year-old Tad of the cleft palate lisping a complaint that "nobody asked me to go," and young Robert Lincoln, just returned from duty, bubbling with stories about his hero Ulysses Grant and the last days of the war; then back to the presidential office to look over the morning newspapers (which Lincoln had once remarked he "never" read, but these were happy days, with good news everywhere), sign two documents, and signal the soldier at the door to admit the morning's first caller, Speaker of the House Schuyler Colfax (who was angling for a Cabinet post and had to be tactfully handled); and so on throughout the day—the historic Cabinet meeting at 11:00 a.m., attended by General Grant himself, that stretched well into the afternoon; a hurried lunch at almost half past two with Mrs. Lincoln (had this forty-five-pounds-underweight man eaten his usual midday meal of a biscuit, a glass of milk, and an apple?); more visitors to see in his office (including the unscheduled Mrs. Nancy

Bushrod, escaped slave and wife of an escaped slave and mother of three small children, weeping that Tom, a soldier in the Army of the Potomac, was no longer getting his pay: "You are entitled to your husband's pay. Come this time tomorrow," and the tall President escorted her to the door, bowing her out "like I was a natural-born lady"; the late afternoon drive in the barouche to the Navy Yard and back with Mrs. Lincoln; more work, more visitors, into the evening . . . until finally, at five minutes past 8:00 p.m., Abraham Lincoln stepped into the White House formal coach after his wife, waved, and sank back to be driven off to see a play he did not much want to see, *Our American Cousin,* at Ford's Theatre . . .

Ellery mused over the black day in silence. And, like a relative hanging on the specialist's yet undelivered diagnosis, Bianca DiCampo sat watching him with anxiety.

Harbidger and Tungston arrived in a taxi to greet Ellery with the fervor of castaways grasping at a smudge of smoke on the horizon.

"As I understand it, gentlemen," Ellery said when he had calmed them down, "neither of you has been able to solve Mr. DiCampo's interpretation of the Lincoln clue. If I succeed in finding the book and paper where DiCampo hid them, which of you gets them?"

"We intend to split the $65,000 payment to Miss DiCampo," said Harbidger, "and take joint ownership of the two pieces."

"An arrangement," growled old Tungston, "I'm against on principle, in practice, and by plain horse sense."

"So am I," sighed the Lincoln collector, "but what else can we do?"

"Well," and the Poe man regarded Bianca DiCampo with the icy intimacy of the cat that long ago marked the bird as its prey, "Miss DiCampo, who now owns the two pieces, is quite free to renegotiate a sale on her own terms."

"Miss DiCampo," said Miss DiCampo, giving Tungston stare for stare, "considers herself bound by her father's wishes. His terms stand."

"In all likelihood, then," said the other millionaire, "one of us will retain the book, the other the document, and we'll exchange them every year, or some such thing." Harbidger sounded unhappy.

"Only practical arrangement under the circumstances," grunted Tungston, and *he* sounded unhappy. "But all this is academic, Queen, unless and until the book and document are found."

Ellery nodded. "The problem, then, is to fathom DiCampo's interpretation of that *3od* in the document. 3od . . . I notice, Miss DiCampo—or, may I? Bianca?—that your father's typewritten copy of the Lincoln holograph text runs the *3* and *o* and *d* together—no spacing in between. Is that the way it occurs in the longhand?"

"Yes."

"Hmm. Still . . . 3od . . . Could *d* stand for *days* . . . or the British *pence* . . . or *died,* as used in obituaries? Does any of these make sense to you, Bianca?"

"No."

"Did your father have any special interest in, say, pharmacology? chemistry? physics? algebra? electricity? Small *d* is an abbreviation used in all those." But Bianca shook her splendid head. "Banking? Small *d* for *dollars, dividends?*"

"Hardly," the girl said with a sad smile.

"How about theatricals? Was your father ever involved in a play production? Small *d* stands for *door* in playscript stage directions."

"Mr. Queen, I've gone through every darned abbreviation my dictionary lists, and I haven't found one that has a point of contact with any interest of my father's."

Ellery scowled. "At that—I assume the typewritten copy is accurate—the manuscript shows no period after the *d,* making an abbreviation unlikely. 3od . . . let's concentrate on the number. Does the number 30 have any significance for you?"

"Yes, indeed," said Bianca, making all three men sit up. But then they sank back. "In a few years it will represent my age, and that has enormous significance. But only for me, I'm afraid."

"You'll be drawing wolf whistles at twice thirty," quoth Ellery warmly. "However! Could the number have cross-referred to anything in your father's life or habits?"

"None that I can think of, Mr. Queen. And," Bianca said, having grown roses in her cheeks, "thank you."

"I think," said old Tungston testily, "we had better stick to the subject."

"Just the same, Bianca, let me run over some 'thirty' associations as they come to mind. Stop me if one of them hits a nerve. The Thirty Tyrants—was your father interested in classical Athens? Thirty Years' War—in seventeenth-century European history? Thirty all—did he play or follow tennis? Or . . . did he ever live at an address that included the number 30?" Ellery went on and on, but to each suggestion Bianca DiCampo could only shake her head.

"The lack of spacing, come to think of it, doesn't necessarily mean that Mr. DiCampo chose to view the clue that way," said Ellery thoughtfully. "He might have interpreted it arbitrarily as 3-space-*o-d.*"

"Three od?" echoed old Tungston. "What the devil could that mean?"

"Od? Od is the hypothetical force or power claimed by Baron von Reichenbach—in 1850, wasn't it?—to pervade the whole of nature. Manifests itself in magnets, crystals and such, which according to the excited Baron explained animal magnetism and mesmerism. Was your father by any chance interested in hypnosis, Bianca? Or the occult?"

"Not in the slightest."

"Mr. Queen," exclaimed Harbidger, "are you serious about all this—this semantic sludge?"

"Why, I don't know," said Ellery. "I never know till I stumble over something. Od . . . the word was used with prefixes, too—*biod,* the force of animal life; *elod,* the force of electricity; and so forth. *Three* od . . . or *triod,* the triune force—it's all right, Mr. Harbidger, it's not ignorance on your part, I just coined the word. But it does rather suggest the Trinity, doesn't it? Bianca, did your father tie up to the Church in a personal, scholarly, or any other way? No? That's too bad, really, because Od—capitalized—has been a minced form of the word God since the sixteenth century. Or . . . you wouldn't happen to have three Bibles on the premises, would you? Because—"

Ellery stopped with the smashing abruptness of an ordinary force meeting an absolutely immovable object. The girl and the two collectors gawped. Bianca had idly picked up the typewritten copy of the Lincoln document. She was not reading it; she was simply holding it on her knees; but Ellery, sitting opposite her, had shot forward in a crouch, rather like a pointer, and he was regarding the paper in her lap with a glare of pure discovery.

"That's it!" he cried.

"What's it, Mr. Queen?" the girl asked, bewildered.

"Please—the transcript!" He plucked the paper from her. "Of course. Hear this: '*On the other hand, let us regard* Mr. *Poe's "notion" turn-about.*' *Turn-about.* Look at the 3od 'turn-about'—as I just saw it!"

He turned the Lincoln message upside down for their inspection. In that position the 3od became:

poε

"*Poe!*" exploded Tungston.

"Yes, crude but recognizable," Ellery said swiftly. "So now we read the Lincoln clue as: '*The hiding-place of the book is in* Poe!' "

There was a silence.

"In Poe," said Harbidger blankly.

"In Poe?" muttered Tungston. "There are only a couple of trade editions of Poe in DiCampo's library, Harbidger, and we went through those. We looked in every book here."

"He might have meant among the Poe books in the *public* library. Miss DiCampo—"

"Wait." Bianca sped away. But when she came back she was drooping. "It isn't. We have two public libraries in Eulalia, and I know the head librarian in both. I just called them. Father didn't visit either library."

Ellery gnawed a fingernail. "Is there a bust of Poe in the house, Bianca? Or any other Poe-associated object, aside from books?"

"I'm afraid not."

"Queer," he mumbled. "Yet I'm positive your father interpreted '*the hiding-place of the book*' as being '*in Poe.*' So he'd have hidden it 'in Poe' . . ." Ellery's mumbling dribbled away into a tormented sort of silence: his eyebrows worked up and down, Groucho Marx fashion; he pinched the tip of his nose until it was scarlet; he yanked at his unoffending ears; he munched on his lip . . . until, all at once, his face cleared; and he sprang to his feet. "Bianca, may I use your phone?"

The girl could only nod, and Ellery dashed. They heard him telephoning in the entrance hall, although they could not make out the words. He was back in two minutes.

"One thing more," he said briskly, "and we're out of the woods. I suppose your father used a key ring or a key case, Bianca? May I have it, please?"

She fetched a key case. To the two millionaires it seemed the sorriest of objects, a scuffed and dirty tan leatherette case. But Ellery received it from the girl as if it were an artifact of historic importance from a newly discovered Fourth Dynasty tomb. He unsnapped it with concentrated love; he fingered its contents like a scientist. Finally he decided on a certain key.

"Wait here!" Thus Mr. Queen; and exit, running.

"I can't decide," old Tungston said after a while, "whether that fellow is a genius or an escaped lunatic."

Neither Harbidger nor Bianca replied. Apparently they could not decide, either.

They waited through twenty elongated minutes; at the twenty-first, they heard his car, champing. All three were in the front doorway as Ellery strode up the walk.

He was carrying a book with a red cover, and smiling. It was a compassionate smile, but none of them noticed.

"You—" said Bianca. "—found—" said Tungston. "—the book!" shouted Harbidger. "Is the Lincoln holograph in it?"

"It is," said Ellery. "Shall we all go into the house, where we may mourn in decent privacy?"

"Because," Ellery said to Bianca and the two quivering collectors as they sat across a refectory table from him, "I have foul news. Mr. Tungston, I believe you have never actually seen Mr. DiCampo's book. Will you now look at the Poe signature on the flyleaf?"

The panther claws leaped. There, toward the top of the flyleaf, in faded ink-script, ran the signature *Edgar Allan Poe.*

The claws curled, and old Tungston looked up sharply. "DiCampo never mentioned that it's a full autograph—he kept referring to it as 'the Poe signature.' Edgar *Allan* Poe . . . Why, I don't know of a single instance after his West Point days when Poe wrote out his middle name in an autograph! And the earliest he could have signed this 1845 edition is obviously when it was published, which was around the fall of 1844. In 1844 he'd surely have abbreviated the 'Allan,' signing 'Edgar A. Poe,' the way he signed everything! This is a forgery."

"My God," murmured Bianca, clearly intending no impiety; she was as pale as Poe's Lenore. "Is that true, Mr. Queen?"

"I'm afraid it is," Ellery said sadly. "I was suspicious the moment you told me the Poe signature on the flyleaf contained the 'Allan.' And if the Poe signature is a forgery, the book itself can hardly be considered Poe's own copy."

Harbidger was moaning. "And the Lincoln signature underneath the Poe, Mr. Queen! DiCampo never told me it reads *Abraham* Lincoln—the full Christian name. Except on official documents, Lincoln practically always signed his name 'A. Lincoln.' Don't tell me this Lincoln autograph is a forgery, too?"

Ellery forbore to look at poor Bianca. "I was struck by the 'Abraham' as well, Mr. Harbidger, when Miss DiCampo mentioned it to me, and I came equipped to test it. I have here"—and Ellery tapped the pile of documents he had taken from his briefcase—"facsimiles of Lincoln signatures from the most frequently reproduced of the historic documents he signed. Now I'm going to make a precise tracing of the Lincoln signature on the flyleaf of the book"—he proceeded to do so—"and I shall superimpose the tracing on the various signatures of the authentic Lincoln documents. So." He worked rapidly. On his third superimposition Ellery looked up. "Yes. See here. The tracing of the purported Lincoln signature from the flyleaf fits in minutest detail over the authentic Lincoln signature on this facsimile of the Emancipation Proclamation. It's a fact of life that's tripped many a forger that *nobody ever writes his name exactly the same way twice.* There are always variations. If two signatures are identical, then one must be a tracing of the other. So the 'Abraham Lincoln' signed on this flyleaf can be dismissed without further consideration as a forgery also. It's a tracing of the Emancipation Proclamation signature.

"Not only was this book not Poe's own copy; it was never signed—and therefore probably never owned—by Lincoln. However your father came into possession of the book, Bianca, he was swindled."

It was the measure of Bianca DiCampo's quality that she said quietly, "Poor, poor Father," nothing more.

Harbidger was poring over the worn old envelope on whose inside appeared the dearly beloved handscript of the Martyr President. "At least," he muttered, "we have *this.*"

"Do we?" asked Ellery gently. "Turn it over, Mr. Harbidger."

Harbidger looked up, scowling. "No! You're not going to deprive me of this, too!"

"Turn it over," Ellery repeated in the same gentle way. The Lincoln collector obeyed reluctantly. "What do you see?"

"An authentic envelope of the period! With two authentic Lincoln stamps!"

"Exactly. And the United States has never issued postage stamps depicting living Americans; you have to be dead to qualify. The earliest U.S. stamp showing a portrait of Lincoln went on sale April 15, 1866—a year to the day after his death. Then a living Lincoln could scarcely have used this envelope, with these stamps on it, as writing paper. The document is spurious, too. I am so very sorry, Bianca."

Incredibly, Lorenzo DiCampo's daughter managed a smile with her "*Non importa, signor.*" He could have wept for her. As for the two collectors, Harbidger was in shock; but old Tungston managed to croak, "Where the devil did DiCampo hide the book, Queen? And how did you know?"

"Oh, that," said Ellery, wishing the two old men would go away so that he might comfort this admirable creature. "I was convinced that DiCampo interpreted what we now know was the forger's, not Lincoln's, clue, as 3od read upside down; or, crudely, *Poe.* But '*the hiding-place of the book is in Poe*' led nowhere.

"So I reconsidered, P, o, e. If those three letters of the alphabet didn't mean Poe, what could they mean? Then I remembered something about the letter you wrote me, Bianca. You'd used one of your father's envelopes, on the flap of which appeared his address: *Post Office Box 69, Southern District, Eulalia, N.Y.* If there was a Southern District in Eulalia, it seemed reasonable to conclude that there were post offices for other points of the compass, too. As, for instance, an Eastern District. Post Office Eastern. P.O. East. P.O.E."

"Poe!" cried Bianca.

"To answer your question, Mr. Tungston: I phoned the main post office, confirmed the existence of a Post Office East, got directions as to how to get there, looked for a postal box key in Mr. DiCampo's key case, found the right one, located the box DiCampo had rented especially for the occasion, unlocked it—and there was the book." He added, hopefully, "And that is that."

"And that *is* that," Bianca said when she returned from seeing the two collectors off. "I'm not going to cry over an empty milk bottle, Mr. Queen. I'll straighten out Father's affairs somehow. Right now all I can think of is how glad I am he didn't live to see the signatures and documents declared forgeries publicly, as they would surely have been when they were expertized."

"I think you'll find there's still some milk in the bottle, Bianca."

"I beg your pardon?" said Bianca.

Ellery tapped the pseudo-Lincolnian envelope. "You know, you didn't do a very good job describing this envelope to me. All you said was that there were two canceled Lincoln stamps on it."

"Well, there are."

"I can see you misspent your childhood. No, little girls don't collect things, do they? Why, if you'll examine these 'two canceled Lincoln stamps,' you'll see that they're a great deal more than that. In the first place, they're not separate stamps. They're a vertical pair—

that is, one stamp is joined to the other at the horizontal edges. Now look at this upper stamp of the pair."

The Mediterranean eyes widened. "It's upside down, isn't it?"

"Yes, it's upside down," said Ellery, "and what's more, while the pair have perforations all around, there are no perforations between them, where they're joined.

"What you have here, young lady—and what our unknown forger didn't realize when he fished around for an authentic White House cover of the period on which to perpetrate the Lincoln forgery—is what's known to stamp collectors as a double printing error: a pair of 1866 black 15-cent Lincolns imperforate horizontally, with one of the pair printed upside down. No such error of the Lincoln issue has ever been reported. You're the owner, Bianca, of what may well be the rarest item in U.S. philately, and the most valuable."

The world will little note, nor long remember.

But don't try to prove it by Bianca DiCampo.

FLANNERY O'CONNOR (1925–1964)

(Mary) Flannery O'Connor was born in Savannah, Georgia, and studied fiction-writing at the University of Iowa Writers' Workshop. She returned in 1950 to Milledgeville, Georgia, and, although weakened by the blood disease which would eventually take her life, produced two novels, *Wise Blood* (1952) and *The Violent Bear It Away* (1960), and two collections of short stories, *A Good Man Is Hard to Find* (1955) and the posthumously published *Everything That Rises Must Converge* (1965). A devout Roman Catholic whose faith informed her view of human nature, she focuses nevertheless in her fiction not on traditional religious practices but on the more bizarre manifestations of spiritual crises, and her fiction has been labeled as a result "southern Gothic." She writes about sin rather than crime, and for her the word "mystery" refers to the human spiritual condition rather than to something subject to detection.

"The Comforts of Home" is a critique, rather than an illustration, of detection, as O'Connor shows by confining the detective's analysis to the final paragraph and treating it ironically. Irony is her main device in the story, from title to ending, and it emphasizes the limitations, or virtual irrelevance, of the investigatory process when confronted with the complexities of the human soul. O'Connor's concern is theological, not psychological: the "old man" who seems to drive Thomas is not the Freudian father but "old Adam" of original sin.

THE COMFORTS OF HOME

Thomas withdrew to the side of the window and with his head between the wall and the curtain he looked down on the driveway where the car had stopped. His mother and the little slut were getting out of it. His mother emerged slowly, stolid and awkward, and then the little slut's long slightly bowed legs slid out, the dress pulled above the knees. With a shriek of laughter she ran to meet the dog, who bounded, overjoyed, shaking with pleasure, to welcome her. Rage gathered throughout Thomas's large frame with a silent ominous intensity, like a mob assembling.

It was now up to him to pack a suitcase, go to the hotel, and stay there until the house should be cleared.

He did not know where a suitcase was, he disliked to pack, he needed his books, his typewriter was not portable, he was used to an electric blanket, he could not bear to eat in restaurants. His mother, with her daredevil charity, was about to wreck the peace of the house.

The back door slammed and the girl's laugh shot up from the kitchen, through the back hall, up the stairwell and into his room, making for him like a bolt of electricity. He jumped to the side and stood glaring about him. His words of the morning had been unequivocal: "If you bring that girl back into this house, I leave. You can choose—her or me."

She had made her choice. An intense pain gripped his throat. It was the first time in his thirty-five years . . . He felt a sudden burning moisture behind his eyes. Then he steadied himself, overcome by rage. On the contrary: she had not made any choice. She was counting on his attachment to his electric blanket. She would have to be shown.

The girl's laughter rang upward a second time and Thomas winced. He saw again her look of the night before. She had invaded his room. He had waked to find his door open and her in it. There was enough light from the hall to make her visible as she turned toward him. The face was like a comedienne's in a musical comedy—a pointed chin, wide apple cheeks and feline empty eyes. He had sprung out of his bed and snatched a straight chair and then he had backed her out the door, holding the chair in front of him like an animal trainer driving out a dangerous cat. He had driven her silently down the hall, pausing when he reached it to beat on his mother's door. The girl, with a gasp, turned and fled into the guest room.

In a moment his mother had opened her door and peered out apprehensively. Her face, greasy with whatever she put on it at night, was framed in pink rubber curlers. She looked down the hall where the girl had disappeared. Thomas stood before her, the chair still lifted in front of him as if he were about to quell another beast. "She tried to get in my room," he hissed, pushing in. "I woke up and she was trying to get in my room." He closed the door behind him and his voice rose in outrage. "I won't put up with this! I won't put up with it another day!"

His mother, backed by him to her bed, sat down on the edge of it. She had a heavy body on which sat a thin, mysteriously gaunt and incongruous head.

"I'm telling you for the last time," Thomas said, "I won't put up with this another day." There was an observable tendency in all of her actions. This was, with the best intentions in the world, to make a mockery of virtue, to pursue it with such a mindless intensity that everyone involved was made a fool of and virtue itself became ridiculous. "Not another day," he repeated.

His mother shook her head emphatically, her eyes still on the door.

Thomas put the chair on the floor in front of her and sat down on it. He leaned forward as if he were about to explain something to a defective child.

"That's just another way she's unfortunate," his mother said. "So awful, so awful. She told me the name of it but I forget what it is but it's something she can't help. Something she was born with. Thomas," she said and put her hand to her jaw, "suppose it were you?"

Exasperation blocked his windpipe. "Can't I make you see," he croaked, "that if she can't help herself you can't help her?"

His mother's eyes, intimate but untouchable, were the blue of great distances after sunset. "Nimpermaniac," she murmured.

"Nymphomaniac," he said fiercely. "She doesn't need to supply you with any fancy names. She's a moral moron. That's all you need to know. Born without the moral faculty—like somebody else would be born without a kidney or a leg. Do you understand?"

"I keep thinking it might be you," she said, her hand still on her jaw. "If it were you, how do you think I'd feel if nobody took you in? What if you were a nimpermaniac and not a brilliant smart person and you did what you couldn't help and . . ."

Thomas felt a deep unbearable loathing for himself as if he were turning slowly into the girl.

"What did she have on?" she asked abruptly, her eyes narrowing.

"Nothing!" he roared. "Now will you get her out of here!"

"How can I turn her out in the cold?" she said. "This morning she was threatening to kill herself again."

"Send her back to jail," Thomas said.

"I would not send *you* back to jail, Thomas," she said.

He got up and snatched the chair and fled the room while he was still able to control himself.

Thomas loved his mother. He loved her because it was his nature to do so, but there were times when he could not endure her love for him. There were times when it became nothing but pure idiot mystery and he sensed about him forces, invisible currents entirely out of his control. She proceeded always from the tritest of considerations—it was the *nice thing to do*—into the most foolhardy engagements with the devil, whom, of course, she never recognized.

The devil for Thomas was only a manner of speaking, but it was a manner appropriate to the situations his mother got into. Had she been in any degree intellectual, he could have proved to her from early Christian history that no excess of virtue is justified, that a moderation of good produces likewise a moderation in evil, that if Antony of Egypt had stayed at home and attended to his sister, no devils would have plagued him.

Thomas was not cynical and so far from being opposed to virtue, he saw it as the principle of order and the only thing that makes life bearable. His own life was made bearable by the fruits of his mother's saner virtues—by the well-regulated house she kept and the excellent meals she served. But when virtue got out of hand with her, as now, a sense of devils grew upon him, and these were not mental quirks in himself or the old lady, they were denizens with personalities, present though not visible, who might any moment be expected to shriek or rattle a pot.

The girl had landed in the county jail a month ago on a bad check charge and his mother had seen her picture in the paper. At the breakfast table she had gazed at it for a long time and then had passed it over the coffee pot to him. "Imagine," she said, "only nineteen years old and in that filthy jail. And she doesn't look like a bad girl."

Thomas glanced at the picture. It showed the face of a shrewd ragamuffin. He observed that the average age for criminality was steadily lowering.

"She looks like a wholesome girl," his mother said.

"Wholesome people don't pass bad checks," Thomas said.

"You don't know what you'd do in a pinch."

"I wouldn't pass a bad check," Thomas said.

"I think," his mother said, "I'll take her a little box of candy."

If then and there he had put his foot down, nothing else would have happened. His father, had he been living, would have put his foot down at that point. Taking a box of candy was her favorite nice thing to do. When anyone within her social station moved to town, she called and took a box of candy; when any of her friends' children had babies or won a scholarship, she called and took a box of candy; when an old person broke his hip, she was at his bedside with a box of candy. He had been amused at the idea of her taking a box of candy to the jail.

He stood now in his room with the girl's laugh rocketing away in his head and cursed his amusement.

When his mother returned from the visit to the jail, she had burst into his study without knocking and had collapsed full-length on his couch, lifting her small swollen feet up on the arm of it. After a moment, she recovered herself enough to sit up and put a newspaper under them. Then she fell back again. "We don't know how the other half lives," she said.

Thomas knew that though her conversation moved from cliché to cliché there were real experiences behind them. He was less sorry for the girl's being in jail than for his mother having to see her there. He would have spared her all unpleasant sights. "Well," he said and put away his journal, "you had better forget it now. The girl has ample reason to be in jail."

"You can't imagine what all she's been through," she said, sitting up again, "listen." The poor girl, Star, had been brought up by a stepmother with three children of her own, one an almost grown boy who had taken advantage of her in such dreadful ways that she had been forced to run away and find her real mother. Once found, her real mother had sent her to various boarding schools to get rid of her. At each of these she had been forced to run away by the presence of perverts and sadists so monstrous that their acts defied description. Thomas could tell that his mother had not been spared the details that she was sparing him. Now and again when she spoke vaguely, her voice shook and he could tell that she was remembering some horror that had been put to her graphically. He had hoped that in a few days the memory of all this would wear off, but it did not. The next day she returned to the jail with Kleenex and cold-cream and a few days later, she announced that she had consulted a lawyer.

It was at these times that Thomas truly mourned the death of his father though he had not been able to endure him in life. The old man would have had none of this foolishness. Untouched by useless compassion, he would (behind her back) have pulled the necessary strings with his crony, the sheriff, and the girl would have been packed off to the state penitentiary to serve her time. He had always been engaged in some enraged action until one morning when (with an angry glance at his wife as if she alone were responsible) he had dropped dead at the breakfast table. Thomas had inherited his father's reason without his ruthlessness and his mother's love of good without her tendency to pursue it. His plan for all practical action was to wait and see what developed.

The lawyer found that the story of the repeated atrocities was for the most part untrue, but when he explained to her that the girl was a psychopathic personality, not insane enough for the asylum, not criminal enough for the jail, not stable enough for society, Thomas's mother was more deeply affected than ever. The girl readily admitted that her story was untrue on account of her being a congenital liar; she lied, she said, because she was insecure. She had passed through the hands of several psychiatrists who had put the finishing touches to her education. She knew there was no hope for her. In the presence of such an affliction as this, his mother seemed bowed down by some painful mystery that nothing would make endurable but a redoubling of effort. To his annoyance, she appeared to look on *him* with compassion, as if her hazy charity no longer made distinctions.

A few days later she burst in and said that the lawyer had got the girl paroled—to her.

Thomas rose from his Morris chair, dropping the review he had been reading. His large bland face contracted in anticipated pain. "You are not," he said, "going to bring that girl here!"

"No, no," she said, "calm yourself, Thomas." She had managed with difficulty to get the girl a job in a pet shop in town and a place to board with a crotchety old lady of her acquaintance. People were not kind. They did not put themselves in the place of someone like Star who had everything against her.

Thomas sat down again and retrieved his review. He seemed just to have escaped some danger which he did not care to make clear to himself. "Nobody can tell you anything," he said, "but in a few days that girl will have left town, having got what she could out of you. You'll never hear from her again."

Two nights later he came home and opened the parlor door and was speared by a shrill depthless laugh. His mother and the girl sat close to the fireplace where the gas logs were lit. The girl gave the immediate impression of being physically crooked. Her hair was cut like a dog's or an elf's and she was dressed in the latest fashion. She was training on him a long familiar sparkling stare that turned after a second into an intimate grin.

"Thomas!" his mother said, her voice firm with the injunction not to bolt, "this is Star you've heard so much about. Star is going to have supper with us."

The girl called herself Star Drake. The lawyer had found that her real name was Sarah Ham.

Thomas neither moved nor spoke but hung in the door in what seemed a savage perplexity. Finally he said, "How do you do, Sarah," in a tone of such loathing that he was shocked at the sound of it. He reddened, feeling it beneath him to show contempt for any creature so pathetic. He advanced into the room, determined at least on a decent politeness and sat down heavily in a straight chair.

"Thomas writes history," his mother said with a threatening look at him. "He's president of the local Historical Society this year."

The girl leaned forward and gave Thomas an even more pointed attention. "Fabulous!" she said in a throaty voice.

"Right now Thomas is writing about the first settlers in this country," his mother said.

"Fabulous!" the girl repeated.

Thomas by an effort of will managed to look as if he were alone in the room.

"Say, you know who he looks like?" Star asked, her head on one side, taking him in at an angle.

"Oh some one very distinguished!" his mother said archly.

"This cop I saw in the movie I went to last night," Star said.

"Star," his mother said, "I think you ought to be careful about the kind of movies you go to. I think you ought to see only the best ones. I don't think crime stories would be good for you."

"Oh this was a crime-does-not-pay," Star said, "and I swear this cop looked exactly like him. They were always putting something over on the guy. He would look like he couldn't stand it a minute longer or he would blow up. He was a riot. And not bad looking," she added with an appreciative leer at Thomas.

"Star," his mother said, "I think it would be grand if you developed a taste for music."

Thomas sighed. His mother rattled on and the girl, paying no attention to her, let her eyes play over him. The quality of her look was such that it might have been her hands, resting now on his knees, now on his neck. Her eyes had a mocking glitter and he knew that she was well aware he could not stand the sight of her. He needed nothing to tell him he was in the presence of the very stuff of corruption, but blameless corruption because there was no responsible faculty behind it. He was looking at the most unendurable form of innocence. Absently he asked himself what the attitude of God was to this, meaning if possible to adopt it.

His mother's behavior throughout the meal was so idiotic that he could barely stand to look at her and since he could less stand to look at Sarah Ham, he fixed on the sideboard across the room a continuous gaze of disapproval and disgust. Every remark of the girl's his mother met as if it deserved serious attention. She advanced several plans for the wholesome use of Star's spare time. Sarah Ham paid no more attention to this advice than if it came from a parrot. Once when Thomas inadvertently looked in her direction, she winked. As soon as he had swallowed the last spoonful of dessert, he rose and muttered, "I have to go, I have a meeting."

"Thomas," his mother said, "I want you to take Star home on your way. I don't want her riding in taxis by herself at night."

For a moment Thomas remained furiously silent. Then he turned and left the room. Presently he came back with a look of obscure determination on his face. The girl was ready, meekly waiting at the parlor door. She cast up at him a great look of admiration and confidence. Thomas did not offer his arm but she took it anyway and moved out of the house and down the steps, attached to what might have been a miraculously moving monument.

"Be good!" his mother called.

Sarah Ham snickered and poked him in the ribs.

While getting his coat he had decided that this would be his opportunity to tell the girl that unless she ceased to be a parasite on his mother, he would see to it, personally, that she was returned to jail. He would let her know that he understood what she was up to, that he was not an innocent and that there were certain things he would not put up with. At his desk, pen in hand, none was more articulate than Thomas. As soon as he found himself shut into the car with Sarah Ham, terror seized his tongue.

She curled her feet up under her and said, "Alone at last," and giggled.

Thomas swerved the car away from the house and drove fast toward the gate. Once on the highway, he shot forward as if he were being pursued.

"Jesus!" Sarah Ham said, swinging her feet off the seat, "where's the fire?"

Thomas did not answer. In a few seconds he could feel her edging closer. She stretched, eased nearer, and finally hung her hand limply over his shoulder. "Tomsee doesn't like me," she said, "but I think he's fabulously cute."

Thomas covered the three and a half miles into town in a little over four minutes. The light at the first intersection was red but he ignored it. The old woman lived three blocks beyond. When the car screeched to a halt at the place, he jumped out and ran around to the girl's door and opened it. She did not move from the car and Thomas was obliged to wait. After a moment one leg emerged, then her small white crooked face appeared and stared up at him. There was something about the look of it that suggested blindness but it was the blindness of those who don't know that they cannot see. Thomas was curiously sickened. The empty eyes moved over him. "Nobody likes me," she said in a sullen tone. "What if you were me and I couldn't stand to ride you three miles?"

"My mother likes you," he muttered.

"Her!" the girl said. "She's just about seventy-five years behind the times!"

Breathlessly Thomas said, "If I find you bothering her again, I'll have you put back in jail." There was a dull force behind his voice though it came out barely above a whisper.

"You and who else?" she said and drew back in the car as if now she did not intend to get out at all. Thomas reached into it, blindly grasped the front of her coat, pulled her out by it and released her. Then he lunged back to the car and sped off. The other door was still hanging open and her laugh, bodiless but real, bounded up the street as if it were about to jump in the open side of the car and ride away with him. He reached over and slammed the door and then drove toward home, too angry to attend his meeting. He intended to make his mother well-aware of his displeasure. He intended to leave no doubt in her mind. The voice of his father rasped in his head.

Numbskull, the old man said, put your foot down now. Show her who's boss before she shows you.

But when Thomas reached home, his mother, wisely, had gone to bed.

The next morning he appeared at the breakfast table, his brow lowered and the thrust of his jaw indicating that he was in a dangerous humor. When he intended to be determined, Thomas began like a bull that, before charging, backs with his head lowered and paws the ground. "All right now listen," he began, yanking out his chair and sitting down, "I have something to say to you about that girl and I don't intend to say it but once." He drew breath. "She's nothing but a little slut. She makes fun of you behind your back. She means to get everything she can out of you and you are nothing to her."

His mother looked as if she too had spent a restless night. She did not dress in the morning but wore her bathrobe and a grey turban around her head, which gave her face a disconcerting omniscient look. He might have been breakfasting with a sibyl.

"You'll have to use canned cream this morning," she said, pouring his coffee. "I forgot the other."

"All right, did you hear me?" Thomas growled.

"I'm not deaf," his mother said and put the pot back on the trivet. "I know I'm nothing but an old bag of wind to her."

"Then why do you persist in this foolhardy . . ."

"Thomas," she said, and put her hand to the side of her face, "it might be . . ."

"It is not me!" Thomas said, grasping the table leg at his knee.

She continued to hold her face, shaking her head slightly. "Think of all you have," she began. "All the comforts of home. And morals, Thomas. No bad inclinations, nothing bad you were born with."

Thomas began to breathe like someone who feels the onset of asthma. "You are not logical," he said in a limp voice. "*He* would have put his foot down."

The old lady stiffened. "You," she said, "are not like him."

Thomas opened his mouth silently.

"However," his mother said, in a tone of such subtle accusation that she might have been taking back the compliment, "I won't invite her back again since you're so dead set against her."

"I am not set against her," Thomas said. "I am set against your making a fool of yourself."

As soon as he left the table and closed the door of his study on himself, his father took up a squatting position in his mind. The old man had had the countryman's ability to converse squatting, though he was no countryman but had been born and brought up in the city and only moved to a smaller place later to exploit his talents. With steady skill he had made them think him one of them. In the midst of a conversation on the courthouse lawn, he would squat and his two or three companions would squat with him with no break in the surface of the talk. By gesture he had lived his lie; he had never deigned to tell one.

Let her run over you, he said. You ain't like me. Not enough to be a man.

Thomas began vigorously to read and presently the image faded. The girl had caused a disturbance in the depths of his being, somewhere out of the reach of his power of analysis. He felt as if he had seen a tornado pass a hundred yards away and had an intimation that it would turn again and head directly for him. He did not get his mind firmly on his work until mid-morning.

Two nights later, his mother and he were sitting in the den after their supper, each reading a section of the evening paper, when the telephone began to ring with the brassy intensity of a fire alarm. Thomas reached for it. As soon as the receiver was in his hand, a shrill female voice screamed into the room, "Come get this girl! Come get her! Drunk! Drunk in my parlor and I won't have it! Lost her job and come back here drunk! I won't have it!"

His mother leapt up and snatched the receiver.

The ghost of Thomas's father rose before him. Call the sheriff, the old man prompted. "Call the sheriff," Thomas said in a loud voice. "Call the sheriff to go there and pick her up."

"We'll be right there," his mother was saying. "We'll come and get her right away. Tell her to get her things together."

"She ain't in no condition to get nothing together," the voice screamed. "You shouldn't have put something like her off on me! My house is respectable!"

"Tell her to call the sheriff," Thomas shouted.

His mother put the receiver down and looked at him. "I wouldn't turn a dog over to that man," she said.

Thomas sat in the chair with his arms folded and looked fixedly at the wall.

"Think of the poor girl, Thomas," his mother said, "with nothing. Nothing. And we have everything."

When they arrived, Sarah Ham was slumped spraddle-legged against the banister on the boarding house front-steps. Her tam was down on her forehead where the old woman had slammed it and her clothes were bulging out of her suitcase where the old woman had thrown them in. She was carrying on a drunken conversation with herself in a low personal tone. A streak of lipstick ran up one side of her face. She allowed herself to be guided by his mother to the car and put in the back seat without seeming to know who the rescuer was. "Nothing to talk to all day but a pack of goddamned parakeets," she said in a furious whisper.

Thomas, who had not got out of the car at all, or looked at her after the first revolted glance, said, "I'm telling you, once and for all, the place to take her is the jail."

His mother, sitting on the back seat, holding the girl's hand, did not answer.

"All right, take her to the hotel," he said.

"I cannot take a drunk girl to a hotel, Thomas," she said. "You know that."

"Then take her to a hospital."

"She doesn't need a jail or a hotel or a hospital," his mother said, "she needs a home."

"She does not need mine," Thomas said.

"Only for tonight, Thomas," the old lady sighed. "Only for tonight."

Since then eight days had passed. The little slut was established in the guest room. Every day his mother set out to find her a job and a place to board, and failed, for the old woman had broadcast a warning. Thomas kept to his room or the den. His home was to him home, workshop, church, as personal as the shell of a turtle and as necessary. He could not believe that it could be violated in this way. His flushed face had a constant look of stunned outrage.

As soon as the girl was up in the morning, her voice throbbed out in a blues song that would rise and waver, then plunge low with insinuations of passion about to be satisfied and Thomas, at his desk, would lunge up and begin frantically stuffing his ears with Kleenex. Each time he started from one room to another, one floor to another, she would be certain to appear. Each time he was half way up or down the stairs, she would either meet him and pass, cringing coyly, or go up or down behind him, breathing small tragic spearmint-flavored sighs. She appeared to adore Thomas's repugnance to her and to draw it out of him every chance she got as if it added delectably to her martyrdom.

The old man—small, wasp-like, in his yellowed Panama hat, his seersucker suit, his pink carefully-soiled shirt, his small string tie—appeared to have taken up his station in Thomas's mind and from there, usually squatting, he shot out the same rasping suggestion every time the boy paused from his forced studies. Put your foot down. Go to see the sheriff.

The sheriff was another edition of Thomas's father except that he wore a checkered shirt and a Texas type hat and was ten years younger. He was as easily dishonest, and he had genuinely admired the old man. Thomas, like his mother, would have gone far out of his way to avoid his glassy pale blue gaze. He kept hoping for another solution, for a miracle.

With Sarah Ham in the house, meals were unbearable.

"Tomsee doesn't like me," she said the third or fourth night at the supper table and cast her pouting gaze across at the large rigid figure of Thomas, whose face was set with the look of a man trapped by insufferable odors. "He doesn't want me here. Nobody wants me anywhere."

"Thomas's name is Thomas," his mother interrupted. "Not Tomsee."

"I made Tomsee up," she said. "I think it's cute. He hates me."

"Thomas does not hate you," his mother said. "We are not the kind of people who hate," she added, as if this were an imperfection that had been bred out of them generations ago.

"Oh, I know when I'm not wanted," Sarah Ham continued. "They didn't even want me in jail. If I killed myself I wonder would God want me?"

"Try it and see," Thomas muttered.

The girl screamed with laughter. Then she stopped abruptly, her face puckered and she began to shake. "The best thing to do," she said, her teeth clattering, "is to kill myself. Then I'll be out of everybody's way. I'll go to hell and be out of God's way. And even the devil won't want me. He'll kick me out of hell, not even in hell . . ." she wailed.

Thomas rose, picked up his plate and knife and fork and carried them to the den to finish his supper. After that, he had not eaten another meal at the table but had had his mother serve him at his desk. At these meals, the old man was intensely present to him. He appeared to be tipping backwards in his chair, his thumbs beneath his galluses, while he said such things as, She never ran me away from my own table.

A few nights later, Sarah Ham slashed her wrists with a paring knife and had hysterics. From the den where he was closeted after supper, Thomas heard a shriek, then a series of screams, then his mother's scurrying footsteps through the house. He did not move. His first instant of hope that the girl had cut her throat faded as he realized she could not have done it and continue to scream the way she was doing. He returned to his journal and presently the screams subsided. In a moment his mother burst in with his coat and hat. "We have to take her to the hospital," she said. "She tried to do away with herself. I have a tourniquet on her arm. Oh Lord, Thomas," she said, "imagine being so low you'd do a thing like that!"

Thomas rose woodenly and put on his hat and coat. "We will take her to the hospital," he said, "and we will leave her there."

"And drive her to despair again?" the old lady cried. "Thomas!"

Standing in the center of his room now, realizing that he had reached the point where action was inevitable, that he must pack, that he must leave, that he must go, Thomas remained immovable.

His fury was directed not at the little slut but at his mother. Even though the doctor had found that she had barely damaged herself and had raised the girl's wrath by laughing at the tourniquet and putting only a streak of iodine on the cut, his mother could not get over the incident. Some new weight of sorrow seemed to have been thrown across her shoulders, and not only Thomas, but Sarah Ham was infuriated by this, for it appeared to be a general sorrow that would have found another object no matter what good fortune came to either of them. The experience of Sarah Ham had plunged the old lady into mourning for the world.

The morning after the attempted suicide, she had gone through the house and collected all the knives and scissors and locked them in a drawer. She emptied a bottle of rat poison down the toilet and took up the roach tablets from the kitchen floor. Then she came to Thomas's study and said in a whisper, "Where is that gun of his? I want you to lock it up."

"The gun is in my drawer," Thomas roared, "and I will not lock it up. If she shoots herself, so much the better!"

"Thomas," his mother said, "she'll hear you!"

"Let her hear me!" Thomas yelled. "Don't you know she has no intention of killing herself? Don't you know her kind never kill themselves? Don't you . . ."

His mother slipped out the door and closed it to silence him and Sarah Ham's laugh, quite close in the hall, came rattling into his room. "Tomsee'll find out. I'll kill myself and then he'll be sorry he wasn't nice to me. I'll use his own lil gun, his own lil ol' pearl-handled revollervuh!" she shouted and let out a loud tormented-sounding laugh in imitation of a movie monster.

Thomas ground his teeth. He pulled out his desk drawer and felt for the pistol. It was an inheritance from the old man, whose opinion it had been that every house should contain a loaded gun. He had discharged two bullets one night into the side of a prowler, but Thomas had never shot anything. He had no fear that the girl would use the gun on herself and he closed the drawer. Her kind clung tenaciously to life and were able to wrest some histrionic advantage from every moment.

Several ideas for getting rid of her had entered his head but each of these had been suggestions whose moral tone indicated that they had come from a mind akin to his father's, and Thomas had rejected them. He could not get the girl locked up again until she did something illegal. The old man would have been able with no qualms at all to get her drunk and send her out on the highway in his car, meanwhile notifying the highway patrol of her presence on the road, but Thomas considered this below his moral stature. Suggestions continued to come to him, each more outrageous than the last.

He had not the vaguest hope that the girl would get the gun and shoot herself, but that afternoon when he looked in the drawer, the gun was gone. His study locked from the inside, not the out. He cared nothing about the gun, but the thought of Sarah Ham's hands sliding among his papers infuriated him. Now even his study was contaminated. The only place left untouched by her was his bedroom.

That night she entered it.

In the morning at breakfast, he did not eat and did not sit down. He stood beside his chair and delivered his ultimatum while his mother sipped her coffee as if she were both alone in the room and in great pain. "I have stood this," he said, "for as long as I am able. Since I see plainly that you care nothing about me, about my peace or comfort or working conditions, I am about to take the only step open to me. I will give you one more day. If you bring the girl back into this house this afternoon, I leave. You can choose—her or me." He had more to say but at that point his voice cracked and he left.

At ten o'clock his mother and Sarah Ham left the house.

At four he heard the car wheels on the gravel and rushed to the window. As the car stopped, the dog stood up, alert, shaking.

He seemed unable to take the first step that would set him walking to the closet in the hall to look for the suitcase. He was like a man handed a knife and told to operate on himself if he wished to live. His huge hands clenched helplessly. His expression was a turmoil of indecision and outrage. His pale blue eyes seemed to sweat in his broiling face. He closed them for a moment and on the back of his lids, his father's image leered at him. Idiot! the old man hissed, idiot! The criminal slut stole your gun! See the sheriff! See the sheriff!

It was a moment before Thomas opened his eyes. He seemed newly stunned. He stood where he was for at least three minutes, then he turned slowly like a large vessel reversing its direction and faced the door. He stood there a moment longer, then he left, his face set to see the ordeal through.

He did not know where he would find the sheriff. The man made his own rules and kept his own hours. Thomas stopped first at the jail, where his office was, but he was not in it. He went to the courthouse and was told by a clerk that the sheriff had gone to the barber-shop across the street. "Yonder's the deppity," the clerk said and pointed out the window to the large figure of a man in a checkered shirt, who was leaning against the side of a police car, looking into space.

"It has to be the sheriff," Thomas said and left for the barbershop. As little as he wanted anything to do with the sheriff, he realized that the man was at least intelligent and not simply a mound of sweating flesh.

The barber said the sheriff had just left. Thomas started back to the courthouse and as he stepped on to the sidewalk from the street, he saw a lean, slightly stooped figure gesticulating angrily at the deputy.

Thomas approached with an aggressiveness brought on by nervous agitation. He stopped abruptly three feet away and said in an overloud voice, "Can I have a word with you?" without adding the sheriff's name, which was Farebrother.

Farebrother turned his sharp creased face just enough to take Thomas in, and the deputy did likewise, but neither spoke. The sheriff removed a very small piece of cigaret from his lip and dropped it at his feet. "I told you what to do," he said to the deputy. Then he moved off with a slight nod that indicated Thomas could follow him if he wanted to see him. The deputy slunk around the front of the police car and got inside.

Farebrother, with Thomas following, headed across the courthouse square and stopped beneath a tree that shaded a quarter of the front lawn. He waited, leaning slightly forward, and lit another cigaret.

Thomas began to blurt out his business. As he had not had time to prepare his words, he was barely coherent. By repeating the same thing over several times, he managed at length to get out what he wanted to say. When he finished, the sheriff was still leaning slightly forward, at an angle to him, his eyes on nothing in particular. He remained that way without speaking.

Thomas began again, slower and in a lamer voice, and Farebrother let him continue for some time before he said, "We had her oncet." He then allowed himself a slow, creased, all-knowing, quarter smile.

"I had nothing to do with that," Thomas said. "That was my mother."

Farebrother squatted.

"She was trying to help the girl," Thomas said. "She didn't know she couldn't be helped."

"Bit off more than she could chew, I reckon," the voice below him mused.

"She has nothing to do with this," Thomas said. "She doesn't know I'm here. The girl is dangerous with that gun."

"*He*," the sheriff said, "never let anything grow under his feet. Particularly nothing a woman planted."

"She might kill somebody with that gun," Thomas said weakly, looking down at the round top of the Texas type hat.

There was a long time of silence.

"Where's she got it?" Farebrother asked.

"I don't know. She sleeps in the guest room. It must be in there, in her suitcase probably," Thomas said.

Farebrother lapsed into silence again.

"You could come search the guest room," Thomas said in a strained voice. "I can go home and leave the latch off the front door and you can come in quietly and go upstairs and search her room."

Farebrother turned his head so that his eyes looked boldly at Thomas's knees. "You seem to know how it ought to be done," he said. "Want to swap jobs?"

Thomas said nothing because he could not think of anything to say, but he waited doggedly. Farebrother removed the cigaret butt from his lips and dropped it on the grass. Beyond him on the courthouse porch a group of loiterers who had been leaning at the left of the door moved over to the right where a patch of sunlight had settled. From one of the upper windows a crumpled piece of paper blew out and drifted down.

"I'll come along about six," Farebrother said. "Leave the latch off the door and keep out of my way—yourself and them two women too."

Thomas let out a rasping sound of relief meant to be "Thanks," and struck off across the grass like someone released. The phrase, "them two women," stuck like a burr in his brain—the subtlety of the insult to his mother hurting him more than any of Farebrother's references to his own incompetence. As he got into his car, his face suddenly flushed. Had he delivered his mother over to the sheriff—to be a butt for the man's tongue? Was he betraying her to get rid of the little slut? He saw at once that this was not the case. He was doing what he was doing for her own good, to rid her of a parasite that would ruin their peace. He started his car and drove quickly home but once he had turned in the driveway, he decided it would be better to park some distance from the house and go quietly in by the back door. He parked on the grass and on the grass walked in a circle toward the rear of the house. The sky was lined with mustard-colored streaks. The dog was asleep on the back doormat. At the approach of his master's step, he opened one yellow eye, took him in, and closed it again.

Thomas let himself into the kitchen. It was empty and the house was quiet enough for him to be aware of the loud ticking of the kitchen clock. It was a quarter to six. He tiptoed hurriedly through the hall to the front door and took the latch off it. Then he stood for a moment listening. From behind the closed parlor door, he heard his mother snoring softly and presumed that she had gone to sleep while reading. On the other side of the hall, not three feet from his study, the little slut's black coat and red pocketbook were slung on a chair. He heard water running upstairs and decided she was taking a bath.

He went into his study and sat down at his desk to wait, noting with distaste that every few moments a tremor ran through him. He sat for a minute or two doing nothing. Then he picked up a pen and began to draw squares on the back of an envelope that lay before him. He looked at his watch. It was eleven minutes to six. After a moment he idly drew the center drawer of the desk out over his lap. For a moment he stared at the gun without recognition. Then he gave a yelp and leaped up. She had put it back!

Idiot! his father hissed, idiot! Go plant it in her pocketbook. Don't just stand there. Go plant it in her pocketbook!

Thomas stood staring at the drawer.

Moron! the old man fumed. Quick while there's time! Go plant it in her pocketbook.

Thomas did not move.

Imbecile! his father cried.

Thomas picked up the gun.

Make haste, the old man ordered.

Thomas started forward, holding the gun away from him. He opened the door and looked at the chair. The black coat and red pocketbook were lying on it almost within reach.

Hurry up, you fool, his father said.

From behind the parlor door the almost inaudible snores of his mother rose and fell. They seemed to mark an order of time that had nothing to do with the instants left to Thomas. There was no other sound.

Quick, you imbecile, before she wakes up, the old man said.

The snores stopped and Thomas heard the sofa springs groan. He grabbed the red pocketbook. It had a skin-like feel to his touch and as it opened, he caught an unmistakable odor of the girl. Wincing, he thrust in the gun and then drew back. His face burned an ugly dull red.

"What is Tomsee putting in my purse?" she called and her pleased laugh bounced down the staircase. Thomas whirled.

She was at the top of the stair, coming down in the manner of a fashion model, one bare leg and then the other thrusting out the front of her kimona in a definite rhythm. "Tomsee is being naughty," she said in a throaty voice. She reached the bottom and cast a possessive leer at Thomas whose face was now more grey than red. She reached out, pulled the bag open with her finger and peered at the gun.

His mother opened the parlor door and looked out.

"Tomsee put his pistol in my bag!" the girl shrieked.

"Ridiculous," his mother said, yawning. "What would Thomas want to put his pistol in your bag for?"

Thomas stood slightly hunched, his hands hanging helplessly at the wrists as if he had just pulled them up out of a pool of blood.

"I don't know what for," the girl said, "but he sure did it," and she proceeded to walk around Thomas, her hands on her hips, her neck thrust forward and her intimate grin fixed on him fiercely. All at once her expression seemed to open as the purse had opened when Thomas touched it. She stood with her head cocked on one side in an attitude of disbelief. "Oh boy," she said slowly, "is he a case."

At that instant Thomas damned not only the girl but the entire order of the universe that made her possible.

"Thomas wouldn't put a gun in your bag," his mother said. "Thomas is a gentleman."

The girl made a chortling noise. "You can see it in there," she said and pointed to the open purse.

You *found* it in her bag, you dimwit! the old man hissed.

"I found it in her bag!" Thomas shouted. "The dirty criminal slut stole my gun!"

His mother gasped at the sound of the other presence in his voice. The old lady's sybil-like face turned pale.

"Found it my eye!" Sarah Ham shrieked and started for the pocketbook, but Thomas, as if his arm were guided by his father, caught it first and snatched the gun. The girl in a frenzy lunged at Thomas's throat and would actually have caught him around the neck had not his mother thrown herself forward to protect her.

Fire! the old man yelled.

Thomas fired. The blast was like a sound meant to bring an end to evil in the world. Thomas heard it as a sound that would shatter the laughter of sluts until all shrieks were stilled and nothing was left to disturb the peace of perfect order.

The echo died away in waves. Before the last one had faded, Farebrother opened the door and put his head inside the hall. His nose wrinkled. His expression for some few seconds was that of a man unwilling to admit surprise. His eyes were clear as glass, reflecting the scene. The old lady lay on the floor between the girl and Thomas.

The sheriff's brain worked instantly like a calculating machine. He saw the facts as if they were already in print: the fellow had intended all along to kill his mother and pin it on the girl. But Farebrother had been too quick for him. They were not yet aware of his head in the door. As he scrutinized the scene, further insights were flashed to him. Over her body, the killer and the slut were about to collapse into each other's arms. The sheriff knew a nasty bit when he saw it. He was accustomed to enter upon scenes that were not as bad as he had hoped to find them, but this one met his expectations.

ROSS MacDONALD
(1915-1983)

Ross MacDonald was a pseudonym for Kenneth Millar, born in Los Gatos, California, and educated at the University of Western Ontario, the University of Toronto, and the University of Michigan for a career as an English teacher. His detective, Lew Archer, who is the protagonist in all but two of Macdonald's novels, is one of the best-known detectives in American fiction. Initially influenced by Dashiell Hammett and Raymond Chandler, Macdonald developed an interest in Freudian psychology that led him to create what have been called "gothic psychodramas," stories of psychically wounded characters whose crimes are the end result of complex family relationships often going back several generations. By emphasizing the familial and psychological history leading up to the crime, Macdonald turned from the hard-boiled school of Hammett and Chandler back to the British tradition of crime fiction rooted in the novel of social manners. Among his best-known novels are *The Goodbye Look* (1969) and *The Blue Hammer* (1976).

"The Sleeping Dog" illustrates a shift to the kind of story in which the detective's character and personality are more central than his method. The private investigator has a personal interest in the case and is drawn into the private lives and complicated domestic tragedies of others. Typical Macdonald touches are the California setting, in which affluence threatens to scar the natural landscape and corrupt the justice system, and the theme of the buried past rising up to disturb the present, suggested by the title with its echo of the warning to "let sleeping dogs lie."

THE SLEEPING DOG

The day after her dog disappeared, Fay Hooper called me early. Her normal voice was like waltzing violins, but this morning the violins were out of tune. She sounded as though she'd been crying.

"Otto's gone."

Otto was her one-year-old German shepherd.

"He jumped the fence yesterday afternoon and ran away. Or else he was kidnapped—dognapped, I suppose is the right word to use."

"What makes you think that?"

"You know Otto, Mr. Archer—how loyal he was. He wouldn't deliberately stay away from me overnight, not under his own power. There must be thieves involved."

She caught her breath. "I realize searching for stolen dogs isn't your métier. But you *are* a detective, and I thought, since we knew one another . . ."

She allowed her voice to suggest, ever so chastely, that we might get to know one another better.

I liked the woman. I liked the dog, I liked the breed. I was taking my own German shepherd pup to obedience school, which is where I met Fay Hooper. Otto and she were the handsomest and most expensive members of the class.

"How do I get to your place?"

She lived in the hills north of Malibu, she said, on the far side of the county line. If she wasn't home when I got there, her husband would be.

On my way out I stopped at the dog school in Pacific Palisades to talk to the man who ran it, Fernando Rambeau. The kennels behind the house burst into clamor when I knocked on the front door. Rambeau boarded dogs as well as trained them.

A dark-haired girl looked out and informed me that her husband was feeding the animals. "Maybe I can help," she added doubtfully, and then she let me into a small living room.

I told her about the missing dog. "It would help if you called the vets and animal shelters and gave them a description," I said.

"We've already been doing that. Mrs. Hooper was on the phone to Fernando last night." She sounded vaguely resentful. "I'll get him."

Setting her face against the continuing noise, she went out the back door. Rambeau came in with her, wiping his hands on a rag. He was a square-shouldered Canadian with a curly black beard that failed to conceal his youth. Over the beard, his intense dark eyes peered at me warily, like an animal's sensing trouble.

Rambeau handled dogs as if he loved them. He wasn't quite so patient with human beings. His current class was only in its third week, but he was already having dropouts. The man was loaded with explosive feeling, and it was close to the surface now.

"I'm sorry about Mrs. Hooper and her dog. They were my best pupils. He was, anyway. But I can't drop everything and spend the next week looking for him."

"Nobody expects that. I take it you've had no luck with your contacts."

"I don't have such good contacts. Marie and I, we just moved down here last year, from British Columbia."

"That was a mistake," his wife said from the doorway.

Rambeau pretended not to hear her. "Anyway, I know nothing about dog thieves." With both hands he pushed the possibility away from him. "If I hear any word of the dog I'll let you know, naturally. I've got nothing against Mrs. Hooper."

His wife gave him a quick look. It was one of those revealing looks which said, among other things, that she loved him and didn't know if he loved her, and she was worried about him. She caught me watching her and lowered her eyes. Then she burst out, "Do you think somebody killed the dog?"

"I have no reason to think so."

"Some people shoot dogs, don't they?"

"Not around here," Rambeau said. "Maybe back in the bush someplace." He turned to me with a sweeping explanatory gesture.

"These things make her nervous and she gets wild ideas. You know Marie is a country girl—"

"I am not. I was born in Chilliwack." Flinging a bitter look at him, she left the room.

"Was Otto shot?" I asked Rambeau.

"Not that I know of. Listen, Mr. Archer, you're a good customer, but I can't stand here talking all day. I've got twenty dogs to feed."

They were still barking when I drove up the coast highway out of hearing. It was nearly 40 miles to the Hoopers' mailbox, and another mile up a black-top lane which climbed the side of a canyon to the gate. On both sides of the heavy wire gate, which had a new combination padlock on it, a hurricane fence, eight feet high and topped with barbed wire, extended out of sight. Otto would have to be quite a jumper to clear it. So would I.

The house beyond the gate was low and massive, made of fieldstone and steel and glass. I honked at it and waited. A man in blue bathing trunks came out of the house with a shotgun. The sun glinted on its twin barrels and on the man's bald head and round, brown, burnished belly. He walked quite slowly, a short heavy man in his sixties, scuffling along in huaraches. The flabby brown shell of fat on him jiggled lugubriously.

When he approached the gate, I could see the stiff gray pallor under his tan, like stone showing under varnish. He was sick, or afraid, or both. His mouth was profoundly discouraged.

"What do you want?" he said over the shotgun.

"Mrs. Hooper asked me to help find her dog. My name is Lew Archer."

He was not impressed. "My wife isn't here, and I'm busy. I happen to be following soy-bean futures rather closely."

"Look here, I've come quite a distance to lend a hand. I met Mrs. Hooper at dog school and—"

Hooper uttered a short savage laugh. "That hardly constitutes an introduction to either of us. You'd better be on your way right now."

"I think I'll wait for your wife."

"I think you won't." He raised the shotgun and let me look into its close-set, hollow, round eyes. "This is my property all the way down to the road, and you're trespassing. That means I can shoot you if I have to."

"What sense would that make? I came out here to help you."

"You can't help me." He looked at me through the wire gate with a kind of pathetic arrogance, like a lion that had grown old in captivity. "Go away."

I drove back down to the road and waited for Fay Hooper. The sun slid up the sky. The inside of my car turned oven-hot. I went for a walk down the canyon. The brown September grass crunched under my feet. Away up on the far side of the canyon an earth mover that looked like a crazy red insect was cutting the ridge to pieces.

A very fast black car came up the canyon and stopped abruptly beside me. A gaunt man in a wrinkled brown suit climbed out, with his hand on his holster, told me that he was Sheriff Carlson, and asked me what I was doing there. I told him.

He pushed back his wide cream-colored hat and scratched at his hairline. The pale eyes in his sun-fired face were like clouded glass inserts in a brick wall.

"I'm surprised Mr. Hooper takes that attitude. Mrs. Hooper just came to see me in the courthouse. But I can't take you up there with me if Mr. Hooper says no."

"Why not?"

"He owns most of the county and holds the mortgage on the rest of it. Besides," he added with careful logic, "Mr. Hooper is a friend of mine."

"Then you better get him a keeper."

The sheriff glanced around uneasily, as if the Hoopers' mailbox might be bugged. "I'm surprised he has a gun, let alone threatening you with it. He must be upset about the dog."

"He didn't seem to care about the dog."

"He does, though. *She* cares, so *he* cares," Carlson said.

"What did she have to tell you?"

"She can talk to you herself. She should be along any minute. She told me that she was going to follow me out of town."

He drove his black car up the lane. A few minutes later Fay Hooper stopped her Mercedes at the mailbox. She must have seen the impatience on my face. She got out and came toward me in a little run, making noises of dismayed regret.

Fay was in her late thirties and fading slightly, as if a light frost had touched her pale gold head, but she was still a beautiful woman. She turned the gentle force of her charm on me.

"I'm dreadfully sorry," she said. "Have I kept you waiting long?"

"Your husband did. He ran me off with a shotgun."

Her gloved hand lighted on my arm, and stayed. She had an electric touch, even through layers of cloth.

"That's terrible. I had no idea that Allan still had a gun."

Her mouth was blue behind her lipstick, as if the information had chilled her to the marrow. She took me up the hill in the Mercedes. The gate was standing open, but she didn't drive in right away.

"I might as well be perfectly frank," she said without looking at me. "Ever since Otto disappeared yesterday, there's been a nagging question in my mind. What you've just told me raises the question again. I was in town all day yesterday so that Otto was alone here with Allan when—when it happened."

The values her voice gave to the two names made it sound as if Allan were the dog and Otto the husband.

"When what happened, Mrs. Hooper?" I wanted to know.

Her voice sank lower. "I can't help suspecting that Allan shot him. He's never liked any of my dogs. The only dogs he appreciates are hunting dogs—and he was particularly jealous of Otto. Besides, when I got back from town, Allan was getting the ground ready to plant some roses. He's never enjoyed gardening, particularly in the heat. We have professionals to do our work. And this really isn't the time of year to put in a bed of roses."

"You think your husband was planting a dog?" I asked.

"If he was, I have to know." She turned toward me, and the leather seat squeaked softly under her movement. "Find out for me, Mr. Archer. If Allan killed my beautiful big old dog, I couldn't stay with him."

"Something you said implied that Allan used to have a gun or guns, but gave them up. Is that right?"

"He had a small arsenal when I married him. He was an infantry officer in the war and a big-game hunter in peacetime. But he swore off hunting years ago."

"Why?"

"I don't really know. We came home from a hunting trip one fall and Allan sold all his guns. He never said a word about it to me but it was the fall after the war ended, and I always thought that it must have had something to do with the war."

"Have you been married so long?"

"Thank you for that question." She produced a rueful smile. "I met Allan during the war, the year I came out, and I knew I'd met my fate. He was a very powerful person."

"And a very wealthy one."

She gave me a flashing, haughty look and stepped so hard on the accelerator that she almost ran into the sheriff's car parked in front of the house. We walked around to the back, past a free-form swimming pool that looked inviting, into a walled garden. A few Greek statues stood around in elegant disrepair. Bees murmured like distant bombers among the flowers.

The bed where Allan Hooper had been digging was about five feet long and three feet wide, and it reminded me of graves.

"Get me a spade," I said.

"Are you going to dig him up?"

"You're pretty sure he's in there, aren't you, Mrs. Hooper?"

"I guess I am."

From a lath house at the end of the garden she fetched a square-edged spade. I asked her to stick around.

I took off my jacket and hung it on a marble torso where it didn't look too bad. It was easy digging in the newly worked soil. In a few minutes I was two feet below the surface, and the ground was still soft and penetrable.

The edge of my spade struck something soft but not so penetrable. Fay Hooper heard the peculiar dull sound it made. She made a dull sound of her own. I scooped away more earth. Dog fur sprouted like stiff black grass at the bottom of the grave.

Fay got down on her knees and began to dig with her lacquered fingernails. Once she cried out in a loud harsh voice, "Dirty murderer!"

Her husband must have heard her. He came out of the house and looked over the stone wall. His head seemed poised on top of the wall, hairless and bodiless, like Humpty-Dumpty. He had that look on his face, of not being able to be put together again.

"I didn't kill your dog, Fay. Honest to God, I didn't."

She didn't hear him. She was talking to Otto. "Poor boy, poor boy," she said. "Poor, beautiful boy."

Sheriff Carlson came into the garden. He reached down into the grave and freed the dog's head from the earth. His large hands moved gently on the great wedge of the skull.

Fay knelt beside him in torn and dirty stockings. "What are you doing?"

Carlson held up a red-tipped finger. "Your dog was shot through the head, Mrs. Hooper, but it's no shotgun wound. Looks to me more like a deer rifle."

"I don't even own a rifle," Hooper said over the wall. "I haven't owned one for nearly twenty years. Anyway, I wouldn't shoot your dog."

Fay scrambled to her feet. She looked ready to climb the wall. "Then why did you bury him?"

His mouth opened and closed.

"Why did you buy a shotgun without telling me?"

"For protection."

"Against my dog?"

Hooper shook his head. He edged along the wall and came in tentatively through the gate. He had on slacks and a short-sleeved yellow jersey which somehow emphasized his shortness and his fatness and his age.

"Mr. Hooper had some threatening calls," the sheriff said. "Somebody got hold of his unlisted number. He was just telling me about it now."

"Why didn't you tell me, Allan?"

"I didn't want to alarm you. You weren't the one they were after, anyway. I bought a shotgun and kept it in my study."

"Do you know who they are?"

"No. I make enemies in the course of business, especially the farming operations. Some crackpot shot your dog, gunning for me. I heard a shot and found him dead in the driveway."

"But how could you bury him without telling me?"

Hooper spread his hands in front of him. "I wasn't thinking too well. I felt guilty, I suppose, because whoever got him was after me. And I didn't want you to see him dead. I guess I wanted to break it to you gently."

"This is gently?"

"It's not the way I planned it. I thought if I had a chance to get you another pup—"

"No one will ever take Otto's place."

Allan Hooper stood and looked at her wistfully across the open grave, as if he would have liked to take Otto's place. After a while the two of them went into the house.

Carlson and I finished digging Otto up and carried him out to the sheriff's car. His inert blackness filled the trunk from side to side.

"What are you going to do with him, Sheriff?" I asked.

"Get a vet I know to recover the slug in him. Then if we nab the sniper we can use ballistics to convict him."

"You're taking this just as seriously as a real murder, aren't you?" I observed.

"They want me to," he said with a respectful look toward the house.

Mrs. Hooper came out carrying a white leather suitcase which she deposited in the back seat of her Mercedes.

"Are you going someplace?" I asked her.

"Yes, I am." She didn't say where.

Her husband, who was watching her from the doorway, didn't speak. The Mercedes went away. He closed the door. Both of them had looked sick.

"She doesn't seem to believe he didn't do it. Do you, Sheriff?"

Carlson jabbed me with his forefinger. "Mr. Hooper is no liar. If you want to get along with me, get that through your head. I've known Mr. Hooper for over twenty years—served under him in the war—and I never heard him twist the truth."

"I'll have to take your word for it. What about those threatening phone calls? Did he report them to you before today?"

"No."

"What was said on the phone?"

"He didn't tell me."

"Does Hooper have any idea who shot the dog?"

"Well, he did say he saw a man slinking around outside the fence. He didn't get close enough to the guy to give me a good description, but he did make out that he had a black beard."

"There's a dog trainer in Pacific Palisades named Rambeau who fits the description. Mrs. Hooper has been taking Otto to his school."

"Rambeau?" Carlson said with interest.

"Fernando Rambeau. He seemed pretty upset when I talked to him this morning."

"What did he say?"

"A good deal less than he knows, I think. I'll talk to him again."

Rambeau was not at home. My repeated knocking was answered only by the barking of the dogs. I retreated up the highway to a drive-in where I ate a torpedo sandwich. When I was on my second cup of coffee, Marie Rambeau drove by in a pickup truck. I followed her home.

"Where's Fernando?" I asked.

"I don't know. I've been out looking for him."

"Is he in a bad way?"

"I don't know how you mean."

"Emotionally upset."

"He has been ever since that woman came into the class."

"Mrs. Hooper?"

Her head bobbed slightly.

"Are they having an affair?"

"They better not be." Her small red mouth looked quite implacable. "He was out with her night before last. I heard him make the date. He was gone all night, and when he came home he was on one of his black drunks and he wouldn't go to bed. He sat in the kitchen and drank himself glassy-eyed." She got out of the pickup facing me. "Is shooting a dog a very serious crime?"

"It is to me, but not to the law. It's not like shooting a human being."

"It would be to Fernando. He loves dogs the way other people love human beings. That included Otto."

"But he shot him."

Her head drooped. I could see the straight white part dividing her black hair. "I'm afraid he did. He's got a crazy streak and it comes out in him when he drinks. You should have heard him in the kitchen yesterday morning. He was moaning and groaning about his brother."

"His brother?"

"Fernando had an older brother, George, who died back in Canada after the war. Fernando was just a kid when it happened and it was a big loss to him. His parents were dead, too, and they put him in a foster home in Chilliwack. He still has nightmares about it."

"What did his brother die of?"

"He never told me exactly, but I think he was shot in some kind of hunting accident. George was a guide and packer in the Fraser River valley below Mount Robson. That's where Fernando comes from, the Mount Robson country. He won't go back, on account of what happened to his brother."

"What did he say about his brother yesterday?" I asked.

"That he was going to get his revenge for George. I got so scared I couldn't listen to him. I went out and fed the dogs. When I came back in, Fernando was loading his deer rifle. I asked him what he was planning to do, but he walked right out and drove away."

"May I see the rifle?"

"It isn't in the house. I looked for it after he left today. He must have taken it with him again. I'm so afraid that he'll kill somebody."

"What's he driving?"

"Our car. It's an old blue Meteor sedan."

Keeping an eye out for it, I drove up the highway to the Hoopers' canyon. Everything there was very peaceful. Too peaceful. Just inside the locked gate, Allan Hooper was lying face down on his shotgun. I could see small ants in single file trekking across the crown of his bald head.

I got a hammer out of the trunk of my car and used it to break the padlock. I lifted his head. His skin was hot in the sun, as if death had fallen on him like a fever. But he had been shot neatly between the eyes. There was no exit wound; the bullet was still in his head. Now the ants were crawling on my hands.

I found my way into the Hoopers' study, turned off the stuttering teletype, and sat down under an elk head to telephone the courthouse. Carlson was in his office.

"I have bad news, Sheriff. Allan Hooper's been shot."

I heard him draw in his breath quickly. "Is he dead?"

"Extremely dead. You better put out a general alarm for Rambeau."

Carlson said with gloomy satisfaction, "I already have him."

"You have him?"

"That's correct. I picked him up in the Hoopers' canyon and brought him in just a few minutes ago." Carlson's voice sank to a mournful mumble. "I picked him up a little too late, I guess."

"Did Rambeau do any talking?"

"He hasn't had a chance to yet. When I stopped his car, he piled out and threatened me with a rifle. I clobbered him one good."

I went outside to wait for Carlson and his men. A very pale afternoon moon hung like a ghost in the sky. For some reason it made me think of Fay. She ought to be here. It occurred to me that possibly she had been.

I went and looked at Hooper's body again. He had nothing to tell me. He lay as if he had fallen from a height, perhaps all the way from the moon.

They came in a black county wagon and took him away. I followed them inland to the county seat, which rose like a dusty island in a dark green lake of orange groves. We parked in the courthouse parking lot, and the sheriff and I went inside.

Rambeau was under guard in a second-floor room with barred windows. Carlson said it was used for interrogation. There was nothing in the room but an old deal table and some wooden chairs. Rambeau sat hunched forward on one of them, his hands hanging limp between his knees. Part of his head had been shaved and plastered with bandages.

"I had to cool him with my gun butt," Carlson said. "You're lucky I didn't shoot you—you know that, Fernando?"

Rambeau made no response. His black eyes were set and dull.

"Had his rifle been fired?"

"Yeah. Chet Scott is working on it now. Chet's my identification lieutenant and he's a bear on ballistics." The sheriff turned back to Rambeau. "You might as well give us a full confession, boy. If you shot Mr. Hooper and his dog, we can link the bullets to your gun. You know that."

Rambeau didn't speak or move.

"What did you have against Mr. Hooper?" Carlson said.

No answer. Rambeau's mouth was set like a trap in the thicket of his beard.

"Your older brother," I said to him, "was killed in a hunting accident in British Columbia. Was Hooper at the other end of the gun that killed George?"

Rambeau didn't answer me, but Carlson's head came up. "Where did you get that, Archer?"

"From a couple of things I was told. According to Rambeau's wife, he was talking yesterday about revenge for his brother's death. According to Fay Hooper, her husband swore off guns when he came back from a hunting trip after the war. Would you know if that trip was to British Columbia?"

"Yeah. Mr. Hooper took me and the wife with him."

"Whose wife?"

"Both our wives."

"To the Mount Robson area?"

"That's correct. We went up after elk."

"And did he shoot somebody accidentally?"

"Not that I know of. I wasn't with him all the time, understand. He often went out alone, or with Mrs. Hooper," Carlson replied.

"Did he use a packer named George Rambeau?"

"I wouldn't know. Ask Fernando here."

I asked Fernando. He didn't speak or move. Only his eyes had changed. They were wet and glistening-black, visible parts of a grief that filled his head like a dark underground river.

The questioning went on and produced nothing. It was night when I went outside. The moon was slipping down behind the dark hills. I took a room in a hotel and checked in with my answering service in Hollywood.

About an hour before, Fay Hooper had called me from a Las Vegas hotel. When I tried to return the call, she wasn't in her room and didn't respond to paging. I left a message for her to come home, that her husband was dead.

Next, I called R.C.M.P. headquarters in Vancouver to ask some questions about George Rambeau. The answers came over the line in clipped Canadian tones. George and his dog had disappeared from his cabin below Red Pass in the fall of 1945. Their bodies hadn't been recovered until the following May, and by that time they consisted of parts of the two skeletons. These included George Rambeau's skull, which had been pierced in the right front and left rear quadrants by a heavy-caliber bullet. The bullet had not been recovered. Who fired, or when, or why, had never been determined. The dog, a husky, had also been shot through the head.

I walked over to the courthouse to pass the word to Carlson. He was in the basement shooting gallery with Lieutenant Scott, who was firing test rounds from Fernando Rambeau's .30/30 repeater.

I gave them the official account of the accident. "But since George Rambeau's dog was shot, too, it probably wasn't an accident," I said.

"I see what you mean," Carlson said. "It's going to be rough, spreading all this stuff out in court about Mr. Hooper. We have to nail it down, though."

I went back to my hotel and to bed, but the process of nailing down the case against Rambeau continued through the night. By morning Lieutenant Scott had detailed comparisons set up between the test-fired slugs and the ones dug out of Hooper and the dog.

I looked at his evidence through a comparison microscope. It left no doubt in my mind that the slugs that killed Allan Hooper and the dog, Otto, had come from Rambeau's gun.

But Rambeau still wouldn't talk, even to phone his wife or ask for a lawyer.

"We'll take you out to the scene of the crime," Carlson said. "I've cracked tougher nuts than you, boy."

We rode in the back seat of his car with Fernando handcuffed between us. Lieutenant Scott did the driving. Rambeau groaned and pulled against his handcuffs. He was very close to the breaking point, I thought.

It came a few minutes later when the car turned up the lane past the Hoopers' mailbox. He burst into sudden fierce tears as if a pressure gauge in his head had broken. It was strange to see a bearded man crying like a boy. "I don't want to go up there."

"Because you shot him?" Carlson said.

"I shot the dog. I confess I shot the dog," Rambeau said.

"And the man?"

"No!" he cried. "I never killed a man. Mr. Hooper was the one who did. He followed my brother out in the woods and shot him."

"If you knew that," I said, "why didn't you tell the Mounties years ago?"

"I didn't know it then. I was seven years old. How would I understand? When Mrs. Hooper came to our cabin to be with my brother, how would I know it was a curious thing? Or when Mr. Hooper asked me if she had been there? I didn't know he was her husband. I thought he was her father checking up. I knew I shouldn't have told him—I could see it in his face the minute after—but I didn't understand the situation till the other night, when I talked to Mrs. Hooper."

"Did she know that her husband had shot George?"

"She didn't even know George had been killed. They never went back to the Fraser River after nineteen forty-five. But when we put our facts together, we agreed he must have done it. I came out here next morning to get even. The dog came out to the gate. It wasn't real to me—I'd been drinking most of the night—it wasn't real to me until the dog went down. I shot him. Mr. Hooper shot *my* dog. But when he came out of the house himself, I couldn't pull the trigger. I yelled at him and ran away."

"What did you yell?" I said.

"The same thing I told him on the telephone: 'Remember Mount Robson.' "

A yellow cab, which looked out of place in the canyon, came over the ridge above us. Lieutenant Scott waved it to a stop. The driver said he'd just brought Mrs. Hooper home from the airport and wanted to know if that constituted a felony. Scott waved him on.

"I wonder what she was doing at the airport," Carlson said.

"Coming home from Vegas. She tried to call me from there last night. I forgot to tell you."

"You don't forget important things like that," Carlson said.

"I suppose I wanted her to come home under her own power."

"In case she shot her husband?"

"More or less."

"She didn't. Fernando shot him, didn't you, boy?"

"I shot the dog. I am innocent of the man." He turned to me. "Tell her that. Tell her I am sorry about the dog. I came out here to surrender the gun and tell her yesterday. I don't trust myself with guns."

"With darn good reason," Carlson said. "We know you shot Mr. Hooper. Ballistic evidence doesn't lie."

Rambeau screeched in his ear, "You're a liar! You're all liars!"

Carlson swung his open hand against the side of Rambeau's face. "Don't call me names, little man."

Lieutenant Scott spoke without taking his eyes from the road. "I wouldn't hit him, Chief. You wouldn't want to damage our case."

Carlson subsided, and we drove on up to the house. Carlson went in without knocking. The guard at the door discouraged me from following him.

I couldn't hear Fay's voice on the other side of the door, too low to be understood. Carlson said something to her.

"Get out! Get out of my house, you killer!" Fay cried out sharply.

Carlson didn't come out. I went in instead. One of his arms was wrapped around her body, the other hand was covering her mouth. I got his Adam's apple in the crook of my left arm, pulled him away from her, and threw him over my left hip. He went down clanking and got up holding his revolver.

He should have shot me right away. But he gave Fay Hooper time to save my life.

She stepped in front of me. "Shoot me, Mr. Carlson. You might as well. You shot the one man I ever cared for."

"Your husband shot George Rambeau, if that's who you mean. I ought to know. I was there." Carlson scowled down at his gun and replaced it in his holster.

Lieutenant Scott was watching him from the doorway.

"You were there?" I said to Carlson. "Yesterday you told me Hooper was alone when he shot Rambeau."

"He was. When I said I was there, I meant in the general neighborhood."

"Don't believe him," Fay said. "He fired the gun that killed George, and it was no accident. The two of them hunted George down in the woods. My husband planned to shoot him himself, but George's dog came at him and he had to dispose of it. By that time George had drawn a bead on Allan. Mr. Carlson shot him. It was hardly a coincidence that the next spring Allan financed his campaign for sheriff."

"She's making it up," Carlson said. "She wasn't within ten miles of the place."

"But you were, Mr. Carlson, and so was Allan. He told me the whole story yesterday, after we found Otto. Once that happened, he knew that everything was bound to come out. I already suspected him, of course, after I talked to Fernando. Allan filled in the details himself. He thought, since he hadn't killed George personally, I would be able to forgive him. But I couldn't. I left him and flew to Nevada, intending to divorce him. I've been intending to for twenty years."

Carlson said, "Are you sure you didn't shoot him before you left?"

"How could she have?" I said. "Ballistics don't lie, and the ballistic evidence says he was shot with Fernando's rifle. Nobody had access to it but Fernando—and you. You stopped him on the road and knocked him out, took his rifle, *and used it to kill Hooper.* You killed him for the same reason that Hooper buried the dog—to keep the past buried. You thought Hooper was the only witness to the murder of George Rambeau. But by that time Mrs. Hooper knew about it, too."

"It wasn't murder. It was self-defense, just like in the war. Anyway, you'll never hang it on me."

"We don't have to. We'll hang Hooper on you. How about it, Lieutenant?"

Scott nodded grimly, not looking at his chief. I relieved Carlson of his gun. He winced, as if I were amputating part of his body. He offered no resistance when Scott took him out to the car.

I stayed behind for a final word with Fay. "Fernando asked me to tell you he's sorry for shooting your dog."

"We're both sorry." She stood with her eyes down, as if the past was swirling visibly around her feet. "I'll talk to Fernando later. Much later."

"There's one coincidence that bothers me. How did you happen to take your dog to his school?"

"I happened to see his sign, and Fernando Rambeau isn't a common name. I couldn't resist going there. I had to know what had happened to George. I think perhaps Fernando came to California for the same reason."

"Now you both know," I said.

ED McBAIN
(1926-   )

Ed McBain was born in New York City and educated at Hunter College. As his various pen names (Evan Hunter, Curt Cannon, Hunt Collins, Ezra Hannon, Richard Marsten) indicate, he is a prolific writer of detective and adventure stories. As Ed McBain, his fame rests on his contributions, spanning three decades, to the police procedural. Set in the fictional city of Isola, which is a geographic mirror image of the real New York City, his stories feature a collective protagonist, the detectives working the city's 87th Precinct. McBain's inventiveness is seen in the various plots and structural patterns with which he continually tests the narrative restrictions of the police procedural. In *He Who Hesitates* (1965), for example, everything is seen through the murderer's eyes and the police are relegated to a minor role. For the most part, however, McBain relies on the flexibility of his urban setting and collective protagonist to overcome the major challenges of the procedural: how to present police routines realistically but not tediously, and how to give them a human dimension without sacrificing credibility. His metropolitan setting provides for an inexhaustible supply of storylines crossing ethnic and class boundaries and his cast of recurring characters—including not only detectives like Steve Carella and Meyer Meyer but a villain known as the Deaf Man—provides continuity and depth. McBain differs from his predecessors in his essentially optimistic view of the city as a place in which, despite the violence, moral order prevails because police are good citizens and laws work.

"Sadie When She Died," which McBain also published in a longer version as a novel, illustrates the "inverted" detective story in which the detective suspects from the beginning the identity of the killer but has to find legal proof of it. As a procedural it shows the team effort involved in solving the crime, the reliance on technology—from fingerprints and photographs to telephone taps—and the individual detective's psychological skills in decoding the eccentric behavior of killer and victim alike. McBain's special contribution to the procedural format, faith in the system tempered by an understanding of human frailty, is shown in the story's concluding juxtaposition of the arrest of the actual murderer against the suicide of the wrongly accused man.

SADIE WHEN SHE DIED

"I'm very glad she's dead," the man said.

He wore a homburg, muffler, overcoat and gloves. He stood near the night table, a tall man with a narrow face, and a well-groomed gray mustache that matched the graying hair at his temples. His eyes were clear and blue and distinctly free of pain or grief.

Detective Steve Carella wasn't sure he had heard the man correctly. "Sir," Carella said, "I'm sure I don't have to tell you—"

"That's right," the man said, "you don't have to tell me. It happens I'm a criminal lawyer and am well aware of my rights. My wife was no good, and I'm delighted someone killed her."

Carella opened his pad. This was not what a bereaved husband was supposed to say when his wife lay disemboweled on the bedroom floor in a pool of her own blood.

"Your name is Gerald Fletcher."

"That's correct."

"Your wife's name, Mr. Fletcher?"

"Sarah. Sarah Fletcher."

"Want to tell me what happened?"

"I got home about fifteen minutes ago. I called to my wife from the front door, and got no answer. I came into the bedroom and found her dead on the floor. I immediately called the police."

"Was the room in this condition when you came in?"

"It was."

"Touch anything?"

"Nothing. I haven't moved from this spot since I placed the call."

"Anybody in here when you came in?"

"Not a soul. Except my wife, of course."

"Is that your suitcase in the entrance hallway?"

"It is. I was on the Coast for three days. An associate of mine needed advice on a brief he was preparing. What's your name?"

"Carella. Detective Steve Carella."

"I'll remember that."

While the police photographer was doing his macabre little jig around the body to make sure the lady looked good in the rushes, or as good as any lady can look in her condition, a laboratory assistant named Marshall Davies was in the kitchen of the apartment, waiting for the medical examiner to pronounce the lady dead, at which time Davies would go into the bedroom and with delicate care remove the knife protruding from the blood and slime of the lady, in an attempt to salvage some good latent prints from the handle of the murder weapon.

Davies was a new technician, but an observant one, and he noticed that the kitchen window was wide open, not exactly usual on a December night when the temperature outside hovered at twelve degrees. Leaning over the sink, he further noticed that the window opened onto a fire escape on the rear of the building. He could not resist speculating that perhaps someone had climbed up the fire escape and then into the kitchen.

Since there was a big muddy footprint in the kitchen sink, another one on the floor near the sink, and several others fading as they traveled across the waxed kitchen floor to the living room, Davies surmised that he was onto something hot. Wasn't it possible that an intruder *had* climbed over the windowsill, into the sink and walked across the room, bearing the switchblade knife that had later been pulled viciously across the lady's abdomen from left to right? If the M.E. ever got through with the damn body, the boys of the 87th would be halfway home, thanks to Marshall Davies. He felt pretty good.

The three points of the triangle were Detective-Lieutenant Byrnes, and Detectives Meyer Meyer and Steve Carella. Fletcher sat in a chair, still wearing homburg, muffler, overcoat and gloves as if he expected to be called outdoors at any moment. The interrogation was being conducted in a windowless cubicle labeled Interrogation Room.

The cops standing in their loose triangle around Gerald Fletcher were amazed but not too terribly amused by his brutal frankness.

"I hated her guts," he said.

"Mr. Fletcher," Lieutenant Byrnes said, "I *still* feel I must warn you that a woman has been murdered—"

"Yes. My dear, wonderful wife," Fletcher said sarcastically.

". . . which is a serious crime. . . ." Byrnes felt tongue-tied in Fletcher's presence. Bullet-headed, hair turning from iron-gray to ice-white, blue-eyed, built like a compact linebacker, Byrnes looked to his colleagues for support. Both Meyer and Carella were watching their shoelaces.

"You have warned me repeatedly," Fletcher said, "I can't imagine why. My wife is dead—someone killed her—but it was not I."

"Well, it's nice to have your assurance of that, Mr. Fletcher, but this alone doesn't necessarily still our doubts," Carella said, hearing the words and wondering where the hell they were coming from. He was, he realized, trying to impress Fletcher. He continued, "How do we know it *wasn't* you who stabbed her?"

"To begin with," Fletcher said, "there were signs of forcible entry in the kitchen and hasty departure in the bedroom, witness the wide-open window in the aforementioned room and the shattered window in the latter. The drawers in the dining-room sideboard were open—"

"You're very observant," Meyer said suddenly. "Did you notice all this in the four minutes it took you to enter the apartment and call the police?

"It is my *job* to be observant," Fletcher said. "But to answer your question, no. I noticed all this *after* I had spoken to Detective Carella here."

Wearily, Byrnes dismissed Fletcher, who then left the room.

"What do you think?" Byrnes said.

"I think he did it," Carella said.

"Even with all those signs of a burglary?"

"*Especially* with those signs. He could have come home, found his wife stabbed—but not fatally—and finished her off by yanking the knife across her belly. Fletcher had four minutes, when all he needed was maybe four seconds."

"It's possible," Meyer said.

"Or maybe I just don't like the guy," Carella said.

"Let's see what the lab comes up with," Byrnes said.

The laboratory came up with good fingerprints on the kitchen window sash and on the silver drawer of the dining-room sideboard. There were good prints on some of the pieces of silver scattered on the floor near the smashed bedroom window. Most important, there were good prints on the handle of the switchblade knife. The prints matched; they had all been left by the same person.

Gerald Fletcher graciously allowed the police to take *his* fingerprints, which were then compared with those Marshall Davies had sent over from the police laboratory. The fingerprints on the window sash, the drawer, the silverware and the knife did not match Gerald Fletcher's.

Which didn't mean a damn thing if he had been wearing his gloves when he'd finished her off.

On Monday morning, in the second-floor rear apartment of 721 Silvermine Oval, a chalked outline on the bedroom floor was the only evidence that a woman had lain there in death the night before. Carella sidestepped the outline and looked out the shattered window at the narrow alleyway below. There was a distance of perhaps twelve feet between this building and the one across from it.

Conceivably, the intruder could have leaped across the shaftway, but this would have required premeditation and calculation. The more probable likelihood was that the intruder had fallen to the pavement below.

"That's quite a long drop," Detective Bert Kling said, peering over Carella's shoulder.

"How far do you figure?" Carella asked.

"Thirty feet. At least."

"Got to break a leg taking a fall like that. You think he went through the window head first?"

"How else?"

"He might have broken the glass out first, then gone through," Carella suggested.

"If he was about to go to all that trouble, why didn't he just *open* the damn thing?"

"Well, let's take a look," Carella said.

They examined the latch and the sash. Kling grabbed both handles on the window frame and pulled up on them. "Stuck."

"Probably painted shut," Carella said.

"Maybe he *did* try to open it. Maybe he smashed it only when he realized it was stuck."

"Yeah," Carella said. "And in a big hurry, too. Fletcher was opening the front door, maybe already in the apartment by then."

"The guy probably had a bag or something with him, to put the loot in. He must have taken a wild swing with the bag when he realized the window was stuck, and maybe some of the stuff fell out, which would explain the silverware on the floor. Then he probably climbed through the hole and dropped down feet first. In fact, what he could've done, Steve, was drop the bag down first, and *then* he climbed out and hung from the sill before he jumped, to make it a shorter distance."

"I don't know if he had all that much time, Bert. He must have heard that front door opening, and Fletcher coming in and calling to his wife. Otherwise, he'd have taken his good, sweet time and gone out the kitchen window and down the fire escape, the way he'd come in."

Kling nodded reflectively.

"Let's take a look at that alley," Carella said.

In the alleyway outside, Carella and Kling studied the concrete pavement, and then looked up at the shattered second-floor window of the Fletcher apartment.

"Where do you suppose he'd have landed?" Kling said.

"Right about where we're standing." Carella looked at the ground. "I don't know, Bert. A guy drops twenty feet to a concrete pavement, doesn't break anything, gets up, dusts himself off, and runs the fifty-yard dash, right?" Carella shook his head. "My guess is he stayed right where he was to catch his breath, giving Fletcher time to look out the window, which would be the natural thing to do, but which Fletcher didn't."

"He was anxious to call the police."

"I still think he did it."

"Steve, be reasonable. If a guy's fingerprints are on the handle of a knife, and the knife is still in the victim—"

"*And* if the victim's husband realizes what a sweet setup he's stumbled into, wife lying on the floor with a knife in her, place broken into and burglarized, why *not* finish the job and hope the burglar will be blamed?"

"Sure," Kling said. "Prove it."

"I can't," Carella said. "Not until we catch the burglar."

While Carella and Kling went through the tedious routine of retracing the burglar's footsteps, Marshall Davies called the 87th Precinct and got Detective Meyer.

"I think I've got some fairly interesting information about the suspect," Davies said. "He left latent fingerprints all over the apartment and footprints in the kitchen. A very good one in the sink, when he climbed through the window, and some middling-fair ones tracking across the kitchen floor to the dining room. I got some excellent pictures and some good blowups of the heel."

"Good," Meyer said.

"But more important," Davies went on, "I got a good walking picture from the footprints on the floor. If a man is walking slowly, the distance between his footprints is usually about twenty-seven inches. Forty for running, thirty-five for fast walking. These were thirty-two inches. So we have a man's usual gait, moving quickly, but not in a desperate hurry, with the walking line normal and not broken."

"What does that mean?"

"Well, a walking line should normally run along the inner edge of a man's heelprints. Incidentally, the size and type of shoe and angle of the foot clearly indicate that this *was* a man."

"OK, fine," Meyer said. He did not thus far consider Davies' information valuable nor even terribly important.

"Anyway, none of this is valuable nor even terribly important," Davies said, "until we consider the rest of the data. The bedroom window was smashed, and the Homicide men were speculating that the suspect had jumped through the window into the alley below. I went down to get some meaningful pictures, and got some picture of where he must have landed—on both feet, incidentally—and I got another walking picture and direction line. He moved toward the basement door and into the basement. But the important thing is that our man is injured, and I think badly."

"How do you know?" Meyer asked.

"The walking picture downstairs is entirely different from the one in the kitchen. When he got downstairs he was leaning heavily on the left leg and dragging the right. I would suggest that whoever's handling the case put out a physician's bulletin. If this guy hasn't got a broken leg, I'll eat the pictures I took."

A girl in a green coat was waiting in the apartment lobby when Carella and Kling came back in, still retracing footsteps, or trying to. The girl said, "Excuse me, are you the detectives?"

"Yes," Carella said.

"The super told me you were in the building," the girl said. "You're investigating the Fletcher murder, aren't you?" She was quite soft-spoken.

"How can we help you, miss?" Carella asked.

"I saw somebody in the basement last night, with blood on his clothes."

Carella glanced at Kling and immediately said, "What time was this?"

"About a quarter to eleven," the girl said.

"What were you doing in the basement?"

The girl sounded surprised. "That's where the washing machines are. I'm sorry, my name is Selma Bernstein. I live here in the building."

"Tell us what happened, will you?" Carella said.

"I was sitting by the machine, watching the clothes tumble, which is simply *fascinating,* you know, when the door leading to the back yard opened—the door to the alley. This man came down the stairs, and I don't even think he saw me. He went straight for the stairs at the other end, the ones that go up into the street. I never saw him before last night."

"Can you describe him?" Carella asked.

"Sure. He was about twenty-one or twenty-two, your height and weight, well, maybe a little shorter, five ten or eleven, brown hair."

Kling was already writing. The man was white, wore dark trousers, high-topped sneakers, and a poplin jacket with blood on the right sleeve and on the front. He carried a small red bag, "like one of those bags the airlines give you."

Selma didn't know if he had any scars. "He went by in pretty much of a hurry, considering he was dragging his right leg. I think he was hurt pretty badly."

What they had in mind, of course, was identification from a mug shot, but the I.S. reported that none of the fingerprints in their file matched the ones found in the apartment. So the detectives figured it was going to be a tough one, and they sent out a bulletin to all of the city's doctors just to prove it.

Just to prove that cops can be as wrong as anyone else, it turned out to be a nice easy one after all.

The call came from a physician in Riverhead at 4:37 that afternoon, just as Carella was ready to go home.

"This is Dr. Mendelsohn," he said. "I have your bulletin here, and I want to report treating a man early this morning who fits your description—a Ralph Corwin of 894 Woodside in Riverhead. He had a bad ankle sprain."

"Thank you, Dr. Mendelsohn," Carella said.

Carella pulled the Riverhead directory from the top drawer of his desk and quickly flipped to the C's. He did not expect to find a listing for Ralph Corwin. A man would have to be a rank amateur to burglarize an apartment without wearing gloves, then stab a woman to death, and give his name when seeking treatment for an injury sustained in escaping from the murder apartment.

Ralph Corwin was apparently a rank amateur. His name was in the phone book, and he'd given the doctor his correct address.

Carella and Kling kicked in the door without warning, fanning into the room, guns drawn. The man on the bed was wearing only undershorts. His right ankle was taped.

"Are you Ralph Corwin?" Carella asked.

"Yes," the man said. His face was drawn, the eyes in pain.

"Get dressed, Corwin. We want to ask you some questions."

"There's nothing to ask," he said and turned his head into the pillow. "I killed her."

Ralph Corwin made his confession in the presence of two detectives of the 87th, a police stenographer, an assistant district attorney, and a lawyer appointed by the Legal Aid Society.

Corwin was the burglar. He'd entered 721 Silvermine Oval on Sunday night, December 12, down the steps from the street where the garbage cans were. He went through the basement, up the steps at the other end, into the back yard, and climbed the fire escape, all at about ten o'clock in the evening. Corwin entered the Fletcher apartment because it was the first one he saw without lights. He figured there was nobody home. The kitchen window was open a tiny crack; Corwin squeezed his fingers under the bottom and opened it all the way. He was pretty desperate at the time because he was a junkie in need of cash. He swore that he'd never done anything like this before.

The man from the D.A.'s office was conducting the Q. and A. and asked Corwin if he hadn't been afraid of fingerprints, not wearing gloves. Corwin figured that was done only in the movies, and anyway, he said, he didn't own gloves.

Corwin used a tiny flashlight to guide him as he stepped into the sink and down to the door. He made his way to the dining room, emptied the drawer of silverware into his airline bag. Then he looked for the bedroom, scouting for watches and rings, whatever he could take in the way of jewelry. "I'm not a pro," he said. "I was just hung up real bad and needed some bread to tide me over."

Now came the important part. The D.A.'s assistant asked Corwin what happened in the bedroom.

A. There was a lady in bed. This was only like close to ten-thirty, you don't expect nobody to be asleep so early.
Q. But there was a woman in bed.
A. Yeah. She turned on the light the minute I stepped in the room.
Q. What did you do?
A. I had a knife in my pocket. I pulled it out to scare her. It was almost comical. She looks at me and says, "What are you doing here?"
Q. Did you say anything to her?
A. I told her to keep quiet, that I wasn't going to hurt her. But she got out of bed and I saw she was reaching for the phone. That's got to be crazy, right? A guy is standing there in your bedroom with a knife in his hand, so she reaches for the phone.
Q. What did you do?
A. I grabbed her hand before she could get it. I pulled her off the bed, away from the phone, you know? And I told her again that nobody was going to hurt her, that I was getting out of there right away, to just please calm down.
Q. What happened next?
A. She started to scream. I told her to stop. I was beginning to panic. I mean she was really yelling.
Q. Did she stop?
A. No.
Q. What did you do?
A. I stabbed her.
Q. Where did you stab her?
A. I don't know. It was a reflex. She was yelling, I was afraid the whole building would come down. I just . . . I just stuck the knife in her. I was very scared. I stabbed her in the belly. Someplace in the belly.
Q. How many times did you stab her?
A. Once. She . . . She backed away from me. I'll never forget the look on her face. And she . . . fell on the floor.

Q. Would you look at this photograph, please?
A. Oh, no. . . .
Q. Is that the woman you stabbed?
A. Oh, no . . . I didn't think . . . Oh, no!

A moment after he stabbed Sarah Fletcher, Corwin heard the door opening and someone coming in. The man yelled, "Sarah, it's me, I'm home." Corwin ran past Sarah's body on the floor, and tried to open the window, but it was stuck. He smashed it with his airline bag, threw the bag out first to save the swag because, no matter what, he knew he'd need another fix, and he climbed through the broken window, cutting his hand on a piece of glass. He hung from the sill, and finally let go, dropping to the ground. He tried to get up, and fell down again. His ankle was killing him, his hand bleeding. He stayed in the alley nearly fifteen minutes, then finally escaped via the route Selma Bernstein had described to Carella and Kling. He took the subway to Riverhead and got to Dr. Mendelsohn at about nine in the morning. He read of Sarah Fletcher's murder in the newspaper on the way back from the doctor.

On Tuesday, December 14, which was the first of Carella's two days off that week, he received a call at home from Gerald Fletcher. Fletcher told the puzzled Carella that he'd gotten his number from a friend in the D.A.'s office, complimented Carella and the boys of the 87th on their snappy detective work, and invited Carella to lunch at the Golden Lion at one o'clock. Carella wasn't happy about interrupting his Christmas shopping, but this was an unusual opportunity, and he accepted.

Most policemen in the city for which Carella worked did not eat very often in restaurants like the Golden Lion. Carella had never been inside. A look at the menu posted on the window outside would have frightened him out of six months' pay. The place was a faithful replica of the dining room of an English coach house, circa 1627: huge oaken beams, immaculate white cloths, heavy silver.

Gerald Fletcher's table was in a secluded corner of the restaurant. He rose as Carella approached, extending his hand, and said, "Glad you could make it. Sit down, won't you?"

Carella shook Fletcher's hand, and then sat. He felt extremely uncomfortable, but he couldn't tell whether his discomfort was caused by the room or by the man with whom he was dining.

"Would you care for a drink?" Fletcher asked.

"Well, are you having one?" Carella asked.

"Yes, I am."

"I'll have a Scotch and soda," Carella said. He was not used to drinking at lunch.

Fletcher signaled for the waiter and ordered the drinks, making his another whiskey sour. When the drinks came, Fletcher raised his glass. "Here's to a conviction," he said.

Carella lifted his own glass. "I don't expect there'll be any trouble," he said. "It looks airtight to me."

Both men drank. Fletcher dabbed his lips with a napkin and said, "You never can tell these days. I hope you're right, though." He sipped at the drink. "I must admit I feel a certain amount of sympathy for him."

"Do you?"

"Yes. If he's an addict, he's automatically entitled to pity. And when one considers that the woman he murdered was nothing but a—"

"Mr. Fletcher . . ."

"Gerry, please. And I know: it isn't very kind of me to malign the dead. I'm afraid you didn't know my wife, though, Mr. Carella. May I call you Steve?"

"Sure."

"My enmity might be a bit more understandable if you had. Still, I shall take your advice. She's dead, and no longer capable of hurting me, so why be bitter. Shall we order, Steve?"

Fletcher suggested that Carella try either the trout *au meunière* or the beef and kidney pie, both of which were excellent. Carella ordered prime ribs, medium rare, and a mug of beer.

As the men ate and talked, something began happening, or at least Carella *thought* something was happening; he might never be quite sure. The conversation with Fletcher seemed on the surface to be routine chatter, but rushing through this inane, polite discussion was an undercurrent that caused excitement, fear, and apprehension. As they spoke, Carella knew with renewed certainty that Gerald Fletcher had killed his wife. Without ever being told so, he knew it. *This* was why Fletcher had called this morning; *this* was why Fletcher had invited him to lunch; *this* was why he prattled on endlessly while every contradictory move of his body signaled on an almost extrasensory level that he *knew* Carella suspected him of murder, and was here to *tell* Carella (*without* telling him) that, "Yes, you stupid cop, I killed my wife. However much the evidence may point to another man, however many confessions you get, I killed her and I'm glad I killed her. And there isn't a damn thing you can do about it."

Ralph Corwin was being held before trial in the city's oldest prison, known to law enforcers and lawbreakers alike as Calcutta. Neither Corwin's lawyer nor the district attorney's office felt that allowing Carella to talk to the prisoner would be harmful to the case.

Corwin was expecting him. "What did you want to see me about?"

"I wanted to ask you some questions."

"My lawyer says I'm not supposed to add anything to what I already said. I don't even *like* that guy."

"Why didn't you ask for another lawyer? Ask one of the officers here to call the Legal Aid Society. Or simply tell him. I'm sure he'd have no objection to dropping out."

Corwin shrugged. "I don't want to hurt his feelings. He's a little cockroach, but what the hell."

"You've got a lot at stake here, Corwin."

"But I killed her, so what does it matter *who* the lawyer is? You got it all in black and white."

"You feel like answering some questions?" Carella said.

"I feel like dropping dead, is what I feel like. Cold turkey's never good, and it's worse when you can't yell."

"If you'd rather I came back another time . . ."

"No, no, go ahead. What do you want to know?"

"I want to know exactly how you stabbed Sarah Fletcher."

"How do you *think* you stab somebody? You stick a knife in her, that's how."

"Where?"

"In the belly."

"Left-hand side of the body?"

"Yeah. I guess so."

"Where was the knife when she fell?"

"I don't know what you mean."

"Was the knife on the *right*-hand side of her body or the *left?*"

"I don't know. That was when I heard the front door opening and all I could think of was getting out of there."

"When you stabbed her, did she *twist* away from you?"

"No, she backed away, straight back, as if she couldn't believe what I done, and . . . and just wanted to get *away* from me."

"And then she fell?"

"Yes. She . . . her knees sort of gave way and she grabbed for her belly, and her hands sort of—it was terrible—they just . . . they were grabbing *air*, you know? And she fell."

"In what position?"

"On her side."

"*Which* side?"

"I could still see the knife, so it must've been the opposite side. The side opposite from where I stabbed her."

"One last question, Ralph. Was she dead when you went through that window?"

"I don't know. She was bleeding and . . . she was very quiet. I . . . guess she was dead. I don't know. I guess so."

Among Sarah Fletcher's personal effects that were considered of interest to the police before they arrested Ralph Corwin was an address book found in the dead woman's handbag on the bedroom dresser. In the Thursday afternoon stillness of the squad room, Carella examined the book.

There was nothing terribly fascinating about the alphabetical listings. Sarah Fletcher had possessed a good handwriting, and most of the listings were obviously married couples (Chuck and Nancy Benton, Harold and Marie Spander, and so on), some were girlfriends, local merchants, hairdresser, dentist, doctors, restaurants in town or across the river. A thoroughly uninspiring address book—until Carella came to a page at the end of the book, with the printed word MEMORANDA at its top.

Under the word, there were five names, addresses and telephone numbers written in Sarah's meticulous hand. They were all men's names, obviously entered at different times because some were in pencil and others in ink. The parenthetical initials following each entry were all noted in felt marking pens of various colors:

Andrew Hart, 1120 Hall Avenue, 622-8400 (PB&G) (TG)
Michael Thornton, 371 South Linder, 881-9371 (TS)
Lou Kantor, 434 North 16 Street, FR 7-2346 (TPC) (TG)
Sal Decotto, 831 Grover Avenue, FR 5-3287 (F) (TG)
Richard Fenner, 110 Henderson, 593-6648 (QR) (TG)

If there was one thing Carella loved, it was a code. He loved a code almost as much as he loved German measles. He flipped through the phone book and the address for Andrew Hart matched the one in Sarah's handwriting. He found an address for Michael Thornton. It, too, was identical to the one in her book. He kept turning pages in the directory, checking names and addresses. He verified all five.

At a little past eight the next morning, Carella got going on them. He called Andrew Hart at the number listed in Sarah's address book. Hart answered, and was not happy. "I'm in the middle of shaving," he said. "I've got to leave for the office in a little while. What's this about?"

"We're investigating a homicide, Mr. Hart."

"A *what?* A homicide? Who's been killed?"

"A woman named Sarah Fletcher."

"I don't know anyone named Sarah Fletcher," he said.

"She seems to have known you, Mr. Hart."

"Sarah *who?* Fletcher, did you say?" Hart's annoyance increased.

"That's right."

"I don't know anybody by that name. Who says she knew me? I never heard of her in my life."

"Your name's in her address book."

"My name? That's impossible."

Nevertheless, Hart agreed to see Carella and Meyer Meyer at the offices of Hart and Widderman, 480 Reed Street, sixth floor, at ten o'clock that morning.

At ten, Meyer and Carella parked the car and went into the building at 480 Reed, and up the elevator to the sixth floor. Hart and Widderman manufactured watchbands. A huge advertising display near the receptionist's desk in the lobby proudly proclaimed "H&W Beat the Band!" and then backed the slogan with more discreet copy that explained how Hart and Widderman had solved the difficult engineering problems of the expansion watch bracelet.

"Mr. Hart, please," Carella said.

"Who's calling?" the receptionist asked. She sounded as if she were chewing gum, even though she was not.

"Detectives Carella and Meyer."

"Just a minute, please," she said, and lifted her phone, pushing a button in the base. "Mr. Hart," she said, "there are some cops here to see you." She listened for a moment and then said, "Yes, sir." She replaced the receiver on its cradle, gestured toward the inside corridor with a nod of her golden tresses, said, "Go right in, please. Door at the end of the hall," and then went back to her magazine.

The gray skies had apparently infected Andrew Hart. "You didn't have to broadcast to the world that the police department was here," he said immediately.

"We merely announced ourselves," Carella said.

"Well, okay, now you're here," Hart said, "let's get it over with." He was a big man in his middle fifties, with iron-gray hair and black-trimmed eyeglasses. "I told you I don't know Sarah Fletcher and I don't."

"Here's her book, Mr. Hart," Carella said. "That's your name, isn't it?"

"Yeah," Hart said, and shook his head. "But how it got there is beyond me."

"Is it possible she's someone you met at a party, someone you exchanged numbers with?"

"No."

"Are you married, Mr. Hart?"

"No."

"We've got a picture of Mrs. Fletcher. I wonder—"

"Don't go showing me any pictures of a corpse," Hart said.

"This was taken when she was still very much alive, Mr. Hart."

Meyer handed Carella a manila envelope. He opened the flap and removed from the envelope a framed picture of Sarah Fletcher which he handed to Hart. Hart looked at the photograph, and then immediately looked up at Carella.

"What is this?" he said. He looked at the photograph again, shook his head, and said, "Somebody killed her, huh?"

"Yes, somebody did," Carella answered. "Did you know her?"

"I knew her."

"I thought you said you didn't."

"I didn't know Sarah Fletcher, if that's who you think she was. But I knew *this* broad, all right."

"Who'd *you* think she was?" Meyer asked.

"Just who she told me she was. Sadie Collins. She introduced herself as Sadie Collins, and that's who I knew her as. Sadie Collins."

"Where was this, Mr. Hart? Where'd you meet her?"

"A singles bar. The city's full of them."

"Would you remember when?"

"At least a year ago."

"Ever go out with her?"

"I used to see her once or twice a week."

"When did you stop seeing her?"

"Last summer."

"Did you know she was married?"

"Who, Sadie? You're kidding."

"She never told you she was married?"

"Never."

Meyer asked, "When you were going out, where'd you pick her up? At her apartment?"

"No. She used to come to my place."

"Where'd you call her when you wanted to reach her?"

"I didn't. She used to call me."

"Where'd you go, Mr. Hart? When you went out?"

"We didn't go out too much."

"What *did* you do?"

"She used to come to my place. The truth is, we never went out. She didn't want to go out much."

"Didn't you think that was strange?"

"No," Hart shrugged. "I figured she liked to stay home."

"Why'd you stop seeing her, Mr. Hart?"

"I met somebody else. A nice girl. I'm very serious about her."

"Was there something wrong with Sadie?"

"No, no. She was a beautiful woman, beautiful."

"Then why would you be ashamed—"

"Ashamed? Who said anything about being ashamed?"

"I gathered you wouldn't want your girlfriend—"

"Listen, what *is* this? I stopped seeing Sadie six months ago. I wouldn't even talk to her on the phone after that. If the crazy babe got herself killed—"

"Crazy?"

Hart suddenly wiped his hand over his face, wet his lips, and walked behind his desk. "I don't think I have anything more to say to you gentlemen."

"What did you mean by crazy?" Carella asked.

"Good day, gentlemen," Hart said.

Carella went to see Lieutenant Byrnes. In the lieutenant's corner office, Byrnes and Carella sat down over coffee. Byrnes frowned at Carella's request.

"Oh, come on, Pete!" Carella said. "If Fletcher *did* it—"

"That's only *your* allegation. Suppose he *didn't* do it, and suppose *you* do something to screw up the D.A.'s case?"

"Like what?"

"I don't know like what. The way things are going these days, if you spit on the sidewalk, that's enough to get a case thrown out of court."

"Fletcher hated his wife," Carella said calmly.

"Lot of men hate their wives. Half the men in this city hate their wives."

"But her little fling gives Fletcher good reason for . . . Look, Pete, he had a motive; he had the opportunity, a golden one, in fact; and he had the means—another man's knife sticking in Sarah's belly. What more do you want?"

"Proof. There's a funny little system we've got here—it requires proof before we can arrest a man and charge him with murder."

"Right. And all I'm asking is the opportunity to *try* for it."

"Sure, by putting a tail on Fletcher. Suppose he sues the city?"

"Yes or no, Pete? I want permission to conduct a round-the-clock surveillance of Gerald Fletcher, starting Sunday morning. Yes or no?"

"I must be out of my mind," Byrnes said, and sighed.

Michael Thornton lived in an apartment building several blocks from the Quarter, close enough to absorb some of its artistic flavor, distant enough to escape its high rents. A blond man in his apartment, Paul Wendling, told Kling and Meyer that Mike was in his jewelry shop.

In the shop, Thornton was wearing a blue work smock, but the contours of the garment did nothing to hide his powerful build. His eyes were blue, his hair black. A small scar showed white in the thick eyebrow over his left eye.

"We understand you're working," Meyer said. "Sorry to break in on you this way."

"That's okay," Thornton said. "What's up?"

"You know a woman named Sarah Fletcher?"

"No," Thornton said.

"You know a woman named Sadie Collins?"

Thornton hesitated. "Yes," he said.

"What was your relationship with her?" Kling asked.

Thornton shrugged. "Why? Is she in trouble?"

"When's the last time you saw her?"

"You didn't answer my question," Thornton said.

"Well, you didn't answer ours either," Meyer said, and smiled. "What was your relationship with her, and when did you see her last?"

"I met her in July, in a joint called The Saloon, right around the corner. It's a bar, but they also serve sandwiches and soup. It gets a big crowd on weekends, singles, a couple of odd ones for spice—but not a gay bar. I saw her last August, a brief, hot thing, and then good-bye."

"Did you realize she was married?" Kling said.

"No. Is she?"

"Yes," Meyer said. Neither of the detectives had yet informed Thornton that the lady in question was now unfortunately deceased. They were saving that for last, like dessert.

"Gee, I didn't know she was married." Thornton seemed truly surprised. "Otherwise, nothing would've happened."

"What *did* happen?"

"I bought her a few drinks and then I took her home with me. Later, I put her in a cab."

"When did you see her next?"

"The following day. It was goofy. She called me in the morning, she said she was on her way downtown. I was still in bed. I said, 'So come on down, baby.' And she did. *Believe* me, she did."

"Did you see her again after that?" Kling asked.

"Two or three times a week."

"Where'd you go?"

"To my pad on South Lindner."

"Never went anyplace but there?"

"Never."

"Why'd you quit seeing her?"

"I went out of town for awhile. When I got back, I just didn't hear from her again. She never gave me her number, and she wasn't in the directory, so I couldn't reach her."

"What do you make of this?" Kling asked, handing Thornton the address book.

Thornton studied it and said, "Yeah, what about it? She wrote this down the night we met—we were in bed, and she asked my address."

"Did she write those initials at the same time, the ones in parentheses under your phone number?"

"I didn't actually see the page itself. I only saw her writing in the book."

"Got any idea what the initials mean?"

"None at all." Suddenly he looked thoughtful. "She *was* kind of special, I have to admit it." He grinned. "She'll call again, I'm sure of it."

"I wouldn't count on it," Meyer said. "She's dead."

His face did not crumble or express grief or shock. The only thing it expressed was sudden anger. "The stupid . . ." Thornton said. "That's all she ever was, a stupid, crazy . . ."

On Sunday morning, Carella was ready to become a surveillant, but Gerald Fletcher was nowhere in sight. A call to his apartment from a nearby phone booth revealed that he was not in his digs. He parked in front of Fletcher's apartment building until 5:00 p.m. when he was relieved by Detective Arthur Brown. Carella went home to read his son's latest note to Santa Claus, had dinner with his family, and was settling down in the living room with a novel he had bought a week ago and not yet cracked when the telephone rang.

"Hello?" Carella said into the mouthpiece.

"Hello, Steve? This is Gerry. Gerry Fletcher."

Carella almost dropped the receiver. "How are you?"

"Fine, thanks. I was away for the weekend, just got back a little while ago, in fact. Frankly I find this apartment depressing as hell. I was wondering if you'd like to join me for a drink."

"Well," Carella said. "It's Sunday night, and it's late . . ."

"Nonsense, it's only eight o'clock. We'll do a little old-fashioned pub crawling."

It suddenly occurred to Carella that Gerald Fletcher had already had a few drinks before placing his call. It further occurred to him that if he played this *too* cozily, Fletcher might rescind his generous offer.

"Okay. I'll see you at eight-thirty, provided I can square it with my wife."

"Good," Fletcher said. "See you."

Paddy's Bar & Grill was on the Stem, adjacent to the city's theater district. Carella and Fletcher got there at about nine o'clock while the place was still relatively quiet. The action began a little later, Fletcher explained.

Fletcher lifted his glass in a silent toast. "What kind of person would you say comes to a place like this?"

"I would say we've got a nice lower-middle-class clientele bent on making contact with members of the opposite sex."

"What would you say if I told you the blonde in the clinging jersey is a working prostitute?"

Carella looked at the woman. "I don't think I'd believe you. She's a bit old for the young competition, and she's not *selling* anything. She's waiting for one of those two or three older guys to make their move. Hookers don't wait, Gerry. *Is* she a working prostitute?"

"I haven't the faintest idea," Fletcher said. "I was merely trying to indicate that appearances can sometimes be misleading. Drink up, there are a few more places I'd like to show you."

He knew Fletcher well enough by now to realize that the man was trying to tell him something. At lunch last Tuesday, Fletcher had transmitted a message and a challenge: *I killed my wife, what can you do about it?* Tonight, in a similar manner, he was attempting to indicate something else, but Carella could not fathom exactly what.

Fanny's was only twenty blocks away from Paddy's Bar and Grill, but as far removed from it as the moon. Whereas the first bar seemed to cater to a quiet crowd peacefully pursuing its romantic inclinations, Fanny's was noisy and raucous, jammed to the rafters with men and women of all ages, wearing plastic hippie gear purchased in head shops up and down Jackson Avenue.

Fletcher lifted his glass. "I hope you don't mind if I drink myself into a stupor," he said. "Merely pour me into the car at the end of the night." Fletcher drank. "I don't usually consume this much alcohol, but I'm very troubled about that boy."

"What boy?" Carella asked.

"Ralph Corwin," Fletcher said. "I understand he's having some difficulty with his lawyer and, well, I'd like to help him somehow."

"*Help* him?"

"Yes. Do you think the D.A.'s office would consider it strange if I suggested a good defense lawyer for the boy?"

"I think they might consider it passing strange, yes."

"Do I detect a note of sarcasm in your voice?"

"Not at all."

Fletcher squired Carella from Fanny's to, in geographical order, The Purple Chairs and Quigley's Rest. Each place was rougher, in its way, than the last. The Purple Chairs catered to a brazenly gay crowd, and Quigley's Rest was a dive, where Fletcher's liquor caught up with him, and the evening ended suddenly in a brawl. Carella was shaken by the experience, and still couldn't piece out Fletcher's reasons.

Carella received a further shock when he continued to pursue Sarah Fletcher's address book. Lou Kantor was simply the third name in a now wearying list of Sarah's bedmates, until she turned out to be a tough and striking woman. She confirmed Carella's suspicion's immediately.

"I only knew her a short while," she said. "I met her in September, I believe. Saw her three or four times after that."

"Where'd you meet her?"

"In a bar called The Purple Chairs. That's right," she added quickly. "That's what I am."

"Nobody asked," Carella said. "What about Sadie Collins?"

"Spell it out, Officer, I'm not going to help you. I don't like being hassled."

"Nobody's hassling you, Miss Kantor. You practice your religion and I'll practice mine. We're here to talk about a dead woman."

"Then talk about her, spit it out. What do you want to know? Was she straight? Everybody's straight until they're *not* straight anymore, isn't that right? She was willing to learn. I taught her."

"Did you know she was married?"

"She told me. So what? Broke down in tears one night, and spent the rest of the night crying. I knew she was married."

"What'd she say about her husband?"

"Nothing that surprised me. She said he had another woman. Said he ran off to see her every weekend, told little Sadie he had out-of-town business. *Every* weekend, can you imagine that?"

"What do you make of this?" Carella said, and handed her Sarah's address book opened to the MEMORANDA page.

"I don't know any of these people," Lou said.

"The initials under your name," Carella said. "TPC and then TG. Got any ideas?"

"Well, the TPC is obvious, isn't it? I met her at The Purple Chairs. What else could it mean?"

Carella suddenly felt very stupid. "Of course. What else could it mean?" He took back the book. "I'm finished," he said. "Thank you very much."

"I miss her," Lou said suddenly. "She was a wild one."

Cracking a code is like learning to roller-skate; once you know how to do it, it's easy. With a little help from Gerald Fletcher, who had provided a guided tour the night before, and a lot of help from Lou

Kantor, who had generously provided the key, Carella was able to crack the code wide open—well, almost. Last night, he'd gone with Fletcher to Paddy's Bar and Grill, or PB&G under Andrew Hart's name; Fanny's, F under Sal Decotto; The Purple Chairs, Lou Kantor's TPC; and Quigley's Rest, QR for Richard Fenner on the list. Probably because of the fight, he hadn't taken Carella to The Saloon, TS under Michael Thornton's name—the place where Thornton had admitted first meeting Sarah.

Except, what the hell did TG mean, under all the names but Thornton's?

By Carella's own modest estimate, he had been in more bars in the past twenty-four hours than he had in the past twenty-four years. He decided, nevertheless, to hit The Saloon that night.

The Saloon was just that. A cigarette-scarred bar behind which ran a mottled, flaking mirror; wooden booths with patched, fake leather seat cushions; bowls of pretzels and potato chips; jukebox gurgling; steamy bodies.

"They come in here," the bartender said, "at all hours of the night. Take yourself. You're here to meet a girl, am I right?"

"There *was* someone I was hoping to see. A girl named Sadie Collins. Do you know her?"

"Yeah. She used to come in a lot, but I ain't seen her in months. What do you want to fool around with her for?"

"Why? What's the matter with her?"

"You want to know something?" the bartender said. "I thought she was a hooker at first. Aggressive. You know what that word means? Aggressive? She used to come dressed down to here and up to there, ready for action, selling everything she had, you understand? She'd come in here, pick out a guy she wanted, and go after him like the world was gonna end at midnight. And always the same type. Big guys. You wouldn't stand a chance with her, not that you ain't big, don't misunderstand me. But Sadie liked them gigantic, and mean. You know something?"

"What?"

"I'm glad she don't come in here anymore. There was something about her—like she was compulsive. You know what that word means, compulsive?"

Tuesday afternoon, Arthur Brown handed in his surveillance report on Gerald Fletcher. Much of it was not at all illuminating. From 4:55

p.m. to 8:45 p.m. Fletcher had driven home, and then to 812 North Crane and parked. The report *did* become somewhat illuminating when, at 8:46 p.m., Fletcher emerged from the building with a redheaded woman wearing a black fur coat over a green dress. They went to Rudolph's restaurant, ate, and drove back to 812 Crane, arrived at 10:35 p.m. and went inside. Arthur Brown had checked the lobby mailboxes, which showed eight apartments on the eleventh floor, which was where the elevator indicator had stopped. Brown went outside to wait again, and Fletcher emerged alone at 11:40 p.m., and drove home. Detective O'Brien relieved Detective Brown at 12:15 a.m.

Byrnes said, "This woman could be important."

"That's just what I think," Brown answered.

Carella had not yet spoken to either Sal Decotto or Richard Fenner, the two remaining people listed in Sarah's book, but saw no reason to pursue that trail any further. If the place listings in her book had been chronological, she'd gone from bad to worse in her search for partners.

Why? To give it back to her husband in spades? Carella tossed Sarah's little black book into the manila folder bearing the various reports on the case, and turned his attention to the information Artie Brown had brought in last night. The redheaded woman's presence might be important, but Carella was still puzzling over Fletcher's behavior. Sarah's blatant infidelity provided Fletcher with a strong motive, so why take Carella to his wife's unhappy haunts, why *show* Carella that he had good and sufficient reason to kill her? Furthermore, why the offer to get a good defense attorney for the boy who had already been indicted for the slaying?

Sometimes Carella wondered who was doing what to whom.

At five o'clock that evening, Carella relieved Detective Hal Willis outside Fletcher's office building downtown, and then followed Fletcher to a department store in midtown Isola. Carella was wearing a false mustache stuck to his upper lip, a wig with longer hair than his own and of a different color, and a pair of sunglasses.

In the department store, he tracked Fletcher to the Intimate Apparel department. Carella walked into the next aisle, pausing to look at women's robes and kimonos, keeping one eye on Fletcher, who was in conversation with the lingerie salesgirl.

"May I help you, sir?" a voice said, and Carella turned to find a stocky woman at his elbow, with gray hair, black-rimmed spectacles, wearing Army shoes and a black dress. Her suspicious smile accused him of being a junkie shoplifter or worse.

"Thank you, no," Carella said. "I'm just looking."

Fletcher made his selections from the gossamer undergarments which the salesgirl had spread out on the counter, pointing first to one garment, then to another. The salesgirl wrote up the order and Fletcher reached into his wallet to give her either cash or a credit card; it was difficult to tell from an aisle away. He chatted with the girl a moment longer, and then walked off toward the elevator bank.

"Are you *sure* I can't assist you?" the woman in the Army shoes said, and Carella answered, "I'm positive," and moved swiftly toward the lingerie counter. Fletcher had left the counter without a package in his arms, which meant he was *sending* his purchases. The salesgirl was gathering up Fletcher's selections and looked up when Carella reached the counter.

"Yes, sir," she said. "May I help you?"

Carella opened his wallet and produced his shield. "Police officer," he said. "I'm interested in the order you just wrote up."

The girl was perhaps nineteen years old, a college girl working in the store during the Christmas rush. Speechlessly, she studied the shield, eyes bugging.

"Are these items being sent?" Carella asked.

"Yes, *sir,*" the girl said. Her eyes were still wide. She wet her lips and stood up a little straighter, prepared to be a perfect witness.

"Can you tell me where?" Carella asked.

"Yes, *sir,*" she said, and turned the sales slip toward him. "He wanted them wrapped separately, but they're all going to the same address. Miss Arlene Orton, 812 North Crane Street, right here in the city, and I'd guess it's a swell—"

"Thank you very much," Carella said.

It felt like Christmas already.

The man who picked the lock on Arlene Orton's front door, ten minutes after she left her apartment on Wednesday morning, was better at it than any burglar in the city, and he happened to work for the Police Department. It took the technician longer to set up his equipment, but the telephone was the easiest of his jobs. The tap would become operative when the telephone company supplied the police with a list of so-called bridging points that located the pairs and cables for Arlene Orton's phone. The monitoring equipment would be hooked into these and whenever a call went out of or came into the apartment, a recorder would automatically tape both ends of the conversation. In addition, whenever a call was made from the apartment, a dial indicator would ink out a series of dots that signified the number being called.

The technician placed his bug in the bookcase on the opposite side of the room. The bug was a small FM transmitter with a battery-powered mike that needed to be changed every twenty-four hours. The technician would have preferred running his own wires, but he dared not ask the building superintendent for an empty closet or workroom in which to hide his listener. A blabbermouth superintendent can kill an investigation more quickly than a squad of gangland goons.

In the rear of a panel truck parked at the curb some twelve feet south of the entrance to 812 Crane, Steve Carella sat behind the recording equipment that was locked into the frequency of the bug. He sat hopefully, with a tuna sandwich and a bottle of beer, prepared to hear and record any sounds that emanated from Arlene's apartment.

At the bridging point seven blocks away and thirty minutes later, Arthur Brown sat behind equipment that was hooked into the telephone mike, and waited for Arlene Orton's phone to ring. He was in radio contact with Carella.

The first call came at 12:17 p.m. The equipment tripped in automatically and the spools of tape began recording the conversation, while Brown simultaneously monitored it through his headphone.

"Hello?"

"Hello, Arlene?"

"Yes, who's this?"

"Nan."

"Nan? You sound so different. Do you have a cold or something?"

"Every year at this time. Just before the holidays. Arlene, I'm terribly rushed, I'll make this short. Do you know Beth's dress size?"

The conversation went on in that vein, and Arlene Orton spoke to three more girlfriends in succession. She then called the local supermarket to order the week's groceries. She had a fine voice, deep and forceful, punctuated every so often (when she was talking to her girlfriends) with a delightful giggle.

At 4:00 p.m., the telephone in Arlene's apartment rang again.

"Hello?"

"Arlene, this is Gerry."

"Hello, darling."

"I'm leaving here a little early. I thought I'd come right over."

"Good."

"I'll be there in, oh, half an hour, forty minutes."

"Hurry."

Brown radioed Carella at once. Carella thanked him, and sat back to wait.

On Thursday morning, two days before Christmas, Carella sat at his desk in the squad room and looked over the transcripts of the five reels from the night before. The conversation on that reel had at one point changed abruptly in tone and content; Carella thought he knew why but he wanted to confirm his suspicion.

FLETCHER: I meant after the *holidays*, not the trial.
MISS ORTON: I may be able to get away, I'm not sure. I'll have to check with my shrink.
FLETCHER: What's he got to do with it?
MISS ORTON: Well, I have to pay whether I'm there or not, you know.
FLETCHER: Is he taking a vacation?
MISS ORTON: I'll ask him.
FLETCHER: Yes, ask him. Because I'd really like to get away.
MISS ORTON: Ummm. When do you think the case (inaudible).
FLETCHER: In March sometime. No sooner than that. He's got a new lawyer, you know.
MISS ORTON: What does that mean, a new lawyer?
FLETCHER: Nothing. He'll be convicted anyway.
MISS ORTON: (Inaudible).
FLETCHER: Because the trial's going to take a lot out of me.
MISS ORTON: How soon after the trial . . .
FLETCHER: I don't know.
MISS ORTON: She's dead, Gerry, I don't see . . .
FLETCHER: Yes, but . . .
MISS ORTON: I don't see why we have to wait, do you?
FLETCHER: Have you read this?
MISS ORTON: No, not yet. Gerry. I think we ought to set a date now. A provisional date, depending on when the trial is. Gerry?
FLETCHER: Mmmm?
MISS ORTON: Do you think it'll be a terribly long, drawn-out trial?
FLETCHER: What?
MISS ORTON: Gerry?
FLETCHER: Yes?

MISS ORTON: Where are you?

FLETCHER: I was just looking over some of these books.

MISS ORTON: Do you think you can tear yourself away?

FLETCHER: Forgive me, darling.

MISS ORTON: If the trial starts in March, and we planned on April for it . . .

FLETCHER: Unless they come up with something unexpected, of course.

MISS ORTON: Like what?

FLETCHER: Oh, I don't know. They've got some pretty sharp people investigating this case.

MISS ORTON: What's there to investigate?

FLETCHER: There's always the possibility he didn't do it.

MISS ORTON: (Inaudible) a signed confession?

FLETCHER: One of the cops thinks I killed her.

MISS ORTON: You're not serious. Who?

FLETCHER: A detective named Carella. He probably knows about us by now. He's a very thorough cop. I have a great deal of admiration for him. I wonder if he realizes that.

MISS ORTON: Where'd he even get such an idea?

FLETCHER: Well, I told him I hated her.

MISS ORTON: What? Gerry, why the hell did you do that?

FLETCHER: He'd have found out anyway. He probably knows by now that Sarah was sleeping around with half the men in this city. And he probably knows I knew it, too.

MISS ORTON: Who cares what he found out? Corwin's already confessed.

FLETCHER: I can understand his reasoning. I'm just not sure he can understand mine.

MISS ORTON: Some reasoning. If you were going to kill her, you'd have done it ages ago, when she refused to sign the separation papers. So let him investigate, who cares? Wishing your wife dead isn't the same thing as killing her. Tell that to Detective Copolla.

FLETCHER: Carella. (Laughs).

MISS ORTON: What's so funny?

FLETCHER: I'll tell him, darling.

According to the technician who had wired the Orton apartment, the living-room bug was in the bookcase on the wall opposite the bar. Carella was interested in the tape from the time Fletcher had asked Arlene about a book—"Have you read this?"—and then seemed preoccupied. It was Carella's guess that Fletcher had discovered the bookcase bug. What interested Carella more, however, was what Fletcher had said *after* he knew the place was wired. Certain of an audience now, Fletcher had:

1. Suggested the possibility that Corwin was not guilty.
2. Flatly stated that a cop named Carella suspected him.
3. Expressed admiration for Carella, while wondering if Carella was aware of it.
4. Speculated that Carella had already doped out the purpose of the bar-crawling last Sunday night, was cognizant of Sarah's promiscuity, and knew Fletcher was aware of it.
5. Made a little joke about "telling" Carella.

Carella felt as eerie as he had when lunching with Fletcher and later when drinking with him. Now he'd spoken, through the bug, directly to Carella. But what was he trying to say? And why?

Carella wanted very much to hear what Fletcher would say when he *didn't* know he was being overheard. He asked Lieutenant Byrnes for permission to request a court order to put a bug in Fletcher's automobile. Byrnes granted permission, and the court issued the order.

Fletcher made a date with Arlene Orton to go to The Chandeliers across the river, and the bug was installed in Fletcher's 1972 car. If Fletcher left the city, the effective range of the transmitter on the open road would be about a quarter of a mile. The listener-pursuer had his work cut out for him.

By ten minutes to ten that night, Carella was drowsy and discouraged. On the way out to The Chandeliers, Fletcher and Arlene had not once mentioned Sarah or the plans for their impending marriage. Carella was anxious to put them both to bed and get home to his family. When they finally came out of the restaurant and began walking toward Fletcher's automobile, Carella actually uttered an audible, "At *last*," and started his car.

They proceeded east on Route 701, heading for the bridge, and said nothing. Carella thought at first something was wrong with the equipment, then finally Arlene spoke and Carella knew just what had happened. The pair had argued in the restaurant, and Arlene had been smoldering until this moment when she could no longer contain her anger.

"Maybe you don't want to marry me at all," she shouted.

"That's ridiculous," Fletcher said.

"Then why won't you set a date?"

"I have set a date."

"You haven't set a date. All you've done is say after the trial. *When*, after the trial? Maybe this whole damn thing has been a stall. Maybe you *never* planned to marry me."

"You know that isn't true, Arlene."

"How do I know there really *were* separation papers?"

"There were. I told you there were."

"Then why wouldn't she sign them?"

"Because she loved me."

"If she loved you, then why did she do those horrible things?"

"To make me pay, I think."

"Is that why she showed you her little black book?"

"Yes, to make me pay."

"No. Because she was a slut."

"I guess. I guess that's what she became."

"Putting the little TG in her book every time she told you about a new one. *Told Gerry*, and marked a little TG in her book."

"Yes, to make me pay."

"A slut. You should have gone after her with detectives. Gotten pictures, threatened her, forced her to sign—"

"No, I couldn't have done that. It would have ruined me, Arl."

"Your precious career."

"Yes, my precious career."

They both fell silent again. They were approaching the bridge now. Carella tried to stay close behind them, but on occasion the distance between the two cars lengthened and he lost some words in the conversation.

"She wouldn't sign the papers and I ( ) adultery because ( ) have come out."

"And I thought ( )."

"I did everything I possibly could."

"Yes, Gerry, but now she's dead. So what's your excuse now?"

"I'm suspected of having *killed* her, damn it!"

Fletcher was making a left turn, off the highway. Carella stepped on the accelerator, not wanting to lose voice contact now.

"What difference does that make?" Arlene asked.

"None at all, I'm sure," Fletcher said. "I'm sure you wouldn't mind at all being married to a convicted murderer."

"What are you talking about?"

"I'm talking about the possibility . . . Never mind."

"Let me hear it."

"All right, Arlene. I'm talking about the possibility of someone accusing me of the murder. And of my having to stand trial for it."

"That's the most paranoid—"

"It's not paranoid."

"Then what is it? They've caught the murderer, they—"

"I'm only saying suppose. How could we get married if I killed her, if someone says I killed her?"

"No one has said that, Gerry."

"Well, *if* someone should."

Silence. Carella was dangerously close to Fletcher's car now, and risking discovery. Carella held his breath and stayed glued to the car ahead.

"Gerry, I don't understand this," Arlene said, her voice low.

"Someone could make a good case for it."

"Why would anyone do that? They know that Corwin—"

"They could say I came into the apartment and . . . They could say she was still alive when I came into the apartment. They could say the knife was still in her and I . . . I came in and found her that way and . . . finished her off."

"Why would you do that?"

"To end it."

"You wouldn't kill anyone, Gerry."

"No."

"Then why are you even suggesting such a terrible thing?"

"If she wanted it . . . If someone accused me . . . If someone said I'd done it . . . that I'd finished the job, pulled the knife across her belly, they could claim she *asked* me to do it."

"What are you saying, Gerry?"

"I'm trying to explain that Sarah might have—"

"Gerry. I don't think I want to know."

"I'm only trying to tell you—"

"No, I don't want to know. Please. Gerry, you're frightening me."

"*Listen* to me, damn it! I'm trying to explain what *might* have happened. Is that so hard to accept? That she might have *asked* me to kill her?"

"Gerry, please, I—"

"I *wanted* to call the hospital, I was *ready* to call the hospital, don't you think I could *see* she wasn't fatally stabbed?"

"Gerry, please."

"She begged me to kill her, Arlene, she begged me to end it for her, she . . . Damn it, can't *either* of you understand that? I tried to show him, I took him to all the places, I thought he was a man who'd understand. Is it that difficult?"

"Oh, my God, *did* you kill her? *Did* you kill Sarah?"

"No. Not Sarah. Only the woman she'd become, the slut I'd forced her to become. She was Sadie, you see, when I killed her—when she died."

"Oh, my God," Arlene said, and Carella nodded in weary acceptance.

Carella felt neither elated nor triumphant. As he followed Fletcher's car into the curb in front of Arlene's building, he experienced only a familiar nagging sense of repetition and despair. Fletcher was coming out of his car now, walking around to the curb side, opening the door for Arlene, who took his hand and stepped onto the sidewalk, weeping. Carella intercepted them before they reached the front door of the building. Quietly, he charged Fletcher with the murder of his wife, and made the arrest without resistance.

Fletcher did not seem at all surprised.

So it was finished, or at least Carella thought it was.

In the silence of his living room, the telephone rang at a quarter past one. He caught the phone on the third ring.

"Hello?"

"Steve," Lieutenant Byrnes said, "I just got a call from Calcutta. Ralph Corwin hanged himself in his cell, just after midnight. Must have done it while we were still taking Fletcher's confession in the squad room."

Carella was silent.

"Steve?" Byrnes said.

"Yeah, Pete."

"Nothing," Byrnes said, and hung up.

Carella stood with the dead phone in his hands for several seconds and then replaced it on the hook. He looked into the living room, where the lights of the tree glowed warmly, and thought of a despairing junkie in a prison cell, who had taken his own life without ever having known he had not taken the life of another.

It was Christmas day.

Sometimes, none of it made any sense at all.

SUGGESTIONS FOR FURTHER READING

DETECTIVE FICTION:

WILLIAM GODWIN, *Things As They Are or, The Adventures of Caleb Williams* (1794)
CHARLES DICKENS, *Bleak House* (1853)
WILKIE COLLINS, *The Woman in White* (1860)
MARY ELIZABETH BRADDON, *Lady Audley's Secret* (1862)
EMILE GABORIAU, *L'Affaire Lerouge* (1866)
WILKIE COLLINS, *The Moonstone* (1868)
CHARLES DICKENS, *The Mystery of Edwin Drood* (1870)
ANNA KATHERINE GREENE, *The Leavenworth Case* (1878)
MARY ROBERTS RINEHART, *The Circular Staircase* (1908)
AGATHA CHRISTIE, *The Murder of Roger Ackroyd* (1926)
DASHIELL HAMMETT, *The Maltese Falcon* (1930)
DOROTHY L. SAYERS, *Gaudy Night* (1935)
RAYMOND CHANDLER, *The Long Goodbye* (1953)
CHESTER HIMES, *A Rage in Harlem* (1957)
GEORGES SIMENON, *Maigret and the Madwoman* (1970)
P. D. JAMES, *An Unsuitable Job for a Woman* (1972)
REX BURNS, *Strip Search* (1984)

CRITICAL WORKS:

BARZUN, JACQUES and WENDELL H. TAYLOR. *A Catalogue of Crime*. New York: Harper & Row, 1971; rev. 1989.

CHANDLER, RAYMOND. *The Simple Art of Murder*. Boston: Houghton Mifflin, 1950.

DOVE, GEORGE N. *The Police Procedural*. Bowling Green, Ohio: Popular Press, 1982.

ECO, UMBERTO. *Postscript to "The Name of the Rose,"* trans. William Weaver. New York: Harcourt, Brace, Jovanovich, 1984.

HAYCRAFT, HOWARD, ed. *The Art of the Mystery Story*. New York: Grosset & Dunlap, 1946.

———. *Murder for Pleasure: The Life and Times of the Detective Story*. New York: Appleton-Century, 1941; Carroll & Graf, 1984.

HUBIN, ALLEN J. *Crime Fiction 1749–1980: A Comprehensive Bibliography*.

JAMES, P. D. "No Gore, Please—They're British," (interview) *The New York Times Book Review*, 9 October 1988.

LANDRUM, LARRY, PAT BROWNE and RAY B. BROWNE, ed. *Dimensions of Detective Fiction*. Bowling Green, Ohio: Popular Press, 1976.

MAUGHAM, W. SOMERSET. "The Decline and Fall of the Detective Story," *The Vagrant Mood*. Port Washington, New York: Kennikat Press, 1969.

NEVINS, FRANCIS M., JR. *The Mystery Writer's Art*. Bowling Green, Ohio: Popular Press, 1970.

OUSBY, IAN. *Bloodhounds of Heaven: The Detective in English Fiction from Godwin to Doyle*. Cambridge, Massachusetts and London: Harvard University Press, 1976.

REILLY, JOHN M., ed. *Twentieth-Century Crime and Mystery Writers*. New York: St. Martin's, 1980; rev. 1985.

SYMONS, JULIAN. *Bloody Murder: A History, From the Detective Story to the Crime Novel*. New York: Viking, 1985.

WILSON, EDMUND. *A Literary Chronicle of the 1940s*. New York: Farrar, Strauss & Giroux, 1950.

WINKS, ROBIN, ED. *Colloquium on Crime*. New York: Scribner's, 1986.

———. *Detective Fiction: A Collection of Critical Essays*. Englewood Cliffs, N.J.: Prentice Hall, 1980; rev. Woodstock, Vermont: Foul Play Press, 1988.

———. "The Genre of Mystery and Spy Fiction Should Get Serious Study—But It Must Be for the Right Reasons," *The Chronicle of Higher Education*, 2 August 1989.